WIFE NUMBER ONE

SAINT VIEW SLAYERS VS. SINNERS
BOOK 1

ELLE THORPE

WWW.ELLETHORPE.COM

Copyright © 2024 by Elle Thorpe Pty Ltd

All rights reserved.

No part of this book may be reproduced in any form or by any electronic or mechanical means, including information storage and retrieval systems, without written permission from the author, except for the use of brief quotations in a book review.

Editing by Studio ENP

Proofreading by Barren Acres Editing

Cover photography by Michelle Lancaster

Cover model: Cooper

Original cover design by Elle Thorpe Pty Ltd

Discreet cover design by Emily Wittig Designs

V: 1

For the women who fell for the 6'2, tattooed bad boy with pretty eyes. Even though he only had one scene and he's probably the villain.

1

KARA

I was never without my veil.

The heavy mesh scratched across my nose and cheeks, suffocating and hot in the crowded church. I'd worn it so long I could barely remember what it felt like not to squint through the material so I didn't trip or stumble over the altar steps.

"May the Lord bless your womb. May he grant you good health to bring forth new life this month. May you carry his seed and nurture it into his disciple."

I nodded at the woman kneeling at my feet, accepting her blessing.

She took the small head bob as her dismissal, and the next in line dropped into the position.

"May the Lord bless your womb. May he grant you good health to bring forth new life this month. May you carry his seed..."

I tuned out, nodding automatically as each new woman took her turn at my feet, before moving on to the next of Josiah's wives and repeating the familiar words.

The other wives didn't wear the same black veil I did.

Their faces were unmasked for all the congregation to see. They breathed freely, the air touching their summer-tanned skin.

They were the fertile.

The blessed.

The women chosen by Josiah, through the Lord's word.

They had each provided the Lord and Josiah with an heir. Some more than one. Josiah's second wife, Camilla, who sat to my left, had provided him four children within the past five years. Laurie, wife three, had delivered two healthy baby boys who were both toddlers now. And Scarlett, the newest and youngest of his wives, a baby daughter just last year.

I had provided none.

Despite being wife number one.

Shame washed over me, as it always did each weekend when this ritual was performed. I lowered my gaze to my lap and prayed silently, hoping that this month, the blessings would finally work. That this would be the month I didn't bleed. That Josiah's seed would take hold and bring forth new life.

That I would finally make him happy.

When that happened, I would be freed of the veil prison I'd lived in the past five years. I would sit like the other wives, honored by the community Josiah had built around his connection to the one true God.

Instead of hidden away behind layers of thick cloth, a disappointment and embarrassment to all.

I just had to pray harder. Be quieter. Sweeter. Love Josiah and the Lord we served harder.

Josiah's other wives had proved over and over again that if you were the perfect wife, you would conceive an heir. It was my fault I had not been blessed. Every person here knew no baby grew in my womb because the Lord had deemed I wasn't worthy.

As Josiah told me every night, I just wasn't trying hard enough.

People filed in, wearing their best clothes, their faces scrubbed clean of dirt and grime that came with the hard work they did here throughout the week. When they had finished paying their respects at our feet, they took seats in the rows of hard, wooden pews, talking quietly amongst themselves while they waited for the sermon to begin.

The church had been extended last year to meet the needs of the growing community, and there were so many people here now I could barely keep track of all the new faces. What had been a small group just five years ago when I'd returned from the outside world, had more than tripled in size, people flocking to join when Josiah and his inner circle had begun actively recruiting new members with a podcast about the Lord and our community here at Ethereal Eden.

My interest snagged on my mother and younger sisters entering with my father, all of them joining the line quietly.

Alice, the eldest of my siblings in attendance and the closest to me in age, stood tall, her head high, and a smile offered up easily for me.

Until my mother poked her sharply in the back. Alice rolled her eyes for my benefit before lowering them obediently.

I didn't bother stifling my smile of amusement, because nobody could see it through the veil anyway.

Samantha and Naomi kept their gazes on the floor, like the good women they were. I knew from every other time we'd done this, they would kneel and bless my womb without any sort of sisterly familiarity we might have once had.

Jacqueline, the last of my siblings, had grown into a young woman over the past few years. She'd become quite the beauty, a fact Josiah reminded me of more than once, while chills raced up and down my spine. The threat barely concealed in his expression.

Jacqueline might not have been a child in the eyes of our community, but she was only thirteen.

I hated the way men stared at her. It reminded me too much of the way a man on the outside had once looked at me. Like I was prey, just waiting to be eaten alive.

My breath caught on the memory, and bile rose in my throat.

But then the one good thing that had come from my time outside walked through the church doors and curiously peered up to where I sat.

Every bad memory disintegrated.

When I looked at her, I was reminded that the best thing in my life had come from the worst.

Hayley Jade.

My heart flickered, squeezing with love for the little girl with her dark hair and big eyes. Day by day, I'd watched from afar as she grew taller, stronger, smarter. But somewhere in her five-year-old face, I still saw the tiny baby who had been placed into my arms, and tears pricked the backs of my eyes.

A woman behind her prodded Hayley Jade forward, urging her along the blessing line.

My fingers curled around the armrest of my chair, fingernails digging into the hard, ornately carved wood. I wanted to stand and shout at the woman for laying a finger on my daughter, even though the touch had barely moved Hayley Jade's small frame.

But that was not my right.

I was no longer her mother.

That privilege had been removed six months after I'd married Josiah when I'd failed to provide him with a child of his own.

The Lord had told him my attention was too focused on the child I had. The one born outside of our community, who brought dishonor to my new husband.

And so she'd been given to another woman to raise. A widow who had no children of her own.

"Kneel down, Jade," the woman urged in a sharp whisper.

I hated that she'd shortened her name.

"But, Mama, it hurts my knees!"

My heart clenched at hearing my daughter call another woman Mama.

"Forgive me," the woman said quietly, taking the girl's hand and pulling her down to the altar steps, forcing her onto her knees. "She's headstrong and still learning her place."

Hayley Jade pouted up at me, a scowl twisting her pink lips and screwing up her button nose adorably.

Everything inside me ached to reach out and touch her. "She doesn't need to kneel before me." My voice was barely above a whisper. "She's perfect, just the way she is."

Hayley Jade's expression morphed into a triumphant smile of pleasure.

I wanted to photograph it. So I would remember the way she'd looked at me forever. But technology had been forbidden at the farm for a long time now. I still mourned the loss of all the baby photos that had been on the phone I'd kept when I'd first come home.

Once Josiah had found it, I'd never seen it again.

"Kara," Josiah snapped from behind me, using the voice he reserved for when I had disappointed him. Which was almost all of the time.

I hadn't even realized he was there, listening, I'd been so caught up in getting this one, tiny exchange with the little girl I'd birthed so many years before.

"Shari is right." Josiah studied the pair with hard eyes, making sure they knew that they did indeed need to kneel before the feet of him and his family. "The girl needs to learn her place."

"She's disobedient, but I'm working on it," Shari assured him. "She will become a good woman in time." She side-eyed me. "When her soul has been properly cleansed of the sins she was exposed to as a baby."

There was nothing I could say about that. My sins were known to all in the community. How I'd left. Gotten pregnant and come back home a year later with a newborn baby in my arms and my tail tucked between my legs.

How my parents had begged Josiah for forgiveness on my behalf.

How they had agreed I would marry him and bring

him the heir he so desperately craved. After all, I had a proven track record of being able to carry a child to term, and at the time, I had been one of the few women in the group of marrying age.

But I had failed at all of it.

"Indeed," Josiah agreed, his gaze sweeping over Hayley Jade. "Her manners need work, but she is growing up into a beauty. How old is she now?"

Anger and disgust bubbled through me. Hayley Jade wasn't disobedient. And she didn't need to learn her place. Or kneel at my feet like she was some sort of servant. She was beautiful and kind and sweet. All qualities I'd admired in her as I watched her from the window of my bedroom in Josiah's home.

The man sharpened his gaze, studying my daughter.

Her good qualities suddenly seemed dangerous.

They drew the attention of men, the same way her aunt Jacqueline did.

My daughter had been removed from my care as a punishment, but when Josiah took too much interest in her, as he was now, I was grateful she was being raised outside his home.

"Thank you for your blessings," I said quickly to Shari. "May the Lord bestow abundance upon your home this week." I ended the conversation so she would be forced to move on down the line, taking Hayley Jade away from Josiah's watchful eyes.

But also away from me.

2

KARA

I took up my place at the end of the line, walking silently behind the other wives and their children. The women chatted about the sermon we'd just heard, the latest episode of Josiah's podcast, and the new dress Laurie had made for herself which had gotten a lot of compliments. Josiah carried his eldest son, four-year-old Mathew, on his shoulders, while the other children skipped around his feet or were pushed in strollers by their mothers.

Nobody paid me any attention, trudging along alone.

When we reached the large, nearly new house Josiah had built for us all to share, I headed for the kitchen as unobtrusively as possible, my stomach rumbling.

Josiah caught my wrist as I reached for the refrigerator door. "Go upstairs, Kara."

"I will," I assured him without really thinking it through, my stomach protesting the fact I hadn't eaten yet today. "I just need something to nibble on first."

A hush fell over the other women, their conversations faltering, and I quickly realized my mistake.

I hadn't been sweet. Or meek. I had spoken back after being given a direct order.

His grip tightened until it hurt. "You eat more than any of the other women, and it shows. I said go upstairs. Pray to the Lord to forgive your greed."

I lowered my gaze to the floor. "Of course, Brother Josiah. I didn't mean to misspeak. I'm sorry."

My apologies didn't change his expression. The anger that hid behind the pale-blue ocean of his eyes. He let go of my arm, and I turned quickly, avoiding the stares of the other wives as I hurried up the stairs and to my bedroom.

I perched on the edge of my neatly made bed and waited.

He would come to punish me for my insolence. He always did.

Downstairs, the household went on about their normal morning routine, the wives making an elaborate brunch of eggs from our chickens and bacon from the last pig we'd had slaughtered. The bread had been baked earlier that morning before we'd all left the house, and the fresh, sweet smell of it still lingered in the air, even up here.

My stomach rumbled again, twisting itself into knots with hunger.

Josiah was right. I was a greedy woman.

I dropped to my knees on the floor, resting my elbows on the bed and steepled my hands in front of my face. "Lord, forgive me for the greed that consumes me. Forgive me for speaking out of turn. Forgive me for the disrespect I've shown my husband..."

The list of my wrongdoings fell from my tongue, barely louder than a whisper. I repeated them, over and over, praying for forgiveness, and that my sins this morning wouldn't taint yet another month of trying to conceive a child of God.

I kneeled there while everyone else gathered around the large kitchen table and food was handed out. My knees ached, pressed against the hard floorboards, while the clinking of cutlery and glasses drifted up the stairs, along with the happy family's laughter.

A family I could join, if only I were a better woman. If only I could do the one thing the Lord asked of me.

The sun got higher outside my window and then began to head in the other direction, sinking toward night.

I stayed there on my knees.

Quiet. Meek. Obedient.

The perfect wife.

It was late afternoon when my bedroom door finally swung open and Josiah strode in.

I raised my gaze in time to catch him blink in confusion, like he'd completely forgotten he'd sent me here to repent for my sins.

"Have you been on your knees all day?" he asked.

"Yes, Josiah."

He nodded in satisfaction, closing the door behind him. "The Lord is pleased with you."

I doubted that, but I didn't voice the thought out loud.

"Get up."

I tried, but my legs protested the movement after being in one position for hours. My knees screamed in pain, collapsing beneath me when I tried to put weight on them. I hit the floorboards, groaning when I tried to straighten my legs through the stiffness that had developed in my joints.

Josiah grabbed my arm and yanked it hard. "I said, get up, Kara. Do you need to spend another day down on your knees praying?"

"No, Brother Josiah." I tried again to get to my feet, but my knees just weren't having it. I whimpered, failing again. Pins and needles shot through my legs from toe to thigh, and though my brain tried to force the limbs to work, they just wouldn't. "I need a moment."

Josiah's glare turned dark. "It's always about what you need, isn't it? You need more food than anyone else. More time. More help. What about what I need?"

I dropped my gaze to the floor once more, knowing I was working him up and I needed to tread carefully, or all my hours of repentance would have been in vain. "What can I provide for you, Brother Josiah? Please. Anything. I'll do it."

He leaned down, sneering in my face. "The one thing I want from you, Kara, is the one thing you've never been able to give me. How hard is it? How hard is it to conceive a child? All the other women do it. And yet you continue to embarrass me. The wife I picked as my number one, proving over and over again how truly worthless she is. Are you trying to make a fool of me?"

I shook my head quickly. "Of course not."

"Then explain to me how you can provide a bastard child to some other man, and yet when you are married, to a man the Lord has chosen as his prophet no less, you provide me nothing? The congregation laughs at me behind my back. You do realize that, don't you? Every time they see that bastard child, they're reminded you spread your legs for another man and grew his seed. And yet you cannot do the same for me." His gaze darted around the room, landing on the small bedside table. He took three big steps toward it and yanked the top drawer open, rummaging through all my belongings. Not that I had many. A tattered book that had been read many times because there weren't many other books available to me. Some paper and a few pens.

Finding nothing of interest, he stormed to my dresser, ripping out my clothes. The neatly folded garments piled up on the floor, until he whirled around, glaring at me again. "Where are they?"

I had no idea what he was talking about, but I didn't dare say that.

Spittle formed at the corner of his mouth. "Are you deaf as well as dumb? I said, where are they?"

He left me no choice but to ask. "Where are what?"

"The pills! You stupid woman. The pills you take so you can't get pregnant. You must have some in here somewhere."

I blinked. "Pills?"

I knew I sounded like the dumb woman he accused me of being, but I had no pills. I knew such a thing existed in the outside world, but how I would get them here, I had no idea. Josiah kept us protected, never letting outsiders cross our fence lines without his escort. Children were thought of as the highest blessing a wife could give her husband. No woman here would deliberately try not to get pregnant. Or help another woman prevent conception.

It would dishonor her husband and be the greatest of sins.

Josiah stormed back, staring down at me on the floor, no offer of help or care.

He lowered the zipper on his pants. "You embarrass me, Kara."

"I'm sorry," I said again.

"Show me how sorry you truly are. Remove your veil and open your mouth."

I did as I was told. There was no other choice.

I choked on Josiah's member while he gripped my hair, thrusting in and out of my mouth, until that wasn't enough to satisfy him.

"Assume the position," he demanded. "I can't bear to look at your face any longer. Not until you remember the vows you took to honor and obey me."

Only now did he help me from the floor, though really, "help" was a kindness he didn't afford me. He dragged me up until I was on all fours, knees and hands digging into the mattress.

The frame squeaked beneath us, rocking back and forth. Our thighs slapped together, and his fingers dug into the fleshy curve of my hips as he took me. I blanked out, just like I always did.

My body might have been here, but my head took me somewhere else.

Not somewhere.

Someone.

Dirty-blond hair. Tattoos winding their way up and down strong arms. Gray-blue eyes that even now, five years later, I couldn't forget.

I buried my face in the blankets, breathing easier at the thought of him.

The one man who had never hurt me.

Josiah pulled my hair, jerking my head back. "Say my name," he demanded.

I held tight to the memory in my head, wishing I could say another man's name instead.

Hayden.

But he was my little secret. One who only lived in my memories.

"Josiah," I mumbled.

"Louder, bitch."

He'd been drinking, I realized suddenly. His true colors shined through when he'd been deep in a bottle.

"Josiah," I said again, louder.

He shuddered behind me and pulled out.

The sound of his zipper drawing up mingled with his labored breathing, his seed leaking down my thigh.

He made a sound of satisfaction. "Stay like that, head down, ass up until it has time to soak in." He made his way around the bed to stand in front of me and used my hair to draw my head up just enough that he could stare me in the eye. "You will have my child this month, Kara. This disobedience of yours cannot continue."

I nodded, like his commands could actually change the way my body had rejected him over and over again.

The door closed, and I flopped down on the bed, the disobedient whore we all knew I was.

Josiah's cum inside me, while I dreamed of another man.

3

HAYDEN

I should have worn a tie.

I cursed low beneath my breath, drawing a dirty look from the middle-aged woman and her teenage son beside me.

"Sorry," I muttered. The back of my neck heated, and I tugged uncomfortably at my collar. I'd really thought the white button-down shirt and the clean pair of jeans I'd pulled on that morning would be enough. That I wouldn't stick out like a sore thumb.

But even the teenager beside me wore a suit, like it was him who was about to walk up on stage and be handed an award by the mayor of the city.

"Hayden!"

I turned at the familiar voice and threw an easy smile at my sister-in-law Mae when she waved me over from the table she'd snagged right beside the stage.

She stood as I approached, her long black dress swishing around her ankles and her blond hair all piled up on her head in an elaborate up-do. Diamonds sparkled on her ears, and there were matching ones around her throat.

I grimaced when she wrapped her arms around me, drawing me in.

"I'm so underdressed," I whispered into her ear, hugging her back.

She stepped back, holding me at arm's length. Without missing a beat, she shook her head. "Well, I'm overdressed but I was so excited to not wear Mom clothes for a few hours, so I went all out. You look great. Your brother doesn't care what you wear. He's just going to be so glad you came."

A burly man from Mae's other side reached out a hand and took mine, shaking it with a firm grip. "You can join my no-tie club. They aren't my thing either."

I grinned at Heath, returning his handshake. He was part of my brother's family, and I'd always liked the guy. He and I were similar in a lot of ways, but it didn't really make me feel any better that his neck was also tie-free. Because his shirt was crisp linen, and his jacket and pants matched. Even his footwear showed mine up, his polished dress shoes, while I hadn't even considered wearing anything other than my old boots. I didn't even own a pair of dress shoes, let alone ones that matched my outfit as nicely as Heath's did.

I went around the table, saying hello to Rowe, the third of my brother's partners, as well as my mom and stepdad, who were busily doting on their grandsons.

I sat next to my brother's eldest, Ripley, and held out a fist to the kid.

He bumped it and grinned. "How you doing, Chaos?"

I rolled my eyes and ruffled his hair. "How many times do I have to tell you, that ain't my name no more."

Ripley sniggered. "It's so much cooler than Hayden, though. Hayden sounds like he works in a bank and eats tuna for lunch every day."

I dropped my mouth open in mock outrage. "And what exactly is so bad about tuna?"

Ripley screwed up his face in disgust. "Have you tried Mom's tuna casserole lately?" He made some quiet gagging sounds for effect.

I elbowed him. "Hey. Don't disrespect your mom like that. I bet she worked real hard to make that tuna taste good. It's your immature, preteen taste buds that are the problem."

Mae glanced over and winked at me. "Thanks for the backup, but he's right. It was awful." She turned a disapproving eye on her son. "But Hayden has asked you before not to call him Chaos. In this family, we respect that, okay?"

He nodded quickly. "I know. Sorry. I was only joking."

Mae smoothed out the hair I'd ruffled out of place, her eyes full of affection for the kid who had grown about two inches since the last time I'd seen him.

QB, my stepdad, had Mae and Liam's younger son, Jay, on his lap, and was keeping the little boy occupied with magic tricks that would only fool a six-year-old. While my mom tried to keep hold of their toddler who, despite his cute suit and tie, clearly wanted to be anywhere but here.

"Where's the man of the hour?" I asked, my gaze flicking around the room and not seeing my older brother in it.

Mae took Casper from my mom and put him on her hip. She swayed back and forth, rocking her overtired son. The ceremony was a formal lunch thing, but Cas was still young enough to need a nap. "Backstage somewhere. He's the first award, so they wanted him ready to go..."

A voice came over the loudspeaker. "Could all guests please take their seats. The ceremony is about to begin."

Mae made a face that was half excitement, half "better do as they say or we'll get in trouble." She took her seat between Rowe and Heath and looked up at the stage expectantly.

I followed suit, sitting as the room quieted. The ballroom was windowless, positioned in the middle of a government building, overhead lights the only reason we could see. They dimmed so the stage could be spotlit.

It was a relief. At least in the dark my wardrobe faux pas wouldn't be as noticeable.

With heels that clip-clopped across the stage, the mayor took to the podium. "Good morning, ladies and gentlemen. I'd like to welcome you all to today's ceremony, and thank you for coming out to support your friends and family who have earned these awards. What an honor and privilege it is for me to be invited to hand these out, and I'm sure you feel the same. These award recipients are the most outstanding members of our community. Their tireless efforts in the areas of sport, health, finance, law, and community service are overdue in being recognized."

She paused for a breath, but the people around me took it as a sign for applause. I joined in, clapping my hands.

The mayor waited for the applause to die down, then

leaned into the microphone. "Please keep that applause going for our first recipient. This award is presented to Liam Banks, for his tireless efforts in the area of law. Liam's work in representing underprivileged and low-income earners in the Saint View area has not gone unnoticed by those in his field. After speaking with him backstage, it's clear to me how much this man truly cares about giving each and every person a fair trial, no matter what they can afford to pay. On top of working at Simonson Lawyers and Partners, Liam volunteers at the local homeless shelter on a weekly basis, not only providing those in need with clothes and a safe place to sleep, but with free legal counsel. He's a dad to three, and despite all he does for the community, I'm told he still manages to volunteer at the school bake sales."

The mayor turned to the side of the stage. "Without further ado, I'd like to ask Liam to join me and accept this award."

Across the table, Heath let out a wolf whistle. Rowe cheered while clapping loudly, and Mae smiled, the pride in her eyes so bright it rivaled her diamonds.

Ripley and I joined in, clapping and cheering for my brother who strode across the stage, a big grin stretching his mouth wide. His dark-blond hair was slicked neatly to the side, and his suit was immaculate. There was zero trace of the jam-smeared dad I knew he could also be, except when he gazed down at his family around me and beamed like their cheers were worth more than the twenty thousand dollar check his award came with.

My brother took the award and the check from the mayor and then took her place at the microphone. "I'd like to thank..."

Liam's words washed over me, déjà vu sinking in. How many times had I sat in the audience, watching my brother receive awards? I couldn't count that high.

Liam excelled at everything he did. From sports to business. Hell, the man had even somehow made his polyamorous relationship such a nonevent that no one batted an eye when he walked off stage to the woman, two men, and the little tribe of kids he called family. I let them all hug him and stood behind my mom and QB, waiting for them to finish congratulating him before they sat to give me a turn.

Liam's grin widened, and he took my offered hand and drew me in for a hug. "What the hell are you doing here?" He stepped back. "I didn't know you were coming!"

I shrugged, but it was with a proud smile. "Mae invited me. Of course I came."

Up on stage, the mayor was moving on to the next award, but Liam jerked his head toward the bar, a question in his eyes.

I nodded, figuring it was after twelve and this was a special occasion, so a drink was warranted. I followed him to the back of the room and the empty bar. I pulled out a stool, Liam did the same, and we settled there, Liam ordering us both a glass of whiskey.

The bartender got busy making our drinks, and Liam set his award and check down on the bar top before turning to me.

Laughing, he punched me in the arm. "You look stupid. Where's your leather jacket and—" He leaned in and made a show of sniffing me. "Is that shampoo I smell?"

I punched him back. "At least I'm not in a suit. And fuck off. I wash my hair regularly. You're just jealous I have so much more of it than you do."

Liam reached around and tugged on the short ponytail I'd tied up at the nape of my neck. "Hey, I could grow mine out if I wanted to. Don't start rumors I'm going bald."

I sniggered as the bartender pushed our glasses toward us. "I don't know, I think that hairline is receding."

It wasn't, but it was part of the brother code to give each other shit every time we saw each other.

Liam took a sip of his drink. "You keeping yours long so no one accidentally thinks you're a fine, young, upstanding member of the community? Or just so women can pull it when you're going down on them?"

I snorted. "Don't say that too loud. You have all these people fooled, thinking you're a classy lawyer and respectable father."

"I am!"

"Pfft," I sniggered. "Hardly."

Except we both knew he was. He was a good guy through and through. He was the successful one. The smart one. The one who had settled down and given my mom grandchildren. He was the man who ran a successful law firm but still volunteered to sew on Ripley's Boy Scout patches.

Once upon a time, I'd resented Liam. I'd been jealous as hell of everything he'd been given. It all seemed to come so damn easily to him. While he'd been excelling at school and earning degrees, I'd been busy doing the opposite, hell-bent on rebelling. For every award Liam got, I would go out and get drunk. Or high. When Liam had been accepted to an Ivy League college, I'd gone out and joined a street gang, just as a fuck you.

I couldn't compete so I hadn't even bothered trying.

But things changed.

People grew up.

I grew up.

So instead of going out and getting drunk at some bar tonight while the world celebrated how great my brother was, I'd showed up for him and hoped like fucking hell that just a little of his success, his drive, and his commitment would rub off on me.

Liam watched me carefully, the teasing smile slowly fading away into something more serious. "How you been? Haven't seen you for a couple of months."

I nodded, running a finger around the rim of my whiskey glass. "Yeah, sorry about that. I know I missed Ripley's school play last month, but I'll be there when baseball starts back up."

"He'll like that. Means a lot to him when you show." He paused, thinking over his words. "Means a lot to all of us. It's been nice having you around more lately the last few years. You know that, right? You don't need an invitation. You're always welcome at whatever we're doing. Or even if you just want to drop in at home sometime. We've always got coffee." He lifted his glass again. "Or whiskey."

"Actually, I haven't been drinking much."

Liam nodded. "I noticed."

I raised an eyebrow. "You did?"

He shifted on his seat. "You think we haven't noticed all the changes you've made over the past few years? Cutting back on drinking. Showing up for family things. I haven't seen you high in years, so if you're still doing that, well, you're doing a good job of hiding it."

"I'm not," I said quietly. "Not in a long time."

Not since...

I swallowed thickly.

Liam had an uncanny ability to read people's minds. It was what made him so well liked. He paid attention. Actually gave a shit about how other people were feeling and made an effort to understand it.

He sighed heavily. "I know it's something we don't talk about, but everything that happened with Kara and those women...that was a rock bottom you needed to hit. Frankly, I'm just fucking glad you made it out alive, because we were well on our way to losing you before all of that happened."

I squeezed my eyes shut and took a thick swallow of amber liquid at just the sound of Kara's name on his lips. I might have been doing better these days, but I never let myself think about her. About everything I'd put her through.

About how she'd left five years ago, and no one had seen her since.

I knew she was safe with her family and that was all I was entitled to know after what I'd done to her.

Liam punched me in the arm again. "Hey. I didn't bring all that up to have you go dark again. I just meant we're all really proud of where you are now."

I gave him a tight smile. His words and praise meant a lot. "I'll try to come by more. I've been doing double shifts at the restaurant and working seven days a week. Just trying to save every penny I can, you know?"

Liam nodded. "I get it. How is the restaurant?"

I made a face before I could think about trying to mask it.

Liam chuckled. "That good, huh?"

I rolled my eyes. "I don't want to complain. I'm grateful for the work."

"But..."

I groaned, unleashing every shitty thought I had about my job. "Simon is driving me insane. He refuses to try anything new. Did you know we've had the exact same menu for the entire five years I've worked there? Five fucking years of the same tired burgers and french fries."

Liam shrugged. "People like burgers and french fries."

"Yeah, I guess so. Place is always busy so I get why he doesn't change things up."

"But you want more."

I lifted my gaze to meet his. "I'm an asshole, aren't I? Simon gave me a job when nobody else would. He taught me everything I know about food—"

Liam held up a hand. "Uh, no he did not."

"He did," I insisted.

But Liam wouldn't hear it. "You just told me the man has had the same menu for five years. So yeah, sure, you owe Simon for teaching you how to make decent mac and cheese, or how to deep-fry potatoes. But I've seen the shit you've been posting on your Instagram. That isn't deep-fried, diner food. Simon didn't teach you that."

That heat started up at the back of my neck again. "You follow my Instagram?"

Liam chuckled. "Mae said I wasn't allowed to tell you that we found it. She thinks it would make you uncomfortable."

"She's right." I hated the idea of my older, much more

successful brother following along my stupid, dinky little Instagram page that had less than a hundred followers. That was embarrassing.

Liam wasn't having it though. "Your food looks like something out of a cooking show. You're an amazing chef."

I shook my head. "I'm not a chef. Just a cook."

Liam rolled his eyes and pulled out his phone. A second later he spun it around to show me a photo I'd taken of the chargrilled tuna steak with salsa verde, shaved fennel, and a green bean salad I'd plated up yesterday after Simon had gone home for the night. My boss had no idea I stayed late, well past closing every night, in order to practice making dishes that weren't on his very basic menu.

I probably needed to shut the stupid Instagram page down. If Liam and Mae had found it so easily, then Simon probably would too. Then I'd be fired for fucking around.

I couldn't afford to lose my job. Not when I was this close to having the down payment for a restaurant of my own. I didn't care that I rented a shitty apartment in the worst part of Saint View. Or that my truck was about as old and run-down as they came. I'd keep putting the damn thing back together with sticky tape if it meant all my money could go toward buying something of my very own.

Something I could be proud of. That no one could take away from me.

I didn't even want to rent a place. Something deep inside me needed to know it was mine. That I couldn't be kicked out at the whim of some asshole landlord. So I'd been saving every cent for years now.

"That is the work of a chef." Liam stabbed a finger over the screen and scrolled through my photos. "As is that. And this. And this, oh damn, what is that? That looks fucking amazing."

"It's lobster thermidor."

"I don't know what that is but am I drooling? Like seriously, my mouth is so full of saliva right now it has to be sliding down my chin." He lifted the phone toward his mouth.

"If you lick that screen, I'll never let you live it down."

Liam let the phone drop away from his face. "Fine. But my point still stands. You're a chef. And you're way too fucking good to be working in that shithole diner, even if they do sell good burgers. You're going to be running your own place in no time." His eyes lit up. "Did you see that place on the main street of Providence is up for auction? That would be the best spot for a restaurant. Not a ton of competition for food like yours either, but the right market for it."

"I've seen it," I said reluctantly, knowing exactly which place he was talking about because I'd been stalking it for weeks. And just this morning my app had reminded me the auction was that afternoon. "It's going under the hammer today. In a few hours, actually. You're right. It's perfect."

So fucking perfect I wanted to cry every time I drove my shitty truck past it. I'd been looking at properties in Saint View for the best part of two years, just waiting for something workable to come up, but it hadn't happened. And then just last week, I'd gotten a ping on my real estate app, and up had popped the space of my dreams.

But of course, it was in fucking Providence, so it was well out of my price range. The two towns shared a border, but it was very much a case of upper-class snobs to the left, broke-ass bitches to the right.

I was one of the broke-ass bitches, unfortunately.

Liam, not so much.

Once upon a time that would have eaten away at me. I would have become sullen and angry about the fact he'd always had so much more.

I didn't want to go back to being that person.

Liam eyed me. "So go for it."

I peered over at him. "Go for what?"

"The place on the main road! Start your own restaurant. You've got the experience."

"But not the money."

Liam's leg bounced. "How much would you need?"

My fingers tightened around my glass. "To get the deposit the bank requires to give me the mortgage? Or to actually be up and running?"

"Both."

I shrugged. "I've got some saved for a deposit. But I'd need a lot more."

Liam pushed his check across the bar top. "Would this cover it?"

I froze. "That's twenty thousand dollars."

My brother nodded. "Yeah, that's what it says."

"I can't take that."

"I mean, sure. Not this check. It has my name on it. But I'll bank it then write one with yours."

I shook my head so fast it nearly fell off. "No. No way."

Liam rolled his eyes. "You need money. I have it. I want to give it to you."

I shoved the offending piece of paper away. "I'm not taking your money, Liam. You have a family to spend that on."

Liam stared me dead in the eye. "What are you, *Brother*?"

I swallowed hard, staring at the zeroes printed on the check. There were so many. It seemed absurd he would want to just give me that much money. I knew he had plenty of it. Hell, with three partners and four incomes, especially Liam having a partner salary from his law firm, I knew this was just a drop in the bucket to them.

But it was everything to me.

Not just money. It was dreams. Security. A legacy.

"I would pay you back," I whispered, barely daring to hope he was actually serious.

Liam shrugged. "Or you don't, and I become a silent investor in your restaurant."

That felt like way more pressure. I'd never even considered searching for investors. I was a nothing from Saint View. The idea that someone would want to invest in me was ludicrous. "What if I fuck it up and the whole place bombs?"

But Liam's gaze never wavered. "You won't." He slapped my arm. "We've all watched you grow up over the last five years. Don't think we haven't noticed you aren't the thug you used to be."

I still felt like him inside though. So much of my identity was wrapped up in "Chaos" that sometimes I still found it hard to just be Hayden.

I touched my fingers to the numbers printed on the

check. My brother was offering me everything I'd ever wanted. All I had to do was say yes.

A slow smile spread across my face. "Don't you need to ask Mae and Rowe and Heath?"

"You're their family too. I'll ask, but I already know what they'll say."

I did too. Because they were good people. So fucking good I surely didn't deserve them. Not after everything I'd done.

But I found myself agreeing anyway.

Liam held his hand out. "Partners?"

Despite myself, I nodded. "Let's buy a restaurant."

4

KARA

I stayed in the position for the required hour, silently praying a pregnancy would come from our joining. When my time was up, the sky had turned dark, and I moved slowly and stiffly to the bathroom to clean myself up.

There was no mirror in the small space, vanity frowned upon in our community, but I was glad for it. I didn't need a mirror to remind me my face and body were a disappointment.

I'd been chosen because of my ability to bear children at a time when Josiah had few other options. But he'd made no secret of his disgust and the fact he had never found me attractive. My face was too round. My thighs too thick. Breasts too full and heavy so they didn't sit high and perky anymore, if they ever had. My stomach wobbled, and silver stretch mark scars from carrying Hayley Jade inside me all those years ago covered my skin.

I brushed my teeth slowly and meticulously, spitting

toothpaste into the basin and rinsing my mouth. Reluctantly, I put my veil back on.

In the silent room, the tiny tap at my window was easily heard.

I glanced over my shoulder, trying to place the unusual sound. It came again, a tiny pebble flicking off the glass window.

I rushed to the windowsill and peered out into the night, squinting through the darkness and trying to make out the shadowy shapes on the ground below.

Alice waved to me frantically from behind a shrub, beckoning me down.

My heart rate increased, nerves racing through me. I shook my head, motioning for her to leave. If Josiah or one of the other wives caught her out there, she'd be punished.

And so would I.

But Alice was insistent. Her mouth pulled into a stubborn line, and her miming turned aggressive. She angrily pointed at me, and then down at the ground, a clear summons.

When I didn't move, she changed tactics, stabbing one finger at her chest, and then toward the front door.

Oh no. She could not come to the door at this time of night and knock. Children would wake, Josiah would be so angry. We weren't permitted guests he hadn't approved and most certainly not after dark.

Alice stepped out from behind the bushes and walked toward the door, glaring up at me in defiance.

"Stop!" I whisper-shouted, placing my palm flat on the windowpane, like that could halt her in her tracks.

To my surprise, it did. But I knew it wouldn't keep her

still long. Clearly, she had something to say and nothing I did was going to deter her. I slipped on my shoes and jacket, closing the thick material around me and belting it at my middle. I poked my head out into the hallway, checking both ways. It was empty. Muffled sounds came from behind the closed doors, the other wives putting their children to bed with lullabies and Bible stories.

I had no idea where Josiah was, but worry plagued me that he could be somewhere in the house or on his way back from a meeting.

The last thing I wanted was for him to catch Alice loitering around outside.

I crept down the stairs, grateful the house was still new enough they didn't squeak. At the landing, I hurried through the darkened living room and reached for the door handle.

"Where do you think you're going?"

I froze, spinning around.

Camilla, wife number two, scowled at me in the darkness. Her youngest was swaddled in her arms, quiet in sleep. I hadn't even seen her, curled up on the couch with her son.

"Camilla." I put my hand over my heart, trying to calm the racing pulse. "You startled me. Is Jonathan colicky again?"

"I've got him off again now. I was just about to take him back upstairs."

I nodded at her. "Of course. Don't let me stop you. I'm just going out for some air. My stomach is a little off, and my room is stuffy. A short, nighttime walk will do me good."

Camilla's eyes narrowed. "It's past curfew."

She was right. We weren't allowed outside the home after darkness fell. I already knew she would tattle to Josiah the minute he returned. The fact she hadn't already called out for him told me she knew he wasn't here.

Jealousy rolled off her in waves, just like it always did when we were forced to interact. Why, I had no real idea. She was the perfect wife. With four beautiful children in such a short space of time, surely she knew she was Josiah's favorite.

But I was wife number one, and it was clear it irked her. Even if I was a failure in every other way.

I needed to get outside before Alice came looking for me. "I'll only be a minute, and I won't go far. But I don't think anyone wants me in here, vomiting and waking the babies up. Do you? You probably should go upstairs now. I may be contagious."

Camilla screwed her nose up and covered little Jonathan's face with the blanket, like that would keep him safe from my cooties. "We'll need to disinfect everything in the morning if you have a stomach virus."

"Indeed, sister. I am truly sorry for the extra work. But please, I must go now. I really do feel quite ill."

Camilla didn't offer any sympathies like Laurie or Scarlett might have. She hurried up the stairs, leaving me blissfully alone to sneak out of the house.

I slipped out, closing the door quietly behind me and searched the darkness for my actual sister. "Alice!" I hissed.

"Took you long enough," she huffed, grabbing my arm and pulling me into the trees that surrounded my house.

I shook her off, casting a nervous glance back at the house, half expecting Camilla to be watching me out the window. "Stop it. You're going to get us both in trouble. What are you even doing here? Does Dad know you're out of the house?"

Alice huffed. "I'm a grown woman. I'll do as I please."

"Don't talk like that," I scolded. I knew all too well how sass and independence got you in trouble. I grabbed my sister's arms and spun her to face me. "You know what happened to me when I started thinking along those lines. Don't follow in my footsteps. What do you want that's so important it couldn't wait until morning?"

Alice swallowed thickly, her expression turning serious. "I think Hayley Jade is in danger."

My mouth went dry, and my heart that was already beating too fast, just because I was breaking the rules, went into overdrive at the mention of my daughter's name. "Is she hurt? Where is she?"

It didn't matter that she no longer knew me as her mother. That it was some other woman who got to tuck her into bed each night. My heart still knew she was my child.

"I'll show you." Alice dragged me into a brisk walk, and this time, instead of protesting, I followed, keeping pace with her quick steps.

"Don't ask me why I was out past curfew. I just was. But when I was sneaking back, I noticed that." She pointed ahead.

Through the darkness, a dull orange light glowed. The sounds of voices floated in the cold night air.

I stopped. "The men are at the bonfire. So what?" It wasn't exactly an unusual event. We didn't have a bar within the community, and drinking in homes wasn't allowed. Women were expressly forbidden to indulge.

But we all knew the men did. It was hardly a secret when they rolled home at two in the morning, too drunk to hide it. Not that they would have bothered trying.

Alice's lips twisted into a grim line. "They have Hayley Jade with them."

My eyes widened in shock, and then I was running through the woods, not caring if anyone heard me coming.

Alice caught me and pulled me down to the ground as the circle of men appeared. "Are you insane?" she whispered, puffing slightly from having to jog to catch me. "You can't just run in there!"

I tried to calm my rapid breathing, but I couldn't suck in enough air at the sight of my little girl, sitting on a man's lap looking tired and confused while he drank from a dark-colored bottle.

"Where's Shari?" I bit out around the lump in my throat. "Is this what she thinks being a mother is? Leaving your child to a group of men she barely knows?" I wrung my hands, fighting the urge to leap out from behind the fallen log we were using as cover and race across the clearing to snatch my daughter from the arms of the man I'd only seen a few times at church. I couldn't even remember his name.

"I don't know." Alice rubbed my hand slowly, soothingly. "But right now, everything is okay. I don't know what's going on here, which is why I came to get you. But Hayley Jade is there. She's safe at least for now. Maybe Shari asked Onith to babysit her tonight?"

I stared at my sister. "So he brought her to a bonfire so

he could get drunk?" I stared back at the possessive hold the man had on Hayley Jade's waist and didn't like it. "You can't seriously tell me you believe that, otherwise you wouldn't have just told me my daughter was in danger."

Alice sighed. "Maybe I'm just being dramatic. This could all be very innocent..."

Except her instincts had been it wasn't. And mine were screaming in alarm at the very sight of one small girl surrounded by so many men.

Drunken laughter came from the woods beyond the far side of the circle, and out stumbled Shari and a man I'd never seen before. Shari tugged at her clothes, trying to straighten them, while the man groped her breasts, fighting against her to free them from her woolen top while she tried to get it back into place.

Alice gasped. "Oh, that slu—"

I cut her off with a glare. "Don't you dare call her a name. Look at her face. You think she has a choice in whatever is going on here?"

Josiah raised an eyebrow at the couple, but his gaze focused on the man. "Well? What do you think?"

"I think your women are very lovely." He sat heavily on one of the wooden seats surrounding the fire. He grinned at the circle of men. "She was real sweet, bouncing up and down on my cock."

They all laughed, while Shari blushed and stared down at the ground, mortification written all over her face.

Josiah nodded like he was pleased and turned his gaze to the man beside the newcomer. I didn't recognize him either.

"Would you like a sample as well? We like all our new

friends to get a taste of what their lives can be like if they join us. Shari here will only be too pleased to accommodate any requests you might have. Our women like to please their men. We teach that the way to serve the Lord is to serve your husband, who was made in the Lord's image. Pleasing our men is the way our women show their faith and commitment to God. Isn't that right, Shari?"

Shari nodded quickly, pushing to her feet once more and holding her hand out to Josiah's guest.

Alice's mouth dropped open. "She's just fucked one guy now she's going to go fuck another?"

"Don't use language like that," I said on autopilot while my stomach churned.

My heart ached for the woman, so clearly being used by Josiah and his friends as bait. Was this how they were luring new members in? With promises of easy women? What else did they promise?

I looked over at my sister, who was glaring at the group with barely controlled anger.

She didn't even seem to see the danger she was in.

She'd been spared so far, but if this was what Josiah was doing, how much longer would it be before it was her, forced to take men into the woods so she could "serve God."

The new man pushed Shari's hand away, his dark eyes focused on Hayley Jade. "My tastes run…younger."

My blood turned to ice.

Alice dug her fingernails into my arm. "Don't," she whispered. "Let Josiah handle it. He's not a monster. He'll put him in his place."

My sister didn't know my husband the way I did.

Josiah motioned for Hayley Jade to come to him.

Onith loosened his grasp on her, and she walked obediently across the clearing to her leader.

Josiah's gaze rolled over my daughter, his eyes hardening. "Kneel before your leader, little girl."

"Shit," Alice mumbled.

I didn't even reprimand her for her poor language. I couldn't do anything but watch my daughter and pray she just did as she was told.

Hayley Jade pouted. "I don't like kneeling. It hurts my knees."

My heart stopped.

She was too much like me.

Josiah leaned forward, so he was face-to-face with her. The anger in his eyes at her refusal to worship him was visible even from a distance. "It's very lucky you're so pretty and worth so much money."

Onith glanced up with interest. "Wait. You're selling her?"

Josiah sat back and picked up his beer bottle again. "I've got a contact interested, and frankly, I can't stand to look at her any more. I've just been waiting, biding my time because she was so pretty I knew I could get a good amount of money for her. But she's what, six now?"

"Five," Hayley Jade said quietly.

Josiah shrugged. "Close enough."

The newcomer's greedy-eyed gaze lifted to meet Josiah's. "What is your asking price? I'll pay."

Onith shot a glance at the new man and then shook his head at Josiah. "I'll pay more than what either of them are offering. I've had my eye on her for a while."

I let out the tiniest of whimpers.

Alice wiped the back of her hand over her mouth. "I'm going to be sick. Does Dad know about this? Does Mama?"

Our father wasn't among the men sitting around the fire, and I wholeheartedly wanted to believe he knew nothing about this. But these were the same parents who had willingly sold me to Josiah, and the same parents who had allowed him to take my child and give her to another woman, so I didn't hold out much hope that they didn't know about Josiah's plans to sell her.

She was an embarrassment to them, as much as she was to Josiah. She was a daily reminder of their failures as parents and a burden nobody wanted.

Nobody except me, and these disgusting excuses for men who had entered into some sort of sick bidding war, three of them arguing now over which could pay the most money for the privilege of owning the child.

Josiah's grin of amusement told me he had probably planned this. Or at least had an inkling it might happen. Eventually, as the bidding war grew louder, he waved his free hand, his beer bottle touching his upturned lips. "Settle down, settle down. My contact will outbid you all. This is pointless. By this time tomorrow, she'll be his property."

Alice turned big eyes on me. "What are we going to do?"

I'd been brave once. I'd left, found my own way out of here, and crossed the country, searching for more.

I'd found it.

But I wasn't that woman anymore. The outside world had beaten it out of me as much as Josiah had.

Listening to these men threaten my daughter terrified

me in more ways than just the obvious. I didn't want to leave the commune. At least here, I knew my place. I had food and somewhere to sleep.

Outside, I had nothing.

But if I stayed and Josiah sold my goddamn daughter to some sick excuse for a human being, I knew I couldn't live with myself. My fingers shook in terror at the words I knew I had to say, knowing if it went wrong, we'd all be dead.

But there was no other choice. "Escape."

5

HAYDEN

"There are so many people here."

Liam looked over at me and shrugged. "This is Providence. Home of the rubberneckers. Most of these people are probably just here because their private chefs called in sick or their tennis coaches said it was too cold to practice tonight. They aren't here to buy. They're here to socialize and get the gossip on who the new owner might be."

I cringed at the thought of these people judging me. "They're gonna be real fucking disappointed when they realize it's a piece of shit loser from Saint View."

Liam thumped me on the back. "That's the spirit!"

I raised an eyebrow.

He grinned with the same snigger I remembered from when we were kids. "The spirit of you being the new owner, I mean. Not you being a piece of shit loser." He squinted at me. "Do you need Mae to give you one of her kindergarten teacher pep talks? She's been working at the prison for so long those pep talks are pretty much the only thing she has left from her time in grade school."

"No," I scoffed. But the thumping of my heart and my clammy palms said otherwise. "Actually, maybe yes? I'm shitting myself here."

Liam slung his arm around my shoulders. "Look around. You have nothing to worry about. This place was always supposed to be yours."

When he said it, his voice so full of confidence, I believed it. The space was even better in person than it was in photos. It was twice as big as I'd thought from the online listing, which had my brain ticking overtime with what I could do with the extra space. Maybe a cocktail bar. More seating. A larger kitchen area. I swallowed down my excitement. "What if we bid on this today and the bank says no?"

"They won't. My guy says with me as your silent partner, we'll get approved for a mil, no sweat."

I wiped my palms on my jeans. This was all happening so fast. Just last night I'd been resigned to at least five more years of working in Simon's kitchen, stashing every penny away until I had enough money for the deposit. And then in one day, my brother had changed everything.

I didn't let myself think past the auction. Or the fact getting a mortgage for this place was just one part of the problem. Liam's good credit rating might seal the deal with the bank, but it was me and the restaurant I'd create inside these four walls that would have to make the payments each month.

Those sorts of thoughts clearly weren't plaguing my brother though. And why would they? He'd never lived paycheck to paycheck. Not since his grandfather had plucked him from our shitty little house in Saint View and raised him like a son anyway.

"When this auctioneer opens things, go in hard and confident. Fuck all the Providence snobs. Let them know you're here, and you mean business." Liam leaned over and tapped a woman on the shoulder.

When she turned, he flashed his phone at her. "My brother is buying this place. This is his Instagram, @ChaosKitchenSaintView, and the food you and your friends will soon be eating. Spread the word."

The woman looked confused, and I couldn't blame her. I grabbed my brother's arm and towed him across the room where the real estate agent was taking registrations.

"You gotta stop that," I mumbled at Liam as we waited in line. "I can't use that Instagram if I'm opening a restaurant in Providence, and besides that, you're embarrassing me."

Liam gave an overexaggerated groan. "You have to sell yourself, little brother! Do I need to hire a marketing firm to pimp this place out?"

I swallowed thickly. "I just want to cook good food that people like. And make an honest living. I don't want to be shoving my Instagram posts down some random lady's throat."

We both looked over at the woman Liam had accosted. She was busy talking to two others, all three of them shooting not-so-secretive glances my way.

When they noticed us watching, one broke away from the group and strode over, holding out her hand to me and staring me up and down with an appraising eye.

"Pamela Lexington. My friend just told me you're bidding on this place?"

Liam elbowed me, and I started, taking the woman's hand and shaking it. "Hey, yeah." Fuck, I was so awkward. When had I become like this? I used to be full of swagger with a confidence that rivalled Liam's.

It had all been for show, a voice whispered in my head. *That was never you and you know it. What you did to Kara and her friends fucked you up so bad you—*

I cut it off, my skin crawling at the thought of Kara and the other women held captive with her.

I wasn't that man anymore.

I cleared my throat and tried again. Pamela was attractive for an older woman. She probably had twenty years on my twenty-nine, but she was well-dressed, her hair neatly brushed, makeup expertly applied. I would have put money on the fact she was a bored Providence housewife. But that meant she knew people. Had friends who would talk. Like Liam said, these people were not necessarily here to bid but to gossip.

I needed to be able to market this place, and maybe that started now. I cleared my throat. "Hayden Whitling. It's nice to meet you. I'm looking forward to bringing you and your friends a hot new restaurant. I hope you'll give us a chance once we're up and running."

Pamela continued to hold my hand, long after an appropriate amount of time for a handshake had passed. Her gaze lingered on my face, her eyes turning heated. "Indeed," she practically purred. She stepped in closer so her tits brushed my chest and her warm breath tickled across my neck. "I do hope you win the bid today. It would be nice to have some...new blood around here. You aren't a local, are you?"

I shook my head, even though it wasn't exactly the truth. But this woman didn't want to hear that I was from the ghetto just across the town border. I didn't want to be known as him either.

At least not today. Not here.

Pamela smiled. "Good luck, Mr. Whitling."

She backed off, and I took a deep breath, though I immediately wanted to cough it all back up since it was heavily laced with Pamela's expensive-smelling perfume.

Liam laughed under his breath as we moved forward. "Oh, Brother. How hard it must be to have that whole 'dirty bad boy' thing going for you."

I whipped my head around to him sharply. "I don't have that look. I ironed my damn jeans this morning."

Liam snorted on his amusement and flicked my chin-length hair. "You think actually doing your laundry hides your muscled arms, your tattoos, and your come-fuck-me eyes?"

He said it in the mocking way only an older brother could and finished the sentence with near hysterical laughter.

Even though I knew he was joking, it bothered me. "Do I really come across like that?"

Liam sobered and gave me a shrug. "You can't help it. Women like your face."

I sighed. It wasn't even just women.

I'd spent years skating by on my looks, using them to avoid the things I didn't want to do, and playing on them as a strength when I did want something. I wasn't smart like Liam. I could barely fucking read long enough to stay in school until I'd dropped out in the tenth grade. My face was all I'd had.

It had led me down a path I didn't want anything to do with.

It was why I liked working in kitchens. Most of the time I was in the back, surrounded only by pots and pans, knives, and fresh ingredients.

Nobody could see my face. Or considered if I was intelligent or dumb as a doormat.

I was judged on the plates the waiters set on the tables.

I was praised because of the work I put into my craft, not just because I'd been lucky enough to be born with a pleasing facial structure.

Every time someone commented on my face, I just felt cheap. It reminded me of every lame come-on line I'd used on women, barely putting in the effort because I knew I didn't have to. It freshened the memories of everyone praising Liam for winning another award, or graduating with another degree, while I fell further and further behind, always in his shadow unless I was picking up someone at a bar who would make me feel better.

Cooking had given me something more. It had opened a different part of me, one I didn't want to lose.

The people in front of us shuffled forward, and we took their spot. The woman behind the desk smiled up at us. Her gaze glanced over Liam and landed on me.

She leaned forward, her tits straining against the vaguely see-through material of her blouse. "Good morning, gentlemen. How can I help you?"

"We'd like to register to bid," I told her.

"Oh, of course." She dragged her gaze away from me and over to Liam. "What was your name, please, sir?"

Liam glanced at me with a slight cringe. "I'm not bidding. He is."

The woman's eyes widened. "I'm so sorry! I misunderstood..." She paused for a second and then gave me a tight smile. "I'm so sorry to ask, but do you have your finances in order? The owners are really only interested in serious bidders."

A new determination settled over me. She hadn't asked Liam if he was a serious bidder.

I needed this restaurant.

I needed people to take me fucking seriously. I was so sick of being nothing.

"My finances are sorted," I told her through gritted teeth.

She dug her teeth into her bottom lip and wrote down the rest of my details as I rattled them off, but I couldn't shake the feeling she thought I was wasting everyone's time.

"Let it go," Liam said quietly, moving away.

Every muscle in my body felt overwound, so tight they hurt. "Easy for you to say. People don't underestimate you."

Liam sighed heavily, but he didn't comment, probably because he knew I was right.

But that wasn't his fault. "Sorry," I mumbled. "I just really want this place."

"I know. Tell me all your plans for it."

"You already heard them."

He elbowed me. "Yeah, but you're like an excited kid

on Christmas morning when you talk about it, and that's the vibe we need to go into this auction with."

He was right. So I spent the next fifteen minutes rattling off every idea I'd ever had for my own space, and minute by minute, the vision came alive before me. I could see the bustling kitchen. Smell the fresh ingredients. Hear the smiles and laughter of the guests in the dining room.

The sense of pride that settled over me was one I wanted to live in.

It was one that washed away some of the bad shit I'd done.

One that made me feel like I could actually call myself a man.

And when the auctioneer clapped some rolled-up papers into his palm, I knew without a doubt I was going to make this place mine.

"Welcome, ladies and gentlemen, and thank you for your interest in this spectacular property. What will it become? A clothing boutique? A bookstore? A lovely little café for our residents to while away a lazy Sunday morning? Seventy-four Main Street, Providence, indeed has many different possibilities, and I know you all agree as we have several very excited bidders here this afternoon, as well as two on the phone, being represented by our agents."

The woman who had registered us earlier and a man about the same age both raised numbered paddles from the sides of the room. Both of them held phones to their ears with their free hands and spoke in quiet tones to the bidders they were representing on the other end.

The auctioneer clapped his papers again. "Okay!

Without further ado, let's get this show on the road. Let's start the bidding. Does anyone want to start us off?"

Liam's words about going in and going in strong were fresh in my mind.

As was the memory of the real estate agent assuming I didn't have the money for a place like this. I raised my paddle. "Nine hundred thousand."

Liam's surprised gaze bored into the side of my face, but I refused to look at him, even when he whispered, "Damn, bro. I said go hard, I didn't say wipe out the entire fund on your first bid."

"I didn't," I whispered back. "We still have a hundred thousand to play with, but what's the point in beating around the bush?"

Liam nodded. "Fair enough. Let's see where this goes."

"Strong opening bid from bidder two seventy. Thank you, sir. Can I hear nine hundred and fifty?"

The agent representing a telephone buyer raised her hand. "Nine-fifty."

"Excellent! Can I hear a million?"

"Steady," Liam warned. "That's a suggested bid, not the one you have to make."

I nodded, raising my hand to bid nine seventy instead, but the auctioneer took a bid from elsewhere in the crowd. "A million! Excellent."

My stomach lurched, and I raised the paddle. "A million and five," I called out. I would find the extra five thousand somewhere, even if I had to steal it. It was only five K.

The agent on the phone lifted her hand. "One million and fifty thousand!"

I sucked in a shocked breath.

Liam grimaced and made a disappointed sound beneath his breath. "Listen, man. It wasn't—"

"One point one," I called out, raising my paddle again.

Liam stared at me. "We don't have—"

"One point one five," the agent called out, then went back to speaking quickly into the phone.

My heart thrummed behind my chest. Anxiety and adrenaline mixed inside me, swirling dangerously. "One point two," I yelled before I could even think about it.

Liam yanked my arm down. "What the hell are you doing? We don't have approval for anything over a million!"

"I'll get the money."

"From where? You going back to running drugs and selling women?"

I froze.

Liam shook his head and swore beneath his breath as the agent on the phone bid another twenty thousand. "I'm so fucking sorry. I shouldn't have said that."

The auctioneer turned my way, peppering me with questions about whether I had another bid in me. I shook my head, letting the paddle drop from my fingers, while Liam's words echoed around my head.

Liam ran a hand through his hair and let out a sharp breath. "Hayden, shit. I didn't mean..."

I pressed my lips into a tight line. "I know," I assured him. "You were right to bring it up. I was in over my head and needed to be reminded of my place. And it ain't here."

Liam tried to grab my arm, but I pulled away, walking out of the building and leaving a dream behind.

6

KARA

I didn't dare take my eyes off Hayley Jade. Firelight flickered over her sweet face, and I'd removed my veil without permission, not caring if I was caught in public without it. I refused to have my vision obstructed by anything when watching my daughter. Making sure she was safe was more important than it had ever been.

Alice tried to convince me to go and pack a bag, but I shook my head stubbornly. There was nothing in my room I wanted. Josiah had long ago stripped away everything I cared about. I had no idea how we were going to get out, or how we'd get away with no money or resources, but none of that mattered when Hayley Jade wouldn't even be here in twenty-four hours if we tried to delay long enough to make a plan. If Josiah had his way, she'd be sold and shipped off.

I'd already lost her once.

I wasn't going to lose her again.

It took another hour, but eventually Shari came back

from the woods for the second time, more haggard and used up than I'd ever seen her. The second man, the one who'd bid on Hayley Jade, had taken his turn with Shari after all. A consolation prize when Josiah had refused him the thing he really wanted. The newcomer zipped up his pants as he returned to the circle, and Shari brushed fallen leaves and dry winter grass from her hair and the back of her top.

I wanted to hate her. For allowing my daughter to be here. For not keeping her safe.

Except, wasn't I just as guilty? Just as helpless?

All I could do was pity the woman who wasn't even protected by the sanctity of marriage. Josiah might have used my body whenever the mood took him, but at least he didn't rent me out to his friends.

"Take the girl home, Shari," Josiah demanded. "Make sure she is clean and presentable tomorrow. I'll need some photos of her so we can get things underway."

Shari hesitated.

Josiah's gaze sharpened. "Is there a problem with that? You were told long ago what the Lord's plans for this girl were. She is not part of our flock. She is tainted with the evil of the man who made her. She cannot be allowed to stay within our walls, especially not as beautiful as she is. You saw what happened here tonight. She is a temptation that will divide our men."

Shari nodded quickly. "Of course. I will follow the Lord's word, Brother Josiah. I will have her ready."

Josiah ran his finger down the side of her face and lifted her chin, so she was forced to look him in the eyes. "That's more like it. The Lord will be pleased by your obedience, as am I. Now take the child and go."

Shari gathered up Hayley Jade who was slumped over on the log seat, too tired to stay awake any longer. She didn't stir as Shari strode from the campfire, Hayley Jade in her arms.

"Go," I said to Alice. "Pack whatever you need but do it quickly and silently." I swallowed thickly, not sure if what I was going to say next was the right thing to do or not. But I had to try. "Wake our sisters and tell them to come with us."

Alice shook her head quickly. "We can't! They'll never come! Naomi and Samantha do everything right. You know they do. They'll alert everyone, and we'll never get out."

She was right, but guilt crushed me at the thought of leaving them behind. "Will you be able to sleep at night if we leave them, knowing what we know now? Jacqueline is barely older than a child, but beautiful enough to turn men's heads everywhere she goes. I've seen them staring at her, Alice! And not just in this perverted little circle where darkness and alcohol make them brave. They stare at Jacqueline in church like they're a pack of hungry wolves and she's a rabbit. No shame that everyone can see them. You know she'll be next. All of our sisters will be."

"Naomi and Samantha long for husbands," Alice argued.

She was right. They did. I bit my lip with a sigh, then finally nodded, agreeing with her. Naomi and Samantha were made for this life in a way that Alice and I were not. I tried to be everything that was expected of me but failed at every hurdle. Alice didn't even try. One of those newcomers could be the man who decided he wanted her, and then Alice's life, which might have been reasonably good up until now, my father somewhat tolerant of her antics, would become identical to mine. She'd be a slave to her husband, there only to serve his needs and raise his children.

He'd eat up every ounce of her sparkle and leave her as dust.

Naomi and Samantha would thrive with those boundaries. Alice would shrivel up and die, and so would my bright-eyed daughter.

I couldn't save them all.

"We leave Naomi and Samantha," I agreed. "You're right. They'll never come. But we have to take Jacqueline."

Alice nodded determinedly. "I can do it. I can make her understand. You get Hayley Jade. I'll get Jacqueline. Meet me outside our place as quick as you can. It's closer to the road." Her eyes were bright with excitement. "We're really doing this?"

Dread pooled in my stomach.

Alice saw this as a big adventure.

While I knew it was anything but. Alice had never been outside the walls that had been erected around our community. She'd been so sheltered, daydreaming about what life beyond the fences would be. Romanticizing it. No idea what the actual reality was.

But I knew. I'd been her once. I'd left and gone exploring, only to realize the world outside was worse than what I had in here. It was dark and depraved, no happiness to be found.

I didn't want to leave the commune.

But Josiah had left me no choice.

Alice disappeared into the darkness, and I did the

same, leaving the light of the bonfire behind me, praying the men would all stay there for hours more, drinking away the night until they were too intoxicated to get up and notice we'd gone.

Maybe if I was lucky, they'd all pass out, the fire would burn low, and the night frost would take them.

Something inside me delighted in the thought of their deaths, but I quickly banished the thought, knowing it stemmed from the evil inside me I hadn't been able to shake in the five years since I'd returned from the outside.

Those demons still lurked inside me. It was yet another reason the Lord would not bless me with a pregnancy.

And I was about to make it so much worse. Step by step into the darkness, I could practically feel my insides blackening.

I was ruined.

But my determination to get Hayley Jade to safety mattered more than the state of my soul.

I caught up with Shari as she left the woods and entered the main area of the commune. We didn't have streets as such, at least not with signposts and names, but there were well-worn paths between the central gardens and the modest homes that had been built around the edges.

Shari took a path I knew well. It led to the small cottage I had once lived in with my baby.

Back before I was wife number one.

My heart ached at the sight of it now. The little home I'd created for my daughter, that had been given to Shari when I'd been given to Josiah. I paused a few feet away and watched Shari enter her home, the lights flickering on and spilling out around the edges of the curtains.

"What now, Kara?" I mumbled out loud, breathing into my ungloved hands to warm them. I could practically hear a clock ticking in my head, counting down the seconds until Josiah would leave the bonfire and realize I wasn't in my bed.

I froze when the door to Shari's cabin opened before I could even decide what to do.

Shari stared right at the shrub I was hiding behind. "Are you coming in or just hanging around out there waiting to get caught?" she whispered.

Shock held me immobile for a moment, but Shari waved me in impatiently again, and slowly, I rose from my crouched position.

"Hurry," she whispered.

I passed by her and into the home I'd once known so well.

Shari closed the door behind me, then the two of us stared at each other in the tiny living room of the cabin I'd once called home. Nothing much had changed. All the furniture was still the same as when I'd left. Only now, the handful of baby toys that had sat in a wicker basket in the corner was replaced with a small desk with crayons and paper, and a ragged doll.

Shari followed my line of sight and picked the toy up off the floor. She held it close to her for a moment and then reluctantly held it out to me. "She'll need this. Here. Take it. The crayons and papers too. She likes to draw."

I didn't dare move, my heart pounding. Was this a trap? Something her and Josiah had conjured up together to test my loyalty?

Shari's expression shifted to desperate. "Take it!" She threw the items at my chest, so I had no choice but to grasp them before they fell to the floor.

Shari found a small backpack in the mudroom closet and started pulling tiny clothing from a laundry basket of fresh-smelling, neatly folded clothes. She shoved as many as she could fit into the backpack and then thrust that at me too.

I stared down at the bag full of Hayley Jade's things and then back up at Shari. "I don't understand."

Shari's expression turned angry. She glared at me with barely concealed hate. "You're taking her, aren't you? Getting her out of here?"

"I..." I closed my mouth, too scared to say a word. My brain screamed this was a trap. That this woman and Josiah were working together to trick me.

Shari moved in until we were practically nose to nose. She stared at me with such intensity I desperately wanted to turn away and yet I didn't dare anger her further.

Shari's eyes blazed as hot as the bonfire. "Listen to me, Kara, and listen to me good. Take that little girl and run. Run as far and as fast as you can." She strode to the couch and lifted one of the sagging cushions. Beneath it, she withdrew an envelope and pushed it at me. "Here. Take this. It's not much, but it should get you a bus ticket."

With trembling hands, I looked down into the open envelope. Inside was a handful of small bills. Maybe two hundred dollars altogether. I snapped my head up in shock. "Women can't have money here."

Shari sniffed. "You think I don't know that? That's why I had it hidden beneath the couch."

"How..."

Shari sighed. "The only way women have ever made money when they have nothing else to give. You saw what happened tonight. You think that's the first time? The newcomers don't know Josiah doesn't allow us women to have money. Many are in the habit of tipping to ease their guilt."

My heart broke for the woman. She was older than me, maybe even closer to my mother's age. I grasped her hand. It was cold, and I rubbed it briskly between mine. "Come with us. You don't have to stay here and keep doing this."

But the woman shook her head. "I can't. I've been saving that money for years, knowing this day would come and I would have to protect that child. But I have nowhere to go. Nobody to help me. If I leave, I'll just end up doing the same thing I'm doing here, but with no home, and no community around me." She stared down the hall to where I knew there was a small bedroom. "I would have done it, for her." She shifted her gaze back to me. "But you have a shot on the outside, Kara. You have a sister out there who will help you, right? I remember seeing her once years ago, when she came to visit your family, back before Josiah closed us off."

I swallowed thickly and nodded. "Rebel."

"You'll go to her?"

I bit my lip. I hadn't spoken to my sister in years. Not since shortly after I'd married Josiah and lost Hayley Jade. "It's the first place they'll look for me."

Shari nodded. "You don't have much choice though. Go. Ask her to help you find somewhere safe. Somewhere they won't find you. That money will get you and Hayley

Jade there, and maybe pay for some food for a day or two. But you're going to need more."

I knew she was right. I had no other contacts. No other way of getting money. The last time I'd left the commune with nothing had ended with me desperate and foolish.

Despite our lack of contact, Rebel would help me. She was a good person. Even though our communication had ended when Josiah had taken my phone, she wouldn't send me away.

"Mama?" a tiny voice called from down the hall.

Both Shari and I turned.

My heart broke in two when Hayley Jade ran down the hallway and wrapped herself around Shari's legs.

When she'd said Mama, she hadn't meant me.

Shari knelt on the floor, so she and Hayley Jade were eye height. "Listen to me, Jade. I'm not your mama." Her voice wobbled, and her eyes brimmed with tears. "I got to be for a little while, and I will always love you like you were my own. But I can't be what you need anymore. You're going to go with Sister Kara, okay? She's your mama now."

Hayley Jade snuck a peek up at me, her eyes filled with fear. "No! I don't want to."

My knees shook, threatening to give out.

Shari's voice wobbled. "I know, sweetheart. But you can't stay here anymore. You have to leave." She wrapped her arms around Hayley Jade quickly, crushing the girl to her chest before urging her to me. "Take her."

"No!" Hayley Jade clung to Shari, digging her fingers into the woman's skirts, her eyes filling with tears. "I don't want to go! Mama, no!"

Shari gave a tiny sob. "Take her, Kara," she urged, her face crumpling and her voice breaking. She pushed Hayley Jade to me again. "Please! Just take her and go. Don't get caught. Make sure she has a good life away from this place. She's your daughter. She always was."

My heart broke in two, gratitude filling me for the woman who had taken my spot but was now giving it back to me. I reached for Hayley Jade, grasping her arm.

She opened her mouth and let out a blood-curdling scream.

I froze, despising that my touch had produced that sort of response in my own child.

Shari shook Hayley Jade hard. "Stop that. You won't say a word. You won't make another sound. Not if you want to be safe. You hear me? Not one. Now do as I say and go."

Silent tears of fear and betrayal fell from Hayley Jade's eyes.

But not a sound left her little lips as I tried to pick her up again. Shari covered her with a black coat and then urged me toward the door.

"Come with us," I begged her again.

But Shari had already closed the door, leaving me outside in the frost with the daughter who feared me, and absolutely no idea what the hell I was doing.

7

HAYDEN

When I was a kid, my mother had peeped out the blinds every time she wanted to leave the house and checked the barrage of locks she'd had installed on the doors and windows. I'd grown up thinking it was normal for that mild level of panic to be present every time you stepped outside.

It made you pay attention to your surroundings. To check for danger at every turn. It was a habit that had only been reinforced when I'd grown up and joined a gang.

My mother might have been a bit paranoid, perhaps trying to protect two young kids from the dangers of our neighborhood. But I'd made it a thousand times worse by joining the Sinners. I'd made myself a real target. One people truly did want to hurt.

I had every reason to pay attention to my surroundings whenever I left my home. Even now.

So I noticed the sleek gray car outside my shitty apartment before I even stepped out of it. The car stuck out like a sore thumb because of how expensive it was, but I would have noticed it anyway. Because noticing changes like that was what kept you alive in a town like this. Even five years after leaving the Sinners, I still waited for the pop-pop-pop of a gun, sure that's how my days would end.

There were no rounds fired, but the driver of the car opened the door and stepped out. "Chaos."

My lip curled, and I strode past the man without acknowledging him.

"Chaos, come on. I just want two minutes of your time."

I glanced over at Luca, a man I barely knew, but what I did know was enough that I didn't want to know any more. "Got places to be."

"Your job at the diner?"

I didn't answer. I didn't want to tell him yes. I hated that he knew where I worked. But of course he did.

Luca Guerra knew fucking everything and everyone.

He didn't move out of my way, so I brushed past him, forcing him back, refusing to budge just because he was one of the biggest crime lords Saint View had ever seen. Though I'd never seen the man get his hands dirty. Oh no, he had idiots like me to do that for him.

He'd *had* idiots like me. I was out. I didn't work for him or for Caleb or for any of his other minions anymore.

Luca put his hands into the pockets of his expensive suit pants. I'd bet they could have paid my rent for a year. Fucking rich people.

"Do you actually like that grubby shithole you serve food out of?" he called.

I pulled my keys from my pockets. "Anything is better

than my previous job," I called back. "Last boss was a real fucking asshole. Maybe you've met him?"

Luca chuckled deeply. "Do you mean me or Caleb?"

"Why not both?" I threw back, hitting the beeper on my keys to unlock my truck doors and cursing the fact this damn apartment building only had street parking. If it were in a nicer neighborhood, I could have avoided this entire conversation with an underground garage. "Plenty to hate about both of you."

Luca followed me down the road. "I'm insulted you'd put me in the same league as Caleb."

Oh, that was rich. "Why? Aren't you the one who had him finding women for you to sell?"

Luca shrugged. "Aren't you the one who held them against their will for him?"

My fingers curled around the keys so hard I was sure it would leave imprints. "I didn't have a choice. He blackmailed me."

Luca tutted under his breath. "Well, if that's true, then I'm sorry. If I'd known..."

If he'd known he wouldn't have done shit, and we both knew it.

I turned to glare at him. "I've already had a fucking shittastic day, and you showing up here out of the blue sure isn't fucking helping. So just cut to the chase, Guerra. What the fuck do you want?"

"I would like to offer you a job. Isn't that great?"

I stared at him. "Are you fucking serious?"

He dropped the fake positivity. "Deadly."

I shook my head, completely astonished by the balls on him. I stepped in close so we were nose to nose. I wasn't some dumb kid anymore. I wasn't scared. And I wasn't falling for his smooth talk. "Hear me when I say, Guerra, I would rather hack my own dick off with a rusty blade than ever work for you again. Now leave me the hell alone and let me get to work. My boss will be pissed if I'm late."

Luca nodded knowingly. "Simon is a cunt, isn't he?"

I paused with my door on the handle. "You really did your homework on this one, huh?"

Luca grinned. "Always do. Want to hear what else I know?"

"Not even a little bit."

Luca went on like I hadn't spoken. "I know you're way too good a chef to be working at his shithole."

I froze.

Luca noticed. "I know all about your Instagram account. That's not the food you're making for Simon."

"No, it isn't," I gritted out, hating that he'd seen my social media. Fucking hell. I should have never started that stupid thing. It had caused me nothing but problems.

"Making all those sloppy burgers and deep-fried potatoes can't be very fulfilling for you when you can make dishes with titles I can barely pronounce."

"My burgers aren't sloppy."

He chuckled. "Of course not. But hardly a test of your skill either."

He was right there. It was completely unfulfilling work. But it was a means to an end.

At least I'd thought it had been. But I'd been outbid so badly at that auction that now I wondered if there was actually any point to having dreams bigger than running Simon's kitchen. Even with my brother's help, which was humiliating enough in its own right, I couldn't afford to get into the game.

Not in Providence anyway. And there was no point serving up Wagyu beef in Saint View, where I probably could afford the rent. No one here had the money or the palette for the sort of food I wanted to serve.

"I heard you bid on a place in Providence today," Luca mused.

I stared at him, anxiety creeping up my spine slowly and insidiously.

Luca Guerra taking this much interest in someone was never a good thing.

He continued, not caring that I wasn't responding. "Great spot on the main street in Providence. Perfect for an upmarket restaurant and bar, don't you agree?"

I agreed so fucking hard I wanted to cry just thinking about what I'd lost today.

"Such a big, beautiful space. Plenty of room for a huge, state-of-the-art kitchen. Low lighting over private tables. A bar serving all the very best top-shelf liquor. Even room for functions and parties in the back."

I hadn't even thought of using the extra space like that. But it was a good idea.

It hurt that all of that had gone to someone else. That I hadn't even been close to being able to afford it. Luca rubbing salt in the wound wasn't helping.

"If you're done trying to get under my skin, I'm going to leave now. See you around." I yanked open the car door and slid into the seat.

"What if I told you that restaurant could be yours?"

I squeezed my eyes shut tight and gripped the

steering wheel, willing myself to close the door and drive away.

But Luca grinned at me through the windshield. "Ah. That interests you. I thought it might after hearing how much you bid for the place. How the hell were you going to pay the mortgage on that?"

I refused to answer.

Luca nodded knowingly, like somehow, with just my silence, I'd spilled all my secrets. "Ah. You couldn't. You were in way over your head."

Anger boiled my blood. I hated that he knew exactly which buttons to push to make me feel like shit. It was the same way I felt every time my brother had been awarded a new trophy for outstanding excellence, while I came home with nothing but a detention notice my mother had to sign with a disappointed expression on her face. It was almost a fucking relief when Liam's paternal grandfather had noticed his talent for everything and plucked him out of Saint View to raise in Providence as his heir.

It had only deepened the divide between my brother and me though. And it was one we were still actively trying to mend, decades later.

I wondered if Luca knew all of that too.

One look at his smug face said he probably did.

I switched the engine on.

"I was the winning bidder, Chaos," he called over the roar of my engine. "And I want you to run the place."

I turned off the engine.

Luca grinned. "It would be everything you want it to be. You'd have full control over the menu. You could make any dish you'd ever desired, in the kitchen of your dreams. You would do all the hiring, and I have a very generous budget in mind so you could attract some real talent to work alongside you. I'd pay you a top-level salary, and your sign-on bonus will include shares. Making you a part owner."

The words hung in the air around me like pictures. Images of the life I'd so desperately wanted but had watched slip through my fingers just an hour before.

Luca was offering it all to me on a silver platter.

He tossed me an envelope, thick with the papers it enclosed. It had my name on it. Not Chaos, but Hayden Whitling.

"I don't sleep on talent, Chaos. That's contracts and shareholder documentation. A draft because my lawyers can only do so much in an hour, but it's a solid deal. Have your brother look it over if you want. You'll see it's all above board." He paused, watching me carefully. "Come work for me, Hayden. I think we both know you want to."

I pulled out the top page of the contract, my gaze catching on the number printed neatly next to the word salary.

It was six figures.

And came with a ten-percent share in ownership.

Luca grinned. "You like?"

There was nothing about that offer not to like.

Except for the man it came from.

I pushed the contract back inside the envelope and stuck my hand out of the open window.

Then let it fall to the road.

Fuck Luca Guerra. My words held a barely concealed snarl. "You can take your offer back to whatever fiery pit of Hell you crawled out from. I wouldn't work for you for all the money in the fucking world."

I was done with that life. I was done with gangs and violence.

I wasn't going to be dragged back in with the lure of everything I had ever wanted.

Regret burned bitter on the back of my tongue.

Apparently, I was done with dreams too.

8

KARA

Alice wasn't at the meeting spot.

I stared up at the house I'd grown up in. It was one of the original properties, built back when these lands had just been a hundred-acre farm, surrounded by a couple of polite neighbors we would wave at as we traveled into town once a month for supplies.

Josiah had bought the land to the south of our property first, and then soon after the property that bordered our northern fence. What had started as a friendship between my father and the new owner next door had grown until we were calling him uncle, and then brother.

I'd been a stupid, naïve kid. I hadn't understood what was happening as the land around us became dotted with small cottages, and more and more people moved in.

But even if I'd been older, like my parents, I doubted anyone could have foreseen what this place would become over the course of the next two decades. Even five years ago, the commune had been nothing like it was today.

The fences had seemed important. Necessary for keeping us safe.

But now I saw them for what they truly were. Designed to keep us in. Small. Scared.

"Come on, Alice," I mumbled, desperately searching the windows for any sign of her moving around on the other side. But there was nothing. Had something happened? Surely a light would have come on if my parents had caught her.

I glanced up toward the road, knowing it was there even though I couldn't see it. It was a mile or two, but it should be an easy walk, since we could follow the main driveway. Once we were beyond that, it was miles more to the nearest town though.

Panic lit up inside me again. This was never going to work.

I glanced down at Hayley Jade beside me. She stared dead ahead, completely silent and unmoving.

But she was here. She was alive. If I didn't do something, that wouldn't be the case in twenty-four hours' time.

"Come on." I tugged her hand, and together we ran across the frosty front lawn of my parents' house. I put my finger to my lips when we reached the stairs, and silently, the two of us crossed the old wooden porch.

They had never locked their doors. Nobody here did. It was easy to turn the handle and push open the heavy wood, though I cringed when it gave a tiny, short squeak of protest.

The mudroom on the other side was familiar. It was exactly the same as it had been when I'd lived here years before. The jackets hanging on the walls and the boots lined up neatly in rows were all larger than I remembered, a clear reminder that while Josiah had kept me sequestered away, my sisters had all grown up.

All except one.

I couldn't leave Jacqueline behind. Or Alice.

"Stay here," I whispered to Hayley Jade, praying she wouldn't try to run back to Shari. "Remember what..." I swallowed hard. "Remember what your mama told you. Be still and quiet and you'll be safe."

She sat on the bench seat I nudged her toward but didn't agree. She didn't seem like she was going to run though.

That would have to be enough. I moved silently through the house, up the stairs that led to the bedrooms and around the corner that led to Jacqueline's and Alice's bedrooms.

"Oof," Alice grunted softly, colliding with me in the hall. She put her hand over her heart when she recognized me. "Shit, Kara, you scared me half to death. I thought you were Mama. I was about to make up some sort of lie about sleepwalking."

I ignored her, my gaze sliding past her to my youngest sister.

Jacqueline's eyes were wide with fear. But a determination shone behind them.

"Are you okay?" I asked, voice barely above a whisper.

She nodded quickly.

She wasn't, but she would be. Somehow. I motioned for the two young women to follow me and I swiveled silently on my heel, heading back the way I'd come

Down the stairs. Through the living area and to the

mudroom where Hayley Jade sat exactly where I'd left her.

Thank God.

"Let's get out of here." Alice shouldered her backpack now that she had room. "We need to get up to the road and through the fence before those douchebags at the fire run out of beer to drink and women to abuse. Sayonara, house. I won't miss you."

Alice gave the finger to the stairs we'd just come down, and Jacqueline gasped. I didn't blame her. I didn't know what had gotten into my sister. She'd always been a bit unpredictable, a little wild, but I'd never seen her this openly disrespectful.

It wasn't the way we'd been brought up.

Alice strode for the door, taking Hayley Jade's hand and pulling her along with her.

I followed, pausing at the doorway to look back over my shoulder at Jacqueline.

She stood frozen, stuck between the life she knew upstairs and the unknown that lay beyond the gates.

I held my hand out to her. "Come on," I urged. "Alice told you why we had to leave, right?"

Jacqueline nodded.

But she didn't move.

She was reacting much the same way Hayley Jade had, reminding me she was barely more than a child herself. She needed me to be the strong one.

Which was a role I was wholly unfamiliar with.

"Trust me." I tried to keep the wobble out of my voice. "I'll keep you safe. You just have to come with me. I swear, it will all be all right."

The overhead light flickered on.

Jacqueline and I both froze.

"What's going on?" Naomi sleepily rubbed her eyes and blinked in the sudden light, even though she was the one who'd created it. Her eyes widened as her gaze landed on me, without my veil on. "Kara? What on earth are you doing here? Does Brother Josiah know..." Her forehead furrowed in confusion when she noticed Hayley Jade's backpack slung over my shoulder, and a similar one strapped to Jacqueline's back. Her shoulders straightened, and any remaining grogginess disappeared. "Why do you both have backpacks?"

I grasped her hand, nothing to say to her but the pure, honest truth. "Jacqueline is in danger. So are you. All the women here are. We're leaving. Tonight."

"Leaving? Leaving where? The house? Where are you going?"

I shook my head fast, my heart pounding at how long we were taking and how every second we stood down here was another second we risked being caught. But I had to try. Try to convince her to come with us. "We're leaving the commune."

Naomi ripped her hand away so quick it was like I'd burned her. And from her expression, I may as well have just burst into Hell-spawned flame.

"You don't have permission," she protested.

Jacqueline's eyes watered. "Kara and Alice heard the men talking about selling women..."

Naomi squeezed her eyes shut tight, like a toddler who thought that if she couldn't see, then no one could see her either. "No. They must have misheard. Now go back upstairs before Mama and Daddy catch you talking such nonsense."

"It's true," I whispered urgently. "Please, Naomi. Just listen to me. You're all in danger."

My sister's eyes narrowed. "The only person we're in danger from is you, Louisa Kara. There's a reason Brother Josiah keeps you locked up in that house. It's so your evil doesn't spread."

My heart split in two at my sister's hard, cold words.

"Naomi!" Jacqueline gasped. "Don't talk like that! She's our sister."

Naomi shook her head. "She hasn't been my sister for a long time."

Her expression hurt more than any of the beatings I'd taken. Any of the cruel words my husband had taunted me with.

The only thing that hurt more was losing my daughter, and I wasn't about to do that again.

I nodded at Naomi and the scorn and indignation in her eyes. She might have hated me in that moment, but I couldn't bring myself to feel the same. There would be no coming back here after this night. This would be the last time I'd ever get to see her. "I'll miss you, Sister," I said quietly, meaning every word. I turned to Jacqueline. "Come on. We need to go."

Naomi grabbed Jacqueline's arm and glared at her. "You are doing no such thing. I don't care what Kara and Alice do. They're grown women, and if they want to disrespect Brother Josiah and our Lord by leaving, then that's on their souls. But they aren't dragging an innocent child down with them. I will scream this house down and have Mama and Daddy here in a second if you so much as take a step outside this house, Jacqueline. You are not going to be dragged down by them. I won't stand for it. You're a good girl."

I was suddenly glad Hayley Jade was outside somewhere with Alice, out of Naomi's sight. If she'd known we were taking her too, she would probably already be screaming.

Unless she believed that innocent little girl was also as evil as the woman who'd given birth to her.

"Let her go," I begged Naomi in a frantic whisper, checking over my shoulder for the others, but I couldn't see them through the open door. "Please. You don't know what you're doing by keeping her here."

"I know exactly what I'm doing," Naomi argued, her voice rising with every syllable. "I'm staring down the Devil, protecting an innocent from his clutches." She shook her head at me with a look of pitying disgust. "There's no hope for you, Louisa Kara. Go. Leave our house and our community, we're all better off without you."

I drew in a sharp breath.

Naomi's eyes softened just the tiniest bit, like maybe she realized she'd gone too far. But she didn't admit it. "Leave Jacqueline and I'll give you a five-minute head start before I raise the alarm."

"Naomi!" Jacqueline whispered. "You can't tattle on them! I won't go, but you can't say a word! If they're caught..."

I didn't even want to think about it. The punishment would be the worst I'd ever received.

But Naomi held her frame tight and shook her head. "I won't have Brother Josiah thinking I was unfaithful or that I kept this a secret. Five minutes is being more than generous."

Five minutes? We were never going to get out in five minutes.

Naomi didn't relent though. "Time is ticking."

I frantically glanced to Jacqueline, knowing I couldn't stay.

She nodded. "Go," she said quietly. "I'll be okay."

I had to hope she would be. I had to pray our father would be man enough to stand up to Josiah if the time came.

I had to accept I couldn't save both her and my daughter.

Hayley Jade had to come first.

I turned and fled from the house, silent tears streaming down my face in the cold, dark night of winter.

My breaths frosted around my lips, and my heart rate tripled until I could barely breathe. Panic coursed through my veins, terror pushing me on.

Alice and Hayley Jade waited for me at the edge of the clearing.

Alice stared at me, taking in my tears and swore low under her breath. "She's not coming, is she?"

I scooped Hayley Jade up from the ground and shook my head, my throat too choked with tears to say anything. But the panic didn't subside.

Naomi was a good woman. She was exactly what Josiah wanted. I had no doubt in my mind that when she said she was giving us a five-minute head start before she raised the alarm, she meant every word.

"Run," I choked out to Alice. "God, please. Run."

9

HAYDEN

I worked twice as hard as I normally did at the diner that night. It was busy, the cheap restaurant in the middle of Saint View bustling with customers I caught a glimpse of every so often as I pushed plates of burgers and fries through the serving window.

With each order I hit the little silver service bell that signaled Carli, our waitress, to come pick up the food and take it out to the customers. Carli and Simon were run off their feet, but I couldn't help them. I was too busy running things backstage. The other cook had called in sick, so I was making do with our busboy as a second set of hands. It was working but only barely.

"Fries on the side of that, please." I passed Toro a plate. "Salad on the second."

"Yes, Chef," he said obediently, doing as I'd asked.

I hid a smile. The kid was trying so fucking hard to impress. And he was doing a great job, despite how far behind on orders we were. He was clearly angling for a cooking position, and I couldn't blame him. Washing dishes fucking sucked.

Creating something beautiful and tasty out of food was infinitely better.

Burgers and fries were beautiful to someone. But I was already thinking about the new dish I wanted to try later that night after we shut up shop and I had the kitchen to myself. It was the only thing that got me here tonight after the auction disaster earlier in the day. My face burned with embarrassment at the very thought of how desperate I'd been.

And at how deeply disappointed I still was that, despite my best efforts, owning my own place was just not in the cards for me.

Unless I wanted to work for Luca fucking Guerra.

I paused in the middle of adding cheese to a burger patty. What was the point of staying late anymore? It was stupid to be practicing dishes I'd never get to serve to anyone other than myself. And it was a waste of ingredients and time. Simon would notice I was using his kitchen without permission eventually, and then I wouldn't get to cook at all. My apartment didn't even have a kitchen. Not a proper one anyway. The single hot plate and microwave didn't count. Simon's diner might have been a shithole, but he'd kept the kitchen fairly well updated. He'd handed it over to me with grease around the burners and a refrigerator that hadn't been cleaned out in I didn't know how long, but it was nothing I hadn't gotten cleaned to sparkling on my first shift.

I'd kept it like that ever since. It might not have been mine, but I treated it like it was.

"Wipe that spill, Toro," I admonished the younger man gently. "Keep your workspace clean."

"Yes, Chef," he barked out like he was some sort of army recruit, and I was his drill sergeant.

"Not a chef," I said for the second time in twenty-four hours. "Just a cook."

Toro didn't argue, just cleaned up his mess and kept on with the tasks he'd been delegated. We worked in silence for the most part, him only opening his mouth to ask a question if he didn't understand my instructions.

The bell over the door tinkled, and a new rush of noise filtered back to the kitchen.

Toro groaned as he leaned around me and peered out through the serving window. "It's the hockey crowd. Game must have just finished."

I cringed but didn't look up. "How drunk are they tonight?"

Toro paused for a second, watching them. "Pretty bad. Simon is trying to herd them to seats in the back."

I shook my head and kept on with chopping a carrot. "Good luck to him. If their team lost, which I assume it did, considering they didn't enter with cheers and shouts like they normally would, they'll all be in shitty, argumentative moods. And will forget to tip."

Toro went back to his workstation. "There's a couple of guys from the Slayers Motorcycle Club out there too. Maybe they'll keep them in line."

I gripped my knife harder and bit back a scoff at the mention of the motorcycle club the Sinners considered their biggest rivals. "Fuck the Slayers," I muttered. "They're more likely to start a fight than prevent one." I might have been out of the game, but it didn't mean I'd suddenly switched teams.

Toro glanced over at me questioningly. "Really? They've always seemed like good guys to me. Scary as fuck, but I've never seen them start any trouble."

I didn't say anything. What was there to say? I wasn't about to tell this eighteen-year-old kid the Slayers were up to their fucking eyeballs in illegal activities.

Or how I knew about it.

They could eat where they liked, but I didn't have to notice. "Stop talking and do your work," I said to Toro, not wanting to think about it anymore.

"Yes, Chef."

"Not a fucking chef," I mumbled again, but it was with no heart.

A crash came from the main dining area, and a roar of drunken laughter came up after it, along with a few cries of dismay. I didn't have to look up to know that the plates Toro and I had just sent out were probably now all over the floor. I sighed and just started replating the orders.

Carli's pissed-off voice shouted over the top of it. "Did you just fucking knock my tray so I would drop them all?"

Toro and I both stopped and peered out through the serving window. Carli was a tough nut, she was used to guys like these, but it was rare for her to lose her patience and yell at them the way she just had.

Simon kept this place pretty family-friendly, and there were kids around. Carli might have grown up in the trailer park, but I'd never heard her cuss like that at a customer. Her tone and the volume of it told me she knew very well that her tray of food and glasses, that was now spread out all over the floor, was no accident.

"Oops!" one of the hockey guys slurred. "Seems like you need an extra set of hands, sweetheart. Let me help you." He staggered out of the booth and made a show of bending to pick up a broken plate from the floor and placing it back on her now empty tray.

He made sure his hand brushed over her boob while he was at it.

"Aw, fuck no." Toro dropped a set of tongs from his fingers right as I dropped the knife.

Fuck no, indeed.

Carli was tough and could handle her shit, but she was one woman against a group of drunken men.

Drunken men who would be leaving and never coming back. 'Cause fuck if some guy was going to indecently grope a teenager in front of me.

I strode through the kitchen, my long strides eating up the small space quickly, Toro right behind me. I pushed out through the kitchen doors right as Carli swung a punch at the groper's face.

He blinked.

And then punched her back.

All fucking hell broke loose.

I let out a shout and doubled my pace, full speed running at the man and crash tackling him to the floor, my fingers already curled into a fist.

I sent it flying into his meaty face so hard my knuckles cracked.

I didn't care. How dare he. How dare he lay a single fucking finger on a woman like that. How dare he even fucking think about it.

I just kept punching, frustration from my run-in with

Luca and the loss of the auction mixing with my anger. I was fast, and the punches were well-aimed.

The guy's feeble attempts at fighting me off were laughable. But his friends shouted from their booth, and I knew it would only be seconds before I was surrounded, so I got in as many good punches as I could.

It was all I could do to find Toro in the crowd, going head-to-head with a guy about my age, and Carli huddled in a corner with her nose bleeding, a phone pressed to her ear.

I had no idea if she was calling the cops or for backup of a different kind. Like in the form of her muscle-head boyfriend and his buddies.

When one of the hockey bros yanked me off his friend and sent his fist straight into my mouth, I considered the fact I probably could have used the backup in either form. Toro was trying his best, but we were well outnumbered.

Two guys got a hold of me, a third sending a quick round of punches into my face and stomach as I fought against my restraints. Pain erupted in each place the man's fist connected, but I was too wired with adrenaline to worry about it.

It was hardly the first time I'd been attacked.

From the other side of the room, the Slayers emerged from their table. I barely got a look at them from the corner of my swelling eye. They were a sea of black leather and denim, swarming across the restaurant while families and teenagers fled out into the parking lot to avoid the brawl.

I groaned when a heavy boot connected with my midsection, the big guy in the hockey jersey who had started this whole thing now back on his feet and out for my blood. His boot came again, and I coughed painfully.

The Slayers joined the fight like the lethal weapon I knew them to be. My head hung, pain slowly breaking through the adrenaline and coursing through my body. My ears rang, the diner around me turning into one painful squeal of noise, and I wondered if my eardrum had ruptured.

That pissed me off.

"You fucking pansies, holding a guy down while you beat the shit out of him," an older guy with a Slayers' vest fitted across his broad chest muttered.

The man was huge, and I thought I vaguely recognized him, but it was hard to tell with my eyes full of sweat. Or was that blood?

My eyesight was fuzzy around the edges, and I doubted I was going to be conscious for much longer.

Simon had disappeared, and aside from Toro who I'd also lost track of, it was me against a pack. I hated the Slayers but I needed someone on my fucking side here.

"Don't you fucking know who we are?" a deep, male voice roared above the din.

Suddenly, the two guys holding me down let go of me. Footsteps crunched over the smashed plates and what was left of the food Toro and I had so painstakingly prepared.

I rolled over onto my stomach, coughing, and pressed up on my hands, ignoring the sting of pain as broken glass speared through my palms.

Fuck this day.

I wiped at my eyes and tried to focus on what needed to be done, but the Slayers joining the fight had evened the score, and the drunken idiots had clearly decided it was no longer worth their while. They took one look at the patches on their jackets and the emblems on their backs and took off running into the night.

Smart.

But I refused to do the same.

Someone slapped me on the back. "Hey, you all right? You need a hand?"

With effort, I glanced up at the man offering his help.

Ah, fuck.

Familiar green eyes stared back at me.

Familiar because five years ago this fucking prick had met with a bullet from my gun.

Hawk realized at the same second I did, and in the one that followed, I was staring down the muzzle of his gun.

Gone was any sympathy his eyes might have held before he'd recognized me. And in them, anger and hate burned hotter than any fire I'd ever seen.

I let out a slow, bitter laugh, wishing again that I hadn't gotten out of bed today. "Too late to change your mind and let that guy kill me. You already helped me."

Hawk's upper lip curled, taking him from stupidly handsome to fucking mean in an instant. "Bullshit." He cocked his head to one side and pushed the muzzle against my forehead. "I can change my mind any fucking time I want." His finger hovered over the trigger.

He'd do it, too. I had no doubt in my mind.

That's how much Hawk Robinson hated me.

But I raised a cocky eyebrow. "Really? Here? We're on the main fucking road in town, and you know Carli over there already called the cops. You in the habit of killing people in cold blood in front of a couple of scared teenagers?"

I jerked my head toward the young woman, shaking in the corner, her trembling fingers clutched around her arms like she was trying to hold herself together. She truly was terrified, her cheeks streaked with tears as an older lady who'd stayed behind helped her hold napkins to her probably broken nose.

Toro stood with two of the other Slayers who had stepped in and helped. I recognized Aloha now. He'd been a member of the Slayers since I was a kid. The younger guy went by Ice, but I didn't know much about him, other than he'd been a prospect back when I'd been held in their basement after they'd picked me up from the side of the road, too injured to fight back.

Hawk didn't falter. Didn't stop to glance over at Toro or Carli. "I wouldn't normally, but I can make an exception for you." He shook his head slowly. "Sinners piece of shit," he taunted. "I should have fucking killed you years ago."

I laughed slowly, and found it felt good, so I did it some more. And then more, until I was laughing nearly fucking hysterically in Hawk's face. Honestly. Just fuck this day. And fuck Hawk. He had a nice pair of rose-colored glasses on. "Five years ago you were too busy lying on the floor crying because I shot you in the leg to do anything. You remember that?"

Hawk's face went red, and he shifted his weight from his right leg to his left, like he was remembering that one had once had a bullet hole with my name on it. Was it his right? Or the left? I couldn't remember.

Only that I didn't regret doing it.

I might have been a Sinners piece of shit once upon a time, but he was the one still in the club life. I might have been the leader of a gang that rivalled his. At least I'd grown up and gotten out.

He clearly couldn't say the same.

Red and blue lights flashed around the diner through the grubby windows, and we both looked over at the cop cars screeching in.

"Shit," Aloha swore under his breath. "That's our sign to get going."

"Our bikes are out there," Hawk bit out. "Can't go anywhere now unless you plan on leaving your bike to get impounded and running away on foot."

Ice shoved his hands in his pockets. "I'm not in the mood to go to jail tonight, Hawk. Can you at least put the fucking gun away before the cops get in here? Jesus."

Hawk rolled his eyes, and with a grimace, withdrew the gun and tucked it into the back of his jeans. "Fine."

The cops stormed through the front door right as Simon appeared from somewhere behind the counter. "Officers! Thank God you're here," he called, like he hadn't just been hiding, sacrificing the rest of us.

The officer took his hat off and surveyed the mess. His gaze came to land on Hawk, Aloha, and Ice, and he mumbled something into the communication device on his shoulder before addressing Simon. "We had reports of a fight? Why doesn't it surprise me to get here and find a handful of the Slayers are involved?"

The officer was an older guy. One I remembered well from my days in the Sinners gang. He clearly knew who Hawk and the other guys were, but I was kind of hoping I might have flown under the radar.

The officer's gaze narrowed with recognition.

Damn.

"You're Chaos Whitling, aren't you?" he asked.

I sighed heavily. No point lying. "I was. Just go by Hayden now."

Two more officers entered the diner, and a third cop car stopped in the parking lot, blocking off the doors.

They were quietly surrounding us. Like we might be getting ideas about running.

The officer stroked his short beard and watched me with squinty eyes. "Leader of the Sinners, right?"

This was getting so fucking old. How many years did I have to wait until my past would stop following me? Ten? Twenty? Would I be eighty and still get stopped by police who remembered the dumb shit I'd done in my twenties? "Again. I was. Haven't been for a long time."

I knew my mistake as soon as I said it. The Providence cops had a God complex, especially when it came to those of us from Saint View. They took any opportunity to remind us that we were just the scum on the sole of their expensive leather boots.

The cop sneered in my direction. "He says he's out, and yet here he is, causing a disturbance with the Slayers. I'm getting déjà vu. Pretty sure we've all seen this before."

The cops slowly surrounding the restaurant clearly made the man brave. "And you know what I remember about the Sinners and the Slayers from back in the day when you were Chaos? I remember how much the two gangs hated each other. How much blood was spilled on these streets over drugs and guns and territory."

I frowned at his memory. He acted like we'd left Saint View littered with bodies. "That's a bit dramatic."

Hawk snorted in amusement but quickly covered it with a scowl.

The officer continued to stare me down. "Is this what we have here, Chaos? A resurgence of violence on these streets that have been real fucking peaceful since you moved away?"

I hadn't moved anywhere. I was just off their radar. And this was why I kept such a low profile, hanging out in Simon's diner or staying home. Because the minute I poked my head out, my past came back to slap me in the face.

The cop's gaze shifted to Hawk. "War know you're in here fighting with the Sinners?" he asked, referring to the Slayers' president, War Maynard.

Hawk gave the officer his most charming grin. One I was surprised he could even muster. "Don't know what you're talking about, sir. The Sinners and the Slayers are the best of friends."

"Gag me with a fucking spoon," I muttered.

Hawk moved in closer to me and whispered back, "I'd really love to, but not in front of the po-po. Now smile like we're best fucking friends so we can get out of here." He slung an arm around my shoulder like we were posing for a tourist photo. "Nothing to see here, Officer. Isn't that right, *Chaos*?" Hawk asked, saying my gang name like the slur it was. "There was a bit of fisticuffs with some drunken fools who wandered over after the hockey game and tried to feel up a waitress, but that's all. We kicked them out, and I was just checking to see if Chaos needed any medical attention."

I shrugged his arm off my shoulders. "I think I'd

rather die in a pool of my own blood if it's all the same to you."

"That's not what you were saying last time I saved your life," Hawk threw back with a smug smirk. "Pretty sure you *begged* me to help you."

I stared at him. "I was fucking unconscious. And then you kept me prisoner in your basement."

Hawk wandered over to the officer and crossed his arms over his chest, mimicking the cop's posture. "I do think he protests too much. Don't you?"

The cop's gaze bounced between us like he was at a tennis game. "He what? He kept you…" Eventually, he sighed and took out a pair of handcuffs. "You're both under arrest."

Hawk dropped the mocking stance immediately. "What the fuck for?"

I cleared my throat and motioned at my black, swelling eye. "Uh, hello? On the floor fucking injured. And I'm under arrest? He's the one with a gun."

The cops eyes widened, and suddenly his friend pounced, one of them tackling Hawk to the floor while another patted him down, removing the gun that had been pointed at my head just minutes earlier.

"Concealed weapon." The cop twisted Hawk's arm up behind him as he dug a knee into his back. "You don't think you should have disclosed that when we first arrived, son?"

"I prefer to go by Daddy rather than son," Hawk bit back, his voice kind of muffled from the officers on top of him. But didn't resist the arrest. His smart-assed mouth earned him another sharp knee to the back though.

I smiled smugly, enjoying watching Hawk get his perfect face smushed into the dirty linoleum floor.

He groaned. "Can you ease up with that? I never said I wanted *you* to call me Daddy. Fuck. Unless you're hiding a sweet set of tits and a pussy that tastes like maple syrup beneath that uniform, you aren't my type. Try pretty boy over there if you want to get your dick sucked." He jerked his head in my direction.

Hawk calling me pretty was fucking hilarious when he looked more like the love child of movie stars than the trailer trash, MC kid he actually was.

Ignoring Hawk, the cop moved in behind me and slapped cold metal around one of my wrists. It had been a while since I'd felt the grating bracelets, and I couldn't say I'd missed them. The cop pulled them tighter, his voice low in my ear. "That true, Chaos? You like to suck dick? You a fucking faggot?"

"Why?" I asked him sweetly. "You want to be my boyfriend?"

It was like I hadn't been out at all.

I'd stepped straight back into that twenty-something asshole who ran his mouth and got himself in trouble all the fucking time.

When I found myself in the back of a cop car with Hawk on the other side of the bench seat, I didn't even know why I was surprised.

10

HAWK

Nothing ever changed at the Providence Police Department. Not the scuffed-up concrete floors. Not the bustle of cops moving around the space, acting like they were the kings of the world. Not the smell of unwashed bodies and shit because the holding cells never got cleaned properly.

I shuddered at the sight of the metal toilet in the corner of the processing room Chaos and I had been locked in.

"That's so fucking unsanitary," I complained, screwing up my face. "I can't even think about how many fucking germs are crawling all over this place." I itched to wash my hands, but they were cuffed behind my back so the best I could do was wipe them on the back of my jeans.

Chaos rolled his eyes from where he leaned against the wall on the other side of the cell. "Wouldn't have picked you to be OCD about germs. Shame you don't have your purse here. I bet you have sanitizer in it."

Behind my back, my fingers flipped him off, even though he couldn't see it. "My OCD about germs is the only reason you're even fucking alive to give me shit right now. Remember how you didn't get an infection and die after we picked your broken ass up off the side of the road and nursed you back to health? Remember how I washed my hands so you didn't get sepsis? Oh! Oh!" I glared at him. "Remember how you *shot* me, but I cleaned the fucking wound and stitched it up, so I didn't die either? That was fucking fun."

Chaos raised an eyebrow. "Do you want a medal?"

I glared at him. "Actually, maybe I fucking do. Or even better, how about you just shut up about me complaining about the germs crawling all over this place?" I shuddered and squinted at the toilet again. "Fuck, it's like I can see them."

The urge to gag rose in my chest.

"Just stop thinking about it," Chaos advised.

God, I fucking hated him. "Don't talk to me."

Chaos huffed out a breath. "Fine by me."

We stood in silence for all of thirty seconds before I couldn't stand it. I'd never liked long silences. They left me too much room for my head to fill in the blanks. "You think they arrested the others too?"

Chaos shrugged. "Probably. It's not like any of us are particularly well-liked by cops round here. Any excuse for them to—"

A guard opened the door to our cell, cutting off whatever Chaos was going to say. "The two of you are up. Get going."

Chaos pushed off the wall, but I beat him to the cell door. I couldn't stand being anywhere near that filthy fucking toilet for another second. "Did someone come to bail me out?"

The guard glanced up from a file folder. "Not yet."

Damn. We had only been here twenty minutes so that was probably too much to hope for. "Where are we going then?"

"The boss wants you both searched and your belongings removed."

Yeah, how about no. "What the fuck for?"

The cop shrugged and looked over at me. "You had a gun on you. Boss wants to see what else you might be hiding."

"We were patted down when we came in," Chaos argued. "Why are they doing it again?"

"Strip search," the cop said. "You're both known gang members. It's standard procedure to check for concealed drugs."

"Concealed drugs?" I asked. "Concealed where?"

The cop just stared at me.

I stopped walking. "No. No fucking way are you checking my ass for drugs."

The cop shoved me in the back. "I don't remember asking for your permission. Just shut up and move. You think I want to check your ass any more than you want me to? Trust me, I don't. But like I said, it's standard procedure."

"Since fucking when?" Chaos snapped. "I'm not exactly a stranger to getting arrested, I think we both know that. I've never been strip searched before."

The cop tapped his pass to a security panel, and it opened the door in front of us. He waited while Chaos and I passed by. "Take it up with the chief when you're released if you want to make a complaint."

Relief sank in. "Let me talk to old Barry." I turned around and walked backward so I could smile at the cop. "We're old friends."

Which was true. We'd been bribing the old ass to look the other way for years. War dropped him the occasional freebie at his sex club, Psychos, and everyone was happy. Barry got his rocks off, and we did our thing without the cops giving us too much hassle.

The officer shook his head. "Barry's gone. Got caught taking bribes. We got a new chief last month. He's from one of the gang taskforces in the city, so guys like you two are a personal pet peeve of his and he's changed the way we do everything around here." He raised an eyebrow at me. "Guess you haven't had a chance to try to bribe him yet, huh?"

Well, shit. A new chief? That was an oversight War probably should have been on top of.

But War's woman was due to have another baby any day now, and he hadn't exactly been around much. Fuck. I was VP. I should have been the one to pick up the slack.

"Be a good little officer and tell the chief the VP of the Slayers would like a word. I'm sure he'll be happy to oblige."

The officer put a hand on my chest to keep me moving backward. "Sure, sure, Hawk," he said in the most condescending of tones. "I'll get right on that. Right after I finish all the paperwork you created for me tonight, take my dinner break, wash my hair, fill my car up with gas..." He raised an eyebrow. "Get in the fucking room already, would you? No amount of your bullshit is getting you an audience with the chief tonight. You want to talk to him? Wait 'til you aren't in fucking handcuffs and he might actually take you seriously."

Chaos sniggered.

I shot him a death stare. "Why are you laughing? You enjoy strip searches?"

Chaos shrugged. "No. But I enjoy watching you embarrass yourself."

I twisted so I didn't have to see his fucking face.

In the next room we were met by another officer who grabbed my arm none too softly and shoved me to a table. The first officer did the same with Chaos, patting him down for the second time that night while explaining how the strip search would work. At the third table, a guy was already half naked, a cop checking his shirt pockets while the guy covered his bare chest with his arms like he had tits he didn't want us to see.

His gaze landed on Chaos. "This is all your fault! I should have known better than to hire some street thug who claimed he wanted to turn over a new leaf."

The cop pushed Chaos up against the table so he could undo his cuffs, and he let out a grunt of irritation. He swiveled his head to face the weedy, older man squawking at him.

"I was defending Carli. What did you want me to do, Simon? You should have banned those hockey dickheads years ago. They're always trouble, and you never do anything about them."

"Trouble!" Simon squeaked, glaring at Chaos. "They're paying customers. You can't just turn away paying customers. You'd know that if you had any business sense. But we both know you don't. That's why you're in the back, and I'm out front."

"Take your pants off, please, sir. Your underwear too," Simon's cop interrupted.

Simon's face crumpled, like he wanted to cry at the officer's command.

I didn't bother hiding my laugh.

"What are you laughing at?" Simon snapped at me. "You're about to get the same treatment!" Then he turned to the cop. "This is all a misunderstanding. I wasn't even in the room when the fight broke out. My only crime was giving that man a chance. He was a street thug, born loser before I took him in. Completely useless in the kitchen until I taught him everything I know. But look where supporting the community got me? I'm being punished for being a good person!"

Chaos stared at his boss, his voice dry with sarcastic humor. "Thanks for all your support, Simon. I'm so glad you taught me all the ins and outs of bad coffee and flipping a few fucking burger patties. It was real damn hard to learn that, so you really should pat yourself on the back."

"You ungrateful—"

"Quit your fucking whining and drop your pants and underwear," the cop said again.

Simon's mouth drew into a thin line as he took off his clothes. "You're fired, Hayden. So fucking fired! I don't care how damn attractive you are, having a bit of eye candy around isn't worth all of this." He lowered his pants to his ankles, his underwear following. He glared at Chaos, anger heaving his chest.

Like he didn't give a flying fuck, Chaos did the same.

He pulled off his grease- and blood-spattered T-shirt, quickly following up by removing the dirty black jeans and a pair of tight black boxer briefs.

Chaos's dick was fucking huge. It hung halfway down his thigh, dark hair thatched beneath the thick base.

I burst out laughing at the comparison to Simon's shriveled pecker. It was the nicest way I could describe it. "Well, that's embarrassing."

I meant for Simon, but Chaos clearly didn't take it that way. I saw the flash of something in his eye before he turned around, letting the officer run his gloved hands all over his body.

The cop traced every line and ridge. His fingers trailed over Chaos's biceps and down his back rippling with strong muscle. He had a lot of tattoos, probably at least as many as I had. But beneath them, scars. So many of them. I searched out each and every one. I knew where they all were because it had been me who'd stitched the asshole back together after he'd been left for dead on the side of the road all those years ago. I knew every inch of his body because I'd been the one who'd washed the gravel out of every cut. I'd been the one who'd taken the bullet out of his upper chest and sewn it back together. And then with the limited knowledge I had, somehow kept him from getting an infection. He had an ugly keloid scar, but fuck, I'd done all right considering I had nothing more than a high school education.

We hadn't exactly been planning on keeping the prick alive. My instructions had been to fix him up so we could get the info we needed from him. Not to become a plastic surgeon.

But that gunshot wound was one that would have killed him if it had been an inch lower.

This prick fucking owed me everything. Even if I hadn't exactly had his best interests at heart.

The cop groped between Chaos's legs before running a hand along the seam of his ass.

Chaos's eye caught mine.

I looked away before he could say a fucking word.

From the other side of the room, Simon was finally silent, his beady-eyed gaze on Chaos like he'd been waiting years to see him with his gear off and now he was going to take his fill.

"Get your clothes off, Hawk," my officer said. "Stop stalling. I don't have all day. This is happening whether you like it or not."

The back of my neck heated. "With Simon the pervert in here? I don't fucking think so. Don't need to be a visual for his spank bank the way Chaos is right now."

Simon let out a babbling protest about how he was a married man and blah, blah, blah.

I didn't care. Whatever took the attention away from the fact I'd been checking out my handiwork on Chaos's scar.

I took off the club jacket and jeans I'd put on that morning. Lost the white wifebeater singlet.

I rarely wore underwear, so that wasn't a problem.

I stared at the wall, but all I could think about was that some prick was getting all up and personal with my ass crack.

Breathe. Just fucking breathe.

I couldn't.

Agitated and searching for distraction, I made the

mistake of glancing over at Chaos again and found him watching me.

I raised an eyebrow as gloved fingers began tracing the same path I'd just watched them make over Chaos's body. "Just making sure your dick is bigger?" I managed to get out while every muscle in my body tensed at the cop's touch.

"I don't need to see your dick to know it is."

"You fucking wish." I was no slouch in the dick department and I knew it. I had no problem showing off what that fucker up in the clouds had blessed me with.

As long as it wasn't some asshole cop touching me when I did it.

The corner of Chaos's mouth lifted when he was guided to a shower room where Simon was yelping like a little girl that the water he was being hosed down with was too cold.

I gritted my teeth for the rest of my search and died a bit inside as I was hosed off with some sort of lice washdown which smelled like chemicals and seemed like fucking bullshit. "Is anyone actually going to charge us with something?" I asked over the din of the spray hitting the metal wall behind me and the gurgling of the drains beneath our feet. I fought the chattering of my teeth. "Or is this all just to remind us that we're Saint View pieces of shit who don't deserve rights?"

I argued with my cop, while Chaos's gave him a fresh prison jumpsuit to put on and told him his clothes were being sent away for testing. Chaos just shook his head and started putting on the clothes like the good boy he was.

For fuck's sake. Have some balls.

"That how you became the leader of the Sinners?" I asked him, voice dripping with derision. "By saying yes sir, no sir, how about I bend over for you, sir? You fuck your way to the top of that gang?"

"You talk a lot," Chaos muttered from where he was toweling off. "You ever try just shutting up for once?"

"I could, but I don't want to. It's called having a personality." I looked over at him as he sat on the bench to pull on a pair of gray woolen socks that seemed scratchy enough to use as an exfoliator. "You should try it sometime."

He glanced up at me. "Would I have to talk as much shit as you do? If so, no thanks."

"Your words cut so deep, Chaos," I said sarcastically. "How will I ever recover?"

He rolled his eyes, and I was semi satisfied I'd gotten to have the last word. It was a cheap thrill, but then so were half the women I slept with, so whatever.

"Whitling!" a cop called from out the front. "There's a lawyer out here to see you. Says he's your brother."

I raised my head in interest. Liam, despite being Chaos' brother, was also a friend of War's. He'd gotten more than one of us out of the slammer over the years.

The guard held the door open, and Chaos stood to walk toward him.

I stepped in front before he could leave the room and grabbed his arm. "Tell Liam he needs to get me out too."

Chaos stared down at my hand on his arm and then back up at me.

I quickly released the hold I had on him, the back of my neck burning for no good reason.

Chaos just leaned in so far his warm breath brushed

over the bare skin of my neck. "I could, but I don't want to," he said, parroting my words back at me. He grinned. "Enjoy spending the night in jail with Simon. He seems pretty obsessed with my dick too, so maybe the two of you will have something to talk about."

11

KARA

My legs throbbed. My chest burned.

I'd spent years basically doing nothing while my muscles withered away, and I ate to curb my depression. I'd never been a small woman to begin with, but now I was at my heaviest and trying to run through the darkness with the added weight of a five-year-old.

My lungs were going to explode.

The road I'd thought wasn't really that far suddenly seemed like a million miles away. My steps slowed with every minute that passed.

Alice glanced over at me worriedly. "Do you want me to take her?"

I nodded and started to hand her over, but Hayley Jade's fingernails dug into my arm.

This poor child. She'd been ripped from the safety of the only home she could remember. It was cold and dark, and she had no idea what was going on.

"I've got her," I promised, picking up the pace again.

A clock ticked in the back of my mind, counting down the seconds until Naomi would raise the alarm.

A horn sounded somewhere behind us.

Alice and I both stopped dead, spinning around when lights came on and the members of our community all staggered from their homes.

In the distance, a group of men stood outside our parents' house, Naomi talking frantically with them.

Time was up.

Neither of us needed to say a word. My burning muscles and breathless lungs suddenly ceased to exist, adrenaline coursing through me. I ran for the cover of the trees, following closely behind my sister, neither of us willing to be sitting ducks on the road.

I pushed my body, running harder and faster as the noises of the community and shouts of our names pierced through the night.

"Oh God, oh God, oh God," Alice mumbled, her eyes wide. "Hurry, Kara!"

I didn't answer. I was too busy trying to keep myself upright. Too busy trying to keep myself going. Panic swelled inside me, and as if she could sense it, Hayley Jade held me tighter.

If this had been anywhere else, any other time, I would have relished the feel of her in my arms. She was so much bigger than the last time I'd been allowed to hold her. With every sharp inhale, the sweet smell of her hair filled my nose and took me right back to when I'd arrived back here with a tiny baby in my arms.

I'd been so stupid.

I'd gotten us into this.

It was up to me to get us out.

"Think, Kara, you stupid, stupid woman," I muttered beneath my breath. But all I could do was put one foot in front of the other. I had no idea what we were going to do once we got to the road. The nearest town was miles away. We could walk, but it would take hours, and in that time the sun would come up.

Josiah would get his dogs.

He'd find us. Drag us back.

Make us pay for our disobedience.

This was not like the last time I'd left. Josiah had raised the stakes a hundred-fold, and not making it out now would mean certain death.

At least for me. I was his wife, and everything I did reflected on him and his leadership.

Maybe he'd spare Alice and Hayley Jade.

Maybe he wouldn't.

He couldn't catch us. That couldn't be an option.

I broke into a run, pushing my exhausted body further than I ever thought I could.

Twigs snapped somewhere not too far behind us, and I stifled the urge to scream. They were catching up. Their flashlights lit up the darkness behind us, filtering out before it could touch us, but they were there. No dogs yet, but people called my name.

My father. My mother. Sisters. The other wives. Josiah. Their voices mingled until it was one big blur of terror.

"We're nearly at the road," Alice promised. "I can see it!"

I raised my weary head. Through the thick trees and the glistening moonlight, a paved road loomed ahead.

It was an empty stretch of asphalt, but in that moment, it looked like freedom.

I hurried, running faster.

"Kara!" Josiah's booming voice cut through the night. "Where are you, sweetheart? Come back to us. Come back to the Lord, and He will forgive your sins."

My fingers trembled, my footsteps faltering.

"Don't you fucking dare listen to him, Louisa Kara." Alice grabbed my arm. "He's a fake and a phony and he's been abusing you for years. Don't you listen."

I nodded, but it was hard. It was so, so hard when it was him I heard in my nightmares. When it was his voice telling me I wasn't good enough, wasn't worthy to receive the blessings of the Lord.

Some part of me wanted to curl into a tiny ball and just let his dogs find me.

Let them rip me limb from limb until I was as nothing on the outside as I was on the inside.

I stumbled on a stick half hidden by fallen leaves, and a sharp pain wrenched my ankle. I went down hard, my knees crashing to the freezing ground.

Pain ricocheted through my entire body, but I cradled Hayley Jade from the brunt of the fall.

She cried out before I quickly clapped a hand over her mouth. My ankle screamed in agony, but I shushed the little girl, whispering reassurances into her ear. "You're okay. I've got you. Just stay quiet and we'll be safe. Okay?"

"Kara get up," Alice whisper-shouted, pausing and reaching back for me.

I shook my head, knowing I couldn't go on with my

ankle the way it was. "Take her. Go. Please, Alice. She can't stay here!"

My sister's determined face got in mine. "Neither can you. They find you, and you're dead."

Josiah's voice filled the air. "Kara! It's all going to be okay. Just come back to us and repent. Your sins will be forgiven if you bring the child back safely."

To anyone else, his words might have sounded sweet. Reassuring.

All I could hear was the underlying malice. The vicious danger he barely concealed in his tone.

Alice knew it too. "For her. Get up and run, Kara. For your daughter."

I nodded, pressing back up onto feet that protested my weight.

A flashlight shined in my eyes.

We were too late.

I closed my eyes against the bright light and pressed my lips to the top of Hayley Jade's head, waiting for someone to rip her from my arms.

It didn't come.

Only Alice's low swear. "Kyle! Oh Jesus Christ, you scared the living shit out of me. Put that flashlight down before someone sees it!"

I blinked at my sister and the man standing next to her.

His face was rounded with youth, though he towered over my sister and me. He had to be around her age. Maybe eighteen or nineteen at most. I'd seen him at church, but he was the son of a newcomer, a family who had moved to the commune only in the last year or so and I hadn't heard anyone call him by name.

I trembled in place, waiting for the young man to shout that he'd found the devil woman who was luring away Josiah's flock.

But to my shock, he lowered the flashlight. His gaze fell on the ankle I was babying.

"She's hurt," Alice said urgently.

Kyle nodded once and moved to touch me, but I withdrew so fast it was like a rattlesnake had bitten me.

"Don't," I seethed, a warning beneath my breath.

"Kara!" Alice snapped. "He's a friend. He's trying to help."

"He's a man," I said through gritted teeth, not willing to take my eyes off him for even a second. "You heard those men around the fire. You heard what they do. What they want when they think no one is watching. You know what happened to me."

Alice got beneath my arm and slung it over her shoulder, taking my weight. "He's a friend. I asked him to come. He has a car."

Kyle nodded fiercely. "I want to help. Please. Alice told me everything."

"Kara!" Josiah shouted from down the hill. "Kara!"

I stared into Kyle's open, innocent face.

All I saw was danger.

But nothing was as bad as the danger that lurked behind me in the woods, slowly closing in on me.

"You have to trust him." Alice shot terrified looks down the hill. "We don't have any other choice!"

She was right.

With her help and guided by the dim light of Kyle's flashlight, we made it to the fence.

I stared up at the prison-style fencing that was probably twice my height and made of chain-link metal.

Josiah had claimed we needed it to keep wild dogs out after some of our animals had gone missing. He'd sold it so convincingly that all the men had agreed, no thought given to the fact these fences might keep out wild animals, but they also kept us in.

Kyle pointed the flashlight at cuts made in the chain-link and pulled back the wire.

There was just enough space for a person to crawl through.

I stared at Alice. "How..."

She shoved me forward. "I told you! He wants to help. Go!"

I didn't let myself think. I couldn't make sense of this anyway. I just moved on autopilot, putting Hayley Jade down, crawling beneath the fence, and then turning back for her as Alice pushed her through.

I dragged her into my arms, the two of us standing there in the moonlight, on the other side of the fence.

We were out.

A sense of pride and achievement burst inside me, but it only lasted a second.

We were out, but that was only the beginning.

As he'd promised, Kyle had an old pickup truck parked just a few feet down the road. It was rusted, but in that moment, with Josiah and the rest of the commune closing in, it felt like the most beautiful mirage.

"Repent!" a chant started up from behind us. "Repent! Repent!"

They were too close.

I ran. Yanked open the back door of the truck and

shoved Hayley Jade inside. Alice climbed into the front seat, Kyle behind the wheel and turning the key. The engine kicking over, blessedly promising a fast getaway.

"Kara!"

I spun, seeing Josiah cresting the top of the hill.

"Get in!" Alice screamed, spotting him at the same time.

I didn't know Kyle from a bar of soap. For all I knew he was going to drive us right back to Josiah's door.

It didn't matter if I died.

I was more than halfway to making my peace with it. I'd been doing that every day since that monster had taken my baby from me.

But my little girl deserved to live.

Alice and Kyle were giving her a chance.

Giving *us* a chance.

I dove into the back seat, and Kyle put his foot down on the accelerator, the tires squealing in protest as we disappeared into the night.

Before we turned the corner, I twisted back to look through the rear windshield.

Josiah stood in the middle of the road watching us go. Flashlight gripped in one hand.

Shotgun in the other.

12

KARA

*K*yle was clearly in love with my sister.

Alice sat beside him in the front seat while he steered us toward Saint View, the little town where our older sister, Rebel, had grown up before our dad had left her to be raised by her mom. Alice stared with wide-eyed wonder at the buildings and other cars as they flashed by in a blur of headlights. Kyle alternated between watching the road and watching Alice, her every smile making him smile too.

I saw it all from where I slouched in the back seat, too scared to raise my head for fear someone in another car might recognize me. We hadn't seen a glimpse of Josiah or anyone from the commune since we'd left. It all felt too easy, though the constant throbbing in my ankle said otherwise.

Hayley Jade had scrambled to the far side of the truck as soon as we'd been on the road and curled herself into a tight ball, her skinny arms wrapping around her knees and her face twisted away.

I'd managed to get a seat belt on her. But she flinched every time I touched her and refused to lift her head when Alice offered her food and water from a bag Kyle had packed for us.

Hours away from the commune, Kyle was forced to stop for gas, and the urge to use the bathroom was too strong to ignore.

"Hayley Jade?" I asked quietly. "Do you need to go to the bathroom?"

She didn't make a sound. Her hunched-over back still rose and fell with her breaths, which only eased a little of my worries, but the fact she wouldn't look at me, speak, eat, or even use the bathroom was concerning.

Alice reached back and squeezed my arm. "Come on. I need to go too." She opened the car door. "Kyle, we need to use the ladies' room. Can you watch Jade for a minute, please? And when I say watch her, I mean you don't take your eyes off her, okay?"

Kyle nodded quickly, eager to please. "Of course." He was filling the car up with one hand on the gas pump, but he braced his other on the doorframe, so he had eyes on my daughter.

I hesitated, not wanting to leave her alone with a man I didn't know, even if that man did have love hearts for eyes when he was with my sister.

Alice rubbed my arm, soothing the spot she'd squeezed a moment earlier. "You can trust him. He's a good guy. He and I have been talking about getting out of that shithole commune for months."

I widened my eyes at her. "What?"

Alice nodded, tugging me toward the facilities. "Kyle

only moved in a year ago. His parents got suckered in by all of Josiah's bullshit—"

I shot her a look on autopilot. "Alice! Don't talk like that."

Alice groaned in frustration with me and tugged open the door marked with a dress-wearing stick figure. "We're out now. You don't have to play the part anymore. You're free."

I didn't want to be free like this. I didn't want to be out here, at a gas station in the middle of nowhere after kidnapping a child from the only home she remembered. I didn't find any excitement in being on the run, knowing that at any minute, Josiah and his crew could pull up and take me and my daughter and my sister. If that happened...

I shot a worried glance back at the car, but nothing seemed amiss, and my bladder protested at traveling for so long without a break. I ducked inside the bathrooms, quickly relieving myself and washing my hands and was back outside, peering through the truck window to check on Hayley Jade before Alice had even finished in her stall.

Relief washed over me when the little girl was still in the same position I'd left her.

Kyle grimaced at me though. "She's pretty scared, huh?"

I wanted to stroke her hair, but it was clear she didn't want me touching her. "I imagine so. It's been...a lot."

He nodded. "Do you want anything from inside? Candy? A sandwich?"

I nodded before I could think about how greedy I was being. "Please. That sounds amazing."

Kyle nodded, his gaze turning adoring as it switched

to Alice climbing up into her seat. I followed, getting into the back seat behind her.

Oblivious to Kyle's love-struck expression, Alice twisted to grumble at me. "You could have waited."

Kyle walked away to go get supplies, and I bit down on my lip watching him. "He's in love with you."

Alice grinned, gaze straying to his retreating form then back at me. "I know. Isn't it great?"

Surprised punched through me. That was about the last thing I'd expected her to say. "You love him too?"

She barked out a laugh. "Oh my God, no. He's sweet but he's...I don't know. He kind of looks like a golden retriever. Or maybe it's just his personality that makes me think that. He's so eager to please, it's sickening."

I blinked, shaking my head. That was a horrible thing for her to say. The way she dismissed him was so unkind. "He's so eager to please that he left his entire life and his family behind to go on the run with you. And you think that makes him the equivalent of a dog?"

She just shrugged.

When Kyle came back with his arms laden down with more snacks and sandwiches and drinks for all of us, I couldn't help but feel like we were taking advantage of him. "Thank you," I whispered, voice full of the gratitude I felt for the man, even if he was misguided to have placed his affections on my sister. "I really do appreciate this."

"Me too," Alice chirped from the front seat, kicking off her shoes and putting her feet up on the dash. She ripped open a package of potato chips and tossed a few of them into her mouth. She wiped her fingers off on her long skirt and then held her hand out to Kyle. "Can I play something on your phone?"

My mouth dropped open as Kyle fished the small device out of his pocket and handed it over to her without hesitation.

Alice pressed her fingertips to her lips and then onto Kyle's smoothly shaven cheek. "Thank you! Four, seven, three, five. That's the password still, right?"

Clearly this wasn't the first time she'd used his cell.

"Where did you even get that?" I asked. "Josiah would never allow..."

Kyle shrugged. "My parents tried to take it away when we first moved to the commune, but I was sixteen. I had a life. Friends. I said I'd leave and go live with my best friend and his family if my parents didn't let me keep it.

"Your parents knew about it?" I asked him incredulously. "Technology has been forbidden for such a long time, they could be kicked out if you'd been caught..."

Alice glanced over at Kyle with a grin. "Lucky we never got caught then, huh?"

He grinned back at her, like they were Bonnie and Clyde on the run and loving it.

All I saw was the naivete. How I'd probably been exactly the same, said the same stupid things when I'd first left.

I'd had so many big dreams.

I was going to become a doctor.

Help underprivileged communities and those who couldn't afford healthcare. I was going to find myself a nice house, nothing fancy, just a small three-bedroom place somewhere in a middle-class neighborhood. I'd meet a nice man, maybe at the hospital, maybe at a little tucked-away café that the locals all loved. We'd fall in love. Get married. Fill that home with babies.

I hadn't even been out of the commune for a week when I'd met Caleb. He'd been charming at first, rich and handsome.

I'd instantly imagined him taking me on dates. Driving me out to the beach where we'd drink milkshakes in summer or curl up with him reading books by a fire in winter.

Those dreams had been shattered after he'd left me crying and bleeding.

A tiny baby growing inside me, all that was left of the hopes I'd left home with.

And that wasn't even the worst thing he'd done to me.

It got so much worse.

I swallowed thickly, turning away from Alice's fingers deftly moving over the phone screen as she played some sort of animated game on Kyle's phone, her tongue sticking out of the corner of her mouth in concentration.

Hours passed with me lost in my head. Miles flew by beneath the tires of Kyle's truck, and I periodically pushed food toward Hayley Jade, which she mostly ignored.

I bit back a cheer when finally, her small fingers reached for a bag of candy I put by her leg. She still refused to look at me, but she lifted her head and ripped the package open with her teeth before gobbling down a handful of the sour worms.

"I'm sorry I don't know what you like," I whispered to her. "I'll learn though. And I'll fill our pantry with all of your favorites. Whatever you want." I paused, praying she'd respond. "Hayley Jade?" I prompted when she didn't say anything.

She put the cap back on her water and went back to staring out the window.

I sighed.

Alice caught my eye in the mirror on the back of her sun visor. "At least she ate something. Maybe it would help if you just called her Jade, like Shari did."

I nodded but didn't comment. I didn't want to talk about Hayley Jade like she wasn't even in the car.

I also despised the idea of calling her anything other than the beautiful name I'd given her.

She'd been named after Hayden.

And he was the one good memory I had from my time in Saint View.

But I would call her anything she wanted if that's what made her happy. I'd say anything. Do anything. "Would you like that?" I asked her. "Would you like me to call you Jade?"

She didn't answer, and I didn't push her any further.

She was here. She was safe. And we were passing the faded sign that read Welcome to Saint View.

I was back. But it was almost the last place I wanted to be.

Saint View wasn't home. It wasn't good.

Just like the commune, it was where happiness died and dreams were shattered.

13

KARA

"The GPS is saying it's only five minutes until we get to your sister's place." Kyle peered through the windshield and grimaced. "Are you sure we're in the right spot? This place is..."

"Bleak?" Alice filled in, a shudder running through her thin frame. She turned back to me. "Is this seriously where Rebel lives? It's..."

"A shithole," Kyle supplied unhelpfully. "I think those people over there are shooting up beneath that streetlamp."

I took a steadying breath, not wanting to look out the windows for fear of seeing the house from my nightmares. The one I'd been held in against my will, on Caleb's orders.

It had been where I'd met Hayden. And where I'd given birth to Hayley Jade.

I thought I'd put all those bad feelings behind me, but being back here now reminded me exactly of why I hadn't been able to stay, even when my sister had offered to let me live with her.

I hated this town and everything in it. And Rebel's place was too close to it.

I cleared my throat. "Rebel's house is in the neighboring town. It's not like this. You'll see. Just keep driving."

Kyle seemed skeptical, and I couldn't blame him. It had always amazed me that two towns so unalike could share a border and there not be an out and out war between its residents.

The haves on one side. The have-nots on the other.

Maybe little battles were fought every day, and I just didn't know about it.

I wanted to keep it that way. Saint View was not the place for me. But neither was my sister's place in Providence. Caleb had been from Providence, proving that evil lurked everywhere, not just in towns with broken windows and abandoned cars. Sometimes the worst evil lurked behind the doors of million-dollar mansions with luxury cars parked in the driveways.

We rolled slowly through the streets, the houses gradually changing from run-down or abandoned shacks, to low-income government housing, to small suburban dwellings, and finally, as we crossed the border into Providence, to mansions that could be in *Home Beautiful* magazine.

"Wasn't expecting that," Kyle murmured, his hesitant staring becoming star-struck gawking. "These places are huge."

"Take a left here," I told him quietly. "This is Rebel's

street. At least, it was the last time I saw her. If she's moved..."

If she'd moved I didn't know where we'd go next. There was no backup plan.

"She hasn't," Alice said confidently. "I've seen the return address on her letters. It's this address."

I stared at my sister. "Rebel has been sending you letters?"

She glanced back at me with a frown of confusion. "Not us. You. Ever since our phones were taken away."

I shook my head, hurt erupting behind my chest. "She never sent me one."

"She did," Alice insisted. "They were always sent to our place. Dad gave them to Josiah to give to you." She shook her head, expression full of anger. "Josiah wasn't passing them on, was he?"

Stupidly, tears welled in my eyes. My older sister had been a lifeline for me when I'd first returned to the commune with my tail between my legs, one that Josiah had quickly cut off once I was his wife. I might not have liked where she lived, but I had missed her every day.

For the first time since Alice had thrown those tiny pebbles at my window, I felt a tiny kernel of excitement.

"That's her house, just there." I pointed. "With the curved driveway."

My sister was behind those doors. I didn't know if she would even want to see me after not speaking for so long.

But something inside me ached to try.

Kyle was still muttering in shock and awe over Rebel's house, and I couldn't blame him. It was more beautiful than I remembered. The two-story home was nothing short of grand. There were floor-to-ceiling windows everywhere, and the flower beds were neatly arranged, a few new beds in place since the last time I'd been here, though they were bare of any flowers at this time of year. A swing set by the fence line caught my eye, and I couldn't help but smile. Rebel's babies would be four by now, not even a full year younger than Hayley Jade. Before we'd gotten cut off, Rebel had told me she was having a set of boy-girl twins, but I'd never even gotten to know their names.

"I wish you'd told me she was still trying to contact me," I said to Alice. "Did you ever read any of her correspondence?" I wanted to know everything that had been in those letters. Wanted to read every word and know every detail of what had been going on in Rebel's life.

But Josiah had kept it from me. Just like everything and everyone else. A constant punishment because I couldn't do the one thing he'd married me for and he resented it every day.

Alice shook her head. "No. But she never stopped writing to you. The last of her letters arrived just last week."

My heart squeezed as Kyle stopped the truck.

"We're here," I told Hayley Jade quietly. "You can get out and stretch your legs. We can't stay too long, but it's nice here. You'll like it."

She refused to move.

Flinched away when I touched her.

I sighed. Any silent truce we'd called when I'd been bribing her with food was clearly over.

The front door of Rebel's house opened, and a huge man appeared on the porch, flinching against the cold night air in just a thin sweatshirt. He squinted through the darkness, clearly trying to place the unfamiliar car.

"Holy shit, who is that?" Alice asked with a slight hitch in her voice.

The corner of my mouth flickered just a tiny bit. "That's Fang. Your brother-in-law."

Taking in her expression of pure lust, Kyle shot Alice a dirty look. "Your brother-in-law, Alice. So maybe roll your tongue up and put it back in your mouth?"

"Can't," she practically panted. "He's so big. Bet he could crack my head between his thighs like it was a walnut."

"Alice!" Kyle reprimanded before I could. "That guy has to be at least fifteen years older than you."

"Fifteen years more experienced then," Alice mused. "I bet he could teach me a thing or two."

I wrung my hands, shocked by the change in my sister now she didn't have the constraints of commune rules to abide by. "You wouldn't have a clue what to do with a man like that. Now get out of the car before he gets suspicious and pulls his gun."

"He has a gun?" Kyle practically squeaked.

"Fang is the one in the motorcycle club, right?" Alice asked.

"Motorcycle club? Like, the kind who go on nice Sunday drives together? Or..." Kyle's unspoken question hung in the air.

Or the illegal kind who were just as likely to be making a gun or drug trade on a Sunday as taking a leisurely cruise. That was what Kyle had wanted to ask.

"Or," I confirmed. "So get out and keep your hands where he can see them."

Alice grinned.

Kyle looked like he was about to wet his pants.

All I cared about was how Hayley Jade was taking it, but she was still completely checked out.

I pushed open the car door and climbed out slowly, Alice and Kyle following my lead.

"Who's there?" Fang called.

"It's me," I called back, and then realized it had been five years since I'd seen the man and he probably didn't recognize me anymore, sister-in-law or not. "Me, Kara, I mean." I straightened and raised my hand tentatively.

Fang took a few steps forward so he could see better then swore low under his breath. He pivoted abruptly and took two quick steps back inside the house, the door closing behind him.

I froze.

"Er," Alice mumbled. "Was it something we said?"

"More like someone you're with." My chest felt tight. "This is my fault. We shouldn't have come here. Rebel isn't going to want to see me after all this time."

For the first time since we'd made it out, Alice's happy-go-lucky expression morphed into one of worry. "We don't have a backup plan. Where the hell are we going to go? I have no money. Neither do you. Kyle drained the last of his bank account paying for the gas to get us here."

I had the few hundred dollars Shari had given me, but that wouldn't get us far. My fingers trembled. It was cold out. Not freezing, but definitely not warm enough for the four of us to sleep in the car.

The front door opened again, and me, Alice, and Kyle all swiveled in that direction.

A tiny pixie of a woman crashed out of the front door, knocking her shoulder hard on the wooden post holding up the porch. But it didn't slow her. She sprinted across the crunchy winter grass, and on instinct, I braced myself for her attack.

She stopped short a mere inch from my toes and stared at me with huge brown eyes that hadn't changed at all since the last time I'd seen her.

She was a couple of inches shorter than me and probably weighed about half what I did.

But she was the big sister who had given me shelter after I'd left that house of horrors. She was the big sister who had nursed me back to health. And she was the only person in the world I'd thought to run to when I'd had to leave my life behind.

A sob burst out of my mouth before I could even try to control it.

Rebel's face crumpled. "Oh, Kara."

And then I was in her arms, wrapped in the fiercest of hugs and wondering how I'd even considered for a second that I couldn't come to this woman for help.

She held me tight, whispering in my ear, telling me that whatever had happened, whyever I was here now, it was all okay. She would make it okay.

Even though I knew that was a promise she couldn't make, I just nodded into her shoulder and let her soothe me.

Fang came out onto the steps again, and when I lifted my head with my eyes stinging from crying, I noticed two other men had joined him.

"Where you been, lady?" Kian grinned at me. Then

his gaze twisted to where Alice stood with Kyle. "Holy shit. Alice?"

"Who are they?" Kyle whispered to my sister.

"More brothers-in-law," she whispered back while she waved enthusiastically at Rebel's partners. "Rebel has three guys. But don't you dare judge her. She's not a slut."

I shot her a look. Rebel was literally *right* there.

But my older sister just laughed and hugged Alice with her free arm. The other was still attached to me. She'd pulled back but didn't let me go, like she wanted to assure herself I was real and actually there.

Or maybe it was me holding on to her for that reason.

Either way, we weren't letting each other go.

At least not for tonight. Tomorrow would be a different story, but at least I would have right now.

"What on earth are you doing here? Dad kept telling me you were fine but you didn't want to speak to me after everything that happened, and I understood, really I did, but then I would find myself writing you letters anyway, and even though I knew you weren't reading them I just kept sending them." Rebel shook her head sadly in the midst of her babble, her short dark hair falling across her eye. "I've missed you so much."

She had barely aged a day since I'd last hugged her. Barely looked any different other than her once-flat belly now held a gentle curve, proof she'd birthed her babies while we'd been apart.

Little had changed with her, but everything had changed with me. I didn't know where to start. How to fill her in on five years' worth of trauma when I could barely even admit it to myself.

An expression of understanding came over Rebel's

heart-shaped face, and then she nodded determinedly, taking control of the situation. "Fuck, come inside. I don't know why we're standing on the lawn. Do you have bags? Where's Hayley Jade?"

I turned back to the car.

Hayley Jade had slipped to the floorboard, scrunched into a ball so tight she could barely be seen.

Rebel took one look at her niece and then stared at me. "Is she okay?"

I touched my sister's arm. "I have a lot to tell you. Can you help me get her inside?"

Rebel bit into her bottom lip and nodded, but despite me, Rebel, and Alice all trying to coax Hayley Jade out, it couldn't be done. I didn't dare get one of the guys to attempt it. They'd scared Kyle, a fully grown man, so I wasn't about to test them out on a little girl, even if I knew they were totally harmless, at least to people they cared about.

Eventually, I picked Jade up and carried her inside, even though she screamed and kicked and bit at me hysterically.

Tears fell down my cheeks as Rebel quickly showed us to a spare bedroom on the ground floor, and I put Hayley Jade down on the bed.

Rebel left us, and I curled up on the fresh-smelling bed covers, my heart breaking over the way my daughter had just completely shut down.

It wasn't long before her sobs quieted and her breathing became even. When I raised my head from the pillow and leaned across so I could get a glimpse at her face, she was asleep. I couldn't blame her. It had been the longest night of my life, and I was exhausted too.

I sighed heavily and got up, untucking the blankets from my side of the bed and using them to cover the sleeping child. "I know you don't understand any of this right now," I whispered to her. "But there was no alternative." I swallowed hard. "I hope you can forgive me one day."

I got up and moved wearily from the bedroom to the sitting room just down the hallway. Inside, the room was full. Alice and Kyle sat next to each other on a couch, chatting with Vaughn and Kian who sat opposite them, hot drinks in their hands. Fang leaned against a wall, watching over his family, and Rebel had settled herself cross-legged on the floor.

She pointed at the coffee table and the steaming mug clearly meant for me. "Tea. I didn't think coffee was a good idea at this hour."

"Peppermint and chamomile?" I asked hopefully. A sip of my favorite hot drink would be heaven right about now.

Rebel shook her head. "Just the regular kind, I think. I'm not sure. None of us drink it. It's only there for guests."

I picked up the mug and took a sip, trying not to make a face because I didn't want her to feel bad. I hated regular tea, but it was hot, and the warm mug was comforting in my hands, and I was so grateful for the gesture.

Rebel's cheeks were tearstained as she watched me sip my drink. "Alice told us everything. I'm so, so sorry, Kara. I had no idea about any of it. How could Dad have let them do that to you?" Her expression crumpled into a mixture of anger and sadness, and she wrapped her arms around herself tightly.

I swallowed hard, knowing that "everything" was just the tip of the iceberg. Alice knew what had happened in the last twenty-four hours, but little of the years before that, other than what she'd observed from a distance.

But I was grateful I didn't have to rehash it all for my sister and her partners. It was too fresh and raw.

Vaughn shifted to stand with Fang, letting me have his seat, and while it was my instinct to protest and insist he didn't put himself out for me, I sank down into the comfy cushions, letting them envelop me in their softness.

Rebel reached over and squeezed my ankle. "Hey. You don't need to worry about any of it anymore. You'll all stay here. For as long as you need. Even if that's forever."

I shook my head fast, though my heart squeezed with love for this woman who hadn't even blinked an eye at me ignoring her for five years. She'd jumped straight back into being the older sister and protector I remembered.

Her heart was so big, but I was a ticking time bomb. One I refused to let explode all over this beautiful life she'd created for herself. "I can't stay here. It's too dangerous. It's the first place they'll search for us." I glanced at Kyle and then at Fang. "His truck can't be out there. They'll be looking for it. Josiah saw us leave."

Fang held his hand out toward Kyle, palm upturned. "Throw me your keys. I'll put it in the garage."

Kyle fumbled through his pockets and a tiny bit of my panic subsided. It was only a few hours. I knew we had to get farther away, find some tiny town in the middle of nowhere where nobody would think to search for us. But Kyle was slow blinking after driving all night, and Alice was slumped into the couch. It was like making it to a safe place had triggered something inside all of us and signaled to our brains that we could rest. We couldn't get any farther right now. None of us could survive on no sleep, and here, surrounded by Rebel's men and the protection of her home, we were safe. I had to believe that after a few hours in a bed, things wouldn't seem so bleak.

Rebel's face fell. "Kara, please. You have to stay. Between me and the guys, there's always someone here. You won't ever be alone. I'll tell Dad to back off and leave you alone."

I shook my head. "Dad is a pussycat compared to Josiah."

Kian swore low under his breath. "I knew there was something up with that guy years ago. Only had to meet him once to know there was something weird going on. We should have done something back then."

I shook my head, not wanting him to blame himself when there was nothing he could have done. "There wouldn't have been any point. You could have kicked down the fence and tried to get us out, but I wouldn't have gone with you."

"I would have," Alice mumbled, like a know-it-all teenager. "That place and Brother Josiah are the worst."

But she said that with no experience of how the real world worked.

How it chewed up women and spat them out.

How there were dangers here that the commune protected us from.

She was as naïve as I'd been, and it put her in danger.

"We should all go to bed." I looked at Alice sharply, noticing the way Kyle's thigh was pressed against hers. I turned to Rebel and whispered, "Separate beds, if at all possible."

Rebel clapped her hands. "Right. No hanky-panky for Alice and Kyle! We're running out of rooms, but Kyle, there's a guest room out in the pool house. Alice, you can have my room. Obviously Kara can sleep in with Hayley Jade."

I shook my head. "No, no. We don't want to inconvenience you."

Rebel winked at me. "I've got three men whose rooms I get to pick from. It's hardly an inconvenience."

My cheeks heated at the implication.

Rebel slung her arm around my shoulders. "I've missed making you blush. More of that in the morning, okay? After you've slept for ten hours."

The thought of staying here that long filled me with fear. The sun would be up soon, and I wanted to be gone soon after. "We need to leave early. As early as possible."

Rebel's mouth pulled into a frown. "I really want you to consider staying. We'll get restraining orders out against Josiah and Dad and anyone else. We'll make sure there's always a guard here..."

The very thought of all of that sent chills down my spine. We'd be sitting ducks. No piece of paper was going to keep Josiah from getting to me.

Five years as wife number one without a baby to show for it had taught me he never gave up.

Even when I begged for him to stop.

There was no begging anymore. No pleading for his

forgiveness. No going back. If he found me, I was dead and Hayley Jade would be sold to the highest bidder.

"We have to leave," I insisted.

Rebel didn't seem happy, but she finally nodded. "I'll transfer money to your account now. And more anytime you need it. As much as you want to get you as far as you think you need to go. As long as you promise me you'll buy a phone and keep in contact. I'll never forgive myself for not insisting I see you when Dad said you didn't want to be in contact with me anymore."

I grabbed her hand. "I would have lied, even if you had. Please. Don't feel bad. There's nothing you could have done."

Rebel gave a reluctant nod and then stood to hug me. She held me so damn tight I almost broke down in her arms again.

It had been so long since someone had hugged me.

But I pulled myself together and moved down the hallway to where my daughter slept. My heart broke as she made tiny, scared whimpering noises in her sleep.

I wanted to hug her to my chest and hold her the way I once had. Soothe her fear and mine too.

I could only pray that one day she would let me.

And that I could hold on and keep her safe, long enough for that day to come.

14

KARA

I woke to bright sun streaming through the gauzy curtains. It spilled across the pretty guest room, lighting up the pale walls and white ceiling. I blinked a few times, trying to clear the grogginess from my eyes, and took in the slightly wilted plant in the corner. A set of wood-stained drawers designed for holding clothes sat beside it.

I twisted to my side, reaching a hand toward Hayley Jade.

Panic flooded my system. I sat up so quickly my head spun, and a scream of terror lodged itself in my throat.

I scrambled out of bed, yanking the door open and sprinting down the hallway. "Hayley Jade!" My voice came out croaky, with sleep or panic I wasn't sure which. I ran, frantically searching every side table, every corner, looking for the little girl's blond hair and pale skin. "Hayley Jade!"

"In here," Rebel called from the sitting room we'd talked in the night before. "Sorry! We didn't go far because I knew you'd be worried, but the kids all get up so early..."

I stopped in the doorway I'd stood in just last night and stared at my sister in the middle of the room, surrounded by children. Including Hayley Jade, who sat quietly in a corner, playing with a Barbie doll.

My heart beat too fast. It took my brain too long to comprehend she was still here. Safe.

Playing.

Oh my God, she was playing!

I twisted to my sister who gave me a small smile and a shrug. "She heard me with the other kids and came out here on her own. I know it probably scared you but—"

I shook my head, slowly taking the seat next to Rebel. "Is she okay?" I whispered.

Rebel made a noncommittal noise and lowered her voice so the kids wouldn't hear. "She hasn't said anything. I asked her if she wanted to color or if she wanted to use the bathroom, and she didn't answer. But she picked out that Barbie doll, so that's something."

I breathed out heavily. "Other than to scream, I haven't heard her make a noise since we left Shari's place. Shari is her..." I couldn't even say it. There was so much shame in it. Here was Rebel, surrounded by her children, and yet I hadn't even been able to hold on to the single one I'd had.

I didn't need to dump all of my baggage on Rebel though. I did a quick head count of the children in the room and widened my eyes at my sister. "Are they all yours?"

She let out a laugh. "You act like I birthed a football team."

"Rebel, you have four kids under five."

She grinned, rubbing her tiny belly. "And one on the way."

My heart panged with both love and excitement for her. And pain for myself.

Other women all seemed to find it so easy to get pregnant.

I wrapped my arms around myself and rubbed my arms.

Rebel watched me for a second then cleared her throat. "Want to meet your nieces and nephews? Hayley Jade already met them all."

I very much did.

Rebel had a sleepy toddler on her lap, her daughter's eyes big as she stared at me silently, a pacifier in her mouth. Rebel stroked a hand over her daughter's hair. "This sleepyhead is Lavender. She's our youngest, or at least she will be for the next few months. Don't take her silence right now to mean anything. She's a tiny terror when she's awake properly, but she's like her mama and not one for mornings."

I smiled. "I remember Kian trying to get you out the door for runs when I stayed with you."

Rebel stifled a yawn. "That still happens a few times a week. Though with getting up to kids in the middle of the night, our 5:00 a.m. runs are often more like seven now. Sleep is precious around here. You'd think with four of us on nighttime duties, we'd all manage to get more sleep than the average set of parents..."

"But you went and had more kids than most people do."

Rebel grinned. "And in the shortest time frame possible."

I smiled at her. "Probably a known hazard of having as many partners as you do."

Rebel shifted on the couch, cuddling her daughter. "You'd think we'd learn to be a bit more careful, wouldn't you? But can I tell you a secret?"

"Of course."

Rebel leaned in conspiratorially over the top of Lavender's head. "I love being a mom more than anything else. I even love being pregnant." She laughed. "And I think they love knocking me up."

A blush crept up my cheeks at the idea of all the sex my sister had to be having.

But she looked so happy, despite clearly being a bit on the tired side.

A surge of jealousy hit me hard, and I silently admonished myself for it.

This was exactly why the Lord would never let me have another child. I coveted the happiness other women had. Jealousy kept my body inhospitable to creating new life.

A dark-haired boy of maybe three rammed a truck against my foot and then grinned up at me mischievously. "Beep-beep!"

"You're a bit late on the horn there, you crazy driver. You already ran your aunty Kara over," Rebel said to him. "Say hello, Wolf."

He sat back on his heels and cocked his head to one side, his little brow furrowed in confusion, like he was trying to work out where he'd suddenly acquired a new relative from.

He was so much like Vaughn it was shocking. I glanced at my sister, my eyes wide.

She chuckled quietly. "There's no doubting who created him, huh? He looks just like Vaughn when he does that thing with his head. Weirds me out too." She lowered her chin onto the top of Lavender's hair. "She does it as well."

"They're both his?" I asked, though it was obvious how alike the two children were, and Wolf was the spitting image of his biological father.

Rebel nodded. "Remi is Fang's though," she explained, pointing to her fair-haired older daughter. "Though only the hair color gives it away. She definitely didn't get any of his height, poor kid. She's a short-ass like I am. And Madden is Kian's. I think I might have told you that in a letter before we got cut off, though…"

I swallowed hard and nodded. "I remember being so shocked that twins could have different fathers."

"You and me both!" She gazed over at her twins fondly. "Wouldn't change them for the world. The guys are such good dads."

"Do the kids call all of them Dad? Or just their biological parent?" I knew I was being nosy, but I couldn't help it. The dynamic of Rebel's family was so different from the household I'd left behind, even though both were polyamorous.

"They're all dad to each of them. But they call Vaughn Dad. Fang is Daddy. Kian has Irish roots and wanted to be called Da. Really, though, any of them yells Dad and all three guys come running. These kids have those big men wrapped around their little fingers, don't you?" She picked up Lavender's hand and pressed a kiss to her chubby baby fingers. "Your dads are big suckers for all four of you."

I glanced at Hayley Jade, my heart squeezing with love. She wasn't lucky enough to have one father, let alone three who doted on her. Hayley Jade's father was a monster, and I was glad he was dead.

Maybe that was the real reason I couldn't conceive.

Because every day, I was silently glad Caleb was six feet under and could never hurt anyone ever again.

But that didn't change the way I felt about the daughter he'd left me with.

She was everything that was good and right. His evil couldn't touch her.

But Josiah's could.

I bit my lip.

Like Rebel could read my mind, she reached out and took my hand. "Please. You don't have to go. We'll keep you safe. We have the MC, and..."

I squeezed her hand back and stood, because there was no point having this conversation again, even if she meant well. "Can I get Hayley Jade something to eat? As soon as she's eaten, we need to get on the road."

Rebel's face fell, but she nodded and reached over to a side table and picked up a small plastic card. "Here. I didn't know if you had a bank account to transfer money into, but I suspected you didn't..."

"I don't. Josiah doesn't allow women to have money of their own."

Rebel's mouth pulled a thin line, but she didn't comment. "I figured as much. This is the card for an account we don't use. We should have closed it ages ago, but it's one of those annoying things where they make you go into the branch to close it, and who has the time or energy to do that? Do you know how quickly four kids can tear apart a bank if they have to wait in line for longer than five minutes?"

"I'm sure your children are very well behaved."

Rebel laughed. "They're terrors, but aren't all kids at this age? They're loud and full of energy and they talk nonstop..."

Her voice trailed away at the comparison between her healthy, confident kids who felt secure enough to be typical children, and Hayley Jade, who hadn't said a word since we'd been here.

Rebel put the card into my hand. It had her name on it. "We put ten thousand dollars in there last night. And we'll put more if you need it. Fang is going to run out this morning and get you a burner phone so you can stay in contact with us."

I stared down at the small plastic card and then up at my older sister in shock. "Ten thousand...I can't accept that." I pushed the card back at her.

But Rebel's gaze was firm. "You will take it, Kara." Her gaze slid to Hayley Jade. "You'll take it for her and give her a better life. I want you to stay, but even if you don't, you need to have your own money." She swallowed hard. "Women do desperate things when they don't have enough of it. I won't have that life for you."

A look of understanding passed between us. Shari had said much the same thing. I tucked the card into the pocket of the skirt I'd slept in, remembering I didn't even have any clothes to get changed into. "Thank you. You have no idea how much this means to me."

Rebel's bottom lip trembled for a second, but she

drew in a deep breath. "Enough of being sappy. If you're sure you have to leave, then let's get you on the road. Hayley Jade, do you want to come have some breakfast with us? We have all sorts of yummy foods, and you can choose anything you want. I know your cousins are going to choose chocolate Pop-Tarts." She glanced at me. "Which is my bad influence on their diet, but I think today is a chocolate for breakfast sort of day."

I held my breath when Hayley Jade glanced up from her dolls and then watched her cousins cheering and running for the kitchen in their sweet onesie pajamas. Slowly, she stood and followed them.

I breathed out a sigh of relief.

Rebel stood, shifting Lavender to her hip. "I'll handle the food. You go get Alice and Kyle up and organized. They'll probably want to have showers and breakfast before you leave too."

"Good idea. From memory, Alice is just like her eldest sister." I grinned at Rebel. "Not a morning person."

I felt bad for making them get up after only a few hours of rest, but we just couldn't afford to linger.

I headed up the stairs to the room I knew was Rebel's from when I'd stayed with her years ago. I knocked quietly on the closed door. "Alice? It's getting late. Time to get up."

There was no sound from the bedroom beyond.

I tried again. "Rebel is making Pop-Tarts for breakfast. I don't know if you remember those from back before…" Before Josiah had come into our lives and changed everything. I remembered Pop-Tarts from when I was a kid, but Alice was younger than I was. Not even twenty-one yet. Would she even remember the foods we'd had back then?

I twisted the door handle and pushed it open.

Rumpled sheets were twisted on the bed, but there was no dark-haired sister curled up beneath them.

I frowned and moved farther into the room, knocking on the door to the adjoining bathroom carefully because I knew it connected to Kian's room on the other side also.

Nobody answered, and I took a chance, sliding open the pocket door.

The sink top was littered with Rebel and Kian's toiletries—deodorant, toothbrushes and paste, an electric razor.

But no younger sister.

"Alice!" I called out loud as I hurried back out of the room and down the hallway to the stairs. "Alice!" I tried to keep the panic out of my voice so I didn't scare the kids eating in the kitchen.

Fang stuck his head out of the door of his room. He had a phone pressed to his ear, but he murmured, "Hang on a second, Hawk," into the phone.

I was too busy stressing about my sister's disappearing act to crinkle my nose at the mention of Fang's MC friend. I'd met that man before and I didn't care to repeat the process.

"You okay?" Fang asked me.

"Alice isn't up here."

But Rebel poked her head out of the kitchen on the ground floor and stared up at me on the second-floor landing. "Did you try the bathroom?"

I nodded, picking up the pace and running down the

stairs with Fang behind me. "She must be out in the pool house with Kyle. I'm going to kill her."

Rebel caught my arm as I ran past. "Hey. She's young and stupid. If you find her naked in his bed—"

I stared at her with huge, horrified eyes.

Rebel's mouth opened into an O-shape. "Oh, I mean, I'm sure they're not. I'm sure she just went down there early for coffee..."

Fang rubbed a hand over his face and grimaced.

He still had the phone pressed to his ear, so I wasn't sure if the face was about whatever Hawk was saying on the other end, or if it was about Rebel assuming my sister and Kyle were having sex the moment we got away from the commune.

But hadn't that been exactly what I'd done when I'd left?

It had ended so badly that was the last thing I wanted for Alice.

I rushed out the back doors and skirted the sparkling blue pool. The small cottage-style house beyond it had the shades all pulled down, everything quiet on the inside.

I didn't bother knocking. I was too intent on stopping my sister from ruining her life by sleeping with some man she barely knew.

"Alice!"

But another empty room met me.

Rebel jogged in a second later and took in the same empty room. "They're not here," she said, stating the obvious.

I spun around and stared at her, the idea of my sister having sex with some guy suddenly the least of my worries. I almost wished I had walked in and found them naked, him pumping into her body while she moaned.

At least I would have known she was safe.

"Where are they?" I asked Rebel.

"I don't know." Her gaze landed on the bed, and she leaned over, picking up a piece of paper half hidden by the duvet. Her eyes moved right to left as she read whatever was written on it, and then she cringed. "Actually, I do. Here."

I snatched the note from her fingers.

Kara,

Sorry for sneaking out, but I knew you'd say no. We'll be back before night falls and then we can get going. I'm sorry. I know you want to go and hide away, but I don't. Just let me have this one day to explore and then we can move on. I've got Kyle with me so I'll be safe, and you can spend the day with Rebel. I know you've missed her, and Hayley Jade should get to know her cousins.

We're free, Kara! Enjoy it!

Love, Alice.

I stared at my sister's handwriting, and then up at Rebel. "What are we going to do?"

Rebel sighed. "I can get Vaughn and Kian to go look for her. Fang has to go bail Hawk's ass out of jail, otherwise he'd go too."

I blinked. "Hawk is in jail? What did he do?"

"Who knows," Rebel shrugged. "It's not like it's never happened before."

I hugged my arms around myself, regrets fighting their way in to battle with my common sense. "I shouldn't have left," I mumbled. "I should have just stayed. This is the sort of men who are out here. Men who are put in jail. What if Alice runs into someone like Hawk?"

Rebel caught my hand. "Hawk is an asshole, but he's not all bad. From what Alice told me last night, Josiah and some of his friends should be behind bars too. Were you really any safer with him?"

I knew she was right.

I wasn't safe anywhere. Neither was Hayley Jade. Neither was Alice.

"They're going to find me," I mumbled.

Rebel's expression took on a determined firmness. "Over my dead body. Alice is going to be fine. I'm going to send Vaughn and Kian out to search all the most popular hangouts in the city, all the places they don't check ID so she'd be able to get in."

"I should go with them."

Rebel shook her head. "The last thing we need is you out there too. If Josiah and his guys really are tracking you, keeping you safe and hidden is our number one task."

Fang appeared in the doorway behind her, catching the end of the conversation. "Sorry to interrupt. I just came to kiss you goodbye. But I caught the end of that. You aren't staying here alone. Neither of you."

Rebel wrapped her arms around his thick waist and stared up at him. "You think those five probably chocolate-covered kids up in the main house won't protect us?" She was clearly trying to lighten the mood.

I didn't find it funny.

Neither did Fang, clearly.

He rubbed his hand along the side of her cheek, cupping her face. "It's family day at the clubhouse.

There'll be food, and we'll get the swing sets and trampolines out. I'll drop you all off on my way to the police station, and then I'll meet you back there."

Rebel looked at me. "What do you think? He's right. As much as it kills the independent woman in me, I don't want the kids in any danger."

I didn't want to go there. It was where I'd been taken after Rebel had saved me. The clubhouse held memories of pain and sadness. It was full of sinful men who did unspeakable things that weren't just illegal but immoral. I didn't want to go back.

But what choice did I have? I had Rebel's money burning a hole in my pocket, promising a better life for me and Hayley Jade and Alice. But none of that could start until she came home.

The house was full of children, and if we were here alone and Josiah found us...

I couldn't even bear the thought.

"Okay," I whispered. "I'll go."

There were demon figures on the gates of the clubhouse, but what did it matter if I passed through them again? I was already in Hell.

15

HAWK

Spending all night in a holding cell at Providence Police Department was somewhere akin to sleeping on the floor of the clubhouse bathroom after an all-night party. The bench seat beneath me was hard and my shoulder numb from lying on it for hours. The toilet reeked of piss and vomit, though that was almost preferable to the chemical smell that clung to my skin and hair after that delousing wash-down we'd been so delightfully subjected to.

None of the other assholes in this cell seemed to have gotten the same treatment. I hadn't bothered making conversation with the three other guys in the small room, but their street clothes and the stench of BO gave away that Chaos and I had been singled out for special treatment thanks to our gang affiliation.

Poor shriveled-dick Simon seemed to have been caught up as collateral damage. Though he'd been sprung almost as quickly as Chaos had.

Fucking asshole.

Wife Number One

Must be nice to have a rich brother.

The locking mechanism on the door made a grinding sound, and a bored cop leaned on the doorway. "Hawk Robinson?"

I looked up from my rock-hard bench. "Yeah?"

He frowned. "Hawk is honestly your legal name?"

"That's what it says on the fucking paperwork, doesn't it?"

The cop chuckled in the face of my irritation. "Your parents really just set you up for this life, didn't they? Giving you a name like that. Your ride is here. You're out."

My parents naming me Hawk was hardly the bad decision that had led me down this path. I'd grown up in the club. Never knew nothing different. If they'd wanted me to be a lawyer or a doctor, the first thing they probably should have done was make sure I actually went to fucking school.

If they had, it would have saved me the hassle of doing my GED now, at the ripe fucking age of thirty-five.

Speaking of... I jerked my chin at the cop. "Hey, what's the date?"

He raised an eyebrow as he waited for me to leave the cell. "Why? You want to note it down in your journal or something? Dear Diary," he mocked. "Today I met my life's potential and found myself in jail. Won't be long until I'm here permanently. Love..." He sniggered. "Hawk."

He said my name like it was the stupidest thing he'd ever heard. Which was fucking hilarious coming from a man whose nametag read Officer Nigel Buttsworth.

Normally I would have made some sort of smart-ass comment about that, but fuck, I really wanted to know the date. "Please," I forced out through gritted teeth, hating the way that word sounded on my lips. I didn't beg people for fucking anything. My old man would be rolling over in his goddamn grave if he'd heard me mumble those words.

But fuck that old bastard. I needed to know.

The officer checked his smartwatch. "It's the eighteenth."

Fuck.

"That mean something to you?" the cop asked as he guided me back to the processing room and passed me a clear bag with my name on it. Inside were the clothes I'd been wearing when I'd been picked up, but I had no doubt they would have been swabbed to within an inch of their life, photographed, and tested for who fucking knows what in the time we'd been apart.

Whatever. They weren't going to find anything. The new chief could go fuck himself.

I snatched the bag of clothes out of the cop's hand and ripped it open. "Just got something I need to do today. None of your business, Officer Buttshole."

The man's face purpled. "It's Officer Buttsworth."

I squinted at him, pulling my clothes on quickly. "Is that really any better?"

The cop flipped me the bird before turning around. "See you soon, Hawk. You might be writing down today's date in your diary, but I'm just waiting on the one where I get to lock you up for good." He banged a fist against a window that led out into the station. "He's good to go."

Fuck him. He sounded just like my old man.

I wasn't spending my life in here like him.

This date did mean something.

Fang waited for me in the reception area, his arms crossed over his giant chest, a scowl fixed on the cops shoving papers at me to sign.

I scribbled something unintelligible in the places they indicated, my handwriting awful as always, and then I made my way over to Fang.

"You good?" he asked quietly, pushing off the wall. He was a couple of inches taller than my six foot two.

"Yeah, fine."

He wrinkled his nose. "Why do you smell like that?"

The smell truly was disgusting. "There's a new chief. Has it in for us apparently."

Fang grumbled low in his chest. "I'll talk to War. Slip him some stacks."

I shook my head. "No, don't worry. I'll do it. After having my ass groped and being sprayed in this shit then left in a cell all fucking night, I've got a few things I'd like to have a word about. War is busy with his family. Bliss popped out that kid yet?"

"Not that I've heard. I think she still has a few weeks left. At least that's what Rebel said."

I nodded. "She'd know. Those two are joined at the hip and like mama ducks with their tribe of kids following them around everywhere. You all need to learn how to pull out."

Fang's mouth lifted a little in one corner. "Bliss makes Rebel happy. Rebel fat and pregnant with babies makes me happy. So fuck off." But it was said with such good humor I snorted.

"You've changed, brother." I shook my head. "Remember when you were all scowls and scary MC enforcer who never smiled and would snap the neck of anyone who looked at him wrong?"

Fang unlocked the club van as we approached the parking lot. "Do I need to snap your neck right now to prove I'm still capable?"

I grinned at him. The man was pure muscle. A wall of intimidation. I knew for a fact he'd taken out three guys in the last month without so much as getting a scratch in return. He was different because he was happy. More often than not, he had a kid in his arms or was using the club van to pick the twins up from preschool. But it hadn't made him any less lethal when it counted.

I didn't need him to prove it. When we called on him, he was there. Just like he always had been.

"Nah." I gripped the holy-shit handle and pulled myself up into the passenger seat of the van. "We waiting on Aloha and Ice to be released too?"

Fang shook his head. "Cops didn't book 'em. Let them go with a warning."

My mouth dropped open. "Fuck off. Seriously? They put me and Chaos through the wringer."

Fang shrugged. "You're the VP... He's the leader of the Sinners. Or was. I don't know who's in charge over there anymore, if anyone. The cops are making an example of you. Why waste their time booking all of us when they can send the same message by getting to the top of our ranks?"

I eyed him. "Doesn't sound like something the old chief would have done."

"The old chief was an idiot. Maybe this one isn't."

I leaned back in my seat, leaning an arm on the windowsill. "We'll see."

We drove in silence for a few minutes, Fang steering the van back through Providence and into Saint View.

"You nervous?" he asked quietly.

I glanced at him sharply. "About what?"

He concentrated on the road, not twisting his head to make eye contact with me. "Your results are out today, aren't they?"

I let out a breath. "I hate that you know about that."

"I can pretend I don't if you want?"

I shook my head. "As long as nobody else knows. I don't need everyone giving me shit."

"I don't think they would..."

I raised an eyebrow at him.

He chuckled. "Okay, fine. You're lucky it's me who collects the mail and saw all those enrollment papers you had sent. I still don't know why you sent them to the clubhouse. You could have just downloaded them."

Easy for him to say. "Yeah, well, I went and bought a laptop after that, didn't I? It's not like I'm a computer genius like you are."

Fang rolled his eyes. "Having an email address and a Facebook page doesn't exactly make me an IT whiz. I don't know how you made it to thirty-five without either."

I smiled at him, making it overexaggerated and sickly sweet. "Was too busy fucking your sister."

Fang flicked up his blinker and spun the wheel to take the bluff road that would eventually lead to the woods. The clubhouse was nestled behind thick trees, deep inside them, surrounded by an even more robust fence line. Fang didn't even bother replying to my barb. We both knew I'd never met his sister. If he even had one. I didn't fucking know. I wasn't in the habit of going around the club and asking all of the members about their mommies and daddies and how many offspring they'd birthed.

It was hard enough to keep up with the amount of devil spawn the club members had produced over the past few years. Half the time the clubhouse was like a fucking nursery.

At least during the day. No kids were allowed after dark unless we were in lockdown, and thankfully, we hadn't had one of those in ages. I couldn't think of anything worse than being trapped at the club with kids twenty-four seven.

I mentally urged the van to hurry up, my results waiting for me on the shitty old laptop I'd bought when I'd first decided to take the course. It had my login details saved on it. Once I got home, I'd be able to check my results. They should have come in at nine, and it was already eleven.

I can't believe I'd fucking gotten arrested. Of all fucking days.

Fuck Chaos. If I'd known it was him getting his ass kicked at that diner last night, I would have left him to become hamburger. Walked right on past him dying on the floor, the way he had when the fucker had sent a bullet straight into my goddamn leg.

By the time Fang drove us up the tree-lined road and waited for the massive iron gates with the Slayers' emblem to open, my leg jumped with nerves and excess energy.

"Settle," Fang warned. "Getting there faster ain't gonna change what's on those results."

Easier said than done. I'd spent four fucking months

taking this class. I'd never studied for anything in my life, and learning how to do that at thirty-five had felt like pushing a boulder up a hill.

But I'd done it because it was the first step in getting into medicine.

I clamped down on my bottom lip, despising that the stupid fucking dream was even in my head when it was so ridiculous to begin with.

Even Fang didn't know about that. I'd told him I was bored and just wanted to take the GED to prove to myself I could. I'd told him I hated that I felt like school had beaten me and I wanted to prove I could beat it right back now that I was older and hopefully slightly smarter than I'd been at fifteen.

Though that was probably debatable.

But I hadn't dared tell him the real reason I'd wanted to do it was because medicine and healing had, somewhere along the line, become all I could think about. It had started long before Chaos had been scraped off the side of the road and left in our basement for me to fix. I'd been sewing up minor bullet wounds and gashes the club members had come back to the house with for years. Somebody had to, and most of the guys were too busy fainting or gagging over the sight of blood. I'd found it an oddly interesting rush to have someone's life in my hands without having a gun pressed to their head.

Though having the muzzle pressed up against Chaos's skull last night had been pretty fucking sweet too.

I'd watched hours of YouTube videos on all sorts of medical topics. Whatever I could find. It was all fascinating to me.

I watched until watching wasn't enough. I itched to

learn more. To learn in a real setting where I could actually develop proper skills.

I'd never wanted a nine-to-five job, but suddenly there was something in my life worth more than going on gun runs, riding my bike, and fucking women.

So I'd enrolled in the stupid GED class because I needed that in order to get into any sort of medical course.

But first, I had to pass.

"You're going to pass," Fang said, like that big fucker could read my mind.

"I know," I quipped back, trying to sound like the cocky prick I normally was.

But it was hard with this. I was so far out of my depth, and I knew it.

I'd studied so damn much though. I had to pass. There was no other option. Without a pass, any hope of getting into a medical job was gone.

The van twisted through the dirt road toward the large, ugly rectangular building me and a bunch of the club members called home.

I groaned at the sight of a full parking lot and people everywhere.

Not just club members.

Wives. Children. Ew.

"Is it seriously fucking family day?" I complained. "Again?"

Fang looked over at me warily. "It's the third weekend of every month. It's not like this should be a surprise to you."

I screwed my nose up at the damn trampoline that had been pulled out of the storage shed Fang and War had made a few years back once their brats were all walking and talking. The two pussy-whipped fools had filled that shed with all sorts of useless kid crap. Swing sets. Jumping ropes. Barbies.

There was a fucking Barbie Dreamhouse in the middle of the Slayers MC. And one day a month, big burly guys like Aloha and Ratchet crawled around outside like they were ponies while four-year-olds giggled hysterically on their backs.

Our enemies would have a field day if they knew that.

Fang parked the van. "You going to join us?"

"Nope."

He flinched slightly, like I'd managed to hurt his feelings. "Come on. You never come to family day. The twins always ask why Uncle Hawk doesn't want to hang with them."

"Did you tell them it's because I'm not actually their uncle?"

Fang narrowed his eyes at me, but I wasn't in the mood for his guilt trips. He wasn't the prez. He didn't get to make demands on my time. And War was smart enough not to give me a hard time about it.

I didn't have a fucking family.

Why the hell would I go to an event literally called *family* day?

Fang had that "disappointed dad" expression on his face. Again. "Whatever. Don't come. All the more chili for me."

My stomach grumbled. I hadn't even gotten to finish my dinner last night at the diner before I'd had to go save Chaos's stupid ass, and it's not like they'd served up a buffet breakfast at the police station. Chili sounded fucking amazing. "Never said I didn't need to eat," I relented.

Fang shook his head, rolling his eyes. "Thought it might go like that."

We walked side by side to the doorway of the clubhouse, dodging ankle biters and Tonka trucks. Fang paused in the doorway and put a hand out to stop me.

"Listen, though. Something happened last night you should probably know about. Rebel's sister—"

I didn't even need to ask which one.

There was only one I recognized, and she was sitting right in the middle of my clubhouse, as uncomfortable and out of place as a nun in a whorehouse.

But, fuck, she was beautiful.

Long dark hair. Big brown eyes. Tits that strained at her top like it was several sizes too small to contain them.

It had been years since I'd last seen her.

Years since I'd felt that same jolt of lust just from one glimpse of her sweet curves.

My fingertips tingled like they had the first day she'd crashed into me in the woods, alive at just the touch of my skin against hers.

I stormed across the room and stopped right in front of her.

She glanced up, and fuck me, standing above her like this, with her gaze locked on mine, all I could think about was how she'd look naked, on her knees, her mouth open for my dick like the good girl I wanted her to be.

"You." The seething word fell from my lips, so different from how I felt inside. "You fucking broke my nose. *Twice.*"

A hush fell over the group, all eyes focusing on me.

Rebel was quick to defend her sister, rushing over from the side of the room. "That was five years ago, Hawk! Get over it."

I ignored her, staring down at Kara some more because I couldn't drag my fucking eyes off her. She barely looked older than she'd been the last time I'd seen her, but her curves were even more pronounced in clothes that had to be Rebel's because *Paramore* was printed on the T-shirt fighting to contain Kara's tits.

I wanted to rip that shirt off her. Bury my face in the swells. Lick her creamy skin until her nipples pebbled beneath my tongue.

Kara shrank back into the couch, cowering away from me like some scared little daisy.

I blinked.

That was unexpected. Sure, the last time I'd seen her she hadn't exactly been full of confidence either, but that hadn't stopped her from swinging her fist right into my nose. Or using the back of her head to break it again when I'd just been trying to fucking help her.

Watching her shrink away from me now sent a jolt of self-loathing through me.

The woman was too confusing, and I didn't need this bullshit today. Didn't need to be reminded about what a piece of shit I was. I already had my dad's voice in my head telling me I was too stupid to pass that test and why would I even bother when I knew I was too dumb?

I turned to Rebel. "Get her out of here. She's not welcome."

Rebel gaped at me. "She's my sister, jackass! If anyone's not welcome, it's you!"

Blood pounded in my head. I was so fucking tired. I

reeked of jail. And all I could think about was the goddamn GED test results that were going to determine the rest of my life.

I didn't need Kara curling in on herself like the last five years had beaten her into a pulp and one hard word from me was going to send her over the edge.

Amber, my favorite club girl, strode across the room, pressing herself against my side. "Hey, baby. Come on. Let's go to your room."

With effort, I dragged my gaze from Kara to Amber. Amber was so familiar. Her blond hair had been wrapped around my fist hundreds of times. Her fake, overly round tits had been in my mouth just two days ago. She'd come on my tongue and screamed my name while she bounced on my cock more times than I could count.

I'd never felt a thing.

Which only made the lust in my blood for Rebel's curvy sister all the more fucked-up. She was a scared little church mouse who I would destroy in seconds.

Amber was the opposite. She could take my shit. With Amber, I wouldn't feel like a lion devouring an injured fawn.

I strode down the long hallway, leaving the party and everyone at it staring at my back.

"He's such a fucking asshole!" Rebel complained, and there were multiple other voices of agreement who chimed in with her.

Each one sent a tiny jab of hurt through me, but it was only because I hadn't slept and those test results were burning a hole in my computer.

I'd get my walls back up. I didn't need the club wives to like me.

Didn't need Kara to like me. Whatever she'd gone through in the last five years that had her curling into the fetal position wasn't my problem.

I unlocked the door to my room as Amber caught up to me. I didn't stop her when she slipped inside and started taking her clothes off.

Ignoring her, I grabbed my laptop from the floor by my bed, but before I could sit, Amber was tugging at the fly of my jeans. "You look like you need to come, baby," she practically cooed, dragging down my zipper. "Let me help you out."

I didn't want her there. I just wanted to check the fucking results alone. But she already had her fingers around my cock, stroking the length.

I wasn't getting hard.

Because it wasn't Amber's hand around my cock that I wanted.

Fucking hell, I hadn't thought about Kara in years.

Liar.

Fine. I'd thought about her. Not every day. And never enough that I couldn't get hard with Amber's mouth wrapped around my dick.

What the fuck was wrong with me?

I sat hard on the bed, dislodging my dick from Amber's mouth, but she scrambled forward, pushing her way between my knees and bobbing over my cock like it was an Olympic sport.

"Come on, baby. Relax," she murmured. "What's got you so tense?"

"You fucking talking," I bit back.

It was mean and I knew it. But she laughed, pulling off to gaze up at me. "You're such a grump today."

I pushed her head down and flopped back onto the bed, resting my laptop on my chest. I hit the power button and waited for the piece-of-shit computer to whiz and whir its way into life.

I closed my eyes while it did its thing.

Kara's image flashed to life behind my eyes.

Her staring up at me.

Like something out of every wet dream I'd ever had.

My dick got hard.

I pretended Amber's mouth was Kara's. Pretended it was her naked in my bedroom, ready and willing to let me touch her. Kiss her. Fuck her sweet holes with my tongue and my fingers and my dick.

I groaned, precum beading on my tip.

I opened my eyes and logged on to the online class dashboard, where a small envelope notification in the top right-hand corner told me I had one new message.

I knew exactly what it would be.

For the tiniest of seconds, I wished there was someone here to hold my hand.

Someone who wasn't Amber.

"Just fucking do it," I muttered to myself.

"Do what?" Amber asked.

"Make me come," I told her, though that wasn't what I'd meant at all.

She lowered her head, licking my balls and making my eyes roll back with how good it felt.

I clicked on the notification.

Skimmed over a bunch of lines about how the scores were worked out.

Scrolled lower to the actual results page.

I slammed the laptop closed. My erection instantly dead. I sat up and pushed Amber away.

She rocked back on her heels, her forehead furrowed in confusion. "What's the matter? You were so close."

"Get out," I muttered.

"You don't mean that." She reached for me again.

I flinched away because I *so* fucking did. "Get out!" I roared.

She blinked at the tone I'd never used with her before, scrambling back, grabbing her clothes, and clutching them to her chest as she ran from my room.

That rush of self-loathing cloaked me again. This time it was half because I'd managed to upset yet another woman. And half because I should have known better than to think some dumb-ass kid from Saint View had a hope in hell of passing those tests.

Thinking I could do anything in medicine had been as stupid as my body wanting Kara.

Neither were going to happen.

16

HAYDEN

I sighed heavily, letting the groan of the diner door cover up my frustration. A fishy sort of smell lingered in the small, grubby space, and I approached the counter, wrinkling my nose at the unpleasant odor. I had to clear my throat to get the attention of the bored waitress scrolling on her phone.

She finally glanced up. "Oh shit. Hey. Sorry. What can I get you?"

It was clear she wasn't used to having people to serve. The place was deserted. And I couldn't blame people for not wanting to eat here. What was that smell?

Nevertheless, I forced a smile I didn't feel. "Was just wondering if the manager is around?"

Her eyebrows dove together, and her demeanor completely flipped to defensive. "Why? You want to make a complaint or something?"

I shook my head quickly. "No, no. Nothing like that. I just wanted to see if there was any work going here. I'm a…chef." I practically choked on the word I'd never been much good at using, but chef did sound better than cook. If I was going to get another job, I needed all the bonus points I could get.

She gestured around the empty restaurant with her overly long, fake fingernails. "A chef, huh? Well, la di da. You want to cook for all our customers?"

She had a point. I pushed back off the counter. "Thanks anyway."

"You ain't even going to buy a coffee?" she called after me.

But I pretended I didn't hear. For all I knew it was the coffee machine producing that foul odor.

Getting back into my car and switching the engine on, I sighed. Fuck Simon. The job in his kitchen hadn't exactly been my dream, but it had been a damn sight better than any of the other places I'd tried to find work. No one in Saint View seemed to be hiring, and I couldn't blame them. The people in this area didn't have a lot of disposable cash, and times were tough. Eating out was one of the first things people cut from their budgets.

There were a few other diners on my list, but it hardly seemed worthwhile bothering. What the hell else was I going to do though? If I couldn't get a job cooking, my next attempts at finding a job would have to be cleaning toilets.

I could go back to the Sinners. Back to selling drugs. Running guns. Back to holding women against their will because some fucking asshole with a higher rank said I had to.

Or I could go to Luca and ask if his job offer was still on the table. The thought of a salary with six figures and a part share in the ownership had kept me up all night, fueled with confusion.

And regret.

I wanted to turn back the clock and change my mind.

I found myself rolling down a familiar street I'd avoided for the last five years because it brought back too many memories. I forced myself down it now, forced my foot to stay on the gas and my fingers to keep the wheel straight.

If I was thinking of accepting Luca's offer, then I needed to be reminded of why I'd left the world he controlled.

I parked a couple of houses down from the decrepit building we'd once used as a clubhouse. It was in even worse shape now than it had been back then. Windows smashed or boarded up. The lawn full of weeds and so overgrown it was probably waist-high. Porch sagging so bad I'd bet the boards wouldn't even take my weight.

It was clear nobody had occupied the house for some time. Same with all the surrounding houses. The street was deserted.

I got out and wandered along the cracked pavement to stand by the rusted mailbox, barely clinging to the pole it was mounted on.

My blood pounded in my veins. My fingers shook with the memories being here produced.

On autopilot, I followed the path, overgrown with weeds up to my knees. The first bedroom window had once been covered by dirty, cracked glass, but now that was in shards, crunching beneath my boots.

The room beyond was where I'd delivered a baby girl five years ago.

Where I'd held her panicked mother's clammy hand, looked her in the eye, and told her she was going to push and get that baby out.

It was also the room I'd kept five women in against their will, because I'd had no other choice.

Caleb and Luca had owned me. They'd owned Kara and the other women. Caleb had threatened my family until I'd been nothing but his puppet, doing whatever my master told me.

But Hayley Jade and Kara had been the beginning of my undoing.

In trying to save them, I'd gotten shot and almost died myself.

It had been worth it. Knowing they'd spent the last five years away from all of this, out of this shithole town, and safe with Kara's family, had been the only way I'd gotten through the days. I'd only let myself ask my brother about her once, and when he'd reported that she'd gone home, I'd tried to put the woman and her daughter out of my head.

That hadn't worked. I thought about them daily. Wondered if she'd married. Wondered what Hayley Jade would look like, now she was older.

I couldn't forget the little girl who had been named after me.

Nor could I forget her mother.

A tiny, out-of-place noise shook me from my memories.

Instinctively, I reached for my gun, only to remember I hadn't carried one in years. Shit. Coming back here unarmed had been stupid.

I froze, scanning my surroundings. The street was

quiet. Nothing but the rustle of a gentle breeze that stroked the long grass, and the distant sounds of traffic on the main road in the distance.

I squinted, slowly swiveling in a circle.

Something had made that noise.

It came again, along with a scrawny creature who crawled out of the long grass to wrap her way around my ankles.

"Fuck, cat. You scared the shit out of me." I breathed out slowly, letting my blood pressure come down before I squatted to stroke the kitten.

I withdrew my hand quickly, the animal covered in fleas. The kitten scratched its itchy spots against my boots and mewled insistently.

"You're probably hungry, huh? You're definitely in need of a bath, though I'm sure you won't like that... Oh, fuck."

A second and third kitten made their way out of the long grass and joined their sibling, scratching themselves on my shoes.

I groaned. "Seriously? I did not have kitten rescue on my bingo card for the month." I shrugged. "Suppose I didn't have getting fired on it either. Or arrested. Or offered the job of my dreams only to refuse it."

The cats ignored my bitching and started up a chorus of noise, each one seemingly competing with the others for who was the hungriest.

"I hate cats," I told them. "I think I'm allergic to you guys."

They didn't care.

I squinted at the wall of grass around us. "Don't you have a mom somewhere to look after you?"

But if they did, she wasn't doing a very good job of it. They clearly had empty bellies. One had a gunky eye that probably needed medication from a vet. And they all needed flea treatment.

A hawk flew overhead, letting out a screech.

Instinctively, I crouched over the little creatures, blocking the hawk's view.

These kittens were easily small enough for a bird that size to pick up and make a meal out of.

I didn't need this. Not today. What I needed was a job, so I was never tempted to come back to this shithole again.

But I had Kara's sweet face stuck in the back of my mind. Her holding a tiny newborn, wrapped in whatever cloth we'd been able to scrounge up. I remembered the feeling I'd had, watching the two of them curled up on a dirty mattress in the middle of Hell.

It was the feeling that had made me turn over a new leaf. It was a high I'd been chasing for years. It reminded me of the man I wanted to be. The one I was still trying to become every day.

I wasn't the sort of man who left the defenseless behind.

So I picked up the three squirming kittens, let their fleas crawl all over my hands, and protected them in the same way I'd so desperately wanted to protect Kara and Hayley Jade five years earlier.

The vet in Saint View rejected me away in under two minutes. They already had two litters of kittens they'd rescued and had no room for more. So I drove the sleeping fluff balls, content now that I'd stopped at the supermarket and bought them some food, into Providence, hoping the vet there might be more willing to help.

As soon as I stepped foot in the door though, I already knew what the answer was going to be. The receptionist shrugged and parroted much the same thing the first vet had told me. There were too many strays, and they couldn't continue to take them in when people willing to adopt them were few and far between.

"Should I try the vet in the city?" I asked her, staring down at the three little bodies all entwined with each other in a food coma tangle. "The other vet said I'd just have to take them to the pound."

The receptionist gave a sad smile. "There's no point trying the vet in the city. They're even worse off than we are and overrun by strays." She reached into the box and stroked a fuzzy kitten head. "Could you keep them?"

"I'm allergic."

She squinted at me. "Actually allergic, or 'you just don't like cats' allergic? You haven't sneezed once since you've been here."

Dammit. She had a point.

I sighed and held the kittens out to her. "How much is this going to cost me?"

She winced. "To get that eye cleared up, give them all shots, deflea them, run a few medical tests to check for other diseases they might have picked up... Probably about a thousand dollars."

I widened my eyes. "Are you for real?"

She shrugged. "It's that or the pound."

I really didn't want to spend a thousand dollars of my savings. It had taken such a long time to build that up. I couldn't get a job anywhere, so I was going to be going through my savings pretty quickly with no income coming in.

But something deep inside me knew I couldn't leave the kittens for dead either.

The receptionist smiled at me as she took the box, clearly realizing I was going to agree. "You're a good cat dad. Your wife is going to love the new additions to your family."

"No wife," I clarified. "Just me and an empty apartment."

She paused. "Oh? Maybe I could come over and help you get the kittens settled in."

I suddenly felt like an idiot for not recognizing that she'd been fishing to see if I was single. When had I gotten so out of practice?

Probably in the five years since I'd last gone on a date, I realized with a jolt.

The woman was pretty. Probably more than pretty, really. Most guys would take a glimpse of her blond hair and big blue eyes and get hard over her All-American, girl-next-door, cheerleader vibe.

But it did nothing for me.

It only made me think about how Kara's hair had been the opposite, long and dark. How her eyes had looked black in some lights, and warm honey brown in others. How her body had been all curves and softness, while providing a home for her baby.

Like I did every time a woman asked me out, I shook my head and turned the receptionist down.

Because she wasn't the one woman I couldn't get out of my head.

The receptionist blushed pink when I explained I'd be fine alone but told me to come back in an hour after the vet had checked out my animals.

Apparently, I owned three fucking cats now.

How the hell had that happened?

I needed a drink to come to terms with that, and I had an hour to kill. I left my car parked outside the vet and wandered around the streets of Providence in search of somewhere I could get a beer with my lunch. I passed a couple of men's clothing stores that sold shirts and pants a damn sight nicer than the ones in the big, budget-friendly department store in Saint View where most people I knew bought their clothes. I caught a glimpse of a price tag on a suit hanging by the door and did a double take.

While residents over in Saint View seemed to be cutting back on the basics like eating out at cheap hole-in-the wall diners, Providence was over here spending a thousand bucks on a single outfit?

Insane.

Then again, I'd just agreed to spend that on my trio of kittens, so maybe I was crazy too.

The cafés were all busy, no available seats to be seen at any of the ones I checked. Each was full of ladies dining with friends, couples sitting opposite each other, or families with well-behaved children quietly drawing on paper or watching iPads while their parents ordered for them.

I stopped in at one that had a menu that made my taste buds tingle and saliva fill my mouth, but was quickly told that without a reservation, I wouldn't be getting seated today. Or even this month. They were that booked up.

I wanted to scream with frustration.

That new restaurant Luca was opening just down the road was going to make an absolute killing.

My feet took me there without conscious thought from my brain.

If I'd truly been thinking clearly, I would have walked the other way. Or even better, run screaming.

But I stood outside the restaurant that should have been mine and wished with everything inside me that things had worked out differently.

I stood there, losing myself in the daydream.

I didn't notice the silver car pull up behind me, or the man who got out of it until he was standing right beside me, his arms crossed over his chest, matching my position. I didn't acknowledge him. Both of us stared at the building that held so much damn potential I wanted to weep.

"You ready to look at that contract yet?" Luca asked.

And fuck me, I hated myself. But with no job, no prospects, and no hope of changing my life, I nodded.

17

KARA

*A*mber scuttled from Hawk's bedroom without a scrap of clothing on, his bedroom door slamming closed behind her so hard we all looked in that direction.

Bliss got to her feet very quickly for a woman as pregnant as she was, calling for all the kids to run outside for a game of tag. Rebel followed her best friend, helping to herd the combo of hers and Bliss's kids out the door and away from the very adult content that had just fled down the hallway to her own room.

"You coming?" Rebel asked me.

I didn't even know what to say. "Is she okay?"

Rebel's eyebrows furrowed together. "Who? Amber? She's fine. This is a regular thing with her and Hawk. He's an asshole, but she's a big girl, tough enough to take his bullshit and give back her own. Honestly, they fight like an old married couple, but they'll be fucking again within the hour. This is nothing to be worried about."

"Oh." I dropped my gaze to my fingers. "I understand."

Rebel cocked her head to one side. "So, you coming out?"

I eyed Hawk's bedroom door. "Actually, could you watch Hayley Jade for me for a few minutes? There's something I want to do."

Rebel shrugged. "Sure. But what are you doing?"

"I want to apologize to Hawk."

Rebel's mouth dropped open. "What on earth for? He just cussed you out in front of everyone. Not to mention he just sent Amber running from his room without even giving her a second to get her clothes on. The fucking pig."

I winced at my sister's sharp words. There was clearly no love lost between the two of them. They hadn't exactly been besties back when I'd been brought here, but things obviously hadn't gotten any better in the years since I'd been gone either.

That didn't mean I didn't owe the man an apology.

I really had broken his nose. Twice. While Hawk was clearly not a good man, he'd been the one to stitch me up and keep me from getting an infection. At the time, I'd been in shock, and too traumatized to recognize that he'd gone out of his way to help me, and I'd done nothing but be ungrateful in return.

It was something I needed to remedy before I could move on.

Another piece of my past that had to be laid to rest so I could start healing from the traumas I'd experienced.

Hawk had never hurt me.

He was one of the men who'd tried to put me back

together, and for that, I owed him an apology and a thank you.

I stood, my legs trembling slightly beneath my weight, my body remembering the feral way he'd shouted at me. I took a few steps toward the closed bedroom door.

"Oh God, I can't watch," Rebel said behind me. "It's like a lamb being taken to slaughter."

I glanced back at her. "I'm fine. Please, can you go watch Hayley Jade? I know how big this compound is and I don't want her wandering off."

Rebel clearly wasn't happy about leaving me alone with the lion, but she nodded and left the clubhouse.

There was nobody else inside. The room was quiet, apart from the sound of my too-fast breathing.

I forced my feet to take me to the door. I knocked quietly.

"Get in here," Hawk called out.

I twisted the doorknob and pushed open the door. "Hawk, I..."

A rush of something foreign shook my body like an earthquake, the foreign feeling springing to life low in my belly and spearing through every part of me.

My arms, my legs, my chest.

Other places that were sinful to think about.

Hawk was laid out on his bed, eyes closed, his shirt pulled up to reveal tawny, well-defined abs. The waistband of his jeans was around his knees, his thick thighs bare but for the light cover of dark hair on his skin.

They were observations that barely registered when the main show was his...member. He had it in his hand, hard and proud, the tip glistening as he jerked it.

"Quit fucking standing there, Amber. Get back here and on your knees."

I didn't say anything.

Couldn't make a sound.

Couldn't move my feet.

Blood rushed around my body in a crazy and unsettling flood of feeling, heat rising in my cheeks and up the back of my neck in embarrassment.

And yet I still didn't budge.

Hawk opened his eyes.

Then narrowed them. "What the fuck do you want, Little Mouse?"

He didn't try to cover up his erection. He paused his movements but didn't unwrap his fingers from his shaft. The tip of him throbbed, tiny beads of moisture spilling over the top.

He stared at me.

I stared at him, unable to move, breathe, or even think, let alone talk.

His voice lowered. "Close the door."

My hand reached for the knob. The door closed with a snick.

Me on the inside of Hawk's room instead of out in the hallway.

His eyes flared like he was just as surprised as I was.

And then something different filled them. His hand slid down his erection, then back up, swiping through the wetness at his tip. He let out a soft groan of pleasure, stroking himself again with the added lubrication of his precum.

His gaze never left mine.

I couldn't look away, my entire body locked tight with whatever curse he'd put on me.

"Fuck, Little Mouse," he groaned. "You just gonna stand there, watching me jerk myself off?"

Is that what I was doing?

His fingers moved faster, up and down his length, and I stood mesmerized by his expression and the way it softened out all his hard lines. His breaths fell from soft, parted lips that had my heart beating fast, thinking about what they might feel like on my body.

My nipples went hard beneath my bra, and his gaze dropped to them, taking in the shape I knew would be all too evident through the too-tight T-shirt I'd borrowed from my sister who was several sizes smaller than me.

I covered my breasts with my arms.

"Show me, Kara. Don't fucking cover yourself up like that."

Like he could control my body with just the growl in his voice, I dropped my hands away.

He hissed out his pleasure, the tone filled with approval. "Good girl. Just like I knew you would be. Fuck."

His hand gripped his member harder, his strokes becoming more urgent, his hips lifting off the bed, so he was thrusting into the tight grip of his hand.

My senses finally got the better of me.

Horror flooded my system, washing away all the good feelings I'd had a moment earlier and leaving nothing but awkward embarrassment in their place. Tears stung behind my eyes. I reached for the doorknob again.

"Don't you fucking dare walk out now, Little Mouse.

Not when I'm about to come just looking at the sweet curves of your body."

All I'd ever known was taking the orders of men.

Hawk's gaze burned me, like there were literal flames behind the green of his eyes. The heat licked across my skin, my panties getting wet with an arousal I didn't want to feel.

He groaned loudly, so loud I knew if anyone had come back into the clubhouse they'd hear. They all knew I was in here. They would know what he was doing in front of me.

I willed myself to walk out.

Hawk wasn't my husband. He wasn't one of the Lord's favorites.

I could disobey him.

And yet I couldn't.

He worked his length fast and hard, and then it was spurting his seed, covering his belly with it while he made indecent noises that hit me over and over again, right between the legs.

His fingers became coated in the sticky white wetness his body had produced while he stared at me.

The devil on the gates wasn't the only one in this compound.

His gaze slowly rolled over me, lingering in places only a husband should see. Then the corner of his mouth turned up, and he shook his head. "Go on, Little Mouse. Run. I know you want to."

I didn't hesitate this time. He was giving me permission, and so I did exactly what he'd said.

I ran.

The cool afternoon air did nothing to calm the burning behind my cheeks. I sat beside Rebel and Bliss, surrounded by other women from the club, but I heard almost nothing of the conversation. Thankfully, nobody asked me any direct questions, because if they had, I wasn't sure I could have answered them.

I kept an eye on Hayley Jade, who quietly obeyed when her younger cousin told her she had to play with him.

I hated that she looked uncomfortable but did it anyway.

But that's what we'd been taught at the commune. That a woman's place was to follow. I had always accepted it, because fighting was futile.

Was that what I'd just done with Hawk?

Only, when he'd made demands of me, I'd *wanted* to obey them.

I was glad when Rebel noticed and called out to Madden, "Hey, quit being a bossy boots. How about you ask Hayley Jade what she would like to do instead of just assuming she wants to play your game?"

He shrugged. "She doesn't talk though."

Queenie, one of the older club wives who'd been the sweetest to me when I'd come here with Hayley Jade as a baby, spoke up. "She can talk, sugar. She just don't want to talk to you."

I shook my head quickly. "Oh, it's not that—" The last thing I wanted was for Rebel to be offended that my child didn't want to play with hers.

But she was laughing and waving off my apology.

"Queenie is right. That boy is too alpha for his own good. Remi is too quiet and easygoing to put him in his place, and the others are too young yet. Queenie fills the void."

I bit my lip. But then Rebel's son was running across the yard to argue with Queenie, who sassed him back good-naturedly.

Hayley Jade stood off to one side, watching the exchange with huge eyes.

Rebel squeezed my hand. "It's fine, really. Queenie loves him and he loves her. Takes a village to raise a well-rounded kid, right?"

I swallowed hard. "Does it?" I whispered. As soon as we got back to the house, I was packing up Alice and leaving the last of my family behind. Kyle could go back to the commune, or stay in Saint View, I didn't care. But after the stunt he and Alice had pulled, I didn't trust him as far as I could throw him. After that, it would just be the three of us.

Or maybe really just the two of us. As much as the thought sent panic into my throat, I couldn't see Alice sitting at home with me and a five-year-old every Friday and Saturday night. I couldn't really blame her. She wasn't built for that sort of life.

It was the whole reason she'd come with me in the first place. Otherwise she would have just stayed and married some man from the commune like Naomi and Samantha would.

But if it was just me and Hayley Jade, what village would we have?

I fought off the fear gripping my throat. There was no other way around it. I was endangering everyone just by being here, and as soon as we got home, after I shook

Alice for running off in the middle of the night, we were getting on the first bus out of town.

The door to the clubhouse slammed, and Hawk strode out, bare-chested with his jeans slung so low on his hips the V-lines either side were visible. "War. Fang. Need a word."

His hair was mussed up in the back.

From lying on his bed.

Stroking his...

It took a second to register he'd called over the president of the club, as well as Fang, who I knew was high up in the Slayers' hierarchy.

He was going to tell them what I'd done.

Expose me for the perverted woman I was.

My fingers trembled. "Can we go?" I asked Rebel in a breathless whisper. "I want to go home."

Not that I had one anymore, but anywhere other than here would do.

Rebel glanced over at me. "Are you okay?" She put the back of her hand to my forehead. "Shit, Kara, you're all pale and clammy. Was it something you ate?"

I shook my head quickly, one eye on the three men huddled together on the other side of the yard, their faces lined with concern and voices low.

They all looked in my direction.

I wanted the earth to swallow me whole.

There would be a punishment the way there would have been back home if I had accidentally stumbled across one of the men doing...that.

Hawk would be within his rights to punish me.

My heart pounded as War and Fang nodded, and

Hawk lifted a walkie-talkie I hadn't noticed before to his mouth.

His gaze burned mine as he mumbled something into it I couldn't hear.

War moved back to stand beside Bliss and stroked a hand over her auburn hair. "Okay, listen up, you guys. I need someone to take the kids inside—"

Rebel stood. "I'll grab them."

But War shook his head. "Queenie, you, please. I need Rebel and her family here with mine. Everyone else, inside. Don't panic, but we have cops on their way in."

I froze. "Police?"

Some of the guys swore loudly, but War waved them toward the clubhouse impatiently. "Keep your shit together. They don't have a warrant. Ratchet is on the gate and he checked. They won't tell him what it's about, but I think we can probably safely assume it's to do with Kara."

I dropped my gaze to the ground, knowing he was right. Josiah had probably called the police on me for kidnapping or something equally horrible. "I'm so sorry," I whispered. "I should have never come here."

War shook his head, steadying me with his sincere expression. "Hey, no. That's not what I meant. You're safe here. You and Hayley Jade. It's good the cops are here. We can find out what Josiah has reported to them."

My gaze flickered around the smaller group of people. Bliss and her men. Rebel and hers.

Hawk.

His eyes held anger that burned bright as molten lava. "They forced you to marry some guy you didn't even know? All these fucking years, he's been keeping you prisoner?"

Fear trickled down my spine as two cop cars trundled slowly along the dirt road that led from the gates to the clubhouse, but I nodded. I couldn't lie to Hawk, even though the truth ate a little piece of my soul every time I thought about Josiah.

Hawk turned away, but not before I caught a glimpse of pure fury in his expression. When the door on the first cop car opened, Hawk stepped between me and the tall officer who emerged.

"Howard," Hawk greeted without much warmth in his voice. "To what do we owe the pleasure? Planning on arresting me again? Twice in as many days is a bit much, even for me, don't you think?"

War raised an eyebrow at the officer they were clearly familiar with. "That better not be what you're here for. If we need to call a lawyer, tell me now."

The officer held up his hands in mock surrender, and a second cop from the car behind joined his friend. "It's not about Hawk." His gaze landed on Fang. "Your legal name is Milo Garrisen. Correct?"

Fang didn't say a word. Neither did anybody else, distrust hanging in the air between them.

The cop sighed and carried on. "I don't know why I asked. I know that's your name and this place is still registered as your last known address." He sighed heavily. "Sir, are you still the current de facto partner of a Rebel Amanda Kemp?"

Rebel shifted slightly but didn't say anything.

Vaughn and Kian both moved in front of her.

Fang, to his credit, didn't even glance in her direction. "Who I'm shacked up with is of interest to you why?"

The cop took off his hat and fingered the brim of it.

"I'm sorry to be the one to tell you this, but we believe your partner to have been the victim of a murder last night."

The tension fell out of the group, and Rebel snorted on a laugh, pushing Vaughn and Kian aside. "Do I look dead to you boys?"

The cops turned to her, Howard's already lined forehead furrowing, his thick brows drawing together in sharp slants. "You're Rebel Amanda Kemp?"

"That's what's on my driver's license. You got the wrong dead girl, I'm afraid."

But the cop was persistent. "Are you in possession of your driver's license right now?"

Rebel bent and retrieved her wallet from the side pocket of a baby bag, otherwise filled with diapers and pacifiers and toy cars. She flipped it open. "Sure. It's just..."

Her finger slid down the row of cards and then paused. She squinted up at them. "Actually, it appears I am not. That's weird. I never take it out. How did the dead woman get my ID?"

The answer flashed through my head, but I rejected it so quickly I could barely consider it.

Only it came again, and again, like a neon sign in the dark that couldn't be ignored.

The cop cleared his throat. "Does anyone else have access to your purse?"

"Alice," I choked out quietly.

Rebel shot me a look of confusion. "What? No..." She shook her head slowly. And then faster, as the horrifying idea took hold for her too. "No. No! She wouldn't have taken my ID."

Except I already knew she would have. If she'd wanted to get into a club or bar, she would have needed ID to prove she was over twenty-one. None of the women at the commune were allowed any form of government-issued ID, not that it would have mattered anyway since Alice wasn't yet of legal drinking age.

I leaned over, trying hard to suck in breaths, but the air suddenly felt like water and breathing felt like drowning. My head spun from the lack of oxygen.

"Fuck." Fang ran a hand through the long strands of his hair. He turned to Howard. "They have a younger sister. Alice. She's a fuck ton like Rebel and she's not twenty-one yet. She might have taken Rebel's ID to try to get into a bar or nightclub."

Rebel shook her head so fast. "No. No, Fang! That woman is dead. It's not... It's not..."

She suddenly stared at me.

The darkness rushed in on me so quickly I didn't even feel myself falling.

18

HAWK

*D*éjà vu was the weirdest fucking feeling. I didn't believe in all that woo bullshit, spirits and past lives and reincarnation or whatever, but catching Kara after she fainted, hauling her into my arms, and carrying her into the clubhouse had a definite sense of "been there, done that."

The very first time I'd met her had been much the same.

Only she'd given me a broken nose before she'd passed out.

At least that was intact this time.

"Get out of the way," I hollered, Kara's limp body in my arms. "Stop fucking gawking at her and clear off that couch so I have somewhere to put her."

Ice jumped to his feet and swept a couple of car magazines onto the floor, while kicking at one of the kid's toys that let out a protesting squeak as it met his boot. "Fucking hell, man," he mumbled. "What did you do to her this time?"

If looks could kill he would have been dead on the spot.

He shut up fast and scuttled back, making way for me and the crowd who'd followed me inside.

In my arms, Kara stirred, her lashes fluttering. She blinked a few times in confusion, her pretty brown eyes completely freaked out. "What happened? Where am I?"

"You fainted. I caught you. Now I'm carrying you inside the clubhouse."

She tried twisting, getting her bearings, and then stared up at me in horror. "What? No! Hawk, put me down. I can walk."

I tightened my grip on her. "Put you down so you can pass out again? Yeah, I don't think so."

"I'm too heavy," she protested.

I paused at the edge of the couch and stared down at her incredulously. *That* was what she was concerned about? "Woman, do I look like I'm fucking struggling?"

She averted her gaze as I lowered her to the couch, settling her gently on the cracked leather cushions. Fuck. Those things were so damn old. I should have had Ice get her a blanket or something first, but it was too late now.

I knelt beside her, taking note of the lack of color in her cheeks, the clamminess of her skin, and the too-fast breathing. Fuck. She was going to pass out again if she kept that up. I reached for her, needing to get my fingers to her neck so I could time her pulse.

She cringed away.

I froze but didn't back off. "I just need to check your heart rate, Little Mouse. Then I'll leave you be."

Her bottom lip trembled slightly, but she nodded, and I pressed my fingers to the creamy softness of her skin.

I frowned at the sluggish blood that pulsed beneath my fingers, but it wasn't the worst I'd felt, by any means.

"Is she okay?" Rebel asked, hovering over me.

"I'm fine," Kara whispered. "I'm so sorry for all the trouble—"

"I need some pillows." My gaze landing on Ice. "Go to my room and get all the pillows off my bed."

To the younger man's credit, he did exactly what I said this time without giving me any of his usual smart-assery. He came back with two pillows encased in the silky black linen I liked. I lifted Kara's feet and shoved the pillows beneath them to keep them elevated.

I racked my brain trying to remember the other things you were supposed to do when someone fainted.

Loosen clothing.

I flushed hot at the thought of peeling off that too-tight little T-shirt that could barely contain her tits. Of removing the ugly gray skirt that seemed like it had been made from a flour sack or something of equally cheap material. Despite its shitty quality, it did nothing to hide the curves of her hips that would be perfect for holding on to while I fucked her from behind.

She was fine. I wasn't loosening any clothing.

Except maybe the denim currently strangling my erection.

I pushed back onto my feet, twisting so no one noticed I was getting hard. Fucking hell. This day had been one extreme to the other. Couldn't get hard for Amber. Then getting hard over the church mouse, of all people. It was probably me who needed a doctor.

I let Rebel and Bliss take my spot, fussing over Kara, and slammed my way into the kitchen. Without thinking about it too much, I opened cupboards, rummaging through each one, searching for where we kept the tea nobody drank.

I slammed a door shut, frustrated when it was full of spices and herbs instead of the stuff I was searching for.

The kitchen door opened, and Rebel came in, pausing as I shut another door too hard and the crack of wood on wood bounced around the room.

Rebel raised an eyebrow but didn't say anything, walking to the cupboard where we kept glasses. She took one out and then moved to the sink to fill it with water. "Sorry to get in your way," she said quietly. "Kara just wanted a drink."

"Yeah, I figured as much," I answered. "Found it!" I pulled out the tea which was likely stale because who knew how long it had been hidden away in the back of that cupboard.

Might have been five years. Since the last time I'd seen Kara drink it.

I studied the package for an expiration date.

Rebel's stare was intense enough for me to notice even though I wasn't looking directly at her. "What?" I snapped.

"That's Kara's favorite tea. Peppermint and chamomile."

"That's why I'm making it for her."

"How did you know that?"

I shrugged. "Just do."

"I didn't even know that until last night, and I'm her sister."

I glanced up over the top of the box of teabags, an uncomfortable awkwardness settling over me. Why the fuck did I know this was Kara's favorite tea? Rebel's scrutiny was pissing me off. "Well, maybe if you were a better sister, we wouldn't be having this conversation, huh, shrimp?"

The insult had the desired effect. She stopped worrying about why I knew Kara's favorite drink and snatched it from my fingers. "You're such a prick."

"I'm well aware." It irked me to watch Rebel make the tea I'd found and carry it out to Kara, but her having it was the main thing.

Kara took a sip from the steaming mug and glanced up in surprise at her sister. "You remembered it was my favorite."

Rebel glanced over at me and opened her mouth to say something.

I cut it off before she could announce it to the whole fucking room. "I'm going to talk to the cops."

I shoved the door open with my shoulder, and it was only when the cold early evening air hit my bare skin that I realized I still didn't even have a shirt on. Fucking hell. I'd been so focused on Kara I hadn't even noticed until she was out of my line of vision.

War glanced over at me when I approached the little huddle he had going on with the two cops, as well as Aloha and Ratchet. He frowned at the way I was rubbing my arms. "Go get a hoodie or something."

But there was no way I was going back inside and having everyone stare at me because Rebel had blabbed about me finding tea for my patient.

That's what Kara was. Someone I took care of because nobody else here had a scrap of medical knowledge or interest. Nothing more.

Despite the fact I'd let her watch me jerk my dick until I'd come all over myself.

That had nothing to do with her, and everything to do with making someone else feel as shitty as I had in that moment, after realizing I'd fucked up my GED.

Rebel was right. I really was a prick.

"I'm fine," I told War.

He rolled his eyes and pulled off his jacket, handing it to me. "I know you love your abs, but you can't go down to the morgue like that. Put it on."

I shoved it back at him. "I'm not going to the morgue."

War raised an eyebrow. "The cops need Kara and Rebel to go down there and ID the body. You think I'm letting them go down there unprotected with Kara's whack job of a husband hunting her down?"

I screwed up my face. "Send Fang!"

War narrowed his eyes at me. "Why are you fucking arguing with me about this, asshole? I *am* sending Fang, as well as you, Ice, and Aloha. If that really is Alice dead on that table, then it means someone is *really* pissed off about them leaving. Kara just became our number one priority, and she doesn't go *anywhere* without protection."

I gawked at my prez. "Are you joking? She's not even one of us!"

He straightened his shoulders and lowered his voice. "She's Rebel's sister. She has a child who has been through hell and back. And she's a woman in danger. That's enough for me. If it's not enough for you, then fucking say so now and let me know you aren't the man I thought you were."

I glared at him, his words sinking in with stabbing

accuracy. "Well, now who's being an asshole? You didn't have to call me out like that."

He grinned and slapped me on the back. "You didn't have to argue when we both know I'm always right. So put the fucking jacket on already."

I shoved it back at him again. "I ain't your old lady. And I ain't your boyfriend. I ain't wearing your jacket. Scythe would probably put a knife through my kidney if he saw me walking around in that."

War sniggered at the mention of his partner. "He probably would."

Like Rebel and Fang, War and Bliss had the whole polyamorous thing going on with two other guys. I tried to keep my nose outta the details, but some of them had been too hard to avoid.

Like War fucking one of the guys as much as he fucked Bliss.

We'd come to terms with that eventually.

But it didn't mean I wanted to wear another guy's jacket and definitely not War's because his boyfriend was psychotic at the best of times, and I hadn't been exaggerating when I said I was worried I might get stabbed.

Scythe and his alter ego, Vincent, weren't to be fucked with.

One of the cops, Howard, cleared his throat. "Do you think the women will be ready to go soon? I know this is a lot, but we do have to move on to other jobs. If you want us to escort you to the morgue we need to leave now."

I snorted. "If we want you to escort us? Do we look like we need your help—"

War elbowed me. "What my VP here means is, he'll go get his own fucking jacket, and while he's there, he'll make sure Kara and Rebel and Fang are ready to go, because we take the threat of *murder* very seriously, and *any* extra bodies to help keep one of our own safe is welcome. That's what you meant to say, right, VP?"

I made no effort to hide the roll of my eyes. "Sure, boss. Whatever you say."

I was fucking cold though, so I did as I was told, like a good little second-in-charge, and strode right through the living area where everyone was still gathered around Kara.

"Hawk," her small voice called out.

I ignored her and practically ran the last few steps to my bedroom, slamming the door closed behind me.

My dick was fucking hard again.

And all she'd said was my name.

19

KARA

I jumped at the slam of Hawk's bedroom door and then quickly glanced over at Queenie.

She smoothed her hand down the back of Hayley Jade's head and gave Hawk's door a dirty look. "There's babies asleep here! I'm going to kill that boy if he doesn't learn some manners." She cringed in my direction. "Sorry, honey. That was insensitive."

I didn't answer, just stared at my daughter, who'd been curled up on Queenie's ample lap, her head resting on the older woman's chest since I'd come to.

I didn't even have space inside me to be upset that another woman was yet again doing a better job of soothing my child than I could. All I could think about was my sister. Someone hurting her. The pain and fear she must have felt that grew until it felt like my own. Panic threatened to overwhelm me, and I had to gaze around the room, at the familiar faces, and remind myself that for right now at least, we were safe.

But Alice...

I focused on Hayley Jade harder, taking in the curve of her back and the golden blond of her hair. "You used to hold her like that when she was a baby," I said to Queenie.

She paused for a second and then nodded. "I guess I did. Held a lot of babies this way over the years. Yours. Bliss's. Rebel's."

"But not your own?"

She shook her head. "Naw. I'm happy to be the honorary Mamaw, but having any of my own wasn't in the cards for me."

There was a slightly wistful tone in her voice, and I felt bad for asking.

I knew all too well what it felt like to be reminded you didn't have the family you'd hoped for.

Hawk came out of his room, a cream hoodie beneath his Slayers' club jacket. He had his boots on and his helmet in his hand.

His gaze met mine, and I quickly turned away.

Despite everything that had happened since, his bedroom was a reminder of me standing there, obeying his commands to watch him come.

I wanted the earth to swallow me up whole.

It was hard to tell with the scruff along his jaw and cheeks, but for a second, I thought maybe Hawk was blushing too.

But then he turned to Fang and acted like I wasn't even in the room. "Cops want Rebel and her sister down at the morgue for a viewing of the Jane Doe they found. War wants you, me, Ice, and Aloha to escort them."

Rebel glanced up, her eyes filled with tears. "I can do it. Kara doesn't need to be the one to go."

Except I already knew I did. There was a slow churning nausea in my belly, and it wouldn't ease until I'd seen for myself. "No. I want to go too. I'm sorry about fainting. I'm fine now. I can do it."

Rebel grabbed my hand and squeezed it. "We don't know it's her. It might not be. She could be waiting at home for us right now."

But we both knew she wasn't. Vaughn and Kian had taken their four kids home about fifteen minutes earlier. They would have called if Kyle and Alice had been sitting in their living room watching movies and chowing down on snacks from Rebel's pantry.

I took my feet off of Hawk's pillows, still astonished the man had let me use them like that when it was so terribly disrespectful. But he didn't seem to care at all.

Fang put his arm around Rebel's shoulders and pulled her tight, her tiny frame dwarfed by his near six and a half feet. "I don't want you doing this. Your morning sickness always gets worse in the night, and we don't know what we're going to find down there. I can ID the body with Kara."

She stared up at him, adoration in her eyes. "I love you so much, but if you don't already know what my answer will be after five years, then I'm going to question our whole relationship."

He sighed heavily and guided her to the door. "It was worth a shot." He glanced back over his shoulder at me, and then beyond to where Hawk walked with Ice and Aloha. "We'll take the van. No one on bikes, especially not the women. Just in case."

I looked up. "Just in case of what?"

"Nothin'," Hawk answered quickly from behind me.

"Just safer if we're all in the one vehicle. Too fucking cold to ride bikes tonight anyway."

Which wasn't really true because I knew they rode bikes in all sorts of weather.

Which told me they were expecting danger.

My fingers trembled, and I tucked them into the pockets of my thick, woolen skirt so nobody would notice.

Hawk grumbled when Fang lifted Rebel into the front seat like she was a tiny porcelain doll and then kissed her lips before moving around to the driver's side. Ice slid open the back door of the unmarked van and held a hand out to me.

"Need a hand getting in, Kara?" he asked politely. "It's a bit of a step."

Holding his hand was the last thing I wanted. Ice had been nothing but polite, but I didn't want any man touching me.

Hawk made a weird noise behind me.

I glanced back at him. "Sorry? I didn't catch that."

He coughed and cleared his throat. "What? I didn't say anything. Go on. Get in."

But he glared at Ice like he'd committed a mortal sin.

Ice screwed up his face, a silent question of "what did I do?" written all over his expression.

Hawk shouldered him out of the way and got in after me.

I took the seat in the very back row of the van, farthest from the sliding door and from the driver's seat. I put my seat belt on but then made myself as small as I could, hunching in on myself and staring out the window into the darkness beyond while the others took their seats and the van rumbled to life.

Every mile that passed beneath the van's tires increased the sick feeling in the pit of my stomach. It spread up my throat and across my tongue until the bitter tang of fear was all I could taste.

It was almost a relief when Fang pulled the van into the empty parking lot, the two cop cars turning in behind us. I stared at the squat, rectangular building, a shiver running down my spine at the thought my sister's lifeless body could be inside.

I pushed my palms together and doubled over, pressing them to my forehead and mumbling the Lord's Prayer beneath my breath, the words barely legible above the squeak of my seat as I rocked on it.

"Please Lord, don't let it be Alice. Please Lord, keep her in your embrace and return her safely to me. Please Lord, forgive me my sins. Don't punish my sister for the mistakes I've made."

The van was silent.

I could feel everyone's eyes on me but I didn't care.

Aloha whispered something, but all I heard was Hawk snap and tell him to shut up. With the addition of his favorite expletive, that was.

It was clear to me Hawk didn't want to be here. That War had forced him to be my chauffeur, and for that I was sorry. He'd already done enough for me tonight. He didn't need to witness my breakdowns as well.

But nobody said anything more until I was done with my prayers. I dredged up the strength to stand, and Hawk held the door open for me.

He didn't try to touch me again, the way he had earlier.

But of course, now there was no reason for him to check my pulse.

I got out, and Rebel linked her arm through mine, Fang flanking her left, while Hawk flanked my right. The two men moved like they were in an action movie, heads swiveling side to side, searching for danger. Talking with their eyes above our heads, communicating with each other in a way only men who'd worked together for a long time could.

Ice was positioned ahead of us, Aloha behind.

The four men should have made me feel safe, and yet my trembling grew worse with every step. I didn't hear the cops talking with the medical examiner. I stood numbly, walking only when told to walk, my brain desperately trying to check out from reality.

But none of it stopped the shaking.

The medical examiner gave us a small smile and then led us down a short hall and stopped at the doorway to a room marked "viewing." "I just want to prepare you for what you'll see on the other side of this door. It's a very simple room, with a metal table in the middle. The body has already been placed there and is currently covered. When we go in, we'll need to uncover the body so you, the family, can make an ID. Do you understand?"

I twisted my fingers around themselves, trying to get the shaking to stop. Rebel looked at me. I nodded. I just needed to get this over with. I couldn't stand not knowing a minute longer.

But taking those steps into that room was the hardest thing I'd ever forced my feet to do. Everything inside me screamed to turn and run, to pretend this wasn't happening.

To go back to the commune and beg for forgiveness.

Nothing good happened inside the commune walls.

But nothing good happened outside them either. There was evil everywhere, and no matter what I did, I couldn't hide from it. This just proved it.

The mortician tucked his fingers into the white sheet and pulled it back, exposing just the face of the dead woman beneath.

Beside me, Rebel froze. "Oh God. I'm going to be sick."

She spun on her heel and pushed her way out of the room, the sounds of her gagging filtering back until the door swung closed behind her.

The medical examiner grimaced at Rebel's departure and then reached out a hand to touch mine in comfort I didn't want.

Hawk stepped between us. "Don't touch her. Don't lay a single fucking finger on her."

I flinched at his sharp tone.

The medical examiner did, too. "I...um. I'm sorry. Kara, is that your sister?"

I stared at Alice's face. At the lack of color in her cheeks. At the vaguely blue tinge of her lips. It was her.

But at the same time, it wasn't. Everything that had made her Alice was gone. The mischievous spark in her eyes. The sassy tilt of her smile. The warmth of her touch.

But the medical examiner didn't care about those things.

"Yes," I croaked out.

"You're one-hundred-percent sure?" the man asked.

Hawk glared at him. "She said it's her, all right? Don't make her say it more than once."

The medical examiner backed off quickly, apologizing profusely. "Of course. Of course. I'm so sorry for your loss. I'll leave you, give you some time alone."

The door swung closed behind him, and silence fell in the tiny room.

Hawk cleared his throat. "I'll leave too. Fang went after Rebel, and Aloha and Ice are keeping guard outside. But I'll be right outside the door. I won't go any farther."

My hand shot out to grab his before I could even contemplate what I was doing.

Hawk stopped and stared at me, and then down at my grip on his fingers.

I let go of him quickly, like his skin had burned me.

"What do you need, Kara?" he asked more softly than I'd ever heard him before.

I didn't know anything other than I didn't want to be alone in this tiny room with a dead body cold on a table.

But my lips wouldn't form those words.

Hawk didn't seem to need them. "I'll stay here, then. Right here. Just behind you."

A tear fell from my eye, and then more, silent streams creating waterfalls down my cheeks that burned across my skin. I tried to suck in air, but it was so cold it hurt my lungs, which only increased the panic inside me. I tried to breathe faster, sucking in shallow gasps that did little to relieve the ache inside my chest. The trembling increased, shaking me from head to toe until my teeth chattered and my muscles hurt. My heart ached, and a low, keening wail started up somewhere deep inside me, a noise I hadn't made since the day Josiah had taken Hayley Jade away from me.

"No," I cried, slumping forward. "Nooo!"

The second was more of a scream of agony.

I was so cold everything hurt. It seeped through my skin like icy needles of pain.

"Make it stop," I moaned pitifully. "Make it stop!"

Warm arms came around me, and I lashed out, hitting at him, scratching and pushing him away. "No!"

There was only the briefest of hesitation in his embrace, and then he tightened it, turning me around so we were chest to chest, my face buried in the warm, clean material of his hoodie that also held the vague leather scent of his jacket.

"Stop," he said quietly into my ear, his voice low and deep as his grip on me tightened to a point that would have been painful if I hadn't been falling apart. "Just stop fighting me, Kara."

His heat chased away the cold. His words soothed the ragged edges torn open inside me.

I stood in his arms, him holding me up.

Holding me together.

Time passed, but neither of us spoke again. My tears slowly subsided, and the incessant shaking reverted into trembles. My breathing evened out, matching his slow, deep breaths that filled my lungs with a scent I now associated solely with him.

In his arms, I could breathe.

He let go before I wanted him to.

I slowly lifted my gaze to meet his and opened my mouth.

He cut me off with a sharp shake of his head. "If you

hate me for touching you, I don't fucking care. You needed me."

I nodded quietly. "I know."

He groaned like my words had hurt him. Embarrassment coursed through me. His hoodie was soaked with my tears and probably my snot. My face was likely red and blotchy. I was a weak mess and I knew it.

Josiah would have been disgusted with me. It didn't surprise me that Hawk was too.

I bet Amber didn't cry all over him.

I bit my lip. "I'm so sorry."

He shook his head. "Don't say that."

"But I am."

"Your sister was murdered, Kara. Fucking hell. If you didn't cry, I'd be questioning if you were the one who did it."

I gasped. "How could you say that?"

Murder was the greatest sin of them all. Was I that obviously bad? That he would assume I could do something like that? Josiah always preached that our sins were visible.

It was why he'd forced me to wear a veil. So everyone else in the commune wouldn't see how bad I truly was, inside and out.

Hawk shrugged carelessly. "Family is always the first suspect."

I stared at him, wondering how he could be so kind in one minute, only to be so cruel in the next.

20

GRAYSON

I squinted at the couple on the other side of my desk, trying to follow the back-and-forth argument.

The man glared at the woman, not bothering to hide the anger in his tone. "Could you be any more of a nag? All you do is complain and whine about my job." He frowned at me. "A job that pays for all the ridiculous hobbies Mandy has. Do you know how many there's been in the last year alone?" He started ticking them off on his fingers. "First there was crocheting. Then there was painting. Tennis. Pickleball. Rug weaving. Oh, and let's not forget when you made me recreate that scene in *Ghost* with the damn pottery wheel!"

She huffed out an irritated snort. "We were supposed to be trying to date each other! It was supposed to be romantic, but of course you complained about the feel of it, and how you didn't like that it was cold and sloppy and staining your perfect fingernails." She too turned to me. "And frankly, I wouldn't need all the hobbies if he wasn't sticking his dick in his receptionist instead of coming home at night."

"Better he stick his dick in his receptionist than in the pottery wheel, I guess," I mumbled, pretending to write something down on my notepad.

"What?" the woman snapped.

I made a show of checking my watch. "Sorry, you two. Our time is up for today. But this was good. We're definitely opening up some old wounds that we can work on next week."

"Clyde is better at opening up the old, withered legs of his receptionist than wounds if you ask me," Mandy accused.

"Only because *your* old, withered legs are permanently closed!"

And that was about all I could stomach of them today. I herded them toward the door, reminding them to make another appointment with reception.

Fuck knows they needed it, though there was no doubt in my mind that no amount of counseling was going to help. They were headed straight for divorce court.

I closed the door to my office and slumped down in my chair. Listening to married people fight over the stupidest shit had not exactly been what I had in mind when I'd specialized in psychology. Though it paid the bills so I knew I shouldn't look a gift horse in the mouth.

At least that had been the last appointment of the evening.

I opened the email account I'd been neglecting all day and answered a couple of the most important queries, one from another doctor within the hospital needing to confirm a patient diagnosis. Another from a drug rep who wanted a meeting.

I skimmed over the rest of the emails, my finger hovering over the close box, when my gaze snagged on the name of one sender.

My heart rate picked up as I clicked on it and read the short, one-sentence message.

Another body was found last night.

I breathed out slowly and then deleted the message, checking it was removed from the trash folder too. I shut down the computer and gathered my keys and wallet from my desk drawer and locked the office behind me.

My offices were on the psych floor of the hospital but closest to the elevator, so private patients could attend their appointments without wandering their way through the entire floor full of rooms and beds for those here on longer stays. I said goodbye to my receptionist and then stuck my head down the hallway to call a goodbye to the nurses at their station.

I went through the motions, the same as I always did, but my thoughts were already across town.

In the morgue.

I hurried across the parking lot and into my car. Normally after work I would have hit the gym, or stopped somewhere for some food, or maybe even caught a movie. But tonight I drove straight to the ugly building with the "Saint View Morgue" sign attached to the chain-link fence.

I turned into the driveway and stopped my car alongside Ron's but eyed the unfamiliar plain white van parked on the other side, along with the two cop cars parked by the door.

"Fuck," I mumbled. Ron hadn't said there'd be anyone else here tonight. Let alone that there were cops hanging around.

Two guys in biker jackets leaned on the outside wall, to the left of the entrance. One was younger, probably in his early twenties, skinny with light-colored hair. The other was almost the complete opposite. Tall and thick, his brown skin a complete contrast to his friend's pale white. They both had cigarettes between their fingers, and they eyed my car with distrust.

The big guy dropped his smoke to the ground, stubbing it out with his boot and pushing off the wall to walk my way.

Clearly, I wasn't going to just be sitting in the car waiting for them to leave like I'd hoped I might. I opened the door, pulling out my briefcase with me, even though I'd never bothered to bring that in with me before.

The door to the morgue opened at the same time though.

A third biker, a huge guy with a messy blond ponytail, escorted a tiny, dark-haired woman out of the building. He took one look at me and shouted back over his shoulder, "Hawk! Heads-up. We've got company," before leveling me with a warning expression as he led his girl into the white van.

A fourth biker, Hawk presumably, followed out behind them with another woman, this one slightly taller and a hell of a lot curvier.

I sucked in a deep breath so fast and sharp it was clearly audible across the parking lot.

Hawk cast a glance my way and froze, twisting so the woman was protected behind him.

"Who the fuck are you?" he called out, voice deep and full of suspicion.

I held up my briefcase, desperately trying to see past him to get a better glimpse of the woman. "I'm a doctor. Fredderick Grayson."

The man shook his head slightly, like he didn't believe me. "You one of Josiah's people?"

I frowned. "Who?"

He narrowed his eyes, but the woman peeked out from behind him.

My heart thundered.

It wasn't her.

Of course it wasn't.

But fuck, she looked so much like her I was having a hard time accepting it. Everything in me screamed to save her in the way I hadn't been able to for a different woman years before.

"Back up, asshole." The man in front of her let out a low growl.

I'd unconsciously walked several steps toward her, and Hawk clearly wasn't happy about it.

I froze, reminded that although I'd done enough fighting in my time that I could probably take one of these guys head-to-head, three, or four if the guy in the van decided to join in, was a recipe for disaster.

I didn't exactly fancy becoming a stiff in the morgue alongside the victim I'd come to see. If these guys were from an MC, there was every chance in the world they were carrying more than just a packet of gum in their back pockets.

I put my hands up in mock surrender and backed up. "Sorry. I don't know any Josiahs."

"Kara?" He didn't take his eyes off me. "You know this guy?"

She peeked around him again.

A wave of familiarity hit me once more. Fuck. Big brown doe eyes framed by dark lashes. They were red-rimmed, like she'd been crying, and everything inside me screamed to know why. To protect her from whatever it was that had hurt her.

But clearly I wasn't the only one who felt like that. Her bodyguard blocked my view of her again, stepping in closer, a warning on his tongue marked by short, sharp words. "Don't. Fucking. Look at her. Look at me."

My fingers instinctively closed into fists, and my muscles tightened, preparing for a fight I knew I'd lose.

The man ran his gaze down my body, centering it on my closed fists. He let out a slow laugh. "Really, bro? You're real fucking brave posturing like you want to throw that fist into my face. I'd like to see you try."

The woman grabbed his arm. "Stop it! He's not one of Josiah's people."

Hawk didn't lower his gaze from mine for another ten or fifteen seconds, but eventually, he grinned, shook himself visibly, letting go of the tension in his body and stepping back, his hand holding the woman—Kara— behind him. "Let's go, Little Mouse. You just saved this guy his teeth."

He herded her toward the van, and the original two members who'd been guarding the door followed. They both shot me dirty looks when they passed.

I ignored them, watching Kara disappear into the dark interior of the van, my gaze clinging to hers until the very last second the shadows ate her up.

Leaving only Hawk to glare at me as he slammed the sliding door.

I stood there watching until the tires spun out on some loose gravel at the top of the drive before finding traction again.

"You okay, sir?" one of the cops asked me.

I hadn't even seen them leave the building or been aware they'd been watching the altercation.

I forced a smile at him. "Sure." I cleared my throat because I absolutely was not okay. Not even a little bit.

His partner eyed me. "The morgue is closed for the night."

Ron called out from inside, the overhead lamps shining on his balding head. "It's okay, Officers. We have a meeting. He can come inside."

The officer nodded, and I passed him with a mumble of thanks.

Ron kicked out the stopper and closed the heavy glass doors, locking them from the inside. We both raised a hand in farewell, the officers climbing inside their cars.

Ron turned to me. "You're early," he accused, leaning one hand on the countertop like he needed it to hold him up.

I checked the cops had actually left the parking lot. "I came as soon as I finished work, like I always do. I didn't know you'd have cops here. What did they say?"

He shook his head. "Nothing, as usual. They're being very tight-lipped about it all."

"But you think it's our guy?"

"No doubt in my mind. You want to see her?"

I nodded and followed him down the hallway.

Ron pointed at a door halfway along. "She's still in the viewing room. That was the family."

I glanced over at him with interest. "The men or the women?"

"Women. They were the victim's sisters."

That explained her tears. I swore low under my breath as we entered the viewing room. Ron flicked on the lights, and a sickly yellow glow washed over the sheet-covered victim on the table.

The dead girl was way too much like her sister for my comfort.

It took me a second to put my doctor's hat on. This wasn't my area of expertise, but I'd been through med school. I knew enough.

Ron was a talker and commentated on everything he knew while I studied the body without touching her.

"There are strangulation marks on her neck. Restraint marks around her wrists and ankles."

"She's dark-haired. Late teens or early twenties, I'm guessing. Just like the others," I added.

Ron agreed.

"Where did they find her?" I asked.

"In a city dumpster. Some poor schmuck from a café found her when he was taking out the trash this morning."

I shook my head, anger filling me. "Dumped her like she didn't mean anything."

"Cowardly," Ron added with a sigh. "You should have heard the cries from her sisters. This girl was loved."

I lifted the sheet and covered the dead girl's face respectfully. "And in an instant someone just took it all away."

"I'll never understand how someone can do it, you know?" Ron mused. "I mean, the dead bodies don't bother me. I see them every day so it would be a bit of a problem if they did. But they're already pale and lifeless when they come to me. I can't imagine watching the color fade from their face or hearing them struggle for breath." He grimaced. "That's messed up."

"I agree." I didn't know how a man could do it. How he could put a cord around a woman's throat and pull while he stared her in the eye and watched the life drain out of her.

But I knew men who did.

"There's a pattern developing." I pulled out my phone and the magnetic stylus from the pocket of the case. With quick fingers, I scrawled notes across the screen, letting the phone turn my scrawls into text. "Do the cops even realize that?"

Ron shrugged. "I don't know."

I shook my head. "The other victims were sisters."

Ron looked over at me slowly. "You think that's a thing for this guy?"

My heart thundered, thinking about Kara.

Kara who was so much like this dead girl beneath the sheet.

Bile rose in my mouth at the thought of standing here next month, staring down at another lifeless face. This had to fucking stop.

Everything inside me revolted at the thought of this happening again.

It was only made worse by seeing Kara in the parking lot, and knowing this killer preyed on women who looked just like her.

21

KARA

Rebel cried the entire way home from the morgue. Her quiet sobs were painful to hear, and agonizing to watch as she curled up on the passenger seat and hugged her knees to her chest.

I couldn't stand the sound. Couldn't stand the way it made me want to do the same when I'd only just managed to pull myself together. I scratched the skin across my wrist, absentmindedly trying to distract myself at first, only to dig my fingernails in harder and harder as the sounds of Rebel's grief continued.

A warm heat settled on me, and when I glanced up, Hawk was watching me, his eyes glued to the mess I was making of my wrist.

I tugged my sleeve over it, twisted away, and tried to stop, but Rebel's cries only intensified and the scratching was the only thing that distracted me from it.

"Give it a rest, would you, short-ass? You barely even knew the woman," Hawk complained obnoxiously.

Rebel's cries cut off instantly, and she twisted on her

seat to glare at Hawk over her shoulder. "Are you fucking serious right now? God, you are the actual scum of the earth, do you know that? You can't even give me one minute to grieve my sister? You think I don't know I haven't been able to see her in years? You think that makes this hurt any less? God, I really fucking hate you sometimes..."

Rebel's anger all pointed in Hawk's direction was a thousand times easier to listen to than her pain.

I stopped hacking at my skin and laid my head against the window, letting the cool surface soothe my flushed face instead.

Hawk watched me for a second, his head bobbing slightly, like the fact I wasn't destroying my skin anymore had been his aim all along. He turned back to Rebel and continued his argument that she didn't get to be dramatic over a sister she'd only met a couple of times.

It was probably lucky for Hawk that Fang was driving because the look he sent him in the rearview mirror was deadly.

I didn't have it in me to deal with any of them. All I could think was that this entire thing was my fault.

Right now there were probably police officers out at the commune, telling my parents their daughter had been found murdered.

Or would they already know?

Would Josiah's men already be back there, covered in Alice's blood?

Or were they hanging around here, just waiting for their chance to spill mine?

Anger took the place of grief, and like the relief Rebel

had found in arguing with Hawk, I found it in letting myself hate the men who had done this.

Josiah. Onith. George or Tyson or one of the many others Josiah considered his inner circle.

Which one of them had been the man who'd put a cord around my sister's neck and tightened it so much she couldn't breathe? Had she even seen them coming? Had she fought?

Or had it been Kyle, who she'd so openly trusted?

He hadn't returned. We'd seen no sign of him or his truck.

Anger boiled my blood.

It was a familiar feeling. One that had tried to eat me alive before, and one I'd had to learn how to conceal.

So I did it again now.

But it was there, a waiting demon, ready to be unleashed.

Josiah had created it when he'd taken away my child, and he'd fed it again now by murdering my sister. He'd known it too. He'd tried banishing the evil from inside me with prayers and beatings and cruel words.

But the demon had only grown stronger.

Maybe that was why I had never left. The demon inside me was drawn to the demon in him.

Rebel and Hawk argued until we got back to the clubhouse, where she got out of the car and slammed the door.

Fang had his teeth mashed together and twisted to glare at his VP. "If that argument hadn't kept her from focusing on her sister tonight, it would be *my* fingers around your throat right now. You hear me?"

Hawk waved him off. "Yeah, yeah. I know. But I got

her to stop crying, didn't I? Give me some fucking credit where it's due."

Fang shook his head. "She's not wrong when she calls you an asshole, you know? You're seriously a fucking prick." He shut the door before Hawk could respond.

He raised an eyebrow at me instead. "You want to tell me I'm a cunt too?"

I cringed at his word choice but shook my head. "I'm not in the habit of calling people names. Excuse me. I need to get to my daughter."

"I'll tell you you're a cunt if you want," Aloha laughed deeply, Ice joining in with a chuckle of his own.

I ducked my head and made my way out of the van door that Ice held back for me. He went to touch my arm to get my attention, then clearly thought better of it when Hawk shoved him out of the way.

"Jesus fuck, Hawk! Quit pissing all over her like a dog marking its territory. I was only going to tell her I was sorry about her sister."

"She doesn't want your grubby fingers all fucking over her, all right? If I see any of you fuckers so much as lay a finger on her, I won't think twice about breaking them."

Aloha laughed like Hawk hadn't just threatened him with bodily harm. "That go for you too? You breaking your own fingers off every time you touch her? Didn't look like it back there at the morgue. Seemed like you were doing a whole lotta touching indeed."

Hawk's growl came back. "You. Saw. Nothing. Now shut the fuck up and get out of my face. I was just doing my job, protecting her like my prez told me to. Shame you two fuckheads couldn't do the same."

I hurried toward the clubhouse and my daughter

inside, trying to block out their harsh words, but hearing each and every one all the same.

Queenie was still in the same armchair she'd been in when I'd left, Hayley Jade sprawled out over her lap, and Queenie's eyes squinty like she might have drifted off for a little bit too.

"She's been sleeping like an angel the entire time," Queenie assured me. "Didn't wake once. She must have been exhausted, poor poppet."

I nodded.

"You want to take her home?" Queenie shifted slightly on the armchair.

Hayley Jade stirred, clutching Queenie's thick arms with her fingers.

Automatically, Queenie ran a hand up and down the little girl's back, soothing her back into sleep.

I didn't know how to answer her question. I had no home to go to. But I had to leave and it had to be now. I bypassed my sister's frightened eyes and landed on Fang. "Can you take me and Hayley Jade to the bus station, please?"

"What?" Rebel yelped. "No!"

"Rebel," I said calmly, needing her to understand. "I have to. They know where we are. We aren't safe here. I should have never come in the first place. If I hadn't, none of this would have happened."

"They would have come for you no matter where you went and they're going to do the same thing now. You think they're just going to give up because you leave Saint View? They killed Alice, Kara! You're Josiah's wife! At least her death was quick. If he's willing to kill Alice just to make a point, what do you think he'll do to you? It won't be quick. He'll make it slow and painful."

I stared at her wide-eyed, fear splintering through me, knowing that everything she was saying wasn't stemming from knowing Josiah personally, but from the traumas she had suffered from a man just like him.

She'd had five years of healing. Five years of men loving her and helping her mend the hurt that man had caused her. Five years of holding children in her arms and doting on them until her own scars throbbed a little less.

I'd never left. I was still stuck in the same old merry-go-round of abuse, with no way of getting out. Staying here and dragging her back into all of this wasn't an option.

I pulled her tight and kissed her cheek. "I have to go. I won't endanger you or your family anymore."

She grabbed my hand. "Don't. Don't let him hurt you. Don't let him push you away from people who love you. People who can keep you safe."

But Josiah's favorite way to torture me was by taking away the people I loved.

And now he was doing it again.

Forcing me out onto the road, away from the one sister I had left on this side of the fence and the only people outside the commune I knew.

A sob rose in my chest, and I reached for my daughter. "Fang, please. If you won't drive me to the bus station, I'll walk."

Queenie had tears in her eyes, but she fit her fingers beneath Hayley Jade's armpits and hefted her off her chest.

The little girl's eyes flew open, panic taking hold in a frighteningly quick space of time.

"Come here," I said awkwardly. "It's time to go."

She shook her head, and my heart plummeted, but I tried again. "We're going on an adventure, okay? Just you and me this time. We're going to go on a nice long drive on a bus, won't that be fun? Have you ever been on a bus?" I reached out to take her, wrapping my fingers around the skinny tops of her arms. "Come on, sweetheart."

Hayley Jade's scream was ear-piercing. She shoved me away violently, throwing her arms around Queenie the same way she had with Shari.

Queenie soothed the screams out of her, until Hayley Jade was sobbing but no longer hysterical.

My heart shattered into a million pieces.

"You'll stay here," Hawk said quietly, but with a tone that dared anyone to argue.

Nobody did. Not Rebel. Not Fang. Not War.

Nobody but me.

I glared at him. "I don't want to be here."

Hawk pulled his jacket off, tossing it onto a couch. His hoodie followed a moment later, leaving him bare-chested, a gun handle sticking out the top of his waistband. He leaned down, bracing his hands either side of me on the back of the couch. "I don't care, Little Mouse. I really don't fucking care. I just want to go to bed because this has been the longest day in the history of for-fucking-ever, and we all know the only safe place for you is right here, surrounded by fences and men who can protect you." He flicked his head toward Hayley Jade. "Don't want to listen to me? Then listen to your own fucking kid. She feels it. She feels the safety. You gonna take that away from her?"

Queenie gave me a helpless look, one that held pity and an unspoken apology, like she felt guilty because it was her Hayley Jade clung to her like a life raft.

Hawk eased off a fraction, blowing out a slow breath that misted across my lips smelling vaguely of mint and tobacco.

"Nod your head, Little Mouse."

I nodded.

He pulled back. "She agrees. She's staying. Queenie, can the kid stay with you tonight? Kara needs to sleep."

I started to disagree, but Hayley Jade had already laid her head down on Queenie's shoulders miserably, her tear-streaked face buried in the older woman's neck.

I could barely breathe for wanting her to find that sort of comfort in me.

But I clearly wasn't the person who could give it to her right now. "Would you mind?" I asked Queenie.

She gave me an understanding nod. "Not at all, sugar. Hayley Jade and I will have a sleepover in my room tonight. Aloha can sleep in the van."

To his credit, or maybe it was the glare Hawk sent his way, Aloha didn't make a sound of complaint. He just grinned, picked up a cushion from the couch, and tossed it in the air, catching it easily a second later. "I'm all good out there. It'll give me a break from Queenie's snoring."

Queenie rolled her eyes. "You ain't fooling nobody, saying that chainsaw-like noise coming from our room each night ain't you." But then she put her hand to his cheek and drew him in, pressing her lips to his. "Thank you. See you in the morning."

She stopped in front of me. "Hayley Jade, you want to say goodnight to your mama?"

Hayley Jade didn't utter a word.

I wanted to tell her I loved her. That I always had and that everything was going to be all right.

But I couldn't even promise her that.

War cleared his throat after Queenie left, his lightly bearded face full of sympathy. "You can stay in my old cabin. I haven't used it in years. Not since Mila was born."

"Okay," I whispered, not even looking at him, too focused on the fact my daughter would rather be with anyone but me. "Thank you."

Ice cleared his throat awkwardly between me and Hawk and War. "Uh, actually, the cabin hasn't been cleaned since the guys from the Ohio chapter came to stay..."

War recoiled. "Why the fuck didn't someone get on that? Jesus fuck, do I have to do everything myself?"

Hawk glared at Ice like he was the one who was supposed to have done it.

Ice shoved his hands in his pockets, his cheeks pink with embarrassment at being reprimanded in front of all of us. "Sorry. The other prospects and I will get on it tomorrow. In the meantime, Kara can have my bed. All the other rooms in the clubhouse are full."

I shook my head quickly, the thought of staying in Ice's room sending panic up my spine. "I don't need a bed," I assured them. "I can sleep on the couch."

I already knew I wouldn't sleep at all.

War nodded. "If that's what you want..." He glanced at Hawk. "That good with you?"

Hawk looked away quickly. "What do I fucking care?"

War snorted on what sounded like amusement. "Yeah. Okay then. Keep telling yourself that. If everyone is safe and has somewhere to sleep, I'm going home. I've got a very pregnant partner who I know won't be sleeping until I report that everyone is okay. We'll sort out the cabin in the morning. A few of us can go down there, if need be, and get it fixed up."

He smiled gently at me. "This place is safe. We've got cameras and someone on the gate twenty-four seven. It's good to have you back here. We've all missed you. I hope you know that. You're one of us. You always have been, and we take care of our own."

"Thank you," I whispered to the kind-eyed leader. But I wasn't one of them. I wasn't a part of anything bigger than myself, really. I hadn't seen Rebel in years. My family had watched a man isolate and abuse me for half a decade and had never lifted a finger to help. And Hayley Jade didn't even know who I was, other than the woman who had taken her from the only mother she remembered.

Everyone said their goodnights, Fang guiding Rebel toward the parking lot to take her home, Hawk, Ice, Ratchet, and the other guys all disappeared into bedrooms, or in the case of Aloha, cars to sleep in for the night.

I curled up on the couch, tugging a thin blanket over my shoulder that I found in the corner.

Even locked in Josiah's house, I couldn't remember ever feeling so alone.

22

HAWK

It felt like a hundred years since I'd last slept. My eyes were gritty and heavy, yet sleep refused to come. I stared at the damn ceiling in my bedroom for at least two hours, willing myself to just go the fuck to sleep.

It was 2:00 a.m. when I gave up.

I sat up, scrubbing my hands over my face with a groan of annoyance that I felt right to my damn toes. Not bothering to get dressed, I jerked open my bedroom door and stared across the room at Kara huddled on the shitty cracked leather couch.

She had her eyes closed, but she was scrunched into a tiny ball, shivering beneath a blanket that clearly was doing shit to keep her warm.

"What the fuck?" I muttered. Goddamn prospects. They hadn't even bothered to get her a blanket or a pillow? I padded down the hallway where there was a cupboard full of shit nobody had a place for. I yanked it open, eyeing the overflowing shelves for something she could rest her head on.

Not a fucking thing.

I don't know why I expected more. I shared this place with a bunch of twenty-somethings who couldn't have cared less whether they slept on a bare mattress or the floor. Most of them probably didn't even know what a washing machine was. Aloha and Queenie weren't as Neanderthal, and I would bet Queenie had clean sheets and blankets in their bedroom, but she was in there with the kid and I didn't want to wake either of them up.

Fuck, the last thing I wanted was to hear Hayley Jade screaming again. It was a sound that was so filled with fear it had eaten me up all the way down to my soul.

I looked back at Kara. I was sure I could hear her teeth chattering. And was that the fucking blanket Ratchet's ugly mutt dog laid on when he stayed here?

In horror, I realized it was.

I stormed back to stand over her and reached down and ripped it off her sleeping body so fucking fast it whipped up and hit me in the face.

Kara woke with a start. "What..."

"You aren't sleeping under a fucking blanket not even good enough for Ratchet's mutt."

Before she could protest, I picked her up, holding her tight in my arms because I expected a fight.

To my surprise, I didn't get one.

Her chilled body sank against mine, so fucking cold she didn't even argue with me, just sought out my body heat.

Goddamn it.

I stormed back into my bedroom and tossed her into my bed, watching her tits bounce with the impact.

My dick thought about getting hard, and I issued a command for it to piss off before I chopped it off.

Kara's eyes were owlishly big. "I can't take your bed. I don't want you to have to sleep on the floor."

"Good. I wasn't fucking going to." I crawled across the mattress and flopped down on the pillow next to hers. I dragged the covers up, not looking at her as I made sure she was properly covered by the thick quilt.

She was stiff as a board next to me. "I can't..."

I sighed. "You can't what? Be warm and comfortable? Yes, you can."

"I can't sleep in your bed, Hawk. I'm married. It would be a sin."

I opened one eye. "You watching me jerk off with your nipples so hard they practically begged for my mouth was the sin. You already committed that. Sleeping in my bed now instead of freezing your ass off on the couch is just human decency. Go to sleep."

I closed my eyes, but I could tell she was watching me.

I opened them again. "What?"

"Thank you."

"For what?"

"For being kind."

An uncomfortable prickle spread along my spine. I rolled over. "Whatever. Tell anyone else and I'll deny it."

"Okay," she whispered.

I closed my eyes again, and this time, a wave of exhaustion hit me hard. I let her quiet breaths and the heat from her body lull me into the sleep I'd been so desperately craving.

23

KARA

I woke early to a brilliant pink-and-gold sunrise spearing through the trees of the woods outside Hawk's bedroom window.

And to his warm body hard against the back of mine.

I didn't know what to do. I didn't want to risk waking him. He'd been exhausted when he'd brought me to his bed, and had fallen asleep nearly instantly. While I'd huddled on the far side of the mattress and cried silently until I'd eventually fallen asleep too.

Hawk mumbled something in his sleep, and his arm flopped across me, drawing me closer. Slowly, he thrust his hips against my backside.

He was hard.

I bit down on my lip, my brain short-circuiting with a mixture of fear...

And something else a whole lot more pleasurable.

He was so very warm. And his bed was soft and comfortable. The couch had been cold and miserable and lonely.

Hawk's bed was the complete opposite.

I knew I should have woken him. Or moved away, but I was already on the edge of the mattress, and there was nowhere for me to go unless I got out of bed completely.

I didn't want to sit alone in the main room and remember that my sister was dead, my daughter was scared of me, and I had nowhere to go.

So I closed my eyes and pretended I wasn't awake.

Hawk thrust his hips again, and his palm flat to my belly. I squeezed my eyes shut, waiting for him to wake and realize I wasn't Amber or Kiki or one of the other skinny club girls he normally had in his bed. They didn't have an ounce of fat on them. He'd feel the difference soon enough.

But in his sleepy state, he clearly didn't notice. His hand slid up beneath my shirt to cup my breast.

I fought the tightening in my chest, keeping my breathing slow and steady.

His thumb rubbed absently over my nipple, and instantly it hardened for him.

Nice feelings spread from his touch, taking me by surprise.

He buried his face in my hair and the back of my neck, his deep, slow breathing telling me he was still mostly asleep, even if he was touching me like he wasn't.

His hand left my breast, and I wanted to cry for the loss of his touch.

But then it slipped below the waistband of my skirt, and without any warning, straight into my panties to cup me between the legs.

I swallowed down a gasp of shock, fear threatening to

rise inside me, the way it did every time Josiah touched me.

Except his touch had never felt like this. It had never been gentle.

Hawk's fingers found the tiny bundle of nerves between my legs and circled it gently, nudging at it with his fingertips while his hips rocked against me from behind. The two actions slowly started a rhythm, one Hawk clearly knew well enough to be instinct.

His finger swept lower, through the slick wetness that had formed between my lower lips, and then it slid inside me.

I gasped, my eyes fluttering closed at the foreign feeling of pleasure instead of pain.

"Always so wet for me, baby," he mumbled. "Fucking want you."

Through my hair, his lips found the skin at the back of my neck, and he licked the tender spot, while inhaling deep. He withdrew his fingers from inside me just long enough to tug the elastic waistband of my skirt and panties down, baring my behind beneath the covers.

He fumbled with his sleep shorts, pulling them down low enough that his erection sprang free, thick, hard, and hot.

In the next second, it was between my legs, pushing between my thighs, seeking my entrance. His hand went back to my clit, rubbing and stroking it, faster this time, sending little spirals of awareness through my entire system.

He thrust between my legs, not penetrating me, but every movement coating his erection in the slick fluid seeping from inside me.

I'd never felt anything like it.

The feeling grew until I was panting, pressing my behind back against his hard body, and God forgive me, encouraging his actions.

"Need to be inside you, baby," he groaned. "Need your tight, wet cunt around my cock. Need to feel you gushing on it when you come."

"Oh," I moaned, my tongue wanton with need and pleasure. "Hawk!"

Hawk froze behind me.

In an instant, his warmth disappeared. His fingers abandoned my clit. His dick disappeared from rimming my entrance.

"Kara? What the fuck...?"

The swirling, pleasurable feeling obliterated at the confusion in his tone. At the disgust.

I snatched my skirt and yanked it up, struggling out from beneath the covers. I'd never been so mortified in my life. My face burned with embarrassment, my body completely flushed from the way his touch had made me feel. The cool morning air hit me hard as I stumbled out of Hawk's bed, but it did nothing to take away the fire that was engulfing me whole.

The one that Hawk had lit like I was tinder, and he was a match.

The man would burn me alive.

"I'm sorry," I whispered, fleeing the room.

Hawk groaned, "Fuck, Kara. Wait."

But I couldn't. I didn't want to turn back and look at him and see the horror on his face after realizing it was me he'd been touching and not one of the other women who normally frequented his bed.

I couldn't bear it.

I ran from the clubhouse, into the woods, and kept on going until I couldn't hear his shouts any longer.

24

HAYDEN

"Quit whining at me, cat. I already fed you," I complained to the mewling creature standing on top of the table like he was king of the castle. "And get off of there."

I scooped the little animal up and put him back down on the floor. How he managed to keep getting up there was beyond me, but he and his two sisters seemed hellbent on destroying my apartment and getting into as much mischief as possible. There were cat toys and litterboxes everywhere, and I was covered in tiny scratches from their needle-sharp claws.

Shame they were so fucking cute and that I was already thinking of myself as their father.

I shook my head at how pathetic I was. "I need to get a life," I mumbled.

"Or just get laid," Liam called from the couch, a pile of papers in his hands, and the movie I'd been watching still playing in the background. "I mean, why start with something as big as getting a whole life, when you can niche down to focus on why you're actually such a stick-in-the-mud?" He glanced up. "How long has it been since you had a girlfriend anyway? You've never brought anyone home to meet us."

I raised an eyebrow at his questioning. "Oh, I'm sorry. I didn't realize I'd invited a teenage girl over. I thought I'd asked my brother over to review a contract, not give me shit about how much sex I'm having."

Liam grinned like I hadn't just given him shit. "That long, huh?"

"Fuck off."

He laughed and went back to poring over the contract while I paced up and down the small living room impatiently waiting for him to be done. I was so wired I was practically crawling out of my skin.

"I could set you up with one of Mae's friends, if you want? Or maybe someone from my office? You're always going to the movies alone, why not take someone with you once in a while? A couple of the women at work asked about you after the award thing the other day."

I stopped pacing. "Why?"

Liam rolled his eyes behind his black-rimmed glasses. "Oh, I don't know. Might have had something to do with the fact you walk around looking all bad boy. According to Mae, that shit is catnip."

I glared at him. "I meant why would you set me up with someone? I don't date. And I don't need to get laid."

"So you're just going to be celibate forever then?" He sighed. "I know that shit with Kara really messed you up."

I cut that shit off real quick. "I don't want to talk about it."

Liam eyed me. "You never do."

"Would you?" I snapped. "I already think about it every fucking day. The last thing I want to do is talk about how I had to deliver her baby in a shitty Saint View slum house. Or about how if I'd let her go, Caleb would have hurt Ripley or Jay. Or you."

Liam wasn't ruffled by the vague hint of panic that still laced my tone whenever I thought about that time.

"That didn't happen," he assured me. "We're all fine."

"Doesn't mean I don't remember it every time I look at one of you." Or every time I thought of her.

Which was the whole reason I hadn't dated in years. Hadn't even touched a woman.

When you'd done the things I had, seen the things I'd seen, you didn't just give yourself a free pass to be happy.

I didn't deserve that, and I knew it.

Liam sighed and tossed Luca's contract onto the coffee table. "Then why the hell are you even considering that contract? You know very well what Luca is involved with. Not much of it is legal."

I gripped the back of my neck with both hands. "I know! I know, all right! But that contract is offering me everything I've ever wanted. And all of that *is* legal, right? I read it all, every word. It's on the up and up, isn't it?"

Liam sighed heavily. "From what I can tell, and from the research my team did into Luca's business investments, yes. He seems to be using the profit from another restaurant he owns in the city as start-up capital for this. It's all above board, taxes filed, all the I's dotted and T's crossed. It's a very good contract. If it were anyone else offering it to you, I wouldn't think twice in telling you to accept it."

I groaned. "You think I should turn it down."

Liam shook his head. "I can't make that decision for you. You know the risks. It's up to you if you want to roll the dice. But if it were me, no. I wouldn't take it."

I let out a huff of air and frustration. It was so easy for him to say that when he had a beautiful house, a job he was passionate about, enough money in the bank that a twenty-thousand-dollar check hadn't felt like a lottery win, and family to come home to at night.

I threw a hand out, indicating the shitty apartment I'd lived in for five years. "If you lived here, in this shithole, had no job, no prospects, no family...would you still turn it down? If that contract was offering you all of your dreams, would you still say no?"

He screwed up his face and then slowly shook his head. "No, you're right. I probably wouldn't."

"The contract is good," I confirmed. "When Luca says he isn't running women anymore, we have no proof to the contrary."

Liam nodded.

I barely hesitated this time. "Pass me a pen."

Liam still didn't seem sure, but he did it anyway.

And just like that, with the ending credits of *Pulp Fiction* playing in the background, I became head chef and part owner of the restaurant of my dreams.

I left Liam continuing our Quentin Tarantino marathon, two out of three cats curled up asleep in his lap. He'd refused to budge before he got to watch the end of *Kill Bill*, but I was too impatient to wait. I got in my truck and drove it into Providence, my heart rate picking up with every mile I passed, and the signed contracts burning a hole in the passenger seat beside me.

I didn't really expect anyone to be at the restaurant, considering the place had only just been auctioned off in the last week, but Luca's car was parked out front, and the lights inside were all on.

I'd only planned to push the signed contracts beneath the door, but when I leaned on it, it gave way beneath my weight. "Hello?" I called out.

The sound of a nail gun stopped, and Luca stuck his head around the corner of a freshly plastered wall.

"Chaos," he called. "Excellent. Come on back. We've got decisions to make."

I slowly walked through the space that had become a construction zone in the short time since I'd last been here. Around the other side of the new wall, a kitchen area was being put together, and beyond that, heavy dark doors were being installed.

I came to a stop beside Luca and squinted at everything going on, a team of three guys bustling around with tool belts hanging off their hips and plaster dust on their boots.

Luca was somehow still neatly polished, though he did have his shirtsleeves rolled to his elbows and a pencil tucked behind one ear.

"You don't mess about," I commented to him quietly.

"Every day this place sits empty with no customers is a day it's not making money. I'm not about that life. Are you?"

I supposed I wasn't. I was itching to get my hands dirty. I'd work out how to install ovens and tile backsplashes if I needed to. Whatever got this place up and running. While it wasn't making money, neither was I. I couldn't do that for too long if I didn't want to blow through every cent I'd ever saved.

Which I definitely didn't.

That money was all still earmarked for a place of my own. One that wasn't majority owned by Luca Guerra.

But this place…it was a start. There was a nervous excitement inside me that hadn't let up since I'd signed my name across the dotted line on that contract.

"When do we open?" I asked.

Luca twisted to look at me, his gaze dropping to the envelope in my hand. "You signed them, then?"

I handed them over to him.

He pulled the white papers with my signature on the bottom out and shook his head. "Well, look at that. I thought for sure I'd have to get down on my knees and blow you to get you to sign."

I gave him a sidelong glance, making it clear I didn't find him funny.

Luca sniggered. "Right. Chaos has no sense of humor and is maybe slightly homophobic. Got it."

"Not homophobic. Just not interested in banging my boss."

Luca slapped me on the back. "Good for you. I like that sort of attitude. Now come and see these plans. I want to show you what's happening."

He motioned me over to a workbench and unrolled a large piece of paper that had a crudely drawn but recognizable sketch of the restaurant. Luca took the pencil from behind his ear and drew circles toward the front of the rectangular map. "This is where we'll have the tables.

Right in front of the front window so anyone walking or driving past can see everyone salivating over the amazing dishes you're going to create. We already had this wall installed which separates the dining room from the kitchen, and we're going to have a mural artist come in and create something that everyone will want to have photos taken with. I want this place to be as social media friendly as possible. We need people talking about it on TikTok and the like, right?"

I shrugged. "I don't know anything about those things. I just make food."

"Sure. But you're part owner now. It's only fair I tell you everything I have planned for this place."

Shit. I was acting stupid. Of course I needed to know everything going on. I couldn't just hide in the kitchen anymore, like I'd done at Simon's place. I gave Luca a nod. "Yeah, okay. Go on."

"The kitchen will be your domain. Everything state of the art."

I watched over his shoulder as he scribbled out more ideas and marked out placements for various things.

I pointed at the lines symbolizing the two heavy wooden doors that led to the back half of the building. "And this is the function room?"

Luca laughed. "Sure. At least that's what we're calling it on paper."

I squinted at him. "What do you mean?"

He leaned one shoulder against the wall. "You ever heard of Psychos?"

I frowned. "The dive bar in Saint View? Yeah. I've heard of it." Anyone who'd lived in Saint View longer than five minutes had probably heard the rumors about Psychos.

"You ever been there?"

I snorted. "Do you think I have a death wish? It's owned by the Slayers' prez and his family. They aren't exactly my biggest fans."

Luca folded his arms across his broad chest. "Then you haven't seen the sex club they transform it into a few nights a month?"

"Seen it? No. It's invite only, right? My most notable run-in with the Slayers was when they held me captive in their basement. I didn't exactly get time off for good behavior."

Luca stared at me. "Shit, really?" Then he shrugged. "Well, that should make you like this all the better. Because it's come to my attention that their little sex club is making them a shitload of money. And frankly, I want in."

I stared at him. "So...what? You want to turn this place into a sex club too?"

"Ding-ding-ding! We have a winner."

I could barely believe what I was hearing. "You are joking, right?"

Luca shrugged a shoulder. "Why would I joke about something like that? Sex sells."

I could barely believe the words coming out of his mouth. This was not what I'd had in mind for my restaurant. Not at all. I wanted something beautiful. Quiet. Somewhere people came because they wanted a quality culinary experience, not because they wanted to chow down some food then go have an orgy in the back room like they did at Psychos. No. No fucking way. "This isn't

Saint View, Luca! Providence is a nice place. The people here have money and...class. This will never be allowed."

"Of course not. But a secret sex club is half the appeal of Psychos, and it'll be the same here. What the town planning committee and the pearl-clutchers don't know won't hurt them. Like I said, on paper, that space back there is nothing more than a function room." He rolled up the plans, fitting a rubber band around them to keep them from unraveling. He tapped them against his palm and looked past me to the street, a smile pulling across his mouth. "Sign's here!" he called to the workmen.

He strode to the door, opening it and directing the two men delivering the huge sign to just put it down against the newly constructed wall until Luca's guys could attach it to the front of the building. The sign was huge, taking both men to carry it and clearly designed to be a statement piece that attracted attention. They edged their way through the narrow doorway, turning once they were inside with more room to play with.

"You have got to be fucking kidding me," I swore beneath my breath. "You cannot call a restaurant that."

But it was clear Luca already had.

Sinners.

He was naming the restaurant after my old gang. That name was associated with everything I just wanted to forget. The life I'd had. The person I'd been. The Slayers were never going to stand for this. After I'd walked away, the Sinners had sunk back into the shadows, while the Slayers had gone on their merry way, running their bar and sex club, and racking up big profits doing it, if Luca was to be believed.

But I had no doubt they were still there. Working for Luca. Waiting for their moment.

Luca was going to reignite a gang war with one simple little word.

Though to his credit, one thing did stand out in my head.

It was a great fucking name for a sex club.

25

HAWK

I watched Kara run off through the trees and swore low under my breath, swiveling around and storming back to my bedroom. I sank down hard on my bed before I even noticed I was naked, my erection bobbing in protest of the fact it was no longer warm between Kara's thick thighs, nestled up against her wet pussy.

I hadn't even realized it was her. I'd barely been awake. I was so used to Amber or Kiki or one of the other women sneaking into my bed in the middle of the night and being naked ready to ride my cock whenever I wanted. I'd just assumed...

Fucking hell. I should have realized her tits were soft and bouncy, nothing like the harder, fake ones Amber had. I should have paid attention to how holding on to her hip felt so fucking different than Kiki's. Kara had been soft in all the places the other women weren't.

I'd never really had much to do with bigger women. All the women at the club, except Queenie, who I sure as hell wasn't ever going to fuck or Aloha would wring my neck, were thin. It just seemed to be a thing. They barely fucking ate, even on family days where we had so much food we could feed a small army, so it was hardly surprising.

I got hard when they touched my dick, and I came when I stuck it in them, so I'd just figured they were my type.

But now all I could think about was how hard I still was after being curled around Kara's soft body.

"Fuck," I swore, pushing to my feet and staggering to the bathroom. I'd nearly fucking sunk my dick into her. If she hadn't said my name, snapping me out of the exhausted fog I'd been feeling her up in, I would have.

I turned the shower on hard, blasting cold water over the tiles, and then stepped beneath them, praying it would shrivel my erection.

It didn't. The fucker still throbbed.

For Kara.

For the little church mouse who'd watched me jack off. Who'd slept in my bed all fucking night when I never let women do that. And who I'd damn near raped because she was too scared of me to wake me up and tell me to go to hell.

My erection died. Vomit rose in my throat, and I was forced to open my mouth and swallow gulps of water to wash it down.

I'd never cared that everyone thought I was an asshole. I could play that part, and I could play it well.

I was a smart-ass, I knew that. I rubbed people the wrong way and didn't give a shit about the consequences.

Rebel had a whole damn laundry list of names she

liked to call me, and not one of them bothered me, because I knew nothing I'd ever done was truly that bad.

Until today.

Today I'd come so close to taking something from Kara that I couldn't have ever given back.

That made me the biggest piece of shit in the world.

Chilled to the bone more with my actions than because of the water, I shut it off. I found a towel and rubbed it roughly over my body and the spikes of my closely cropped hair, rubbing hardest at my dick until it fucking hurt.

The compound was starting to come to life outside my door, and I put on jeans and a hoodie and a pair of work boots. From the back of the bathroom cupboard, I found a caddy of cleaning supplies.

Prospects got the grunt jobs, like unblocking toilets, laundry, and scrubbing kitchens. We threw all the shittiest jobs at them, to see which ones just shut up and got the job done and which ones bitched and moaned and went home crying to their mommies, the MC life clearly not for them.

That hadn't been any different for me and War, just because we'd been the club founders' kids.

It had been a long time since I'd been a prospect, and I hadn't missed it one bit. All the shutting up and just doing as I was fucking told had never suited me well.

But now I pulled together everything I needed and yanked open my bedroom door.

Kara sat at the bar, a bowl of cereal in front of her.

My gaze slammed into hers, and every memory of what I'd done to her came rushing back, every single one coated in regret.

I'd never been one for apologizing. Wasn't sure I could ever even remember saying the words "I'm sorry."

But they almost fell from my lips in that second. Because I'd never been sorrier for something in my life than I was for what I'd done to Kara that morning.

Ice pulled his headphones from his ears and shook a cereal box at me. "You want some? I'll get another bowl."

I drew my gaze away from Kara reluctantly. At least she'd come back. Even if she couldn't look at me, at least she wasn't blindly running through the woods. She would have hit the fence line eventually. She'd have had no chance of getting through it or over it in her long skirt and with no shoes on, but I was still glad she wasn't out there. I liked knowing she was here, even if I wasn't staying. "No. I'm going down to War's old cabin to fix it up."

Ice frowned and put the cereal box down. "The other prospects and I are going down there once they're all awake. Just give us a day to get it done."

I shook my head, still remembering Kara shivering on that fucking couch because I couldn't even trust the prospects to do something as simple as get her a blanket. I'd told them to clean out that cabin weeks ago and they'd ignored me. Ice acting like I was the one being unreasonable pissed me off. "You had your chance to do it and you chose not to. Get 'em to do something else. Clearly, if I want something done, I have to do it myself."

"You sure?" Ice asked, suitably guilty for not doing his damn job. "It was pretty filthy last time I was down there. How long's it been since you did any cleaning? The kitchen and bathroom probably both need to be really scrubbed. No one has lived down there for ages."

I glared at him, my earlier irritation growing at him

insinuating I wasn't capable of basic tasks. Kara was sitting right there, listening to the entire fucking thing. The last thing I wanted was her thinking I was useless. "This is why you're still a prospect, even though you've been hanging around here for years. Learn when to shut up. I know how to clean."

Ratchet wandered over, his hair a wild mess from sleep. "What was that? Hawk is cleaning?" He sniggered as he reached for a spoon. "I'm so coming down later to get video of you scrubbing that toilet."

I flipped him the bird, took one last peek at Kara who was steadfastly ignoring me, and hoped the toilet was the filthiest one I'd ever seen.

Because if cleaning up a place for Kara was my penance, then I should at least earn it.

I trudged through the woods, taking the leaf-littered path opposite the one I normally took when I came out here. This one led out to the old cabin War had once lived in, back before he'd become a pussy-whipped fool who couldn't stop knocking up his woman. Though to be fair, that could have been any of Bliss's partners. I wasn't about to ask which kid belonged to which baby daddy. They both called war Dad, as would the new baby, I assumed, so it hardly mattered if they were biologically his or not.

The cabin had been a lot nicer when War had lived here. Now we only used it when we had a lone wolf roll into town who was brave enough to ask for somewhere to stay, or when Slayers' members from other chapters came into town to talk business with me and War.

The business talk only ever lasted a few hours and the

rest was filled with drinking, fucking, and partying. When they finally dragged themselves back onto their bikes, sometimes the next day, sometimes weeks later, the mess they left behind always pissed me off.

We never turned away other chapters. It was written into our laws that all the Slayers were brothers. But some of them were brothers I'd be happy to never have in my home because they were disgusting and thought nothing of leaving their shit everywhere for our prospects to clean up.

I stomped up the steps to the cabin, the wooden floorboards creaking underneath my weight. When the door swung open, I almost turned around and walked straight back out. If I hadn't royally fucked up that morning with Kara, I absolutely would have.

The entire place reeked of stale piss, shit, body odor, moldy food. I gagged on the stench and then stormed around the main room as well as the bedroom and bathroom, opening up every window and letting some fresh air in.

I dry heaved over the mess in the bathroom, staring at it in horror.

I wasn't a complete neat freak. But I wasn't a twenty-year-old kid anymore, and my interest in medicine had led me down many a germ-and-bacteria rabbit hole. Once you'd learned some things, and worse, seen some photos, it made you want to keep things clean. How the fuck did fully grown men make a mess like this and then just get back on their bikes and ride on out the gates like it was no big deal?

"Pigs, the lot of you," I said between rounds of

gagging. I pulled a bandana out of my pocket that I usually used for keeping insects out of my mouth when I was on my bike, but now I prayed it would keep out some of the stench of this room.

The toilet had to be first. I squirted a bunch of cleaner in there, found the brush, and then got down on my knees to get to work.

A small gasp came from behind me.

I whipped around, only to come eye to eye with Hayley Jade. I squinted at her, peering behind her for an adult in tow but not finding anyone. "What are you doing down here, kid? Where's your mom?"

She didn't answer, but her face was screwed up.

I couldn't blame her. I was sure mine was too. "Smells bad in here, huh?"

She nodded, covering her nose and mouth with her sleeve.

"Yeah, I agree. You should really probably go back up to the main house. This isn't something a little girl like you needs to see."

She didn't say anything, just gazed around the cabin in interest.

"You come to check out your new digs? I know it doesn't seem like much right now, but just give me a couple hours and I'll have it so sweet you won't even recognize the place."

Hayley Jade cocked her head to one side, and this time when she screwed up her face, it wasn't with disgust but with disbelief.

Jesus, why did no one think I was capable of doing something this basic? "Hey! I can clean! Why the hell does no one think I can clean?"

Hayley Jade didn't respond, but she didn't make a move to go back up to the clubhouse either.

I shrugged. "Fine. Stay. Whatever. No skin off my nose if you're a sucker for punishment too. You want a job to do?"

She nodded her little blond head.

"Good for you, kid. At least you aren't a lazy shit like the prospects are. They should have done this ages ago." I realized what I'd said. "Oh, shit. I mean, sugar. Crap. Am I allowed to swear in front of you? Are you old enough for that?"

She didn't answer.

"Yeah, probably not, right? You really don't talk, do you?"

Still nothing.

I shrugged. "Okay, I can respect that. Fuck knows I talk enough for the both of us. Shit! I mean, fudge, not fuck. Fuck." I sighed. "I give up. I swear a lot, kid. Sorry."

To my surprise her lips twisted into a giggle.

I shoved the toilet brush around the porcelain. "So you can smile, huh?"

The grin instantly dropped from her face.

I shook my head at her. "Nuh-uh. Too late. I already saw it."

It crept back across her mouth, and a sense of satisfaction settled over me. Her smile was really damn similar to Kara's.

Not that Kara was going to be smiling at me anytime soon.

Without me providing any guidance, Hayley Jade found a garbage bag in the cleaning caddy I'd brought down from the clubhouse and with nimble fingers, she shook it out and circled the cabin, collecting empty beer bottles and open chip bags as she went.

I watched her for a second, wondering if I should stop her, but hell, she was doing a good job, and she was smiling for the first time since they'd arrived, so who was I to stop her?

We cleaned quietly, both of us working in the same space, me filling the silence with whatever random bullshit popped into my brain. "Did you know that the country of Australia is wider than the moon?"

Hayley Jade's eyes got big over that, and she paused in her cleaning to look at me, so I offered another useless fact. "You know shrimp? Their hearts are in their heads. Weird, huh?"

She mulled that over for a while as she brought me the bag full of trash.

"You need me to tie that up for you?"

She nodded.

I took it and twisted the end into knots. "There you go."

"Thank—"

Her eyes went huge, and she covered her mouth with her hand, terror suddenly filling her eyes.

Not wanting to make it worse, when talking clearly freaked her out, I pretended I hadn't heard. "Did you know sloths can hold their breaths longer than dolphins?"

A tiny breath of relief slipped out of her, and she carried the bag to the cabin's front porch.

I watched her small frame struggle along with the heavy bag. Her not talking wasn't normal. I didn't need to know much about kids to know that. Rebel's and Bliss's kids talked nonstop, twenty-four hours a day, seven days a week. The constant babble was endless and drove me insane.

Except Hayley Jade's silence was worse. It was unnerving.

But she'd spoken to me.

Maybe I could get her to speak some more.

By the time I had the bathroom and kitchen shining, Hayley Jade had pretty much completed clearing the living and bedroom area of trash and had wiped off the surfaces. I leaned against the wall and surveyed the room. Then held my hand out to her. "High five. You did a good job."

She grinned up at me but didn't tap her palm against mine.

I frowned at her. "You gonna leave me hanging? No high five?"

She cocked her head to one side, then shook it in confusion.

"Jesus," I muttered. "They clearly taught you how to clean but not how to high five? Well, that's fucking depressing."

She hid a giggle at my swearing.

I picked up her hand and tapped it against mine. "That's a high five. It means 'good job.'"

She beamed at me.

Well, fuck. That was about the cutest thing I'd ever seen.

"Come on. We're done here for now. Let's go back up to the main house."

She nodded, and I picked up the two black garbage bags full of trash and hauled them over my shoulder. On the way, I threw more random facts at her. "Did you know a blue whale's tongue weighs as much as a baby elephant?"

They were all useless, stupid things I'd distracted myself with when I'd been a kid who didn't want to participate in the real world. The real world sucked. Thinking about weird stuff made it suck just a little less.

Queenie and Aloha were out in front of the clubhouse when we made it back up there, and Queenie put a hand over her heart. "Lawd, baby girl. Where on earth you been? Thank God your mama fell asleep on the couch and didn't realize you were missing."

Hayley Jade ducked her head subserviently.

That bothered me.

"She wasn't missing." I tossed the bags into the dumpster at the far corner of the clubhouse. "She was with me. Weren't you, Hayley Jade?"

She nodded quickly but still didn't lift her eyes.

Queenie tried again, her voice softer this time now she wasn't panicking over the kid's whereabouts. "You want to go play with some toys? None of the other kids are here today, so you have them all to yourself."

Hayley Jade looked up at me.

I tried to decipher her expression, but I didn't know how to read kids. She wasn't making a move for the toys though, so I guessed she didn't want to play by herself.

"I'm going into town to buy some new sheets and pillows for the cabin." Kara wasn't going to be sleeping under a fucking dog blanket ever again. Nor could she be sleeping in my bed since I clearly couldn't be trusted.

She had nothing here. No clothes or underwear or toiletries. Maybe I could find some of that shit while I was at it.

I glanced over at Hayley Jade. "You want to come?"

The cute grin that spread across her face told me she did.

Queenie frowned. "Uh, I don't think that's a good idea. Kara is asleep. Fell asleep on the couch sitting up, poor thing. She's had a rough couple days."

"All the more reason for me and Hayley Jade to let her get some rest, right then, kid?"

She nodded enthusiastically.

Queenie shook her head. "You aren't putting that child on your bike, Hawk."

I glared at her, insulted. "Do I look that stupid?"

"Yes," Aloha shot back with a grin.

I flipped him the bird then looked to Hayley Jade. "Come on. Let's go." On instinct, I held a hand out to her.

Before I could think about what I was doing, her small fingers wrapped around mine. Warm and clenching my fingers tightly.

"Never in a million years did I think I'd ever see Hawk holding a little girl's hand like that," Queenie muttered to Aloha when my back was turned.

Aloha answered just as quietly. "He never had Kara's daughter to hold before now."

"I heard that," I called back. I yanked open the door to the van and hoisted Hayley Jade up into the passenger seat and clicked the seat belt across her chest.

"Then tell me he's wrong," Queenie called. "You hate Rebel's and Bliss's kids."

I didn't hate them. I just didn't care about them.

I slid into the driver's seat and glanced over at Hayley Jade.

Her hair was light, but everything else about her reminded me of Kara.

And Kara had always been real fucking hard not to care about.

Apparently, her daughter was the same.

26

HAYDEN

It only took Luca's guys about thirty minutes to mount the Sinners sign above the restaurant door, and within the next hour, they had a sticker on the glass window below.

"You like it?" Luca asked as one of his guys used a scraper to remove air bubbles. "That's your name up there."

It seriously fucking was. The sticker was huge, taking up the full length of the shop front window, my name and 'head chef' printed right there for everyone to see. I stared at Luca. "I only just signed the contracts."

Luca thumped me on the back. "Yeah, but I knew from our first conversation that you would. I had this printed a week ago. I was just waiting for you to come around before I had the guys put it on."

I hated that I'd wanted this so bad I'd been that obvious about it. But there was no denying, Luca was handing me everything I'd ever wanted on a silver platter. Though my head screamed warnings, especially after seeing his plans to turn that back room into an underground sex club, I couldn't bring myself to complain.

All I could do was grin like an idiot at my name on the front of a restaurant. A restaurant that was at least partly mine.

Pride swelled within me.

"You like it," Luca said more as a statement than a question.

"I love it," I admitted. I glanced over at him. "I need this place to be a success."

"You and me both. Ninety percent owner over here, remember? You don't make money, I don't make money. The bank will have us out in under three months if we don't have this place up and running and making good coin. You know how much I paid for this fucking building. It's good, but it didn't go cheap, so neither is the mortgage."

I nodded, the reality of banks and mortgages and payments settling on my shoulders. "We should talk more about this club idea..."

Luca grinned. "Plans are on the table there, but I've got to go check on my other businesses. Tomorrow?"

It was getting late anyway. The shops around us were all starting to close, and Luca's guys had already packed their trucks, ready to call it quits for the day.

I lingered though, not having anywhere else to go.

Like he could read my thoughts, Luca pulled a set of keys from his pocket, tied together with a piece of simple brown string. "Stay as long as you want. I'll be around until we get her on her feet, but this place is yours now. Your name is right there on the window after all."

A thrill ran through me as Luca pressed the key into my palm and I closed my fingers around it.

Mine.

This was mine, at least in some ways.

I waved off Luca and the others and went back inside, just standing there like a damn fool. The street outside was busy with people grabbing their last-minute items from the closing stores, and all I could imagine was at this time each day, we'd just be opening. People would be arriving in nice outfits, laughing and smiling with their friends as the maître d' showed them to their tables. The waiters would bring drinks on arrival and present them with fresh, modern menus. Ones where I'd carefully created every dish. Excitement bubbled up inside me, and I pored over the floor plans again.

Luca's scrawl on the rectangular room at the back, marked "sex club" drew my eye, and I sighed, but it was a little less heavy this time.

Restaurants failed all the damn time. I knew that.

This wouldn't be one. If that meant we had to supplement our income with something else, then who the hell was I to complain? Luca might have had his finger in many an illegal pie, but my brother had done his homework. Luca also ran more than one well-established, legitimate business.

If he said we needed a sex club, then maybe we needed a sex club.

As long as I didn't have to perform, then Luca could do what he wanted in the back there, and I'd keep to myself in the kitchen.

I could make snacks for people. Having an orgy surely would work up their appetite.

I sniggered to myself.

"Sinners!" someone shouted from out the front. An accompanying thumping of a fist against the clean glass window followed it. "Are you...fudging serious, Chaos?"

I glanced up and groaned.

Hawk glared at me through the glass window. With one hand, he pointed angrily at the sign, my name proudly displayed beneath it. His other held the fingers of a small girl. "Sinners!" he yelled again. "Really?"

"Hey, what do you know. You can read," I called back.

It was probably stupid to antagonize him, but I couldn't stand obnoxious people, and Hawk was the most obnoxious of them all. As proven by the way he was standing on the sidewalk, in the middle of Providence, shouting like he was a teenager having an argument with his parents.

Hawk stormed to the door, the kid trotting along behind him.

I didn't stop him from entering. I wasn't stupid enough to think he wasn't armed, but what was he going to do with his daughter right there beside him? Shoot me? I didn't think so. Even Hawk wasn't that stupid. Though I swear he acted it sometimes.

I eyed the little blond girl and then dragged my gaze back up to her father. "Didn't know you had a kid."

"I don't," he spat back just as quick.

I raised an eyebrow. "Not sure if you're aware, but there's a small child attached to your hand."

"She's not mine."

I glanced at the girl. "You're real lucky then. I wouldn't want a dad like him either."

Hawk stepped in front of her, blocking her from my sight. "Don't fuc...fudging talk to her."

I sniggered. "Fudging?"

"She's not used to people swearing."

"Definitely not your kid then."

"Like I said."

I wasn't used to seeing him in anything other than jeans and his club jacket. In sweat pants and a hoodie, his hair shorter and neater than mine, he could almost pass as a dad just out and about with his daughter.

It was a good look on him.

Awareness prickled over me, and I realized neither of us had said anything in an uncomfortably long minute.

I broke the silence before he got weird and mouthy, like he had last time. "Did you actually want something, Hawk? Or are you just going to keep staring at me the same way you did the other day?" The memory of his gaze wandering over my naked body and centering on my dick was fresh in my mind.

He snorted. "Don't flatter yourself. I wasn't staring at you."

Liar.

I raised an eyebrow. "No? You weren't checking out my..." I remembered he had a kid there and coughed around a grin. "Salami?"

"Salami? Don't flatter yourself. You mean your pig in a blanket." Hawk sniggered.

I stepped in, close enough I was in his space, just because I knew it made him uncomfortable. I was petty enough to enjoy pushing at his barely cloaked homophobia. "No problem for you to swallow it down then, huh?"

He stilled, me too close to him to see his expression, but I heard the hitch in his voice.

For the tiniest of seconds, I wondered if it was because he was thinking about what getting down on his knees for me would be like.

In the same second, surprise heat barreled through me at the thought.

But he shoved me away and leaned over the table that I had Luca's plans rolled out on.

I cringed, knowing what he'd spotted.

I'd been too busy thinking about him getting on his knees for me to remember the sex club plans were right there in plain sight.

He went nose to nose with me. We were almost identical heights and similar builds, but his eyes flashed with anger. "You're turning this place into a—"

I coughed and glanced down at the kid, staring up at us with big eyes, taking in every word.

Hawk took half a step back, reminded we weren't alone, and tried again. "You're turning this place into a... strawberry club?"

Laughter bubbled up my throat that couldn't be contained. "I'll be sure to invite you. We'll have solo strawberries, group strawberries." I eyed him suggestively. "Male-on-male strawberries is going to be a specialty, I believe. That's right up your strawberry alley, isn't it?"

But apparently Hawk had lost his sense of humor. His eyes darkened. "You know War and his family own Psychos in Saint View. That club is their livelihood."

I shrugged. "I've heard. I'm sure Psychos won't mind a bit of friendly competition though, right?"

He shook his head, no trace of any earlier amusement left. "You're playing with fire, Chaos. Starting up a rival club. Calling it Sinners. For a man who says he's not in the game anymore, sounds a whole lot like you want back in."

I didn't say anything.

Because his warning was fair.

I'd spent five years trying to get out. In the space of a week, I'd thrown myself firmly right back in.

And yet I didn't want to stop. For the first time in a long time, my blood rushed around my body. My heart beat for some other purpose than just keeping me alive.

I wanted this. I wasn't giving it up just because Hawk and War were scared of a bit of friendly competition.

"Invite will be in the mail," I promised the other man, refusing to back down.

He shook his head with something that edged on regret. "Your funeral." He looked down at the kid. "Come on, Hayley Jade."

I froze at the little girl's name. Hawk took a step away, but I grabbed his shoulder, spinning him around.

"Her name is Hayley Jade?"

Hawk opened his mouth to reply, then quickly shut it.

He didn't answer, just picked the kid up and walked to the door, like he'd realized he'd said too much.

Hayley Jade watched me over his shoulder, her big brown eyes so like her mother's I didn't need Hawk to confirm who she belonged to.

She was Kara's daughter.

The one I'd delivered on the floor of a shitty run-down house in Saint View.

The one she'd named after me, even though she wasn't mine.

Bullshit, she isn't fucking mine. She's been mine since the day I delivered her.

And so has her mother.

The thoughts hit me so hard it was like a physical blow to my gut, a punch I hadn't seen coming.

But I should have.

Kara was the reason I hadn't touched a woman in five years.

I rushed to the door. "Is Kara back?"

Hawk kept on walking toward a white van parked farther down the street.

"Hawk!" I shouted.

He yanked open the passenger side and put the little girl down in the seat before shutting the door.

He owed me nothing, but I had to fucking know. "Hawk! Does she even know I'm alive?"

He turned and glared at me. "She's married. And that kid ain't your daughter, even if she was named for you. You're too late, Chaos." His voice dropped to something sadder. "We were all too fucking late."

He didn't even give me a chance to question what that meant before he got into the van and the engine roared to life.

I watched him drive away but refused to heed his warnings.

I wasn't too late. Everything I had ever wanted was falling into place.

All I needed to have everything was that little girl.

And her mother.

27

KARA

An ambulance siren whirred in my head. The sky around us black, but red-and-blue lights reflecting off the dark, wet road outside.

Pain throbbed through my body. Every inch of me tender and sore from birthing my sweet girl just days before.

But in the front of the ambulance, her father sat behind the wheel. His face twisted into pure malice. A gun aimed at the man in the passenger seat.

Boom.

The crack of the gunshot splintered my ears, and the tiny baby in my arms screamed until her tiny face was scarlet.

It matched the blood spreading across the man's chest.

"No!" I screamed, lunging forward but unable to get to him.

He looked back at me. He wasn't supposed to be a good man. He'd done bad things. Things that would send him straight to Hell.

And yet he'd been kind. Sweet. He'd held my hand when I'd wanted to give up and convinced me to try again.

He was the only reason I was alive. The only reason my daughter was breathing and in my arms.

I was the reason he was dead.

I woke up with a start, drenched in sweat. "Hayden," I mumbled around the lump in my throat.

Queenie glanced over at me, a chunky romance hardback in her hands. "What was that, sugar?"

I shook my head, blinking a few times and trying to orient myself. My heart pounded with adrenaline from the dream I'd had so many times in the past five years. That day playing out in my nightmares in horrifying detail, so I could never forget it.

"Nothing." I scrubbed a hand over my face, the exhaustion I'd felt in the dream seemingly following me into the real world as well. The room was so busy I wondered how I'd managed to sleep through it. Besides Queenie and her book, Ice and the other prospects sat around a round table playing cards. Aloha and a man they called Crow sat at the bar, nursing beers while they chatted. Kiki and Amber had a phone out and were dancing in front of it to tinny music from the speakers, laughing when one of them got a step wrong, and then starting over.

Hayley Jade was nowhere to be seen.

I'd fallen asleep and had no idea where my child was.

Panic flooded my system. "Where's—"

Queenie reached over and put a hand on my knee. "She's fine. She's with Hawk."

Hawk's name sent a flush of heat through me before Queenie's words even registered.

"Where are they?"

Queenie frowned. "He took her into town."

"What!" I shook my head, pushing to my feet. Terror gripped me, the thought of Josiah's sharp-nailed fingers getting a grip on my daughter too much to bear. I knew he was out there, just waiting and watching for his moment to take her from me.

Again.

Men always took her.

First her father, not long after that night in the ambulance.

Then Josiah.

Now Hawk.

"No!" I yelled, the terror bubbling up my throat because it had nowhere else to go and I couldn't contain it a second longer. "No! She can't go into to town. Josiah will—"

"Josiah will meet his so-called fucking God if I ever get the displeasure of seeing his ugly face," Hawk said from the doorway. He dumped an armful of shopping bags on the floor and leaned on the doorframe, his gaze immediately latching on to mine.

I ran to him, my chest so tight it hurt. "Where is she?" Leftover panic from my dream ripped its way through my body. All I could see was Caleb's black eyes the night he'd killed Hayden. Josiah's evil laugh while he made plans to auction off my daughter to the highest bidder.

I dug my fingers into Hawk's shirt and tore at the fabric. "Where is she, Hawk? Where the hell is my daughter? You can't take her from me! Not again! Not again!"

I couldn't breathe. I clutched at my throat, clawing at my skin, desperate for air when the room had none. "Please!" I begged him. "Please, give her back."

Hawk stared at me in shock, his big body frozen as he

took in my breakdown and the pathetic, sniveling mess I was. He reached for me, but his touch burned like fire, and I cried out, flinching away from him.

His voice remained calm. "You're having a panic attack."

I shook my head, my lungs screaming for air.

He pointed down his leg. "Breathe, Kara. She's right here."

Hayley Jade peeked out from behind his legs, her eyes huge with fright, a new purple-and-pink unicorn stuffie clutched in her arms.

My legs gave out, and I sank to my knees in relief, tears pricking at the backs of my eyes. I held my arms out for her, needing to touch her soft skin and assure myself she was really there.

She stood there frozen, her face pointed at the floor and her entire body trembling.

My heart broke into a million pieces.

She was so scared of me.

I didn't know how to be her mother. That much was clear. What child was scared of their own parent?

Queenie frowned. "Kara..."

She read the desperate plea for help in my expression and sighed, putting her book down and standing. She moved across the room to Hayley Jade's side and picked her up.

Hayley Jade went willingly, laying her head down on Queenie's shoulder much like she had the night before.

Like Queenie's arms were the only safe spot she had.

Tears spilled down my cheeks again as Queenie carried my trembling daughter from the room. Queenie glanced back at me at the last second and covered Hayley

Jade's ears. "You two need to sort your shit out." She glared at Hawk. "I told you not to take her without Kara's permission, but do you ever listen to anyone? No, you most certainly do not."

I waited for Hawk to snap back at her, because I'd never heard him take a dressing down well.

But he didn't say a word.

Queenie's gaze slid to mine. "You're her mother. I know you don't feel like it right now, but you are, and she needs you."

She turned and moved down the hall, shutting the two of them into her bedroom once more. The door shut with a soft snick, but I flinched as if she'd slammed it in my face.

I couldn't get up. The entire room had gone quiet, all eyes watching us, but I couldn't bring myself to stand. I had nothing left in me to propel me to my feet.

All I had was sadness, grief, and pure fear.

This wasn't the life I'd wanted. But I couldn't even imagine one that included happiness. Not with Alice's body lying cold in the morgue. Not with Josiah out there somewhere, just lurking in the shadows, waiting for his time to bring me home.

Not with Hayley Jade not talking and so scared of me she preferred anyone else.

"Get up," Hawk said quietly.

I couldn't. My body was entirely boneless, my muscles all refusing to work.

"Get up, Kara," he said again. He reached down and lifted my chin so I was forced to look into his green eyes.

I knew he was right. I couldn't just sit there on the

floor. I pushed to my feet, but he still towered over me from his six-foot-plus vantage point.

He picked up his shopping, his eyes flaming. "Come with me."

I didn't dare disobey or complain. I'd already disrespected him so badly by yelling at him in front of his entire clubhouse. I followed him out into early evening, the sun slipping beneath the horizon but the last light rays of the day giving us enough to see the path through the trees.

I walked with my head down, not bothering to place my feet as carefully on the uneven path as I would normally because what did it even matter if I twisted my ankle and fell? I deserved whatever pain and punishment came my way.

I followed him to a cabin in the woods and straight up the stairs, not questioning why he'd brought me here.

That wasn't my place.

Only knowing that I'd spoken out of turn. That I'd yelled at him in front of everyone and I would now be punished for the disrespect I'd shown him.

He might not have been my husband, but he was the vice president of this club. He demanded respect, and while I lived here, I owed him that. I knew my place.

He opened the door, dumping the bags by the couch, and I followed him inside.

He whirled on me the second I closed the door behind me. "What the fuck was all of that?"

I didn't say anything. Trying to explain myself only ever made Josiah angrier. It was better to just be quiet.

Quiet as the church mouse Hawk had said I was.

His body was tense with anger. "Kara, I would never

hurt a kid! Or let anyone else hurt her! What kind of fucking monster do you think I am?"

A tremble ran down my spine at his harsh, sharp words.

He paced up and down the cabin, running his hands through the short lengths of his hair. He stopped abruptly. "Look, Queenie told me not to take her. But fuck, she was smiling and happy and she wanted to come. You were sleeping. I told Queenie to tell you where she was when you woke up so you wouldn't worry. Maybe it was a bad idea. But she held my hand the entire fucking time we were out. She was safe, Kara. If Josiah had tried anything I would have taken him to his grave before he could lay a finger on her."

I'd insulted him. That much was clear. Questioned his manhood. His ability to protect his flock. Josiah would have never stood for that sort of behavior. I didn't blame Hawk for not accepting it either.

"Are you seriously just going to say nothing?" he asked.

"I'm sorry," I mumbled.

He stared at me, anger flickering behind his eyes. "Why the hell are *you* sorry?"

One night at dinner I'd questioned Josiah when he'd said that Hayley Jade would need to get her ears pierced because one day her husband would want her to be pretty.

We'd been newly married. It had only been me and him at that time, wives number two, three, and four not yet in the picture. He'd sat there across the table from me and let me go on and on about how she should have the right to choose what she does with her own body.

I'd been too stupid to see the darkening in his eyes. The growing fury that I dared to disagree with him.

He'd told me to go to my room and assume the position so he could remind me who was the man and who was the woman.

Who got to have opinions and who didn't.

Hawk was powerful. He was the VP of this club, and he could so easily throw me back out on the streets.

Josiah existed beyond the gates. Hiding in the darkness. Just waiting for me to mess this up so he could bring me home and sell my daughter.

I couldn't let that happen.

Slowly, I toed off my shoes.

Then with my eyes glued to Hawk's, I reached beneath my skirt and lowered my panties.

Hawk hissed at the sight of the garment screwed up in my fingers. "What the hell are you doing?"

On shaky legs, I crossed the small cabin to the only bedroom. Beyond the open doorway, a king-sized bed sat on the other side, bare of sheets.

That gave me pause for a moment, but Josiah had always wanted me on the bed, and I didn't know what else to do. I crawled across it, so I was kneeling on all fours, my knees and hands digging into the soft mattress.

"I said it once, and now I'm begging you to fucking answer," Hawk growled from behind me. "What the fuck are you doing?"

"Apologizing," I said quietly. "I'm sorry I questioned you. I know that isn't a woman's place." I lowered my head to the mattress, behind still raised in the air.

I buried my face in my arm, and with the other, reached back to lift my skirt for him.

Shame and humiliation burned my face, but Josiah hated when my skirts got in the way. He never wanted me fully naked though, because all the weight I'd put on repulsed him.

Hawk made a strangled noise from behind me. "What the actual fuck, Kara?"

I twisted to look at him.

At his horrified expression, I quickly turned around and covered myself up. I hunched in on myself, instantly realizing I'd done the wrong thing. Again.

"I'm sorry," I whispered, shameful tears pricking the backs of my eyes.

The mattress groaned as Hawk put one knee on the edge of it and grasped my chin. "Stop fucking saying that! I'm the one who needs to apologize to you! And not just for taking Hayley Jade. Queenie was right about that, it was stupid, and I shouldn't have taken her without asking you."

I shook my head quickly. "A man doesn't need to ask a woman's permission..."

The growl that came deep in his chest was so feral it stopped my words dead.

"Is that what all of this was about? You do something wrong, and I don't even have to ask permission to..." The color drained out of his face at the realization before it morphed into a blind fury. "I'm going to kill that Josiah fucker. Rip him limb from limb."

I shook my head. "It's not my place to question a man."

He let out an angry breath. "That's what happened this morning in my bed, then? You didn't say no because he made you think you weren't allowed to?"

A flush of heat rushed through me at the memory of what we'd done in his bed. His fingers rubbing over my sensitive places. The moisture slicking between my legs. His erection hard and thick, nudging my entrance, seeking its place deep inside me.

I couldn't lie. Lying would only bring punishment. If not from Hawk or Josiah, then from the Lord himself. "No," I said in a tiny voice, barely able to force the word from between my traitorous lips.

I was a married woman and a daughter of the Lord. Hawk was not part of His flock. The demons on the gate proved that.

"Kara, I was a damn breath away from plunging my cock inside you. Why the hell didn't you say no?" Hawk sounded like he was in physical pain.

But so was I. I didn't want to lie. But I didn't want to admit the truth either.

"I didn't want to say no," I finally whispered, swallowing hard.

Hawk froze. "What?"

The embarrassment and shame ate me alive. I couldn't stand to be in the room a second longer. "I should go." I needed to leave before I made a fool out of myself by crying.

But Hawk slowly shook his head. "No, Little Mouse. There's no fucking way you're dropping a bomb like that and then walking out of here. I've felt like a piece of shit all day, cleaning this fucking cabin from top to bottom as a penance for what I almost did to you, shopping at all these women's stores where I was sorely out of place, and then you open those sweet fucking lips of yours and tell me you didn't want to say no?"

"I'm married," I murmured, no idea how else to explain my behavior.

"Like I fucking care." He moved up the bed, and I scuttled backward until my spine hit the headboard. "Like I care about anything other than one, simple question."

We were eye to eye. His warm breath coasting over my lips. His gaze dropped to my mouth and stayed there for an agonizingly long second before finally drawing back up.

"What?" It was almost more of a breath than a word, but suddenly it was the only sound I could make.

"I need to know if you didn't say no because you just wanted to please me. Or did you not say no because you liked what I was doing to you?"

I should have denied it. Should have told him that the Lord punished those who went outside their marriage for personal gratification.

And yet, Hawk's expression demanded truth. He was so close, he was all I could see. And every part of me was burning with a fire I didn't know myself capable of.

"Tell me the truth, Little Mouse. I'll know if you're lying. Did. You. Like it?"

He pushed me back on the unmade bed, so I was laid out flat on my back. With his knees either side of my thighs and his weight braced on his arms, he hovered over me. Not touching me, though my skin tingled with awareness at how close he was.

Tingled with the memory of what he'd felt like nestled in behind me, his dick pressing between my legs, searching for an entrance while his fingers worked my clit in a maddening rhythm.

Slowly, he lowered himself on top of me, giving me every opportunity to stop him.

Just like that morning, I said nothing.

He was hard behind his gray sweatpants. He rubbed his erection against my skirt, letting me feel every inch of him though the fabric kept us apart. Behind the thin T-shirt, my nipples went hard from the friction of his chest on mine.

I gave up a tiny mewling sound that he breathed in like it was oxygen.

His nose ran the length of my neck and up to my ear. His lips brushed my cheeks when he whispered, "You did nothing wrong. You have nothing to apologize for. I was the one who was out of line. It's me who needs to apologize. But, Kara?" His mouth was on my neck. "I've never been much good at words."

His lips caught the sensitive spot beneath my ear, and he sucked my skin in a way that sent a sharp ripple of pleasure through me, so fast and unexpected I gasped at his touch.

"But I need yours. I need you to tell me you want me to put my fingers back where they were this morning."

He moved his hand between us and touched his fingers to the sensitive spot at the top of my slit. I moaned, pressing back against his touch, increasing the friction, chasing the memory of the feeling he'd given me earlier.

He rubbed me through my clothes, murmuring his approval when my legs dropped open and he fit himself in between. "Words, Kara. Your body is giving me all green flags, but that isn't enough. I need to know your head wants me as much as your sweet, wet pussy does. You're wet for me, aren't you, Little Mouse?"

"Yes," I moaned, closing my eyes and jerking my hips with his touch, begging for more.

"Yes I can make you come? Or yes you're wet for me?"

The feeling rocketing through my body took hold of my tongue. "Yes to both."

A long time ago, I'd heard Rebel and her friends talk about orgasms. About how good "coming" felt. It wasn't something I'd ever thought about though.

Not until Hawk was on top of me, fully clothed, and saying things that would surely get us both sent straight to Hell.

In the moment, I knew I didn't care. His touch was the first nice thing I'd felt in so very long. It had the added bonus of focusing my attention down to that one point where he touched me. It was hard to think of anything else when his fingers were working my clit.

Hawk lifted my skirt, settling it around my hips and baring my naked flesh beneath.

He didn't give me a chance to second-guess myself though. I let out a shout of ecstasy as his fingertips slid over my clit and then lower to the silky opening below.

"So fucking wet for me, Little Mouse. You're such a good girl. I knew you would be. Tell me you want my fingers inside your sweet pussy."

"Yes," I groaned, pleading for more than what he'd given me so far. The feeling building inside was the same one I'd had this morning, the same one that had my breasts desperate and needy, aching to be touched.

Like he could read my mind, he issued his next demand. "Shirt off, Little Mouse. Bra too. I need to see those fucking tits. I've been thinking about them since you watched me come for you."

I'd never heard a man talk like this. Never imagined I would like it.

But my body responded to every word. Every command. I didn't know what I was doing, but his demands gave me guidance when I didn't know what I needed. I pulled my shirt off, but he didn't even give me a chance to do the same to my bra. He yanked the strap roughly down one shoulder and flipped the cup, letting one breast tumble free.

That was good enough.

He lowered his head, fitting his mouth over my nipple and sucked hard.

"Oh!" I gasped, fingers clutching the back of his head absentmindedly as he tongued the tip of my breast into a hardened, wet peak for his mouth.

At the same time, his finger pressed inside me and up against my inner walls.

My skirt around my middle covered my fat rolls, and I was grateful. It was bad enough he could see the cellulite on my thighs, but maybe it was dark enough in this room that he hadn't noticed. Neither of us had turned a light on, and the sun had well and truly set since we'd been in here.

He pushed a second finger up inside me and rubbed his thumb over my clit. I cried out again, forgetting every concern because none could exist when he touched me like this.

"I need..." I muttered, except I didn't know what I needed. Him. More. This feeling to never end because inside it, everything felt good. Nothing bad could touch me, as long as he just kept his fingers and tongue moving.

"You need to come, Little Mouse. You're drowning my fingers."

That didn't seem like a good thing, and yet he said it in a way that gave me goosebumps. That made me want to be even wetter, just because he seemed to like it.

"He ever make you come, Mouse? He ever touch you like this?" Hawk practically purred.

I shook my head, grasping his shoulders, his T-shirt bunching in my fists. "No."

Hawk chuckled into my breast, teasing the other from my bra. "You ever touch yourself like this?"

I gasped, "Of course not!"

Such things were not allowed. It let the Devil in.

Though apparently that wasn't something I could consider when it was Hawk touching me.

He groaned into my breasts, his tongue tracing patterns around the swells and dipping in between. "So fucking soft. Come for me."

He dropped his head down my body, bypassing the rolled-up skirt and licked between my legs.

My eyes flew open at the sensation, and my internal muscles clamped down hard. I shouted in surprise at the feel of him inside me, at him being there to stroke me from the inside out in a way that had my eyes rolling back. His tongue assaulted my clit, and some voice in the back of my mind said it was dirty and a sin, but I was completely helpless to make him stop.

I just wanted more.

My hips moved of their own accord, writhing against his face, his fingers buried so deep within my folds. I rode his fingers shamelessly, pleasure everywhere he touched and everywhere he didn't.

The feeling slowly began to fade, and I stared at the ceiling, trying to catch my breath, my head spinning with dizzying thoughts I could barely make sense of.

I untangled my fingers from the short lengths of his hair, realizing I'd been twisting it in a way that had to have hurt him. Absentmindedly, because my head was still halfway between earth and the clouds, I changed the touch, stroking my fingers across his scalp instead, soothing the area I had to have damaged.

My chest heaved as I tried to catch my breath.

I suddenly understood why Rebel and her friends had talked so favorably about orgasms. That had been...new.

Exciting.

So very different from anything I'd ever experienced that tears pricked behind my eyes.

Hawk pulled his fingers from inside me and sat back on his knees. His fingers glistened with my arousal, and I flushed hot, embarrassed at the sight.

"Look at me, Little Mouse. Watch me taste you."

He slid all three fingers into his mouth, sucking them clean. His grin did strange things to my insides.

I realized I was still bared to him and clutched at my clothes to cover myself up, but he caught my wrists and gently pushed them away.

Then he pulled down my skirt and flipped the cups of my bra back into place. He got up off the bed, his erection still evident through his sweats, but he didn't mention it. From the floor he grabbed my T-shirt and pulled it on over my head for me, waiting while I put my arms through the appropriate holes, and then dragged it down to cover my chest.

Then he dropped to his knees at my feet. "You need your panties back on before you can go back up to the clubhouse. I can't be thinking about you up there, pantyless in front of all my brothers." He held them out for me. "Step in."

I'd never had someone take care of me the way he was. I'd only been with two men, Caleb—Hayley Jade's biological father—and Josiah. Neither had so much as looked at me after they were done, let alone helped me to get dressed again.

And Hawk wasn't even...done.

I glanced down at his sweats. "You... You didn't..."

"No. I didn't."

"I can..."

He shook his head. "I owed you that orgasm, Little Mouse. That was my way of saying sorry." He crossed his arms over his broad chest, a smile pulling at his perfect mouth. "Now I only owe you one more."

I was so self-conscious I wanted to die. "You don't owe me anything. Your apology is accepted."

He raised an eyebrow. "Good, I'm off the hook for the apology orgasm then. But I came just from watching you in my bedroom. You didn't. That doesn't sit right with me. I don't want you ever leaving my room without coming, you hear me? That'll never happen again."

I shook my head, so flustered by this man I couldn't even look at him. Had he just *licked* between my legs? With his tongue? The horror of that was slowly sinking through the afterglow of how good it had felt. "We can't... I can't do that again."

He winked. "Sure you can. All you have to do is come to my room, and I'll know. You don't even have to ask."

"I won't do that," I said in a hurry. "I'm married."

Hawk laughed like my protests were all futile. "You'll be on my cock by the end of the week. I'll have you naked, tits in my face, your pussy stretched around my dick, taking you slow and then fucking you hard before the weekend rolls around."

My mouth dropped open.

He reached over and closed it for me. "You'll see." He walked to the door with the confidence of a man who had never been turned down in his life. He pointed to the bags he'd bought while he was out with Hayley Jade. "I bought new sheets, blankets, pillows. A bunch of other shit Hayley Jade and I thought you might like. Candles or whatever. Use them."

He left the cabin, the front porch boards groaning beneath his weight as he jogged down the stairs and disappeared into the evening light.

I watched him go and then sank to my knees, praying to the Lord to forgive my sins.

And to grant me the willpower to resist making them all over again.

28

KARA

I spent the next few days hiding in my cabin. I washed the sheets Hawk and Hayley Jade had bought, marveling over how soft and luxurious they were. The bags had a boutique stamp on them from a shop with a Providence address. All I could think about was Hawk, in his dirty jeans and leather jacket and motorcycle boots, picking out these nice, expensive things for me.

Things I definitely didn't deserve.

But they were so beautiful it was hard not to want them.

I convinced myself it was okay to take them because eventually Hayley Jade would move down here with me, and she could be the one to enjoy the high-thread-count sheets and the candle that made the cabin smell like freshly baked cookies.

I wanted her here so badly I could barely breathe.

But she was still sleeping on a cot in Queenie and Aloha's room. She couldn't do that forever though. At some point, she was going to have to come back here, and when she did, I wanted to be ready.

I was also avoiding Hawk.

Or more accurately, avoiding his bedroom and the things he'd promised would happen if I went in there.

I had to close my eyes and clench my thighs together every time I thought about what he'd done to me on that bed. It sent goosebumps spreading across my skin every time I entered the bedroom.

But if I was being honest, I liked it.

I liked remembering the way he'd smelled. The way his body had felt, pressed on mine. The way his tongue had…

I swallowed thickly as Rebel snapped her fingers in front of my face. "Earth to Kara. Did you hear what I said?"

I blinked, focusing on my sister. She'd come over earlier, only Remi with her, the other kids at home with one of the guys. I shook my head. "Sorry, no. I got distracted."

Rebel twisted on the front porch swing, hooking one leg up onto the seat so she could face me. "I asked how Hayley Jade was doing? Any changes?"

I stared out at my daughter following her younger cousin around, Remi leading in a game she'd made up that seemed to involve searching for fairies in the shrubs. The only reason Hayley Jade had come down to the cabin was because Rebel and Remi were here. Rebel had herded both girls down to me after she realized Hayley Jade was up at the clubhouse and I was down here alone.

I lifted a shoulder to answer my sister's question. "No, not really. Queenie says she's eating normally, but she still won't talk." I swallowed hard, remembering the last day I'd heard her voice.

I so desperately wanted to hear it again.

Rebel squeezed my leg. "There's a clinic at the hospital. It's free. I thought maybe we should take Hayley Jade? Just get her checked out, you know?" She grimaced at me. "Please just ignore me if I'm overstepping. But it's been on my mind. As is getting her into school. She should really be going."

My eyes went wide. "She can't. They'd find her and take her and I'd never see her again."

Rebel reluctantly nodded. "Homeschool then. You could teach her."

My heart sank. "She won't even sit in the same room as me. How am I going to teach her anything when she's terrified of me?"

Rebel sighed and watched the two girls playing. "You're right. She's only five. Making sure she's okay mentally and physically is more important than anything else right now."

I put a finger to my mouth and chewed on the nail. "I do think she needs to see a doctor."

Rebel nodded. "The clinic doesn't require ID or insurance. I checked. There'll be no record of either of you there. It'll be safe. But you still can't go alone. Fang or one of the other guys will take you and stay with you until it's time to bring you back."

I didn't know how to tell her that wasn't even my biggest worry. But that actually getting Hayley Jade there was.

I didn't think I could take another round of her screaming and crying and fighting to get away from me.

She'd go with Queenie, but I really wanted to be the one who took her. And Queenie couldn't protect her.

Hawk could. She'd trusted Hawk enough to let him take her into town once. She was still carrying around the stuffie he'd bought her while they were out, and I hadn't missed the way she took notice of everything he said.

Which was probably not great because the man swore like a drunken sailor.

But at least she wasn't scared of him.

That was all that mattered in getting her to a doctor.

I cleared my throat. "It's okay. I know Fang is busy. I'll ask Hawk to take us."

Rebel paused. "Seriously? Hawk?" She screwed up her face in disgust.

"Don't do that," I said quickly.

Her expression was still twisted in dislike. "Do what?"

I pointed at her expression. "You make faces every time his name comes up in conversation."

"Yeah, because he's the worst." She drew her knee up to her chest and wrapped her arms around it. "He's such a pig."

"He's not the worst," I said quietly. "We both know that's not true."

Hawk might have been obnoxious and sarcastic and even self-centered, but there were men who did much worse things than that.

He was not the worst.

She glanced over at me and sighed. "Yes. We do. Sorry. But I can't see Hawk agreeing unless War makes him."

She was probably right. "Hayley Jade likes him. Maybe if I ask him nicely…"

"Uncle Hawk!" Remi shouted, stopping in the middle of her game.

Hayley Jade stopped playing as well, and to my surprise, waved her little hand at the figure coming along the path.

Rebel swore softly under her breath. "Well, damn. She does like him. That's the first time I've seen her wave to anyone since you two got here."

I'd stopped listening. I was too busy staring at the man, my heart pounding louder with every step closer he took. His gaze sought mine and held it, and the heat threatened to consume me.

His eyes were so green they were all I could think about. His lips were so perfectly shaped and had fit over my clit so well it was like I could feel them there right now.

His mouth quirked up like he knew exactly what I was thinking about.

Because he was thinking about it too.

Rebel cleared her throat in a way that somehow sounded disapproving. "Your kid has poor taste in men, Kara. Please don't tell me it's hereditary."

I snapped my head in her direction. "What?"

Why on earth had that come out kind of breathless? Why did my skin suddenly feel so hot it could peel off?

She gripped my arm, her eyes widening in shock. "You like him!"

I swatted at her, panic creeping up my throat that she would realize the truth in her words. That she could somehow sense what I'd let him do to me in the bedroom just behind us. "Stop it!" I hissed. "I'm married."

Rebel narrowed her gaze. "You're married to a

monster. Nobody around here is going to judge you for not honoring wedding vows you were forced into making."

I didn't want to talk about it. I wasn't like Rebel and Bliss who could talk about sex and orgasms like they were chatting about the weather.

The only person I wanted to talk about orgasms with was the man walking up my front steps and leaning on my porch railing like he owned the place.

Rebel glowered at him. "Look who showed up to wreck the day. Go away."

"Nope." He popped the P, just to piss her off. "It's Kara's place, and she likes me. Isn't that what you just said?"

I glared at my sister, mortified Hawk had heard her.

She grimaced. "Oops."

He leaned in, his lips to my ear so only I could hear. "Don't worry, Little Mouse. Your sweet, wet pussy and the way you came on my fingers told me exactly how much you like me. Rebel's big mouth didn't tell me anything I didn't already know."

I wanted the ground beneath the porch to open up so I could throw myself into it.

Hawk didn't seem affected by it at all though. He straightened and jerked his head toward the main clubhouse. "Cops are here searching for the two of you. Can you come up? I don't want them coming down here, knowing which cabin you're staying in. Better that no one other than club members know that."

My heart rate increased again, but this time it wasn't because of the ridiculously attractive man waiting on me.

I stood, nodding my thanks to Hawk as I passed him.

Rebel followed me, though I doubt she acknowledged Hawk the way I had. She paused at the bottom of the steps. "Girls? We need to go back up to the main house, okay? There's some police officers up there that Mommy and Aunty need to go talk to."

Remi jogged over to her mother's side and grinned. "We found five fairies!"

"Five?" Rebel asked. "That's amazing!"

"I called one Pix. Like Daddy calls you."

Rebel grinned at her daughter and ruffled her hair. "That's very sweet, kiddo. What are the other ones called?"

"Madden, Wolf, and Lavender."

Rebel chuckled. "Well, I'm sure your brothers and sister will all be pleased to have fairies named after them. You said five, though, and that's only four. Did you ask Hayley Jade if she wanted to name the last one?"

Remi looked over at Hayley Jade, who shot a quick glance at Hawk.

Remi dissolved into giggles like Hayley Jade had just said the funniest thing ever. "She wants to call the last fairy Hawk," Remi announced.

Hawk stopped and turned back, an eyebrow raised.

Rebel glanced at me, and we both looked down at Hayley Jade, who was watching for Hawk's reaction with bated breath.

I didn't know how Remi had worked out what Hayley Jade had wanted without a single verbal word spoken between the two of them, but it was clear she'd interpreted Hayley Jade's meaning correctly.

I was very scared Hawk was not going to deal well with having a fairy named after him.

"A fairy named Hawk, huh, Hay Jay?" he asked slowly. "You want to name the dainty little fairy after me?"

Hayley Jade nodded.

Hawk's grin widened. "Best fairy name ever."

The expression on Hayley Jade's rounded face was priceless. Her grin widened until it matched his. He took a few steps back toward the girls then he broke into a run, scooping the two of them up beneath his arms and spinning them around in circles while they squealed and giggled. "Fairies gotta fly!"

The two girls reached their arms out and kicked their legs in the air, their laughter contagious as Hawk flew them up the path to the clubhouse, where two police cars sat in the parking lot.

Rebel shook her head, watching them go. "Who was that, and what have they done with the real Hawk? He's never paid Remi any attention, let alone flown her up the path so she could be a fairy."

I smiled softly to myself. "I told you he's not the worst."

Rebel let out a soft sigh. "Or maybe he's even worse than I thought. Because if he makes you fall for him and then he breaks your heart—"

"Stop saying things like that. It's a sin." What had happened between Hawk and I wasn't going to happen again. There wasn't going to be any opportunity to break my heart because I couldn't have feelings for someone while I was married to someone else.

Rebel shook her head slowly. "I hope you don't truly believe that, little sister. Because from the look on your face, you're already halfway gone."

29

KARA

Even without uniforms on, the police were so out of place in the Slayers' clubhouse. The rumpled suits made from cheap material weren't the only giveaway. It was the uncomfortable glances at the club members lingering around the room.

The men pretended to have a reason to be there, busying their hands by playing pool or reading magazines. But they were all terrible actors.

They were there for War, who sat across the table from the cops, his arms folded over his solid chest, his gaze narrowed on the two men and their female colleague. He glanced up when we entered and waved us over. "Rebel. Kara. The detectives here would like a word."

Rebel twisted her neck to one side, cracking her neck. "This should be good," she muttered, sliding down into the seat beside War and glaring at the trio across the table.

I knew there was no love lost between my sister and the police after what she'd been through with her mother's murder. War's expression made it clear he was about as interested in being at this little tea party as he was in waxing his legs. A mug of coffee sat in front of him, but he hadn't touched it.

I took the seat next to Rebel.

A second later, Hawk slid into the seat on my other side.

I searched for Hayley Jade. "Where's—"

"Kiki and Amber are playing Barbies with the two girls outside." He leaned forward, resting his elbows on the table and eyeing the cops as distrustfully as War and Rebel were. "Figured they didn't need to hear whatever rubbish these jerks have brought here."

The female detective sighed. "We aren't here to start anything."

War raised an eyebrow. "Really? So I don't need to go call my lawyer?"

The woman shook her head. "No, you really don't. This isn't an interview. If we had wanted to do that, we would have had Kara and Rebel brought into the station. Instead, we came here. Are we good?"

Hawk gave a rumble under his breath. He didn't like that they were here.

But I was glad they'd come. Rebel had called the police station a few times, trying to get information about what was happening with Alice, but each time she'd been told it was too early for them to give out any information, and we just needed to wait until the detectives had made their initial round of inquiries.

It had been days without any news, and I was desperate for information.

"Did you arrest them?" I asked, too impatient to wait for whatever they were going to say.

The female cop cocked her head to one side quizzically. "Which 'them' are you referring to?"

Rebel kicked me beneath the table, a warning to be quiet, I assumed.

But I didn't care. I need to know. "Josiah Turnbull."

The woman stared down at her notes. "Leader of the Ethereal Eden group, right? Formerly known as Ridgemont Homestead. Where Alice lived?"

I nodded quickly.

The woman shook her head. "He has an alibi. As does every other member of the group."

My mouth dropped open. "They're lying. They came after us when we ran. I know they did. They wouldn't just let us leave with no repercussions."

One of the male cops raised an eyebrow. "They say you all left of your own free will. That nobody tried to stop you."

"They're full of shit," Rebel argued. "She was terrified when she came to my place that night. They were sure they were being followed by Josiah and his posse."

"Did they actually say you couldn't leave, Kara?" the female detective asked. "Did you see any of them following you?"

I opened my mouth to answer but shut it abruptly, not sure that in five years, Josiah had ever actually said the words, "I forbid you to leave." I racked my brain, but it was hard to remember. My days after Hayley Jade had been taken from me were so full of sadness and grief, beatings, and abuse, that it was all a blur.

Could I have left?

But I instantly knew the answer was no.

Even if he'd never come right out and said it, our marriage vows bound me to Josiah. He'd cut me off from my family, he'd made me weak and reliant on him. Even if he'd left the gates wide open, there was always an unspoken threat, that I was his, and he'd come for me if I ever tried to walk away.

That wasn't all in my head, even if he'd never said the words out loud.

His actions spoke louder than his words ever had.

But I had to tell the police the truth. "I didn't see any of them following us."

"So you have no proof Josiah or any of his colleagues were in Saint View the night Alice was murdered?"

Reluctantly, I shook my head.

Except I knew in my heart they were. I knew with every fiber of my being that Josiah hadn't just watched us drive away, shrugged, and decided to carry on with his life.

That wasn't the sort of man he was.

I'd wronged him, and there would be punishment for it. Josiah never left a sin to go unpunished. My chest tightened at the memory of all the punishments I'd received from him. My leg bounced uncontrollably beneath the table, adrenaline flooding my system at the memories.

The room felt too small. I wanted to get up and run. Or stand and scream. But I couldn't do either. So I concentrated all that feeling into my leg instead.

The female detective jotted something down on her pad. "Good. Because that checks out with their alibis as well as some other information that has come to light about Alice's death."

"What information would that be?" Hawk asked the cops. Beneath the table, his hand came to rest on my leg.

I sucked in a breath at his touch, the heavy weight pinning my leg so it stilled.

The male detective cleared his throat. "That's what we came here to discuss. We have other persons of interest in this case."

"Who?" Rebel demanded.

The detective folded his hands on top of his paperwork and directed his attention to my sister. "Kyle, the young man who left with Alice and Kara for one. We haven't been able to locate him."

"Kyle?" Rebel asked. "That kid was so in love with Alice, I could see it from the moment he stepped foot out of the car." She looked at me. "Do you think he had it in him? He seemed like a nice kid."

"Unrequited love is often a motive for murder," the female cop explained. "The boy's parents told us he'd been quite infatuated with your sister for some time. That she'd been found in his room a few times."

I shook my head. "No. I don't believe that."

"They've said she was quite promiscuous. They believe she lured him away from their community."

"What?" I shouted. "That isn't true! We had to leave. Kyle helped us. Alice never forced him to do anything. How could she? She had nothing! Women aren't allowed anything of their own."

The detective looked up at me. "We'll get to the

bottom of that when Kyle is located. It's not something you need to worry about. We just wanted you to know we don't believe it was anyone from the Ethereal Eden commune, and they've assured us they have no interest in where you are or what you're doing. The message from Josiah was..." She flipped open her notebook once more to read from the scrawl written across one page. "The Lord has many paths to His kingdom, and Kara is on her own journey. We wish her all the best on her spiritual quest."

War groaned and rolled his eyes. "Excuse me while I choke on that bullshit."

Rebel argued with the cops, questioning where they'd searched for Kyle and how they could have no leads on a kid who had no money and no resources to survive in the world by himself. "Josiah and his cult of freaks have to be hiding him. You do know that, right? Josiah is probably the one who sent him with Alice and Kara in the first place! What if that was his plan all along? For Kyle to stay with Alice just long enough for him to report back to Josiah and—"

"Ms. Kemp," the female detective interrupted. "Like I said, we'll explore all those possibilities when Kyle is found."

Rebel kept arguing, as was her nature. She was a dog with a bone when it came to the people she loved.

Hawk kept rubbing my thigh. His touch was all I could concentrate on. It was the only thing that focused me long enough to consider the words the detective had actually said. "Persons," I said quietly.

Everyone paused mid argument and stared at me.

Hawk squeezed my leg. I wasn't sure if he meant it as

a sign of encouragement, but I took it as one and cleared my throat. "You said you had persons of interest. Meaning more than just Kyle. Who else?"

The detectives grimaced at each other, and then the woman turned back at me. "Due to the way your sister died and the marks on her body at her time of death, we have reason to consider...other suspects."

I shook my head. "I don't understand. What does that mean?"

The detective pursed her lips together. "I'm sorry, at this time we cannot comment further on the matter. All we have right now is circumstantial evidence, and nothing is set in stone."

I squinted, trying to make sense of what they were saying, but I couldn't. "The police won't release her body until further investigations have been completed, but she needs to be buried. Our religion believes in reincarnation and that Alice's soul will be kept captive in her body until she is buried. Her sins can't be forgiven and she can't enter Heaven until her soul is released. She isn't at peace until then. So please, tell us what you know. I need to know you're getting closer to working this out so I can bury my sister. Who do you think the other suspect is?"

The officers wouldn't answer.

My stomach twisted into knots. What if they thought it was me? I knew they'd targeted Rebel for the murder of her mother and stepfather at one point, what was stopping them from doing the same to me?

Absolutely nothing.

I turned to Hawk in terror. "They think it was me, don't they?"

Hawk glanced over at the police and then back at me.

Slowly, he shook his head. "No, Little Mouse. What they're refusing to say is they think there's a serial killer out there."

30

KARA

After three solid weeks of wandering around the Slayers' compound, it had begun to feel like as much of a prison as the commune had. While I appreciated that we were safe here, and that we had food and protection, I was quickly realizing those things, while satisfying basic human needs, couldn't sustain me forever.

They weren't enough for me. And they weren't enough for Hayley Jade.

Who was getting more and more withdrawn, rather than getting better. She stared listlessly at an old iPad Rebel had brought over for her, a cartoon playing on the screen, but Hayley Jade's expression never changed.

Rebel tried to bring Remi over as much as she could, and Hayley Jade did seem to perk up a bit in the presence of her younger cousin. But Remi couldn't be here all the time. And when she left, Hayley Jade went right back to being listless and unenergetic.

Yesterday she'd taken a three-hour nap, even though she didn't have a fever or any signs of a physical illness. That wasn't normal behavior for a five-year-old.

Rebel was right. She needed to see a doctor. And we both needed to get out of this compound.

I'd been avoiding the outside world and all its terrors long enough. Staying here, hiding from them, was creating a bigger fear than all the others.

The fear I was doing my daughter permanent damage by keeping her inside these gates.

I left Hayley Jade on the couch with her cartoons and crossed the room, moving a little way down the hall to Hawk's bedroom.

I'd been avoiding it ever since he'd vowed to give me the second orgasm he apparently owed me if I ever knocked on his door.

But I couldn't avoid it anymore. The clinic at the hospital was today, and if I missed it again, it would be another week before I could get her there.

I honestly didn't know if I could take another week of watching her deteriorate the way she had been.

I forced my knuckles across the heavy wooden door.

"What?" Hawk snapped from behind it.

My instinct was to shrink away or apologize for bothering him. But one quick glance at Hayley Jade reminded me I couldn't. "It's me." I called out, trying to make my voice stronger than I felt. "Kara, I mean."

The door flew open.

Hawk grinned at me from the other side, his smile so handsome it made my insides flutter uncontrollably. My tongue seemed to lose all control of itself as tingles surged across my skin at just the sight of him.

I hadn't seen much of him since the police had come. He'd been busy with club stuff. I'd been busy hiding in my cabin or quietly watching my daughter from a distance.

Like the church mouse he'd correctly labeled me as.

I couldn't be that person today. I needed to be stronger and to ask for what I wanted.

But he took my breath away every time and made it so darn hard to speak.

Hawk's eyes darkened in the face of my hesitation. "Get in here, Little Mouse. Get in here and tell me what you want."

His fingers circled my wrist, and he gave it a tug I was helpless to resist. He went to close the door behind me, but I knew in a heartbeat if he did, I would find myself naked and on the receiving end of that second orgasm. I couldn't do that.

Not today.

I caught the door before he could close it properly. "I need you to take me to the hospital."

Any dark, sexual desire that had been lingering in his eyes disappeared, and his gaze swept over me quickly. "Why? What's wrong? Are you hurt?" His gaze darted to Hayley Jade. "Is she?"

I hushed him, not wanting to scare her. "I want to take her to the clinic they have there. Rebel said they have pediatricians and that they don't ask for ID or payment."

Hawk rubbed a hand across the back of his neck. "Yeah, they do." He glanced over at Hayley Jade. "You think she's getting worse."

It was a statement, not a question. Everybody knew she was.

I swallowed down a lump in my throat. "She's traumatized from what I did…"

He grasped my chin so I couldn't turn away. "She'd be traumatized a whole lot worse if you'd left her at that commune to be auctioned off to the highest bidder."

Logically I knew that, but it didn't make it any easier to bear.

My actions had caused her hurt, and there was nothing I could do to take that back. All I could do was try to help her now. "Please. Can you take us? I don't know what else to do."

"Clinic closes in an hour. If we're going, we need to go now."

I nodded, then cocked my head to one side. "How did you know that? About the closing time, I mean."

He shrugged. "Not important." He looked past me to the main recreation room. "Hay Jay! Wanna get out of here for a bit?"

She glanced up at him with interest. Then her gaze landed on me, and she shook her head quickly.

I should have been used to her rejections by now, but each one still hurt.

"Nah, Little Mouse. You don't take that personally. She's hurting right now. That ain't about you."

Except it was. She didn't know what Josiah had planned for her. All she knew was I'd taken her from the only mother she could remember and the only home she'd ever known.

Hawk picked up his jacket from a chair and shrugged it on. In the doorway, his boots sat waiting, and he shoved his feet into them, stooping to do up the laces. "Tell her we'll get her rainbow ice cream," he said quietly.

"Ice cream?"

"*Rainbow* ice cream. Specifically rainbow. She doesn't like the other flavors."

I stared at him in surprise, and he sighed.

"Just fucking ask her, Mouse. The clinic ain't gonna wait for us."

"Ice cream," I blurted out to Hayley Jade. "Do you want some ice cream?"

"Rainbow," Hawk hissed.

"Rainbow flavor," I clarified for Hayley Jade.

She sat up gradually, her gaze darting between me and Hawk, and then she slowly nodded.

Hope lit up inside me. It was the first time she'd responded to my gentle questions in days.

It was something. But it also wasn't the full truth of where we were going, and I didn't want to start rebuilding a bond with lies.

I knelt in front of her. "Would it be okay with you if we went to see a doctor first? I promise, he or she will be very nice, and I think they might be a safe person for you to talk to. If you want that, of course."

I hoped with everything I had that she did.

She didn't say anything or nod, but she did pick her shoes up from the floor and pulled them on her feet.

I glanced at Hawk.

He shrugged. "She didn't say no," he said loud enough so only I could hear.

She didn't say no.

It was a start.

The hospital clinic was overrun with people. Hawk, Hayley Jade, and I all stopped just inside the automatic sliding doors, joining the line of people waiting.

"Fucking hell. This is going to suck," Hawk mumbled.

A harried woman behind the registration desk glanced up and shot him a dirty look, clearly not at all bothered by his MC jacket or the bad-boy scowl he wore effortlessly.

In fact, if anything, his appearance seemed to piss her off even more. She narrowed her eyes at him. "Did I just hear you whining no less than three seconds after you got here, when some of these people have waited hours without so much as a peep? You offering to volunteer your time to help out, Mr. Bad-boy Biker? No. I didn't think so. Everybody is so willing to complain, but we're all volunteers here, so listening to people whine isn't on my to-do list today."

Hawk blinked as the woman went back to taking the details of the patient at the front of the line. He nudged me. "Who pissed in her Cheerios this morning?"

I hushed him. Clearly the woman had supersonic hearing, and I didn't want to risk her turning us away. "We can wait like everyone else. You don't have to stay."

His eyes darkened. "You think I'm going to leave you here alone in a room full of strangers?" His laugh was humorless. "Not a fucking chance."

I tried to hide the breath of relief I let out.

I didn't want him to go.

I didn't want to do this alone.

We got to the front of the line, and the woman gave Hawk a glare then turned to me. "Name?"

I cleared my throat and tried to find my voice. "Um. It's for my daughter. Her name is Hayley Jade..."

"Last name?" The woman's fingers hovered over her keyboard, waiting for my reply.

I didn't know what to say. I didn't want to give my last name, or even Shari's. I didn't want there to be any record of us being here. I couldn't really imagine Josiah having a contact at a hospital hundreds of miles from the commune, but fear made me paranoid. Fang had promised to get fake IDs for both me and Hayley Jade, but his contact hadn't come through with them yet.

I had no idea what to say.

"Robinson," he replied, giving his last name. "Hayley Jade Robinson."

The woman looked between the two of us, her thinly plucked eyebrow raised. "That so?"

I glanced at him, not wanting to lie, but my heart doing weird things at hearing my daughter with his name.

I pinched myself through my skirt, the sharp stab of pain a reminder it didn't mean anything. Nor did I even want it to mean anything. He'd just been helping me out when my brain had frozen.

But a little part of me had melted into a puddle.

"Yes, please, ma'am," I said quietly.

The woman watched me as she typed in the name without even looking at the screen. "What's a nice girl like you doing with a man like him?"

Irritation prickled at the back of my neck. Hawk was

abrasive and rude sometimes, but this woman didn't know him. She'd judged him solely on the fact he had an MC jacket on.

I tried to defend him. "That's not your—"

But she was already leaning around us to address the next patient. "Follow the green line to go on through to triage. Next!"

I tried again. "No wait. Excuse me, but you don't even know him—"

Hawk's fingers fit around my elbow, and he firmly steered me away from the desk before I could say anything more.

"I ain't worth getting kicked out over, Little Mouse." The corner of his mouth lifted. "Cute of you to try to defend me, but you don't know me either."

We followed the green line painted on the linoleum, Hayley Jade walking a few steps ahead of us, her feet sticking to the line religiously, like she was walking a tightrope.

"I know you aren't as awful as you let other people think you are," I argued when she was out of earshot, though I kept my eye on her determinedly.

He laughed. "Got any proof of that?"

"You let me stay at the club when I had nowhere else to go."

"That was War's call."

I blinked. "Fine. You cleaned out that cabin for me. That was nice."

He gave me a grin. "You're right. I am nice." He put his arm around my neck and drew me in close, so his lips brushed my ear when he spoke. "I remember you thinking I was real fucking nice when I had three fingers buried in your pussy and my tongue on your clit."

I pushed him away, horrified he would talk like that in a public place. "Stop it!"

Only, my nipples had instantly hardened.

And my clit tingled like it might want a repeat.

His voice sounded thick when he spoke again, like he knew the effect he was having on my body. "You haven't come to my room to claim that second orgasm I owe you, Little Mouse."

"And I won't be," I promised, side by side again.

"Unacceptable answer," he quipped back. "When getting my tongue to your pussy again is all I can think about. Not just your clit, this time, Kara. I want to taste you everywhere. And I mean, everywhere. All the places I didn't put my tongue last time."

I widened my eyes at him. "What does that even mean? You already..."

I blushed hot pink at the memory of his tongue between my thighs. And the realization that although he had licked me there, he hadn't once kissed my mouth.

Something silly and girlish lit up inside me at the thought of him kissing me the way Fang or Vaughn or Kian kissed Rebel. It was the same way men kissed women in movies, sweeping them into their arms, and her melting into him while their mouths fused.

I'd never been kissed like that.

All I knew of kisses were ones I'd never wanted.

I could barely imagine what it was like to sink into a man's embrace, to wrap my fingers around his neck and actually want his mouth on mine.

But with Hawk, I could imagine it.

My breath hitched at the thought of him wanting me like that.

"I already what, Kara?" he murmured, keeping his voice low so the people passing us and Hayley Jade ahead of us couldn't hear. "I already licked your clit, but you haven't ridden my tongue. I haven't thrust it inside you until you screamed. I haven't slid it down your sweet slit until I got to your ass."

I stared at him. "My what?"

He chuckled. "He never touched you there either, huh?"

"Of course not. Why would he?"

His look was smug. "Because you have no fucking idea how good it feels." He winked at me.

I couldn't breathe for thinking about it. Did people really...do that?

I couldn't even imagine. I needed to ask Rebel. Or Bliss. Or anyone but Hawk because I already felt like an immature, inexperienced child in his presence.

We caught up with Hayley Jade at the triage station, where the green line ran out.

It was only as Hawk gave Hayley Jade's fake name again that I realized Hawk hadn't once mentioned kissing me.

He'd talked about putting his mouth to my pussy and to my...

But he didn't want to kiss me.

I couldn't deny the way that hurt. Even though I had no business kissing anyone.

"Okay, Hayley Jade," the nurse said with a smile. She was a lot friendlier than the woman at reception had been, though this one hadn't heard Hawk complaining the minute he'd walked in the door, so that was probably understandable. "My name is Freya, and I'm going to do a few checks while I have a chat with your parents. Is that okay? First one, all we need you to do is pop this monitor on your finger. Do you think you can do that for me?"

Hayley Jade nodded and held a finger out.

Nurse Freya smiled. "Great job. Just sit for a moment and let that register, then we'll move on."

The nurse focused on us and explained, "The doctors know that patients who come to this clinic often haven't seen a doctor for a long time, or maybe ever. So we run a few basic tests while we chat about what brought you in today."

Hawk glanced at me, letting me take the lead.

I drew in a breath. "Hayley Jade went through something quite traumatic a few weeks ago. She hasn't spoken ever since. I thought it was just shock, and that it would just take her a few days, but it's been weeks, and if anything, she's getting worse, not better."

The nurse's eyebrows drew together. "Can you tell me more about the event you believe triggered this?"

"Um." I wanted to. I wanted to tell her exactly what had happened so they had all the information they needed to help Hayley Jade. But every time I thought about it, I wanted to shut down too. My heart rate picked up until it was uncomfortably fast. My breathing turned shallow. And my throat felt like it was closing in on itself.

I could only imagine it would be so much worse to be five years old, trying to make sense of that night, and all the nights that had come after.

If that was what was going through Hayley Jade's

mind every time she thought about speaking, I understood exactly why she didn't.

The feeling was overwhelming, and I just wanted to make it stop.

Hawk glanced at me and then at the nurse. "Kara's husband is a prick," he said bluntly. "Your imagination can probably fill in the rest."

The woman nodded slowly and then turned her attention back to Hayley Jade. "Right! Let's take a look at that reading then, shall we?"

Hayley Jade let her take the monitor off her finger and fit another around her skinny arm.

But I was still firmly back there.

Running through the darkness.

Terror gripping me.

Josiah's voice calling my name.

Across the room, someone dropped a metal tray of instruments, and the clanging noise sent a shudder through my system.

A hot sweat flushed across my skin, and the room suddenly felt too hot, even though the air-conditioning blew gently across my skin.

I tugged at the collar of my shirt, the fabric choking me.

"Breathe, Little Mouse," Hawk said quietly beneath his breath. "She's watching."

I snapped my head up to meet Hayley Jade's dark-eyed gaze staring at me intently.

The relaxed expression fell from her face, and she suddenly shook her head, pushing at the nurse.

Nurse Freya fought to keep the blood pressure cuff on her patient. "No, no, sweetie. Just gotta keep this on a few more moments. I know it's not very comfortable..."

Hayley Jade yanked at the arm cuff, her eyes wide, her gaze firmly stuck on me.

The nurse glanced over at me, taking in my clammy skin and the way I was breathing. "Mom, how about you go get a cup of water? There's a waiting area just around the corner there that has a dispenser."

I nodded and backed away.

I was clearly not helping here. I was clearly making her worse.

"Kara," Hawk warned, one hand already wrapped around Hayley Jade's trying to reassure her, while they both stared at me.

"Stay with her," I told him. "I'll be fine. I'll be back in just a minute after I get some water."

I could tell he didn't like it.

His expression said he hated the idea of me walking around the hospital by myself, where he couldn't see me.

Couldn't protect me if Josiah or one of his guys had followed us here from the clubhouse.

But I was hurting Hayley Jade.

And I was going to keep hurting her until I faced everything I'd done.

That meant reliving it all. Not just the escape. But every day of the past five years. The thought alone slammed closed doors in my brain, stopping the flow of images. "Stay with her," I said again, imploring him to listen to me.

I needed to know she was safe.

He reluctantly gave a short nod.

As if I hadn't been able to move my feet until he let

me, they suddenly unlocked. I hurried from the room in search of somewhere I could repair the mental walls that kept me from breaking down in front of a hospital full of people, and the one little girl who needed me to be stronger than I was.

31

GRAYSON

The green curtain that partitioned off various sections of the hospital's free clinic slid aside, and Harriet's stressed-out face popped through. "How many more do you want to take? It's already after five."

I peered past the *"Volunteers Wanted. No Medical Training Required,"* sign that we always had up because we were perpetually understaffed, and into the crowded waiting room. "As many as are out there. Nobody gets turned away."

She shook her head. "You're always the last one here. Dr. Tahpley bailed an hour ago, and Zigley didn't even show for her shift."

I finished up the last of my notes from the patient before and handed the file over to Harriet. She groaned good-naturedly at the essay I'd written on the top page that someone—probably her—would have to transcribe into the system later.

"I'm not the last one. You're here too."

"I'm as big a dope as you are."

I slung my arm around her shoulder and squeezed it. "But isn't this so much more rewarding than anything else we get to do here?"

She grumbled about actually getting paid being somewhat rewarding but I knew she didn't mean it.

I'd meant every word. The hours I volunteered at the clinic were one of the best parts of my week, and I never left until the last patient had been seen, even if that meant I was here hours after closing time.

"Timothy Jones," Harriet called. "You're up next."

Timothy stood from a seat to my left, and I moved to greet him.

But my gaze slid past him to the triage area at his back, and I froze.

The triage nurse, Teri, was battling to get a blood pressure cuff on a blond-haired girl of about five, who clearly wasn't having it. But it was the two adults with her that had my muscles locking into place.

The man was familiar, and his jacket gave away why.

A Slayers MC patch sat proudly over his chest, and though he was preoccupied with getting the little girl to cooperate, I remembered him from the night at the morgue.

When he'd been protecting a woman I hadn't been able to stop worrying about since.

Kara.

She stood beside him now, unshed tears glistening in her eyes as she watched on. She said something to the man, and he shot something back at her, but she was insistent, and when he eventually gave a nod, she hurried from the room, disappearing down the hallway.

Without even thinking about it, I followed.

"Gray!" Harriet called. "Where are you going?"

I blinked and turned back.

She had confusion written all over her expression.

The patient looked equally baffled. "Should I sit back down or..."

I was here to do a job. These people, especially *these* people who couldn't afford insurance, needed me to be on my A game.

Normally, I was. I was one of the best. I wasn't arrogant, it was just the truth.

But I couldn't do my job when she was here. I glanced back at the hallway she'd disappeared down, the sense of urgency to follow her completely overwhelming.

"Just...wait," I told the patient. "Wait in the cubicle. I'll be back, I promise. I'll be back."

I apologized as I walked backward, until my ass hit Harriet's desk. She squinted at me with questioning eyes, and I told her the same thing. "I just need a minute. Don't send anyone home. Just...wait."

I spun around and sprinted down the hallway.

She couldn't have gone far.

I glanced at the man and the girl as I passed. He'd pulled her onto his lap and was holding her tight, keeping her calm while the nurse performed the initial basic tests.

That was good. I didn't feel like getting into a fight with him today. We'd come damn close that night at the morgue, and fighting there would have been one thing.

But here, in the hospital I worked at, where I was supposed to protect my patients, would have been completely unacceptable.

I rounded the corner and stopped in the empty hallway. It was long and had an unobstructed view from where I stood with my heart pounding. If she'd run up there, I'd see her, surely. She was half a foot shorter than I was. There was no way she could be that fast on short legs.

Plus if that child back there was hers, instinct told me she wouldn't have gone too far.

I opened the nearest door and stuck my head inside. "Hello?"

A sharp gasp from the corner and big brown eyes, wet with tears, locked on mine. Her gaze slid down my face to my white doctor's coat, and she moved for the doorway I was blocking.

"I'm so sorry," she mumbled. "I know I'm not supposed to be in here."

But I was standing in the doorway, blocking it completely.

And I couldn't move for staring at her.

She was pretty, all that dark-brown hair, pulled back in a simple ponytail that tendrils had escaped. They framed her soft face, kissing her temples and jaw.

I raised a hand on autopilot to tuck the stray strands behind her ear.

She flinched away.

I blinked. Realizing what I'd been about to do.

Fuck.

The expression in her eyes instantly changed to one of fear, and horror rocketed through me. Scaring her had been the absolute last thing I wanted.

I drew my hands back, putting them up, fingers open,

palms facing her, as nonthreatening as possible. "Please don't go. I came in here to cry too, and it would be nice to not be the only one."

She stopped. Blinked. But at least she didn't seem so scared anymore. She'd also stopped crying. "Really?"

I gave her a half-smile, just relieved the fear had disappeared from her expression. "Okay, no. But I swear, I'm harmless." I picked up my doctor's badge. "I'm a doctor. Dr. Grayson. See? But you don't have to call me that. Most people just call me Gray. Or you can call me Fred, if you want."

She blinked. "Um...I think Dr. Grayson is fine."

I let out an overexaggerated sigh of relief. "Oh, thank God. Because Fred gets shortened to Red, and then to..." I gave a fake shudder. "Ed." I screwed up my face at her. "I cannot pull off Ed."

A muscle near her mouth twitched, and something inside me celebrated like I'd just made a touchdown from the twenty-yard line.

If she thought I was even remotely funny, then my entire day was made.

I wanted this woman to like me. I could already tell she wasn't the type to care about money or the doctorate I'd worked my ass off for.

Which only left me with funny. And sweet.

Or whatever the hell else she wanted me to be. But I was betting on funny and sweet for right now at least.

"Maybe you should just stick to Dr. Grayson," she admitted.

I dropped my mouth open in mock outrage. "You mean you don't think I can pull off Ed either? This is very upsetting." I picked a glove from the box mounted on the wall and breathed into it like I was hyperventilating.

Then winked at her and blew one long, deep breath into it, inflating the glove into a balloon and tying it where it would normally snap around your wrist. "That's your daughter out there, right?" I jerked my head back toward triage.

Her mouth pulled into a straight line. "Yes."

"With your husband?"

She shook her head quickly. "Oh, no. He's just a friend."

Interesting. There was no wedding ring on her finger, but that guy out there had protected her like she was his.

I'd always respected marriage vows. I'd never once hit on a woman wearing a ring. Never had any desire to try to tempt one away from their partner like some of my college roommates had made a sport out of doing. It had been a whole thing. Picking up lonely wives in bars whose husbands ignored them. Young college guys and lonely wives went together like peanut butter and jelly.

Just not for me.

But this woman, hell. Maybe I would have been tempted. But all the better if she was single.

I hid a smile and picked up a Sharpie from the container of pens and markers on the exam room table, scribbling some little marks over my makeshift balloon.

Then I flipped it upside down and presented it to her. "It's an elephant," I explained. "See? The thumb is the trunk..."

She cocked her head to one side, studying my creation, clearly trying to decipher my squiggles and lines.

Clearly, I wasn't as clever as I thought.

"I promise, I'm a much better doctor than I am an artist." I pushed it toward her again. "Maybe your daughter will like it though."

She took it from my fingers, holding it gingerly, carefully, like it was breakable. "That's very kind of you. Thank you. I should get back to her."

I didn't want her to leave. Not because I liked the way her lips softly curled into a smile when her daughter was mentioned. It wasn't even that she reminded me of someone else. It was that she was in danger, and I didn't want to see the pink in her cheeks replaced with the bluish tinge of her sister's in the morgue.

The tinge all dead bodies had once the life had been strangled out of them.

"Can I make a suggestion?" I asked her. "As a doctor who has studied psychology."

She paused. "That's your specialty?"

I frowned at her. "No, my specialty is glove balloon animals. Was that not obvious?"

She let out a small laugh. "Right, of course. My mistake."

I moved out of the doorway, so she didn't feel caged in, and leaned my ass back against the bed. "You're clearly upset, and kids feel that, even when you think you're hiding it well. I'm a good listener. It's kinda what I get paid for, and people generally feel better when they share what's on their minds."

She touched her face self-consciously. "Is it that bad?"

Not a thing about her face was bad. "You just seem like you're having a rough day."

She plucked at the trunk of my balloon elephant,

squeezing the tip between her fingers. "It's not just today. It's every day."

I frowned, concerned again for her, but this time for a different reason. "Your friend out there...he's not hurting you, is he?"

She shook her head quickly. "No. It's not him." She looked up at me. "Have you ever lost someone close to you?"

The question took me by surprise. I wasn't used to having patients question me about my thoughts and feelings, and it was oddly uncomfortable.

The urge to make a joke came on strong, but there was a pleading in her eyes. A desperate need for her to not be the only person in the room going through something.

One I recognized because I saw it often in patients.

Even though I saw their pain, it had been easily kept away from my own.

But Kara's pushed past the barriers I'd put up in an instant. In the same way she'd gotten under my skin the very first time I'd laid eyes on her just because she reminded me of someone else.

I found myself saying, "I lost my wife. It was a very long time ago. But she was murdered."

Kara gasped. "My sister was murdered too. Just a few weeks ago."

I swallowed hard. I didn't want to lie to her. "I know. I saw you at the morgue the night you identified her body."

She blinked, and then recognition settled on her pretty face. "I'm sorry. I didn't even recognize you." She bit her lip. "And I'm sorry for the way Hawk spoke to you that night too. You didn't deserve to be attacked like that for just doing your job."

I didn't tell her I hadn't been there on the hospital's dime. It was understandable why she'd assume I might be. Medical professionals weren't completely out of place in morgues, and I didn't want to get Ron in any trouble for letting me in.

I cleared my throat. "Have you talked to the police about your sister? About the way she was killed?"

Kara nodded. "They have some suspects."

"Did they mention the possibility of a serial killer by any chance?"

Kara looked at me sharply.

That expression was all I needed to know they had. She had that fear in her eye again, and so I spilled forth details I hadn't said out loud to anyone in a very long time. "My wife was killed in the same way your sister was."

Kara shook her head. "The police said that was a possibility, but there are other people...people much more likely to want her dead."

I wanted to reach out and squeeze her fingers. Reassure her in some way, except there were no reassurances here.

I stared into Kara's worried eyes. "I don't want to scare you. Truly, that's the last thing I want. But my wife had a sister too."

Kara stilled in front of me. "Why are you telling me that?"

I didn't want to tell her, but for her own safety, she needed to know. "Because she was murdered too. Just a few weeks before my wife."

She shook her head, stepping backward toward the door. "That doesn't have anything to do with me."

Except it did. My gut instinct swore that this was history repeating itself.

But this time, I had the ability to stop a woman from dying. I'd failed once before, and I didn't want to do that again.

I couldn't stop myself reaching for her hand, stopping her from walking away. "It does, Kara. I'm sure of it. I saw the marks on your sister's body. They're nearly identical to the ones that were found on my wife and her sister."

She tried to pull away, but all I could see was my wife's cold, dead, strangulated body. Her eyes no longer warm and brown like Kara's. Her cheeks no longer flushed pink with good health.

All I saw was the deathly blue tinge in her lips. The waxy sheen on her skin. The heart-stopping knowledge that no matter how many times I pumped her chest, no matter how many breaths I breathed past her cold lips, she wasn't coming back.

"No!" Kara's voice held a hint of panic. "No! Let me go!"

I blinked, staring down at where my hand held hers.

My fingers were wrapped around hers. Horror filled me at the realization I was scaring her.

Hurting her.

I instantly let go.

Hawk's fist connected with my face. Something cracked, though I wasn't sure if it was my nose or his knuckle. Pain exploded in my face, and I stumbled back, my vision blurring and blood pouring.

I hadn't even seen him coming.

I smacked into the counter, catching myself before I could hit the floor, and blinking rapidly, trying to shake off the fuzziness in my head.

By the time it cleared, Hawk was gone.

And so was Kara.

32

HAWK

I drove home in a blind fucking rage, furious at myself for being so stupid. Hayley Jade sat in the back seat, quiet as always. She hadn't even gotten to see the doctor.

I'd heard Kara cry out. Heard the fear and pain in her tone.

I'd picked up Hayley Jade and run down the hallway like I was fighting for gold in the one-hundred-meter sprint at the Olympics.

I'd never punched a guy out while holding a kid in one arm, but fuck, seeing that asshole from the morgue with his hands on Kara had sent me over the edge.

Now all I could do was curse myself.

Like Hayley Jade wasn't already scared enough.

Like Kara wasn't already so fucking traumatized she could barely function.

I'd gone and let her walk away from me, completely unprotected, and look what had happened.

I couldn't fucking breathe.

Kara didn't try to talk to me on the way home. She made idle chitchat with Hayley Jade, who didn't respond.

My chest tightened with every mile that passed, buildings, trees, and the beach all flashing by outside the van windows.

At the Slayers' gates, Kara finally looked my way and then picked up my phone from the center console.

"What are you doing?" I snapped.

"I need your passcode, please."

"Seven, eight, three, two," I rattled off, no fucks given that I was handing over access to everything in my phone. Kara wasn't exactly the type to go rifling through my texts. Not that she'd find much there anyway. Some old dirty texts from Kiki. Maybe a nude from Amber. But anything of club significance got deleted or wasn't said in a text in the first place. So she could have the fucking thing if she wanted it.

She tapped her fingers across the screen a few times and then put it to her ear.

I waited for Ice to open the gates, ignoring him when he indicated he wanted to talk, and drove past, leaving him in the cloud of dust the tires kicked up when I put my foot down on the accelerator too hard.

I couldn't talk to anyone right now. I needed every brain cell just to keep the van on the road and my chest sucking in oxygen.

"Queenie, hello. No, it's me. Kara. We're just coming in the gates now. Could you meet us out the front and get Hayley Jade inside for me, please? I need Hawk to come down to the cabin with me. There's some things we need to talk about."

I huffed out a breath. Damn fucking right we had some things to discuss.

Like why the fuck she'd gone off on her own.

And why the fuck I'd let her.

That was never happening again.

Queenie was waiting in the doorway when I stopped the van.

Kara got out and helped her get Hayley Jade inside, and even losing sight of Kara for a millisecond as she stepped into the clubhouse had me strangling the steering wheel as that same feeling I'd had back at the hospital engulfed me once more.

Kara came back alone a moment later and slid wordlessly back into the passenger seat.

We were silent until I navigated the van along the path to the cabin. It was barely even wide enough for the vehicle, the track mostly worn into the grass only by bike tires or feet. I got out first, and she followed, neither of us making a sound until the cabin door closed behind her.

I whirled around on her. "Never again!" I shouted. "Never. Fucking. Again do you leave my sight like that, Kara! What the fuck were you thinking?"

To my surprise, she didn't cower. She didn't flinch like she normally did whenever I got loud. Which was a lot because I just didn't do soft and well spoken.

"You're right," she agreed.

I stopped. "What? No, I'm not. I'm being completely unreasonable, yelling at you for walking away when you clearly needed a minute to compose yourself."

She shook her head. "I put myself in danger."

I moved in on her so quickly, I actually had to catch her as she stumbled to avoid colliding with me, her back hitting the door. I cradled her head, so it didn't thunk on the wood, and pressed my body into hers, breathing hard, her face mere inches from mine. "I put you in danger. You were my responsibility, and I let you go."

"You were just doing what I asked you to do. Hayley Jade needed you."

"You needed me, Kara. *You*." I inhaled her scent, letting it fill my lungs properly for the first time since I'd seen that asshole with his hands on her. I put my lips to her neck, the smell of her not enough to convince me she was safe beneath my body. I kissed her neck, opening my mouth to lick her skin.

She shivered beneath me, her fingers coming to my arms, resting lightly on my biceps. "You were scared for me."

I'd never admitted to being scared of anything in my life, and yet that cry she'd let out when he'd grabbed her was stuck on a loop in my brain, continuing the rush of adrenaline I hadn't been able to shake.

I'd been scared.

I'd been sure that Josiah cunt had her in his grips and that I wasn't going to get to her in time.

The feeling was wholly unsettling. I wanted to deny it. Put on the fake bravado I used as a shield because it stopped this feeling. This feeling I fucking hated.

It felt a lot like having something to lose, and in this world, that was a liability I didn't want to have.

And yet I couldn't lie to her. I couldn't pretend I hadn't been terrified.

I was still terrified, and she was right here. Right in my arms.

I was terrified she didn't want me the same way I wanted her.

I took a step back, but nothing had changed. She still had those huge eyes that just quietly took in the world. She still had those curves I'd wanted to run my hands all over since the very first day I'd met her five years ago. She still had lips so damn kissable I hadn't let myself near them for fear of getting so attached I'd never stop.

I breathed hard, fighting the damn ache in my chest that reminded me over and over that some other man had put his hands on her tonight.

"I'm sorry," she whispered again.

I wanted to kiss her. I wanted to kiss her so fucking bad my lips ached. My fingers shook with the need to reach out, shove my fingers into the back of her hair and draw her in. Put my mouth on hers. Taste her, and not in the dirty, filthy way I'd taunted her with earlier.

Kiss her slow and deep. Trace her lips with my tongue. Suck on her until she moaned into my mouth.

I couldn't do any of that. I didn't know how to be gentle. Didn't know how to kiss her like I wanted to. All I knew was fucking. Slamming my cock inside a woman's body, making her tits bounce and her pussy clench until she didn't care I hadn't kissed her. Didn't care about anything other than the orgasm ripping through her body.

I couldn't be like that with Kara.

She was my Little Mouse.

I would be the trap that broke her.

I wrenched myself away, needing to put distance between us. I went into the bedroom and yanked open the window, needing the evening air to wash over the heat emanating from my body before I set the entire room on fire.

"I'm sorry," she said again, following me in. "Please, Hawk... I need you to..."

I turned around. "Look me in the eye and tell me what you need, Little Mouse. Give me some sort of direction here, because damned if I'd know what you need. Or what I need. Or what the hell we're doing. I don't know anything, so just tell me what you need."

She stared me in the eye and sucked in a breath. "I need you to punish me. I want your forgiveness. I don't deserve that until you punish me."

I blinked. That had been the last fucking thing I'd expected to hear from her lips.

But there was nothing but sincerity in her words.

She thought she'd disappointed me. She thought she was the one who'd done wrong. Again. She always blamed herself, and one day, I'd put a bullet through Josiah's skull for conditioning her to feel like that.

She couldn't have been further from the truth.

But she was removing her shoes. Lifting her skirt and sliding off her panties. Crawling across the bed like she had the last time we'd been in this room. Settling herself on all fours, and then raising her skirt to reveal her perfect, rounded ass.

My dick went hard. So damn hard it ached behind the denim of my jeans.

She was expecting me to take her, the way that fucking asshole Josiah had.

I wouldn't do it.

I refused to make her feel better by hurting her.

I got on the bed behind her, trailing my fingers up the

backs of her thighs and over the rounded globes of her ass. I kept going, skimming the sides of her body, until I got to her tits where I scooped my hands around, taking two indecent handfuls of her and drawing her up so she was off her hands and kneeling.

With my chest to her back, I massaged her tits through her clothes and spoke into her ear. "I want you naked. Every scrap of clothing off. Now."

She drew in a sharp intake of air as I fit my fingers to the hem of her long-sleeved shirt and lifted it, exposing her stomach.

She grabbed the top, holding it in place, and twisted to look over her shoulder at me. "I'm fat."

I stopped and squinted at her. "What?"

She shook her head. "I'm not like Amber and Kiki. I'm fat."

I didn't understand what she was getting at. "I'm not blind, Little Mouse. I know what your body looks like."

"I have stomach rolls."

"So?"

"Stretchmarks. Cellulite."

"Yeah? Great. If you'd let me take your clothes off, then maybe I'd get to see that for myself."

I twisted my fingers in her shirt and drew it over her head. Put my lips to her shoulder, kissing the skin on the side of her bra strap.

She batted me away. "Hawk! Stop it! This is cruel!"

I moved so I could see her face.

She seriously fucking meant it.

I narrowed my eyes. I just wanted to see her in the light. See every damn inch of her body when I made her come.

She covered herself with her arms. "At least turn the lights off. Please."

I stared at her. "No."

Her bottom lip trembled. "Why?"

I could see the hate she had for herself. The hate that her prick of a husband had drilled into her with his actions, if not his words.

Had he ever had her fully naked? Had he ever wanted to see every inch of the woman he'd married, or was she just a hole to stick his dick into in the hopes of producing some heir to his messed-up throne?

In an instant, I saw it all in her eyes. Her expression told me I was spot-on.

That she'd never had a man worship her the way I had been craving to do.

The tiny taste I'd had wasn't nearly enough. It had merely stoked the flames inside me that burned to know her body inside and out.

I slid the bra straps off her arms. Undid the clasp. "You wanted to be punished, Little Mouse. This is how I punish you. The light stays on because I want you to watch everything I do to you. I want you to see exactly how your body responds to my touch. I want you to see how much I want the beautiful body you only see as fat."

I drew the bra away from her skin, growling at the red marks it left behind. I licked at them with my tongue, soothing over the places the fabric had been too tight. I cupped her tits with my hands for a second, only allowing myself the briefest squeeze of her nipples before dragging down the elastic-waisted skirt.

Without me having to say anything, she lifted her knees and let me toss it to the floor.

The overhead light left nothing to the imagination. It kissed her skin, lighting her up, showing off every part of her I had only gotten to feel in the darkness last time.

Kara clutched at her arms. "Please turn the light off," she whispered brokenly.

I swore low under my breath and got off the bed. I pulled my shirt off and then went for my jeans, unbuttoning them and undoing the zipper. "Look at me."

She glanced over, her eyes trailing low across my chest and over my abs.

I kicked my boots off, then dragged my jeans down my legs, freeing my erection.

The fucking thing was hard as rock, straining in her direction.

I palmed it, taking long, greedy strokes just to relieve the pressure the tiniest bit.

Her eyes dropped to what I was doing, heat flaring in her gaze as she watched me jack off over her.

Again.

How many fucking times did I have to do that before she believed it was her who got me hard?

I'd do it every fucking day if she'd let me.

Precum beaded at the tip of my cock, and my balls tightened, ready to come already.

Fucking hell, I hadn't wanted to come that quickly since I was a goddamn virgin. I had to drop my dick before I embarrassed myself.

She was still covering herself up, acting like her body wasn't everything I'd been craving.

"Get on your hands and knees again, Kara."

She did it quickly, taking up the fucking "position" her husband had taught her.

I moved in behind her, rubbing my dick between her legs, hissing when I got my first touch of her wet pussy.

My cock glanced over her clit, and she shivered.

Back and forth I stroked her slit, soaking my cock in the juices seeping from deep inside her, watching her back as her breaths increased.

Every slide was agonizing. I wanted to plunge inside her. Dig my fingers into the curves of her hips and hold on while I fucked her deep.

But she wanted to be punished.

Apparently, so did I.

Not fucking her was the biggest punishment of them all.

Her hips started a slow, mindless rock, back and forth, chasing the friction igniting between our bodies.

I slapped my palm against her ass, hard enough for it to sting.

And was rewarded with a cry that had her knees shaking.

I chuckled. "You aren't supposed to like punishments."

Her skin turned the prettiest shade of pink, and I slapped the other cheek, leaving a matching mark.

Again, my reward was a moan of pleasure that made me just want to do it all over again.

She had her forearms down on the mattress, her head buried in the crook of her arm.

I leaned over her, taking a hold of her ponytail and using it as leverage to turn her face to the side of the room where I'd hung a full-length mirror after my shopping trip to Providence.

"Want to see your face when I spank your pussy, Little Mouse."

She didn't lift her head, but we both looked over at the mirror.

Her gaze met mine in the reflection.

Reluctantly, because my dick was really enjoying the slip and slide I'd created between her folds, I pulled back, sitting back on my feet so I could see every inch of her.

From behind, everything she had was on full display. Her clit, swollen from the way my dick had been playing with it. Her pussy, dripping with arousal. Her sweet asshole, just fucking tempting me with a new way of giving her pleasure.

I slapped her between the legs, making contact with the areas I'd already been working into submission.

She cried out, and her pussy clenched around nothing. And then again. And again.

She moaned loudly, shaking at the force of the feeling.

Holy shit. She'd come without me even penetrating her.

I watched her in the mirror, letting the orgasm die off and pink embarrassment heat her cheeks.

"You came before I was ready to let you," I accused.

"I'm sorry."

I shook my head. "Stop fucking saying you're sorry. Do you have any idea how sweet your pussy is, fluttering like that, wet and dripping?" I bent over her back, wrapping my arms around her, and whispering into her ear, "But the next time you come, it's going to be with my cock buried inside you."

I flipped her onto her back, laying her out on the

mattress and immediately spreading her legs wide. I dove to her tits, sucking one into my mouth, as much of it as I could fit, while I groped the other, squeezing her nipples until she gasped.

I nipped at the one in my mouth, then sucked it hard, drawing it into a stiff peak for my tongue to worship.

Her legs were spread wide, me kneeling in between them, and I let my mouth travel down her stomach. She had old, faded scars beneath her belly button that were silver in the light and so pretty they could have been tattoos. The skin there was different too, softer, and I kissed every inch until I got to her snatch.

I wasn't used to women with hair. Kiki and Amber plucked themselves bare everywhere.

Kara had a sweet triangle that did nothing to hide the good stuff between her folds. I spread her wide with my fingers and ran my tongue from her swollen clit to her glistening opening.

I set up camp there, lying on the mattress between her legs, thrusting my tongue in and out of her entrance, fucking her with my tongue.

Her hands landed lightly on my hair, and I groaned at her touch.

"What do you want? You want to come on my fingers? My tongue? Or my cock?" I grinned up at her. "If you choose my fingers or my tongue, just know there'll be more orgasms until one eventually lands on my dick."

I needed her too bad. Needed to bury myself inside her.

I licked two fingers and let them take the place of my tongue, thrusting in and out of her while I licked her clit instead.

Her thighs clenched around my head, and I rejoiced in the squeeze of her soft skin and the muscles buried deep beneath.

"Wrap your legs around my head. Take what you need."

My dick nearly punched a hole in the mattress when she locked her ankles behind my head, drawing me even farther into her core. I buried my face, her arousal coating my lips and the stubble around my mouth. I added a third finger, finding her G-spot buried deep inside and then when her pussy opened up even farther, a fourth.

She was so damn wet. So damn responsive. And she was taking everything I'd offered like the good girl I knew she was. The urge to push her, to see how much she could take was like a dangling carrot, so damn tempting.

But there would be time for that.

After I'd made her come again.

I picked up the pace, and the rocking of her hips met my fingers, telling me she wanted to receive it as badly as I wanted to give it.

I sucked her clit hard, sending her over the edge. She cried out, smothering me with her thick thighs so damn sweetly I didn't give a fuck if I couldn't breathe. All I could taste and smell was her, and there wasn't a thing in the world I wanted more. She clenched and spasmed around my fingers, but the moment her legs unlocked, releasing me, I was there, ready to fill her with my cock.

I thrust into her, hard and deep, my dick catching the last of her orgasm and hitting her just right until the ebbing feeling became stronger, her third orgasm taking a hold.

Her eyes went wide, panic in her gaze, like she had no idea what her body was capable of. The pleasure she could get from sex, as long as the man between her thighs wasn't her cunt of a husband.

Her pussy claimed my cock. Swallowed every inch like I'd been made for her. She shouted my name. Bucked off the bed. Dug her fingernails into my shoulders as she shook and shuddered, the last orgasm the strongest of them all. Tears filled her eyes, but I didn't stop. I fucked her hard, knowing those tears weren't ones of pain because she was fucking me as much as I was fucking her. Her greedy hips thrust up to meet my every move, and her moans and pants told me exactly how much she'd needed it.

Those tears were surprise. Pleasure. And when one dripped down her cheek, I licked it away.

And then I pulled out, dick shuddering, and sprayed her pussy with my cum.

33

KARA

I moaned as Hawk's essence hit my most private parts.

Cried out as he massaged it into my sensitive, swollen clit.

We both stared down at the mess he'd made of my body, and my core clenched at the sight.

I'd never had a man pull out like that. Mark me like I was his, instead of just trying to fill me with his seed.

Hawk trailed his fingers through the mess, using it as lubricant to play with my nipples again, until I was sure I would self-combust.

I didn't dare tell him to stop. That wasn't allowed in the commune.

But for the first time in my life, I didn't want to. I wanted him to just keep doing it. Making me feel things I'd never felt before. Working my body into such a frenzy that nothing else existed except his touch and the way it caused pleasure where I'd only ever felt pain.

I was so hot. So sticky and sweaty. So utterly spent I couldn't move.

And yet if he'd demanded another orgasm, I would have just opened my legs.

"You're making little noises like you're hoping for a fourth," Hawk murmured into my shoulder. "I would give them to you all night, but you'd be sore as hell tomorrow."

I closed my eyes and enjoyed the feel of his lips brushing across my neck. Tears pricked behind my eyes again, not from the overwhelm of pleasure this time, but for the fact he didn't want to hurt me.

He dragged himself up off the bed and disappeared into the bathroom. A moment later, the water turned on, and then he was back, with a warm, wet washcloth that he wiped carefully over my body.

I was too sated to even feel self-conscious. After everything he'd done to me, it was impossible to feel anything but relaxed.

"Why don't you let anyone else see this side of you?" I asked quietly, watching him gently remove the products of our joining from my skin.

He glanced up. "What? The naked side?"

I frowned. "The gentle side. The side that isn't...mean."

He paused, his washcloth resting on my lower belly. "I'm not gentle."

"The way you're touching me now says otherwise."

He went back to cleaning my skin, swiping the cloth through the patch of hair on my mound, and then lower to clean his cum from my folds. "Is this okay?"

I nodded. "It feels nice."

"I've never done this before."

I bit my lip. "What do you normally do with women when you've finished having sex with them then?"

He glanced at me. "Like I said. I'm not gentle. You really want to know what I do with a woman after I've had her?"

I nodded.

He sighed. "I tell her to fuck off. I can't stand them sleeping in my room, and I can't stand staying in theirs. There's a reason people think I'm mean, Kara. It's because I am."

He didn't know mean. Maybe he was crass and uncaring. Maybe he was selfish.

But Josiah was mean. Caleb had been mean.

Hawk had touched me like I mattered. Like I was worthy of pleasure. Like I was a person, and not just a vessel for a man or the Lord he served.

I took the cloth from his hands and rolled off the mattress, taking it to the bathroom. I stayed there for a lot longer than necessary, using the facilities, brushing my teeth, and putting on a robe that Bliss had brought over for me with a bag of clothes she'd cleaned out of her wardrobe for me. We were the same size, and I was grateful to not have to squeeze into my tiny sister's clothes any more.

I liked the clothes Hawk had picked out for me too. But Bliss's hand-me-downs had filled out my wardrobe nicely.

I rinsed the cloth out beneath the hot water and listened, but I couldn't hear anything from outside the room.

I opened the door and took a single step out.

Hawk watched me from the bed, still gloriously naked, though he'd pulled a sheet up high enough to cover his manhood. It did nothing to hide the ridges of his abs. Or the thick lines that ran either side of his hips, a silent invitation to see what was beneath the sheet.

Even though I'd only just seen it minutes before, I wanted to see it again.

Feel it inside me.

Take it inside my mouth and suck until I made him feel as good as I had.

Instead, I went back into the bathroom, made the cloth hot again, and brought it to him.

"You didn't leave," I said quietly, crawling across the bed and kneeling in front of him. Slowly, I lowered the sheet, exposing his now soft member. Like he had for me, I cleaned him with caring, gentle strokes.

"Is that what you were waiting for?" he asked.

"You said that after you were with someone you..." He'd been crude in what he'd said. I tidied it up a little. "Asked them to leave."

His dick moved beneath my hands, but I kept cleaning him, wiping off the residue of multiple orgasms and sex that had lasted for hours instead of minutes.

"I did say that," he agreed.

"But you didn't do it."

"No."

"Why?" I knew he wasn't lying. I'd seen him throw Amber out into the hall buck naked, not even giving her a chance to put underwear on.

And yet he was still here in my bed. Taking care of me. Letting me take care of him.

He ran his fingers along the edge of the soft sheets. "Maybe I just wanted you to touch my cock again?"

I looked up at him. He was getting hard, so I supposed that was a possibility.

I stroked his cock until it was stiff, and then lowered my mouth toward it.

He stopped me. "What are you doing?"

"That's the only reason you stayed, right?" I challenged, feeling brave after he'd spent the last few hours building me up. "You only stayed so I'd touch your dick. That's what you said."

He frowned at me. Then grabbed my wrist, dragging me down onto the bed beside him. I landed on the soft mattress with an "oof" of surprise.

The surprise turned to shock when he rolled me onto my side and then fit his big body behind me, his knees meeting the backs of mine, his heavy arm pinning me in place.

"What are you doing?" I whispered to him.

"Snuggling."

I widened my eyes. "Snuggling?"

Like he realized he'd said something sweet, on top of not disappearing the second he'd had a chance, he mumbled, "I'm too fucking tired to go up to the clubhouse. I fucked you hard for a really long time. Shut up and go to sleep. Your body needs time to heal so I can do it again in the morning."

The words were back to harsh.

But he didn't move his arm from around my middle.

I was sure no one would believe me when I told them, but Hawk lay like that, wrapped around me, for the entire night.

Snuggling the overweight, worthless woman who'd been kicked to the curb one too many times.

Snuggling the bad-boy biker who was maybe not as prickly as he seemed.

34

HAWK

Kara's hair smelled of fresh apples and honey. Which I could only recognize because I'd read it on the shampoo bottle in her shower when I'd been looking for a washcloth. It was girly, but I liked it a whole lot more than the cheap-ass soap I normally used. I sucked in deep breaths, vaguely pleased that if I moved my head lower, to her skin, the scent of me still clung to her.

Or maybe that was the scent of the sex we'd spent half the night having. We'd cleaned each other up, but neither of us had showered, falling asleep with her in my arms more important than washing off.

She breathed softly now, her robe falling open in her sleep to display her tits. The hem had crept up around her ass, and if I hadn't been worried about her being sore from the night before, I would have cupped her breast and exposed that sweet pussy, waking her up in the best way I knew how.

Instead I just lay there, feeling her warmth, oddly comforted by the feel of her there in my arms.

The panicked feeling from last night when I thought I'd lost her had been replaced by a weird calmness.

I didn't want to run. I didn't even want to leave the bed. The thought of getting up for a shower or food seemed like a poor choice when the other option was to stay here and hold her.

"Hayden," Kara mumbled in her sleep, rolling over. "Hayden..."

I froze.

All the good things disappeared.

I pulled my arm out from beneath her so abruptly her eyes flew open.

But I was already out of the bed, searching the floor for my jeans and T-shirt.

"Hawk?" she asked sleepily. "You're leaving?"

I glared at her, so damn angry at myself for staying. I should have left, like I always did. I should have fucked her, then picked up my shit and gone back to my own bedroom like I always did. If I had, I wouldn't have had to hear her mumbling fucking Chaos's damn name, after I'd spent the night in her bed. "Yeah. I'm leaving."

She pushed herself up to a seated position, and I wanted to groan at the sight of those full tits spilling out of her robe. I wanted to crawl across the bed and take them in my mouth. Or lube them up, straddle her chest, and slide my dick in between them until I came all over her neck.

But not if she'd been thinking about another man all night, pretending I was him.

I was nobody's sloppy seconds. Nobody's runner-up

prize. That was for saps like War and Fang, who didn't mind sharing their women.

She frowned. "Are you upset? Did I do something wrong?"

I glared at her. "Why? Are you going to ask me to punish you again? To make you come so many times you can barely walk straight?" I shook my head bitterly. "Go ask…"

I swallowed hard, not wanting to say his name. She didn't even know he was still alive and yet she'd spent all this time pining for him anyway?

I should have just told her so she could go running into his arms.

But I was too fucking selfish. The thought made me want to hunt him down and put a bullet through his head.

Or to wind back the clock five years and leave him on the side of the road to die instead of nursing him back to health.

Chaos wasn't a good guy. He was the sort of man who would chew Kara up and spit her out.

But then so was I.

I yanked on my shirt, pulling it down to cover the skin that still smelled like her.

Now I needed a shower. Right. Fucking. Now.

She reached out and caught my hand.

I wanted to jerk my fingers away.

But I couldn't.

She stared up at me with those big brown eyes. "I don't know what I did. Please. Last night you were sweet and kind. And now you're…"

I leaned down so my face was barely an inch from

hers and shook my head bitterly. "No, Little Mouse. This time it's not me who's the asshole. You were the one who let me fuck you all night and then slept with your head full of another man."

She blinked, confusion creasing her brow. "What other man? I didn't...I don't remember..." She squinted her eyes. "What did I say?"

"You said his fucking name!" I roared.

"Josiah?"

"Chaos!"

She drew back, shaking her head. "No, I... Chaos is dead. I don't..."

We both knew she was lying.

She looked up at me sadly, face full of resignation. "I can't help who I dream about. It doesn't mean anything."

I picked up my jacket from the floor. "Just like I don't." I scrubbed my hands over my face, hating every word falling from my mouth, and the ridiculous hurt tone that accompanied them. "I'm not your boyfriend. You can dream about whoever you want. I'm out."

I strode out of the bedroom, picking up my boots from the other side of the bed and continuing without putting them on. I didn't know where the van keys were, but I wasn't stopping to find them either. I'd walk back up to the clubhouse barefoot. And then I'd get on my bike and drive as far away as I could, so I didn't have to think about the jackass I was making of myself right now.

Kara caught me at the door, grabbing my arm, pulling me back with a strength I'd never associated with her. "Wait!"

Her entire robe had come undone. It hung from her shoulders, completely wide open, showing me everything she had beneath, and hardening my dick in an instant because it was a sucker for her body.

She breathed heavily, tits rising and falling, her eyes dark with a mixture of anger and hurt.

Good. 'Cause that's how I fucking felt too.

At least her anger was distracting her from covering herself up. She hadn't been self-conscious at all since we'd started arguing.

"I don't want you to go," she said eventually, ending the staring contest between us.

"Yeah, well, go tell that to Chaos."

Her bottom lip quivered. "That's cruel," she accused. "He's dead. He only lives in my memories. I didn't mean to dream about him. And I didn't mean to say his name."

Except he wasn't dead.

He was alive and living just to ruin my life every chance the asshole got.

"Are you in love with him?" I demanded, hating myself for even saying it. I wasn't her boyfriend and I sounded like a whiny, pathetic loser.

Except some part of me really needed to know.

Kara paused. She opened her mouth, then closed it.

I knew the answer even if she didn't.

But she was a fool. I twisted our positions so her back was to the wall, my body pressed against hers. "Just fucking say it, Kara. Say you're in love with a ghost."

Because that's what he was to her. And that's what he needed to stay. Over my dead body was she going to go to him. If she didn't want me, fine. What-the-fuck-ever. She would eventually find some nice accountant or something. Get married. Have a couple more babies and make Hayley Jade a big sister.

I could live with that.

Even though the thought made me want to punch something.

But the Sinners were scum, and Chaos had been their leader. He'd been the one mixed up with Caleb. Didn't she remember what they'd done to her? Didn't she remember how he'd held her hostage? How Caleb had taken Hayley Jade from her arms, the exact same way her cunt of a husband had. Didn't she see Chaos was cut from the same goddamn cloth?

She had some savior complex because he'd shown her a scrap of human decency when she'd had nothing else. That asshole shrink at the hospital probably would have diagnosed her with Stockholm Syndrome if he hadn't been so busy chatting her up.

I'd never done jealousy. Never had anyone I cared enough about to get jealous over. Amber and Kiki had fucked all the guys at the club, and I didn't feel a thing, watching them go off with them instead of me.

They could have gone off with Chaos and I wouldn't have given a damn.

But Kara wasn't them.

"I barely even knew him," she said softly.

"And yet you love him anyway."

"Hawk..."

I shook my head. "Don't. Don't fucking look at me with those big eyes and say my name."

"Hawk," she whispered, doing the one thing I'd asked her not to.

She touched the side of my face, and it felt like death and ecstasy all mixed into one. I hated it and wanted it.

Her other hand joined, cupping my face, hands sliding to the back of my neck.

When she pulled me down, I was helpless to resist.

I slammed my mouth down on hers, stealing her gasp as I picked her up, using the wall and my body as leverage.

My tongue battled a war with her lips until she opened for me and I dove inside, tasting her mouth.

She kissed me back, legs locked around my waist, mouths hard and fast, one hand fumbling between us for my only half-done-up fly and the erection straining between us.

I groaned when my jeans fell around my ankles and my dick made contact with her pussy.

I shifted, getting a better position, lining up my tip with her pussy and driving it up inside her.

She cried out, the sound so full of pleasure I wanted it engraved in my brain forever. I fucked her fast and hard, pistoning my hips, slamming my body into hers, greedy and selfish like the asshole I was.

I couldn't let her go to play with her clit, didn't want to put her down when she felt so damn good in my arms and wrapped around my cock.

But I needed her to come. Come with me. "Touch your clit, Little Mouse. Play with it like I would."

She went to shake her head, but I claimed her mouth again, kissing any disagreements right off her lips. "Make yourself come. Rub your clit while you take my cock. I want to feel you come on me."

She moaned, hot for the words I growled in her ear, just like she'd been the night before. Her fingers came between us, grazing the topside of my cock as she found her clit.

"Faster," I whispered in her ear. "Need to feel you clench around me."

Her head tilted back, exposing her throat. I licked a path up it, biting at her jaw, so she'd lower her head and kiss me.

Our mouths connected.

Her pussy pulsed.

I came inside her so deep and hard and fast, no care given to how irresponsible it was to screw her without a condom, not once but multiple times.

I didn't care. Just needed to be in her.

She shouted my name, squeezed her arms around my neck, clamped down on my cock, and milked it until I was dry.

Fucked me until I couldn't breathe for how good it felt.

Fucked me until I remembered she would never be mine.

I carried her from the wall to the couch. Laid her down gently. Covered her body with the robe still clinging to her shoulders.

This time when I went for the door, she didn't stop me.

It was what I should have done last night.

Fucked her.

Then left.

I staggered back to the clubhouse, hating every step that took me away from her.

Hating myself even more for caring.

Amber sat on a chair outside the clubhouse, an oversized shirt that probably belonged to one of the guys swamping her petite frame. Her nipples showed through the sheer fabric but did absolutely nothing for me. Not compared to the way Kara's soft tits had fallen from the confines of her robe just now.

A cigarette dangled from Amber's fingers as she looked me up and down. "Big night?"

I just kept walking.

Why was it so easy with her, and yet it had felt like agony when I'd done the same to Kara?

I needed a shower. An ice-cold shower that got rid of her smell and her taste and her memory.

War glanced up when I stormed through the room. I didn't even know what he was doing here at this hour, and I didn't care. Fang was there too, as well as Ice, and Aloha, and all the other guys. All of them up oddly early.

"Hawk," War called.

I just kept going.

"Hawk!"

I stopped, grinding my teeth together in annoyance that he'd used his prez voice I couldn't ignore instead of the best friend voice that I could tell to go to Hell. "What?" I snapped.

His gaze narrowed. "Didn't you get my text? I called everyone to church. Where the hell were you?"

I swore under my breath. I hadn't even glanced at my

phone since we'd gotten back from the hospital last night. It was probably still in the van. Church was sacred. It meant the club had something important to discuss that nonmembers weren't privy to.

I wasn't happy with myself for missing the message. As VP I was supposed to have War's back and set an example for the other guys.

But where I'd been last night wasn't his business, prez or not. I wasn't going to blab to the entire club about what Kara and I had been doing.

Amber strode past on her way to the kitchen. "He was in Rebel's sister's cabin. Fucking up a storm by the look of him. Saw him doing the walk of shame back up the path."

Oh, she was a spiteful bitch when she wanted to be. I glared at her, and she flipped me the bird. "What? You were, weren't you?"

"Is that true?" Fang asked, slowly getting up from his seat, his eyes darkening with anger. "Tell me that's not fucking true."

I couldn't deny it.

Fang's shout was deafening. "You piece of shit! You know what she's been through! She's not one of your club sluts who you can just use when you want to and throw away like they never mattered, Hawk! She's Rebel's little sister, for fuck's sake!"

My fingers clenched into fists, but I didn't have a leg to stand on. He was right. Him and Amber both. I fought the urge to drop into a fighter's stance and defend myself from the blows Fang was no doubt about to rain down on me.

"Fang," War said quietly.

Fang stopped.

That was what made Fang good at his job. His complete and utter loyalty to War was admirable and had probably saved me from a black eye just now.

"You, in there." War pointed at me, and then at the room behind me holding nothing more than a single long table with enough chairs for all members. Prospects didn't get a seat at the table until they were patched in and had to stand around the edges of the room if War deemed them worthy of attending.

Apparently, the room was also about to be used to chew my ear off about what a piece of shit I was, because War seemed no happier than Fang. I didn't blame him.

I shoved past Ice who was gawking like the dumbass he was and took my frustration out on him. "Why the hell are you even here?" I snapped at him, the words unnecessarily harsh. "Fucking good-for-nothing prospects."

He stepped aside quickly, a fleeting expression of hurt on his face.

I wanted to groan. He hadn't deserved that. I was just taking my shit out on the weakest person in the room, and that was some cowardly bullshit if ever I saw it. But what's done was done. I didn't apologize. Especially not to a prospect. I'd buy him a beer later.

Like that would ease all the guilt I seemed to have opened a window to when Kara had walked back into my life.

War shut the door behind him, blocking out the others, and then leaned back against it, folding his arms across his chest. "So you fucked your church mouse?"

I glared at him. "Don't call her that."

War raised his eyebrow. "You do."

"Doesn't mean you can."

He let out a deep laugh. "Oh, you dumb asshole. Look at you. You fucking *like* her."

"I'm getting my dick wet. Nothing else."

"Bullshit. You could get your dick wet with Amber or Kiki any damn time you want a whole lot easier than it would be to get into Kara's panties."

A low growl emanated from my chest. "Talk about her panties again and I will put a bullet in your brain, War. I swear, don't push me. I am not in the mood."

His eyes widened in mock shock. "You like her *and* you're jealous?" His chuckles turned into full-blown laughter at my expense.

As much as I would have liked to hit him, he wasn't wrong. And fuck, I clearly needed help. "Can you stop fucking laughing at me and just tell me what to do, you asshole?"

Surprise pulled War out of his laughing fit, and this time the shock on his face was actually sincere. "Oh, shit. You're actually seriously asking me for advice?"

I waved a hand at him impatiently. "Well, who the hell else am I gonna ask? Fang wants to murder me. Aloha got Queenie so long ago he's probably forgotten how. You're the one with partners coming out your ears. Tell me what to do."

He squinted at me. "So, let's just recap. You like her."

I grunted at him, not able to make my lips move to say those words when the feeling inside me felt way more dangerous than just "like."

It felt like obsession, and that was not a good thing for a man like me.

War took my monosyllabic response as confirmation.

"And you've somehow managed to sweet talk her into bed."

"Don't know that there was much sweet about it, but I didn't force her, so don't look at me like I did."

War's gaze darkened. "I don't think that. If I thought you were the type of man who would force a woman, VP or not, you'd be out of this club quicker than you can rev an engine."

That settled something inside me. War's respect meant something to me. I'd known him a long time. That sort of friendship didn't come around often, and I'd pushed it once before, when he'd been falling for Bliss and Scythe.

It wasn't an experience I wanted to repeat.

I sighed. "I've spent my entire life screwing women. More than I should, probably. But..." I stared at the ceiling, not able to look my friend in the eye.

"But you've never had a girlfriend."

I snapped my gaze to him. "She's not my girlfriend," I said too quickly.

Amusement crept into War's expression again. "But you want her to be, don't you? Isn't that why you're in here asking me for dating advice?"

I went to argue but then realized he was actually hitting the nail on the head.

Kara didn't feel like a quick fuck that I sank my dick into and then walked away.

"Fine!" I spat at War. "Tell me what the hell I'm supposed to do if I want to make her my girlfriend."

War grinned widely and crossed the room to clap me on the shoulder. "Well, first, you let me sing, 'Kara and Hawk, sitting in a tree, K-I-S-S-I-N-G—'"

"I just lost all respect for you. You've been watching too many of Lexa's little kid shows."

War screwed his face up. "Yeah, fair enough. That was a bit much. Okay, back to the actual problem. But you really don't have one. She obviously likes you. She was barely a shell of a person when she got here, but we've all seen the way she is with you. You're some sort of safe place to her. That's the hard bit. The easy bit is all you have left."

"Which is...?" I prompted.

He grinned. "Ask her on a date."

I stared at him. "What, like I'm fifteen and asking her to go to prom? I don't date."

"Yeah, and that's why you've never had a girlfriend. But if you want one, you actually have to be, you know. Nice."

"I'm nice," I protested. "I made her come three times last night."

War rolled his eyes. "Well, that's very generous of you. I dub you the new saint of cunnilingus. Good for you. But if you want more, fuck, man, just take her out. She's been stuck in this damn compound for weeks. She'd probably like to go for a meal somewhere. Or to a movie. Or even just for a walk. Take her anywhere other than bed."

I wanted that. I wanted to take her out to a restaurant. A nice place in Providence somewhere...

Her mumbling Hayden's name in her sleep speared through my brain, causing an instant headache. Yeah. Great fucking date that would be. I take her out, we sit down at a restaurant, she looks across the road and sees him standing there, outside the place with his name on the damn window.

While I get to sit there like a damn chump while she runs across the road and throws herself at him, even after everything he'd done.

The jealousy was so debilitating I slid into a seat. "She's still in love with Chaos," I admitted to War.

He jerked at the revelation, his eyes widening. "What the fuck?"

"She talks about him in her sleep."

War shook his head slowly. "That's problematic."

"Yeah, you don't say. I have to tell her he's alive, don't I? I have to let her decide if it's him she wants to go back to."

War's eyes darkened. "Normally I would be all for giving her choices, but he held her captive. He held *five* women captive in that room for weeks, and I don't give a flying fuck if it was because Caleb ordered it. He had a choice. And he fucking chose wrong."

Anger flushed my skin at just the memory of how we'd found Kara after the weeks she'd spent locked in that house with four other women. She'd been hurt. Weak.

And so damn insistent that Chaos was a good guy, even when we all knew better.

War cleared his throat. "She can't live here and be involved with him, Hawk. That puts all of us in danger. I looked into that restaurant he's opened."

I lifted my head. "And?"

"It's majority owned by Luca Guerra."

I stood so fast my chair went flying. "Oh, you have got to be fucking kidding me? That human trafficking piece of shit Caleb worked for?"

"One and the same."

Chaos could draw her back in a heartbeat. She was still so brainwashed that all it would take was one smile, one touch, and she'd be right back in the clutches of a human trafficker. Bile rose in my mouth.

War gripped the table, his face pale like he was imagining the same things I was.

Women held captive.

Women forced into sex work.

Little girls stolen and sold to the perverted creeps who lurked on the dark web.

I knew he was picturing his daughters.

But there was also Bliss. Rebel. Amber. Kiki. Remi. Lavender.

Hayley Jade and Kara.

All of them in danger if she went back to Chaos.

The thought was horrifying.

There was no longer any doubt in my mind, and it was clear there was none in War's either.

He glared at me. "If she still thinks he's dead, then leave it be. It's safer and kinder that way. She can't live here if she goes back to him. She can't have contact with any of us. It's cruel to make her choose between the man she's been brainwashed into thinking she loves and the family who actually does."

Turmoil raged inside me. Not telling her felt wrong. But knowing we'd all lose her if she knew, knowing she'd be out there beyond the fences, unprotected and at the whims of men who did unspeakable things to women, was unbearable.

Kara had named her goddamn daughter after that prick. She still dreamed about him five years later.

Chaos had her as brainwashed as Josiah did.

That sort of influence was all she'd ever known.

I wasn't fucking telling her.

I was going to take her on a date. Dress up nice. Say sweet things.

I was going to make her happy.

And we were all going to forget that Hayden Chaos Whitling had ever walked this earth.

35

KARA

Something was going on up at the clubhouse. Queenie had brought Hayley Jade down to the cabin and chatted my ear off about the men all being up in "church," though their church wasn't anything like the chapel we had at the commune.

Hayley Jade played quietly with a basket of Barbies she'd brought down with her. She dressed them all carefully, pushing their arms through the appropriate holes on the little T-shirts and jackets. When lunchtime rolled around, I made sandwiches for all of us and watched Hayley Jade nibble at the edges of the ham and cheese I'd placed in front of her.

"Would you prefer something different?" I asked her. "You can choose anything you like."

She glanced at me.

My heart soared at the eye contact I'd been so desperately seeking for weeks. "Anything at all," I promised her. "Candy? Ice cream?"

Queenie chuckled. "You gonna send her right on into a sugar high, girlie. What you playing at?"

But she was laughing when I got up to go to the freezer and pulled out the tub of chocolate ice cream someone, probably Hawk, had stocked the cabin with.

Hayley Jade's eyes lit up.

Okay. She liked chocolate as well as rainbow. At this point, I was willing to give her ice cream for every meal if it just meant she gave me a chance.

I spooned swirls of the creamy chocolate into a bowl, heaping it up as much as I could before setting it down for her.

"You gonna say thank you to your mama, sugar?" Queenie asked gently.

Hayley Jade put her spoon down and dropped her gaze to her lap.

"It's okay," I told her. "I know you're thinking it, right? You don't have to say it out loud if you don't want to."

She gave me the tiniest of nods, and my heart squeezed.

I pushed the spoon back into her hand. "Enjoy it."

"Ice cream isn't going to win her over, sugar," Queenie said quietly, watching Hayley Jade scarf down her treat.

I knew, and I hated that I didn't know what else to do. I had no experience being a mother. That opportunity had been taken away from me. I envied the easy confidence that seemed to come to Queenie naturally. Even Hawk, of all people, seemed better with her than I was.

Hayley Jade finished her lunch and put her bowl into the kitchen sink, like the good little girl she was. Shari had taught her that. Shari was the one who was her mother. Not me.

I was just the monster who kept taking things away from her and trying to make up for it by feeding her sugar.

Hayley Jade picked up her doll again. But instead of playing with it, she just held it.

"Have you had enough of that game?" I asked her. "You could play something different..."

My words trailed off as my daughter held the doll out to me.

I just sat there for a second, not knowing what to do.

"Take the doll, Kara," Queenie whispered.

That startled me into action. "Oh, of course!" I reached for it, my fingers brushing Hayley Jade's sweet skin as she handed the doll to me.

I hugged it to my chest, wishing it were my daughter.

Then she chose another doll and went back to dressing it up in a beach outfit.

I quietly slid to the floor, settling in the spot next to her, and did the same with the one she'd given me.

We weren't playing together as such.

But playing side by side felt almost as good.

Even though I knew she wouldn't respond, I spoke out loud as I slipped a skirt over the doll's hips. "I think my doll is going to work today. She's putting on a very pink suit, and I think maybe she's going to her job as an architect. I definitely think she looks like a doll who likes to draw houses. What about you, Hayley Jade? Your doll looks like she might be ready for a day of fun at the beach. Did you know there's a beach here in Saint View? It's been a long time since I saw it, but I know it's there."

Hayley Jade glanced up at me in interest, and I continued on.

"I bet you've never even seen the beach in real life, have you? I hadn't either until I came here. Maybe we could take your dolls down there one day?'

Queenie watched on like a proud mother hen.

Hayley Jade didn't respond, but she definitely seemed interested.

That was enough for me. She might not have been complaining out loud, but it was clear she needed to get outside these walls as much as I did.

I'd ask Hawk to take us. It was too cold to swim, but we could play with her toys and maybe go for a wander along the boardwalk. Build a sandcastle. Dip our toes into the ocean.

Swing her around in circles.

Hug her.

Hold her.

God, I wanted all those things so badly, it hurt. Tears filled my eyes, and like she could read my mind, Queenie squeezed my arm. "Patience, sugar."

I really, really hoped so. Because I wanted that day to happen. I wanted it so bad I could practically taste it.

Aloha called Queenie about an hour later, and I was still sitting on the floor with Hayley Jade. My legs screamed in pain from sitting in the one spot so long, but I couldn't drag myself away. Our dolls had been through multiple outfit changes, and mine had followed Hayley Jade's around, trying to engage and not getting much in return but really just thrilled to be in her presence.

"I've got to head on up to the clubhouse. My man is trying to cook dinner, and if we want it to be edible, I'm going to have to get up there and supervise." She glanced at Hayley Jade. "You want to stay here, sugar?"

Hayley Jade shook her little head quickly, jumping up to put her hand in Queenie's.

It hurt, but I tried not to let Hayley Jade see. "I liked playing with you," I told her softly. It was on the tip of my tongue to tell her I'd ask Hawk to take us to the beach one day.

But I didn't want to promise something I couldn't deliver on.

Hawk had left the cabin upset this morning, and I didn't even know if he was planning on coming back.

Or if he even wanted anything to do with me anymore.

I couldn't blame him.

I wondered if I'd always dreamed of Hayden. Josiah never slept in my bed, always leaving to go back to his own. I'd never woken up with a man the way I had that morning with Hawk.

It was probably lucky Josiah had always liked his own space. If I'd spoken another man's name in his presence, I'd probably be dead now.

At least Hawk had just walked away. Though that somehow felt just as bad.

I waved goodbye to Queenie and Hayley Jade. Queenie promised to save me some of the chili Aloha was making, if it turned out to be edible, that was.

I mouthed a silent thank you at her, meaning it for more than just the food.

"She's helping me as much as I'm helping her," Queenie promised.

I didn't push her on that because it seemed like it stemmed from a place of hurt. I knew all about the sort of pain that came from not having the children you wanted. So I didn't ask her to elaborate or share her story.

I'd only just sat on the couch when the telltale squeak of the front step gave away someone was out there. I stood, quickly hurrying back to the door to open it. "Did you forget something?" I asked, expecting to see Queenie.

Hawk stood on the other side, his hands shoved into his pockets. He lifted his gaze to meet mine. "Yeah. This."

He stepped in, cupping my face with both hands and tilting it up so he could claim my mouth with his. My body sank into his, and I kissed him back, clutching his shirt. Our tongues tangled as the kiss deepened.

He tasted vaguely of bourbon and smoke, and it thrilled me as much as the feel of his body against mine. Kissing him sent longing through my entire body, until I was sure it was something I'd never be able to get enough of.

I'd had no idea kissing could make you feel like flying and falling all at once

When he pulled back, it was barely an inch. His lips hovered over mine. "I shouldn't have done that this morning."

"I liked it," I admitted. The memory of him taking me hard and fast, up against the wall, was burned into my brain as the most erotic thing I'd ever done. Something I would have been shamed for at the commune, but it had lit me up inside, knowing he wanted me so bad he couldn't even leave without having me one last time.

Nobody had ever wanted me like that. After so much rejection, it was a heady feeling that I craved more of. I leaned in and kissed his neck, the same way he'd spent hours kissing mine just last night. The stubble of his short beard prickled my lips, sending jolts of pleasure to my nipples and that place between my thighs.

Bolder than I'd ever been with any man, I slid my hands over his chest, feeling the strong muscles of his pecs and shoulders. I pushed his jacket off so I could trail my fingers over his biceps and forearms. Both were thickly corded with strong muscle that Lord knew he'd needed in order to hold me up on that wall.

I'd let him see me naked. Let him see every lump and bump and roll.

He'd still come back.

I so desperately wanted to keep him coming back. Again and again. He'd done things to me last night that I hadn't even known were possible. He'd made me feel things I'd only known as wrong and bad, and taught me they were good.

They were oh so very good.

I just wanted him to feel the same way.

I dropped to my knees.

I might not have had any experience with what pleased me, but I knew exactly what pleased men. Josiah had been all too willing to teach me that.

"Kara," Hawk warned quietly. "What are you doing?"

I undid his jeans. "I want you in my mouth," I whispered. "I know men like that."

He groaned and pulled away. "No. Stop."

I blinked, feeling stupid as he did his jeans up.

I scrambled back onto my feet and turned away. "I'm so sorry," I mumbled, moving into the kitchen. "That was forward of me."

He grabbed my arm and spun me back to face him. "That was fucking hot of you, and trust me, all I've thought about for days is you getting down on your knees like that for me."

I breathed out a fast, hot breath. "Then why...?"

He scrubbed his hands over his face and groaned. "I'm so fucking bad at this." He drew his hands away and stared at me. "War said I should ask you out. Like, on a date."

I blinked. "War said you should?"

He answered in a rush. "Yeah. I mean, he was trying to give me advice. I don't fucking know. This isn't what I do, Kara. I don't hang out with women. I've never met one I actually wanted to talk to."

"Are you asking me on a date then? Or just telling me what War said?"

He shrugged, eyeing me warily like I might bite him. "Do you want that? Or is that dumb? It's for high schoolers, right? Who are too scared to just get naked and do it?"

I'd never been on a date either. I'd never been to high school. Never gotten to socialize with anyone. It was one of the big reasons I'd left the commune in the first place.

But even then, it wasn't like anyone on the outside had awkwardly stood in front of me like Hawk was now, and turned down a blow job in order to ask me to spend time with him.

Fully clothed time.

He might have been uncomfortable, but all I saw was the good in him. The side that he'd shown me last night. The part of him he hid from everyone else.

I couldn't think of anyone else I wanted to go on a date with more. "I would love to go on a date with you, Hawk."

A look of pure relief settled over him. "Dinner then? Or a movie? That's what War said we should do."

"Both sound nice."

We eyed each other.

He palmed the back of his neck. "Okay, but after the dinner and the movie..." His gaze raked over me slowly. "Do I have to kiss you at the door and then go home?"

"Or you could come inside, and I could get back down on my knees for you."

He groaned.

"Or I could do it again right now." This time when I dropped to the floor, he didn't stop me. He let me tug his jeans down, exposing his thick cock.

He caught my chin before I could put my mouth to his erection though. "Little Mouse."

"Mmm..." I darted my tongue out to lick his tip.

He hissed in pleasure but tried to focus himself. "I don't want you dreaming about Chaos Whitling."

I opened my mouth to explain I couldn't help it, but he pushed his cock past my lips instead. I moaned around the salty-sweet, warm taste of him.

He took out the elastic holding back my ponytail. "I know. I know. You can't help who you dream about. But I ain't him. I do bad shit. I'm not a gentleman. I'm an asshole almost all of the time. I won't ever hurt you though. I won't ever hurt any woman the way he did."

It was my automatic instinct to argue. To tell him he was wrong about Hayden. That Hayden had been the one who'd helped me when Caleb had taken everything I had, including my spirit.

But none of them knew him the way I had. None of them had been there in that house. They hadn't seen the way Hayden had taken care of me. How he was the only reason Hayley Jade was still alive. Rebel, Fang, Bliss, War...all they saw in him was the bad.

But just like with Hawk, I saw past that to the man he'd been inside.

I pulled off Hawk's erection and stared up at him. "It doesn't matter anymore. He's dead."

Hawk's fingers brushed my hair back from my face and then slid into my hair, encouraging my head forward. "Suck me, Kara. Suck me until I come, and then I'm going to take you out to eat. We're going to go to a movie, and then when we get home, I'm going to kiss your mouth, tweak your nipples, lick your pussy, and start working on that sweet little ass of yours, so that one day, I can take you there as well."

I breathed out a hot breath and opened my mouth, taking his cock deep inside.

"I'm going to fuck you every night, Kara. In every hole." He scraped his nails over my scalp. "Until you no longer dream of him."

36

KARA

Hawk and I left the compound before it got dark. I'd put on the nicest outfit I owned, a long floral skirt, paired with a long-sleeved top in a deep purple that matched the violets in the material that swished across my thighs. I'd thrown a light denim jacket over the top and brushed my long hair, deciding to leave it down instead of tying it back into my regular ponytail, since Hawk seemed to like it that way.

He'd picked me up from the cabin wearing fresh clothes and a knitted pullover instead of his regular beat-up Slayers jacket. I had been sucking in deep lungfuls of his cologne while we waited for our dinner.

"Sorry this place isn't that nice," he said awkwardly. "I should have taken you into the city."

The diner was on the main strip in Saint View. It wasn't exactly the nicest of areas, but I was just thrilled to be out of the compound. We sat in a booth for two, and it was warm and cozy, with a hum of conversation around us that gave the illusion of privacy.

"I like it," I told him with a soft smile.

The restaurant reminded me of him. Beat-up and rough on the outside.

A little bit sweet on the inside.

Not that I would tell him that. I knew he'd be horrified if I said it out loud. It was a side of him he kept protected from everyone except me, and I wouldn't ruin that by speaking of it.

It was enough for me to know it was there.

A young waitress came over and took our order. Burgers and fries for both of us. She left, and we settled back into watching each other.

Hawk drummed his fingers awkwardly on the table. "So. What do we talk about on a date?"

I gave a small laugh. "You, Hawk, who never stops talking, doesn't know what to talk about?"

He shrugged. "I talk a lot of shit. I don't want to talk shit with you though."

That warmed something inside me. "Then tell me something that's not...rubbish."

The corner of his mouth turned up. "You can say shit."

"I'd prefer not to. It's bad enough you have me saying...other things."

He leaned in, a wicked glint in his eye. "Like cock? I think you said you wanted to suck my cock earlier."

I blushed pink but refused to be derailed into dirty talk. That was his safe zone. It was easy for him. Getting him to tell me something more than that he wanted to lick my pussy was the real challenge. "I did not, and we both know it." I'd said I wanted him in my mouth and I would get down on my knees for him. But not that I wanted his cock. "Tell me something real."

"Like what?"

The conversation I'd had with Hayley Jade earlier about the various jobs her dolls could have played in my mind. "When you were a kid, what did you want to be when you grew up?"

"A biker," he replied. Except he said it so fast it was like it was the answer he'd been programmed with.

"You wanted to be like your dad?" I asked. "He was in the club too, right?"

Hawk nodded. "He was friends with War's old man. I grew up with the club. Never wanted to be anything else." He looked away. "Never had the chance."

"Your family expected you to be a biker too."

He shrugged. "Wasn't even just my dad. It was War's old man. The other members. My mom. The other women. It just is what it is. As soon as War and I were old enough to get a license, we were made prospects. I don't remember anyone asking if we ever wanted to do anything else."

I could relate to that. "Sounds a lot like the way I grew up. Nobody ever asked me if I wanted anything more either. Women don't do anything in the commune, other than cook and clean and go to church and have babies. I had a vegetable garden. I did like planting seeds and watching them grow into food we could eat. But nobody ever asked me if I wanted anything more than a life inside the commune."

Hawk watched me. "So what would you have been then? If those pricks had given you the chance?"

"I like helping people," I replied. "So maybe I'd have

been a schoolteacher or a nurse." I sighed. "But you need an education to do those things. I don't have that. Not an official one anyway." We'd been homeschooled, but we'd never taken the SAT exams or had the opportunity to go to college.

Hawk let out a long breath. "Story of my life." He watched me for a minute and then sat back in the booth. "I tried to get my GED a couple weeks ago."

I widened my eyes at him. "Really? That's fantastic."

He shook his head. "I failed."

He was so crestfallen I reached across the table and squeezed his hand. "Okay, so you failed. You'll try again."

He moved his hand away quickly, screwing up his face and shaking his head. "Not a fucking chance."

I frowned at him. "Why not?"

"What's the point? If I can't even get a fucking high school degree, there's no way they're going to let me into any sort of medical program."

"You want to do something medical?" I was surprised, as it was so far from his current life of bikes and machines and all the illegal stuff I didn't want to know about it. But the more I thought about it, the more it made sense.

Years ago, when Rebel had first brought me to the club, I'd been a mess. I'd had a head laceration that had needed a hospital, but I'd been so traumatized I'd refused to go.

Even though I'd broken his nose, it was Hawk who had stitched my head up. It was him who'd fed me antibiotics and watched me for a fever and changed the dressings on my wounds.

"You'd be an incredible doctor," I told him.

He shrugged. "I'm too old anyway. Can't teach an old dog new tricks."

"Does that go for me too?"

He looked at me sharply. "You can do whatever the hell you want."

"Then why can't you?"

He set his jaw in a stubborn clench. "Because I'm thirty-five and can't even pass a freaking high school equivalency exam."

I hated that he'd written himself off so quickly. "I've never passed it either. We could do it together. Study. Pretend like we're actually in high school. Might be fun?"

Our waitress reappeared and placed two plates of food down in front of us. We both thanked her and dove into our food. My stomach growled with hunger after working up an appetite with him earlier, and the meal, though simple, was delicious.

We ate in silence for so long it took me by surprise when he paused, his burger halfway to his mouth. "Would you really want to do the test with me?"

I nodded honestly, excitement flickering inside me at the thought of doing something like that. Josiah had never wanted me to have a single thought about anything, other than providing him with a baby. The idea of studying and learning and bettering myself because I wanted to, not because he controlled me, was so incredibly appealing. "I very much would. I'm so grateful for the safety and protection of the Slayers. Please don't take this to mean that I'm not. But I can't hide in there forever either. Hayley Jade needs to go to school. I don't want to homeschool her the way I was. I want her to have all the opportunities I didn't have. I want her to go to a classroom and have friends and learn things that aren't just about the Lord and what He wants from us." I picked up a fry, tapping it against my plate to knock off the excess salt. "I want that for myself too. I don't know anything. We studied a lot, but so much of it was religion. I was taught to read and do basic math, but I know nothing of anything more. I watched a documentary on leeches the other day, and did you know they still use them in modern medicine?"

He swallowed the bite of hamburger he'd been working on and shook his head. "I didn't."

"I found that fascinating."

"Everything about medicine is fascinating," he murmured, trying to hide the earnest tone in his voice but doing a poor job of it.

I watched him. "You know the hospital clinic needs volunteers. I saw the poster in the waiting room when we were there the other day."

Hawk scoffed. "What would I volunteer to do there? Disinfect the tables? Roll bandages? I'm not doing that. I'm not qualified to do anything that would actually help anyone."

"Neither am I. But I've been thinking about applying." It was a lie. I hadn't really been thinking about it.

But it was right up Hawk's alley. Who cared if he had to do the grunt work? The clinic clearly needed help, and it would be a foot in the door to the career he wanted.

The life he led...it was dark and hard and dangerous. If it wasn't what he wanted, if it wasn't what got him up in the morning, then how long could he do that for? How long could he waste his life doing something that didn't bring him any joy, just because he'd never been given the chance to do anything more?

His eyes darkened. "You are not going back to that hospital with that creep doctor there."

I'd barely had a chance to think about what the doctor had said, except now it all came back in a rush.

With a clear head, in this safe spot in a diner, without fear paralyzing me, and Hawk punching people, I considered the warning.

"He said his wife had been killed the same way Alice had and that I was in danger too. What if he's right?" I asked quietly. "The cops think there's a serial killer. That doctor clearly does too. What if we've been barking up the wrong tree by assuming Josiah is responsible for Alice's death?"

Hawk put his burger down and breathed out a long rush of air. "It seems incredibly coincidental, don't you think?" His eyes darkened. "That doctor prick gives me the creeps. I don't want you near him."

But he hadn't seemed like a creep. He'd seemed like a nice man who'd tried to make me laugh. And one who didn't want to see me end up in the morgue with my sister.

"You don't want anyone near me," I argued with a sigh. "Hawk, I need to leave the compound. Keeping me there, keeping me behind those fences is exactly what Josiah did to me."

He froze. "Don't fucking compare me to him."

I grabbed his hand, squeezing my fingernails into his palm to make sure he was listening. "You aren't like him," I promised him. "God, Hawk. You're so different from him in so many ways. He kept me behind bars because he wanted to own me. You do it because you want to protect me."

His mouth flattened into a tight line, and he accepted my explanation. "But at the end of the day, the result is the same."

"I'm a prisoner," I said softly.

He looked away and swore low under his breath. "Fuck. That's not what I want. I just want you to be safe."

"I know."

"The medical thing at the hospital," he said slowly. "The volunteer thing. You really want to do that?"

I hadn't even truly considered it. But it did tick a lot of boxes for me. Hayley Jade would be in school soon. She had to be. She needed friends to play with and to learn.

And maybe so did I. There was so much suffering at that clinic. So many people who needed help, and the people there were doing their best.

I couldn't believe a man who studied medicine, who gave up his time to care for people who couldn't afford medical treatment, could be all that bad.

Gray hadn't hurt me.

If anything, he'd been trying to warn me. Trying to keep me safe.

That made him no different, no more dangerous than the man who sat across the table from me now. If I could trust him, then I could give Gray a chance to explain.

At the same time, I could give Hawk something he clearly needed. If anyone needed this program, to be surrounded by medicine and healing, it was him.

If that was what inspired him to get his GED and take the next steps to chasing his dream, then that was what we'd do.

I was so sick of having dreams crushed. "I want to volunteer."

He eyed me. "You want me to let you wander all over that hospital with some jackass doctor who thinks there's a serial killer after you, while Josiah the Lord and Savior of fucking nothing is still out there, probably waiting to drag his wife back home by her hair and sell her into slavery? That's what you're asking me to do?"

It was that or I went back to sitting alone in that cabin, day after day, for how long? Forever? "That's what I'm asking you to do," I told him.

He sighed. "If you're volunteering, then so am I. You aren't doing it alone."

I smiled down at my plate and put another bite of food into my mouth before he noticed what I'd done.

37

HAYDEN

I knew better than to drive my truck right up to the Slayers' gates and demand they let me see Kara. That would only result in a point-blank bullet to the brain.

So I'd spent days parking my truck on the main road and walking in on foot, slowly finding tracks through the woods around the compound until I could get in and out easily in about a forty-minute trek.

A few days ago, I'd caught a couple of glimpses of her from my hiding spot, which had made every step and every blister worth it. Like an addict, it hadn't been enough. I kept coming back because I needed more.

But the fences rose tall all around the Slayers' property, cameras covering the full expanse. They'd forced me to stay deep in the woods, just watching, getting more and more frustrated that my days were spent living my fucking dream, while my nights were spent being tortured by memories.

The restaurant was coming along. Luca's guys had

installed a state-of-the-art kitchen in under a week, and the thing was straight out of every daydream I'd ever had about becoming a chef. The front dining area had small square tables with black tablecloths and red cloth napkins. The bar had red pendant lights suspended over it. The entire theme of the place was sin and lust, from the furniture to the menus I'd designed with Luca hanging over my shoulder, telling me it needed to scream sex from the minute they walked in the door.

Day by day, I'd come around to his ideas.

It was all class out front, dirty and dangerous in the back. It had taken me a minute, but I could see it now. His vision. This would be the place to be. The venue that set a tone from the very minute you came in the door in your fancy dress and high heels, to the minute you left via the back, rumpled, well fucked, and completely damn satisfied. Everything bored, rich housewives wanted. Everything conceited, wealthy businessmen desired.

This wasn't Psychos. This was all class and would attract the rich clientele we needed.

We'd be opening soon.

When we did, all these visits to the Slayers' compound would have to stop.

So I just needed a look long enough to satisfy me that she was okay with Hawk and the rest of the assholes who called that club home.

Until I could make her mine.

Fuck, I was an arrogant prick, thinking I could waltz on into her life after all this time and make her happier than whichever lucky prick she'd walked down the aisle with.

Arrogant or a completely obsessed stalker. I wasn't sure which was worse, but neither stopped me.

I trampled through the woods, following the barely-there path that was now familiar, the Slayers' absurdly long gravel driveway running parallel maybe one hundred yards away. The flashlight on my phone lit the way, highlighting the tree roots and fallen twigs and branches I needed to avoid, but I'd have to turn it off in a few more steps.

My weeks of watching the place had told me the gates were the main source of action. The clubhouse itself and the other buildings were mostly deep inside their property, harder to see from the edges where I lurked.

A few more steps and the gates would be in view.

I always turned my flashlight off before I got that far.

A roar of engines had me ducking down and slamming the phone into the dirt three steps before I normally would have. I cringed into the darkness, holding my breath, hoping the half a dozen bikers coming up the road hadn't seen my light.

The six men stopped at the gate. Talked to whoever was manning it, and then slowly, the gates opened. Engines revved, bikers started their engines again, but second by second, the noise grew louder, and I swore beneath my breath as more headlights appeared along the driveway. It wasn't just the six. There were more. So many fucking more my heart pounded. Dozens of them wound their way along the driveway, all in black, all with the Slayers logos on their backs, though these men had an additional patch, ones that marked the chapters they came from.

I couldn't stay here. If I was noticed, I'd be dead in

seconds, no questions asked. I'd been outnumbered just with the Saint View chapter of the Slayers, but with all their associated clubs here too? This was just suicide.

But the thought of Kara inside with all of them made me feel sick. The urge to storm the fence and hoist myself over it was there, but I wasn't going to be any good to either of us if I was dead.

I'd walked out of the Slayers' compound one time.

I wasn't stupid enough to think they'd let me do it twice.

"She's not your problem anymore," I muttered. "She's a grown fucking woman who you have no business with. She's smart and sensible and…"

So fucking beautiful I'd never been able to wipe the image of her from my head.

"And she doesn't need you reappearing and reminding her of the hell you put her through," I finished my barely audible reminder.

That was what it came down to. That was really why I hadn't jumped that fence.

I'd never given a fuck about my own life. Every year I'd been given felt like borrowed time, the reaper's hands always reaching for me and just missing. I was dumb enough to walk back in there, even knowing they'd try to kill me.

For her, I'd do it.

But I wasn't what she needed. I had my doubts that Hawk was either, but Hayley Jade had seemed very comfortable with him, and so what the fuck did I know? Who was I to come out of the woodwork and ruin whatever scrap of happiness they'd found? If she was married, or with Hawk, that wasn't my business.

The bikes continued to stream along the road and into the compound.

While I used the cover of darkness and the roar of the engines to back out.

The evening was still young, and nobody expected me back at the restaurant until tomorrow morning. I should just fucking go home.

The thought of spending another night alone with my goddamn cats was too fucking depressing to bear when all I could think about was having her there beside me. Tucked up on the couch beneath my arm. Hayley Jade asleep in the spare room I would decorate in pinks or purples or whatever fucking color she liked.

"You're a dumbass," I whispered to myself, storming through the woods, leaving the Slayers and their party to themselves. "You're so fucking stupid." Who did this? Who kept a woman hostage then spent five years thinking about the damn connection between the two of you that you'd never been able to find again? Who thought about spending nights on the couch with her while her daughter slept in their spare room?

My head was so messed up. I needed therapy. Or bourbon. Or...

Her.

For fuck's sake.

I drove my truck into town, cursing myself at every stoplight and fighting the urge to turn the vehicle around and use it to ram down the Slayers' gates. I was delusional.

My phone rang, and I snatched it up, barking a "What!" down the line because whoever it was, I wasn't in the mood. Unless it was Kara, which was impossible, I didn't want to talk to anyone.

"Your phone manners leave a tad to be desired," Luca said dryly. "Having a bad night?"

He didn't know the half of it. "Something like that."

"You're about to be the head chef and part owner of the hottest new restaurant in Providence. What's to be mad at?"

I sighed, not wanting to confide in Luca but so freaking worked up I also wanted to explode. All I could do was breathe out a ragged breath.

"Ah," Luca said knowingly, like that one release of air told the man everything I wasn't saying. "It's a woman problem. That sweet little thing the Slayers have stashed away?"

My fingers gripped the steering wheel so hard it was surprising it didn't crack. "How do you know about that?"

Luca laughed down the line. "You and Hawk had a screaming match about it on my security cameras."

I frowned, irritated by the fact that moment had been watched by someone else when I hadn't even been aware of it. I still remembered the prickle of heat that had passed over me at being so close to Hawk while we'd argued. "So you've just been watching me when you're not there?" I accused. "What the fuck for?"

"I make it my business to know everything about the people I get into business with, Hayden."

The words sounded eerily familiar. "You sound like Caleb." The prick who'd blackmailed me into keeping Kara hostage in the first place.

Luca scoffed. "Don't be insulting, comparing me to that piece of shit."

Anger flushed through me. "If the shoe fits."

"Don't you do your research on who you work with?" Luca asked. "You didn't have your brother look into me and my business practices before you signed that contract?"

I ground my teeth, because of course I had.

Luca took my silence as confirmation. "Exactly. Don't act like it's a bad thing."

"It is if you're blackmailing someone with the information you found."

"Am I blackmailing you? Have I threatened your family? Your life? Your three fucking cats? Honestly, why do you have so many cats anyway? You can say you like pussy without turning your house into a cat sanctuary, you know."

It was truly disturbing how much he knew. But he was also right. Unlike Caleb, Luca hadn't forced me to do anything.

Yet.

Luca sighed. "I only called to ask if you could come in an hour early tomorrow for a delivery. But I don't like seeing you all tangled up like this either. It's been going on for weeks. You're distracted. I need your head in the game."

"My head's in the game," I argued.

"Your head is full of daydreams of big brown eyes, tits, and hips."

I clenched the steering wheel harder. "Don't talk about her like that."

"Am I wrong?"

He wasn't. The thing between me and Kara was so much more than just physical. Hell, I'd met her when she was days away from giving birth, dirty, and helpless, Caleb's prisoner.

But it hadn't mattered.

Something had clicked between us that couldn't be undone.

"No," I answered Luca, hating he was right. "She's in that fucking compound, and there's Slayers' chapters pouring in by the minute."

It was one thing for her to be staying with the Saint View guys. Her sister was one of them, and maybe that afforded Kara some level of protection.

But with a hundred extra men in there tonight, all drunk and high and handsy, no clue who was a club woman, free for use, and who was off-limits, no woman would be safe.

Especially not one as tempting as Kara.

The thought of those men circling her, outnumbering her thirty to one, came on so strong it obliterated any earlier sense I'd talked into myself. What the fuck was Hawk doing, keeping her in there?

What the fuck was I doing, driving away?

Luca sighed, and I would have bet anything he was shaking his head at poor, stupid Chaos, twisted up in knots over a woman. "She means a lot to you, huh?"

"Yes," I admitted. What was the point in denying it? He'd already seen me running down the street after Hawk, begging him for information about her. That wasn't the behavior of a man who didn't care.

"And I want your full concentration for opening week, and I'm clearly not going to get that if you're worrying about her. You want your girl? Meet me at midnight.

Somewhere near the Slayers' compound. On the bluff road."

I didn't want hope to light me up inside. I didn't want to trust Luca, because I knew that no matter what he said, how smooth his words and promises were, he couldn't be trusted.

But that clubhouse was overrun with bikers.

And I didn't trust Hawk even more than I didn't trust Luca.

I couldn't stand the thought of Kara in that clubhouse, men surrounding her, taking her body while she screamed.

And Hayley Jade...if she was in there too...I couldn't stand the thought of her having to see her mom like that.

I couldn't get them out alone. I had no fucking friends since I'd left the Sinners.

But Luca had people. Contacts. Money. He could get her out.

I swallowed hard, resigning myself to making a deal with the devil for the good of the angel behind the gates. "There's a fire trail turn-off about three miles from the Slayers' compound."

Luca made a noise of approval. "Good. We'll meet you there. And Hayden?"

"Yeah?"

"We have one shot at this. One shot to get in and get your girl, without anyone getting hurt. If that's what you want, don't be late."

I didn't hesitate. "I won't be."

I ended the call, but there were still hours until midnight.

I needed a movie. They had always been my go-to

thought eraser, starting from as far back as when Liam had been chosen to live a bigger, better life, and I'd been left behind without my brother.

Losing myself in somebody else's story made it easier to forget that I was always ruining my own. Right now, it would stop me thinking about what could be happening to her at a Slayers' party. Stop me thinking about other men putting their hands on her. Thinking about how she might not like it.

Or worse.

That she would.

The Saint View theater ran movie marathons on weekends. Back-to-back screenings on Friday and Saturday nights from early evening through to dawn.

At least I couldn't drown myself in the fucking cat's water if I was around other people.

I parked my truck and got out, wandering inside and pulling out my wallet as I looked up at the movie board.

The marathon was all four *Twilight* movies. And the foyer was filled with women.

I was sorely out of place.

But what-the-fuck-ever.

Better to watch someone else's unrequited, hopelessly doomed love story, rather than think about my own.

38

KARA

*D*ating felt nice. We finished our meal, and Hawk drove us to the theater, stopping the van in the parking lot and slipping his hand into mine as we got out.

I glanced down at our joined fingers and then at the crowd milling around us. There were a lot of people here, waiting in line for tickets or the concession stand, or just hanging around the lobby, waiting for the theater doors to open. A woman around my age did a double take when she laid eyes on Hawk, her expression turning into one of confusion when her gaze traveled down his arm to find him holding my hand. She stepped in to her group of friends and said something, and they all glanced back at me.

He cleared his throat. "That okay?"

I dragged my attention back to him. "That you're holding my hand?"

"Mmm."

I rubbed my thumb across his knuckles, tracing over

an old scar that ran across three of them. "You aren't embarrassed to be seen with me?"

He stopped. "What? No. Why the fuck would I be?"

I shrugged, pulling my jacket across my breasts and then glancing back at the group of women.

They were all watching.

I could practically imagine what they were thinking.

Hawk looked good. I'd thought he was attractive in dirty jeans, wifebeater T-shirts, and his club jacket. But he was a whole different sort of hot tonight. Tonight he didn't only appeal to the women who wanted a bad boy.

Tonight he appealed to anyone with an X chromosome.

I was very much aware I was not the sort of person who would normally attract his attention.

The red-haired woman who'd first noticed him and was busy gossiping with her friends was probably exactly his type though. She was older than me, clearly more experienced, and definitely more confident. She watched us openly, and when he turned her way, she lowered her eyes to peep at him through her lashes.

I didn't know how to do that. I didn't know how to flirt or be cute and pretty. I didn't know how to use makeup, and he hadn't given me time to ring Rebel and ask her to come over with her case of foundations and mascara to help me.

He stopped walking and tugged me around to face him, sliding his hand from mine and circling it around my waist instead. He dipped his head, tilted it to one side, and laid his mouth on mine.

In an instant, every worry disappeared. They melted into the hold he had on me, and on instinct, I circled my arms around his neck, fingertips stroking the hair at his nape.

I forgot where we were. Forgot there were other people watching. I let my heart flitter away with my brain and Hawk kiss me until nice feelings replaced the doubts and worries.

He might not have been good with words, but the man's actions told me everything he wanted me to know.

His tongue stroked against mine, and I joined him, needing more of his taste and more of the way he made me feel. I kissed him back, more familiar with him now after kissing earlier that day, but no less thrilled by the way his lips felt when they were on mine.

His hands slid to my ass. When he finally pulled his head back an inch, his lips hovering over mine, I was dizzy in a cloud of lust.

"We're in public," I murmured. But that was about as much complaint as I could put up when my brain was already thinking about ditching the movie and going home so he could do that again with no clothes on.

He grinned against my mouth. "Every time you let that bullshit self-doubt creep in, I'm going to kiss you like that. No matter who's watching." He rubbed his lips over mine. "And then I'm going to take you home and punish you, my way, for thinking so fucking little of me." His warm breath misted over mine. "I don't just want you in my fucking bedroom, Kara. I want you everywhere. If it wouldn't get us arrested, I would have you up on that concession counter, your skirt around your waist, your pussy the only sweet thing I want to taste. All these people, especially those bitches staring at us, be damned. Let them fucking watch."

He'd said it loud enough that everyone around us would have heard. There was no doubt in my mind that had been deliberate.

I didn't even care. He was so attractive; he could have any woman he wanted. But he'd picked me, not just as his dirty little secret, but as something more. That knowledge silenced the memories of Josiah's harsh, sharp words and the disgust I was so used to seeing when men looked in my direction.

All I could think about was letting him do exactly what he'd said on the counter back in my cabin. My knees went weak at the thought of my legs spread wide, his face buried between my thighs, his tongue licking through my center.

He'd push his fingers inside me like he had before, and my hips would rock until I was so wet I was dripping. Desire pulsed through me, hot and needy.

Wanting a man was an entirely new experience for me, and one I was quickly getting addicted to.

He winked at me. "Do you really want to watch this movie?"

I shook my head quickly. "Not at all."

"You want to go home, Little Mouse? You want to go home and let me sink my tongue between your folds, finger you until you're moaning, and then fuck you until you're begging me to let you come?"

A beat pulsed between my legs, made all the stronger by the fact I was sure that woman could hear his dirty promises. My arousal soaked my panties, and an ache bloomed inside me so strong I knew I wasn't going to make it home before I came. Everything between my legs throbbed, begging to be touched.

"I need a minute," I whispered. "Just give me a minute to go to the bathroom."

He grinned at me, like he knew exactly why I needed to go in there. He leaned in and kissed my cheek. "You going to put your fingers inside you? You gonna go hide in the bathroom and make yourself come because you can't wait until I get you home?"

I opened my mouth to deny it, because that wasn't something I ever did, but the thought left me panting. "Is that what you want me to do?"

He groaned. "I'm getting us some popcorn to go, and then I'll meet you outside the restrooms." His gaze went lusty. "Go come for me. And when I get you home, be prepared to come all night."

I'd never run for a bathroom so quickly in my entire life.

An attendant at the auditorium door pulled on the handle at the same time, opening up for people waiting. I fought against the surge of bodies all excited to get to their seats while all I could think about doing was being alone so I could ease the ache inside me that was threatening to engulf me whole.

I pushed on the door to the bathroom, finding two women touching up their makeup in the mirrors and the rest of the bathroom blissfully empty.

I headed for the stalls, my core throbbing with need from Hawk's embrace and the dirty words I couldn't stop thinking about.

The door opened again behind me, and one of the women shouted, "Hey! This is the ladies' room!"

I spun on my heel, smile wide, knowing it was Hawk who'd followed me. I didn't even care what these women thought. I just wanted him to sweep me into his arms, put his mouth on mine, and walk me backward into a stall so I could have his erection inside me.

I froze at the sight of the man who stood in the bathroom, his blue-gray eyes locked on mine.

Like he had every right to be there.

Like he had every right to stare at me.

Like he had every right to be alive.

A cry fell from my lips. A gasp from somewhere deep inside me that had longed to see this man for every day of the last five years.

"You can't be in here!" the woman said again, her gaze bouncing between the two of us.

I had no words to say. Shock held me in its grip.

All I could do was stare at Hayden.

He moved before I could. He took two steps toward me, grabbing my wrist, and dragging me into the nearest stall, locking the door behind him.

"Damn," one of the women said from the sinks. "I wish my man did that to me once in a while."

Tears pricked the backs of my eyes. The women outside and anyone new coming and going disappeared in the roaring of blood in my ears.

My throat clogged with emotion, and I trembled from head to toe, shock refusing to let go of me.

Caleb had shot him. Left him on the side of the road to die.

He was alive.

His gaze searched mine. "I only have a minute. I know Hawk is out there."

I blinked. Hawk. I was in here... I was supposed to be doing...

Now I was here, with the man who'd haunted my dreams for what felt like a lifetime.

The man I couldn't forget.

The man everyone said I should hate, and yet even when I thought he was dead I never could.

Something pulsed in the air between us. A crackling of chemistry that had always been there. That connected us every time we were together.

"You're not dead," I whispered, hands hovering over his chest, not daring to touch him in case this was a dream and he was nothing more than a figment of my imagination.

"Hawk didn't tell you then?" he whispered back, that familiar grumble of his voice seeping through my skin, burying itself inside me until I couldn't breathe. "I saw him the other day, with Hayley Jade...Kara, she's so big."

Nobody had told me. Nobody had said a word.

They'd all let me think he'd died that night on the side of the road.

They'd all lied.

Tears spilled down my cheeks.

In an instant, he cupped my face, his thumbs wiping away my tears. "Don't cry," he murmured. "Shit. Please, baby. Please don't cry."

He'd never called me baby before. But there, in that moment with my chest splayed wide open and everything inside me splintering into pieces, it was the sweetest word I'd ever heard.

I couldn't stop the tears.

He wasn't who they thought he was.

He was the man who'd saved me. Who'd kept me and my daughter alive. He was the man who'd connected with me on such a soul-deep level I'd named my daughter after him.

He wasn't real and yet he was right there, his heart beating too fast beneath the press of my palm against his chest.

"You need to go," he told me. "Hawk will be waiting outside, and if you're too long, he won't think twice about coming in here searching for you."

My fingers clenched in his shirt, and I shook my head frantically. I couldn't lose him again.

But he was right. Hawk was waiting for me on the other side. Waiting to take me home. Waiting to do things to my body I hadn't even imagined possible.

Red hot rage poured in, freezing the lust and desire.

Everyone had lied. Hawk. Rebel. War. Bliss. Had they all known and just said nothing? Thinking me the stupid brainwashed woman who didn't deserve to know the truth so she could make her own decisions?

Hayden's gaze locked with mine. "I know you're staying at the clubhouse. Pack a bag for you and Hayley Jade and meet me. I'll come to you, tonight. Late. I have a way of getting in."

He couldn't do that. He'd be risking his life.

He gripped my face harder. "Say no and I'll walk away."

I should have said no. I should have let him go.

But my lips didn't move. My heart was too busy beating its way out of my chest and my brain was locked up in thoughts of the past, when this man had been the only thing keeping me alive.

"Don't say no, Kara. Say you'll meet me. At the back

gate. I'll tell you everything. We'll work something out. Just fucking say yes. *Please*."

I couldn't say anything.

Hawk was a liar.

And Hayden was still alive.

39

HAWK

Kara's face was flushed when she came out of the bathroom, her skin wet like she'd had to splash water on it to cool down.

All I could think about was her in there, fingers buried deep in her pussy, muffling her cries while she came, and the fact she'd been so turned on she hadn't even been able to make it home so I could do it for her.

I gave her a cocky grin. "Feel better?"

She didn't say anything, just walked past me.

I frowned and followed her, catching her gently by the elbow. "Hey. Are you okay?"

She pulled her arm out of mine. "I've changed my mind. I want to watch the movie."

"Okay..." I had to jog a few steps to catch her.

She didn't say anything.

Doubt crept in. Fuck. I'd pushed her too far. I'd been nudging at her limits, knowing she had no experience. I'd gotten off on breaking apart the walls she'd put up and unveiling the woman she hid inside. One whose body came alight when I touched her.

Telling her to go come in a public bathroom had clearly been a step over the line.

I followed her into the auditorium and sat beside her in the darkness, shooting glances at her for the next two hours while she steadfastly stared at the screen, her hands firmly on her lap.

If the movie hadn't been so full of people, I would have been tempted to try to coax her into letting me apologize. With my tongue buried between the lips of her pussy.

But considering that was basically what had got us to this point, it was probably better that the auditorium was full and there was no chance for me to get on my knees.

My dick was hard for her again, but I forced myself to watch the movie.

When it finished, we walked out into the light, and I slipped my arm around her shoulders. "So, what did you think?"

She cringed away from my touch. "Take me home, please."

There was a distinct chill in her voice I'd never heard before.

I'd heard her scared. Tired. Happy. Turned on.

Never angry the way she was right now.

I followed her to the car, running over the entire night in my head. I had no experience with dates, but I thought it had been going pretty well. We'd talked. I'd said more to Kara tonight than I had ever spoken to Amber or Kiki in the years I'd known them. I'd told her things only my best friends knew. She'd been insecure about being with me in public, but I thought I'd done a good job of reassuring her that the things I wanted from her were more than just a quick fuck at the clubhouse. I thought I'd shown her how much her body did it for me, even if I'd never been with anyone like her before.

But I'd done something wrong.

I opened the passenger-side door for her and cursed beneath my breath as I closed it after her.

This wasn't just her getting a little overwhelmed and needing a minute to calm down. This was her shrinking away from me like she couldn't stand my touch. Like it was me she was scared of.

I'd clearly fucked up. Royally. This was more than me just wanting her to come in a public place. She'd been into that. I knew it.

I jogged around to the driver's side and got in, starting the van.

Kara refused to look at me. She twisted to one side, staring out the window. I got us out of the parking lot and along the bluff road that would lead us back to the compound. It wasn't a long drive, but the minutes felt like hours, each one so painfully silent that by the time we pulled into the Slayers' driveway, I couldn't take it anymore.

"What did I do, Kara?" I asked quietly.

She didn't answer.

Her silence was deafening.

I strangled the steering wheel, fighting the urge to demand she talk.

If I demanded it, she probably would. Fuck, I'd told her to drop her arms so I could see her hard, greedy nipples through her shirt that first night she'd walked into my room and caught me fucking my hand. She'd stood there, watching me come, just because I'd told her to.

But while I liked bossing her around in the bedroom, this felt different.

This felt fragile.

Like if I made demands of it, I could break into so many pieces it could never be repaired.

So I pressed my lips together and forced my concentration to the road.

Taillights up ahead had me slowing, peering through the darkness at the bikes maneuvering through the gates. Fang waved me over as I approached, and I rolled the window down. Music from within the compound filtered through the night air, and I jerked my head toward the gravel drive that led down to the clubhouse. "What's going on? Who was that?"

Fang sighed heavily. "You're late to the party, brother."

"What party? We weren't having a party tonight?"

"We are now. And it's a full house. Guys from the Louisiana chapter have been arriving for hours."

I frowned, irritated they'd shown up here without so much as a word of warning. "What the fuck for?"

He shrugged. "No idea. War was waiting for you to get back before we take their prez and VP to church."

Awareness prickled over the back of my neck. "War called all the Saint View crew in?"

Fang nodded grimly. "You're the last to arrive. We've just been keeping everybody happy. We've been supplying the alcohol. They brought a few women. Everyone is having a nice time." He glanced down the hill. "So far anyway. War ain't happy about them just showing up here uninvited."

Not that he could say that. There were laws between chapters. Rules that had been set in stone from the club's conception. The Slayers were a family, no matter which chapter you were a part of. You never turned away a brother when they arrived on your doorstep, wanting a roof over their heads or a bourbon in their hands.

I glanced over at Kara and then back at Fang. "Are Kian and Vaughn at your house with Rebel and the kids?"

"I sent them all over to War's place. Vincent and Nash are there too." He leaned past me to talk to Kara. "Hayley Jade as well. Rebel picked her up on their way. They're all waiting for you."

That was smart. Keeping all of their families together. Kian, Vaughn, and Nash could all hold their own in a fight, but Vincent was lethal. Kara would be safe with them. A hell of a lot fucking safer than she'd be here tonight, with fifty extra bikers all hoping for a good time. "Tell War I'll be back in twenty. I'll just take Kara and then we can call church."

"No," Kara said sharply.

Fang and I both looked over at her.

I reached over and squeezed her leg, but she flinched away from me, like we were right back where we started, and like I hadn't just had my hands all over her in the lobby of that theater. What the fuck was going on?

"Kara, there's probably a hundred people down there, throwing what will likely be an all-night party," Fang explained gently.

"Great," she bit out through gritted teeth. "Sounds like fun."

I stared at her. "Fun? No. Not fucking fun. You have no idea what a Slayers' party is like. Especially not one with out-of-towners. You've only ever been to family events. That's nothin' like what's going on down there tonight. I'm taking you to War's place. You'll be safe there."

My mouth dropped open when Kara yanked on the handle and shoved the door open. She unclicked her seat belt and got out of the van, storming around to the front and through the gates, lit up by my headlights.

Fang and I stared wide-eyed.

"What the fuck did you do to her?" he asked me.

I shook my head. "I honestly have no idea."

"I've never seen her act like that. Should I go get her? I mean...she can't go down there."

It was what my gut instinct said to do as well. To keep her away. Keep her locked up safe and sound at War's place while I dealt with whatever the hell was going on.

"Kara," I called.

But she didn't stop.

"For fuck's sake," I muttered to Fang and then shook my head. "I'm not gonna carry her out of here kicking and screaming. Are you?"

He stared at her stomping down the driveway. "If you tell me to, I will. But I won't be very happy about it."

"Me neither."

"So what's the other option?"

Her accusations that we were keeping her imprisoned the same way Josiah had played over and over in my head. She wasn't mine to control. She was a grown woman. She had a child. Who was I to tell her what she could and couldn't do? "Rebel and Bliss both had to learn what Slayers' parties were all about. Kara does too. We can't protect her from everything, and if she's going to be my woman, she needs to know what she's getting herself into."

Fang stared at me. "If she's going to be your woman..." He leaned back against the gate and stared at me hard. "Are you for real, Hawk? I've known you a long time, and you've never once looked at a woman as anything other than a warm place to sink your dick. If you're fucking with her, getting your rocks off on toying with her because she's so innocent she's practically Bambi, then—"

I glared at him. "Then nothing. Because I'm not fucking with her." I pulled at the stupid cable-knit sweater that made my arms itchy. "You think I'd wear this shit for a woman I didn't like? You think I'd take her out and spend hours talking to her? You think I'd spend every minute of every fucking day thinking about how sweet and good and sexy she is?"

Fang stared at me. "You gonna put her on the back of your bike?"

I sucked in a breath.

He might as well have asked me if I was in love with her.

It was the same thing in our world. No woman rode on the back of your bike unless you were willing to put a ring on her finger.

My brain said no.

My stupid fucking heart screamed yes.

I twisted on my heel and got back in the van. Screw Fang. Screw his stupid questions. He wasn't in a position to ask me shit like that.

I got in the van and went after Kara.

All I could think about was how she'd feel, her sweet thick thighs wrapped around mine. Her soft tits pressed to my back. Her arms wrapped around my middle.

Every person we passed knowing she was off-limits because she was on the back of my bike.

She was my Little Mouse.

My woman.

Mine.

40

KARA

I struggled down the track in my wedge shoes, battling to not twist my ankle with every step on the dark, uneven road. Party sounds grew louder as I approached the clubhouse, the music thumping and unfamiliar. Shouts and laughter. Beer bottles and glasses clinking together.

The parking area was full of unfamiliar bikes, and a group of men stood by the doorway, all with drinks in their hands, nudging each other. I didn't recognize any of them, but they all wore Slayers' patches like Hawk and War and the others did.

Anger had gotten me this far, but nerves broke through the red haze as I neared the men. I just needed to get inside and find Queenie, or a familiar face, and then the nerves would disappear so I could sink back into the anger.

I was a balled-up mess of confusion. I felt things for Hawk. Things just a couple hours ago I'd been so excited to explore further.

In a split second everything had changed.

If he'd lied about Hayden, what else had he lied about? Did he actually want me? Or did I actually mean no more to him than Kiki or Amber? Everyone had tried to warn me. Queenie. Rebel.

But I'd been so sure there was another side to him. One he'd saved for me.

How stupid to think I was that special.

Josiah's voice rang loud and clear in my head. *You aren't special. You aren't worthy. You're nothing but a hole to fuck, one that can't even produce a child, so what's the fucking point other than a warm place to stick your dick?*

"Hey, sweetheart," one of the bikers said, leaning an arm on the doorway at head height so I couldn't pass. "Haven't seen you here before. You new?"

"Don't fucking look at her," Hawk growled from behind me.

It took me by surprise. I knew he'd follow me down here. Where else was he going to go? But I hadn't even noticed the van, or him striding across the lot to catch up with me. I'd been too caught up in the whirlwind of emotions seeing Hayden had stirred to life.

But anger was the biggest one. It was like Hawk's betrayal had opened some floodgate inside me and let out everything I'd been keeping inside for weeks and months or maybe even years. His lies. Josiah's abuse. My parents' lack of care. My daughter being ripped from my arms. My sister's murder.

I hadn't let myself truly feel any of it until seeing Hayden had disintegrated every barrier I'd ever put in place.

And now I was drowning. Drowning in a sea of emotions that I couldn't make sense of and couldn't stop.

The guy stared at Hawk and then down at me. He had a "president" badge sewn beneath the Slayers' emblem over his chest, just like War did. "You want me to stop looking at you, sweetheart?"

He was handsome. His hair peppered with gray and his eyes framed by thin lines. He smelled oddly good too, like some sort of rich cologne that I breathed in deeply.

I glanced back at Hawk whose face was a storm cloud.

I was so sick of men looking at me like that. So sick of always having to be the good girl they all expected of me when all they did was lie and cheat and make demands.

This older man could look at me if he wanted to. Hawk didn't get a say in that.

I took the glass from the man's hand and put it to my lips, swallowing down several large mouthfuls of the bitter liquid.

"Kara," Hawk said quietly. "What the hell are you doing?"

I didn't know. But drinking was what everyone else did to forget their problems, so if it was good enough for them, then maybe it was good enough for me too. "I'm getting another drink. Leave me the hell alone."

The Louisiana prez let out a laugh and shooed Hawk away like he was a nuisance. "Go on, then. Off you go. You heard the lady."

Hawk stepped in, going eye to eye with the man. "She doesn't fucking drink, asshole. It's against her religion."

The prez raised an eyebrow, pouring another hefty shot into my glass and nudged the bottom of it up toward my lips.

I swallowed it down quickly, this glass not tasting nearly as bad as the first one had and leaving behind a pleasant warming sensation.

It felt nice when the rest of me felt so damn cold.

"Another," I held my glass out.

As it filled, I glared at Hawk, seeing only the lies he'd told. The words he *hadn't* said, so much louder in my head than the sweet ones he had. "I have no religion anymore," I told him. "And so I'm getting drunk. Really fucking drunk, Hawk."

The Louisiana prez held his hand out to me. "I'm Riot."

I took his hand, letting his big fingers engulf mine, but staring at Hawk the entire time. Everyone else had a road name. Maybe it was time I embraced mine. "I'm Little Mouse."

Hawk's nostrils flared.

Riot's gaze bounced back and forth between me and Hawk.

"Kara," Hawk said again, but this time it was with the growling undertone of a warning.

"What?" I challenged him. "Who says you're the only one allowed to call me that? It's not like you asked me if I liked it, did you?"

He grabbed my arm, pulling me in tight against his chest. "Because we both know damn well you do. We both fucking know every time I use that name on you, you get a tingle down your pretty little spine that settles right between your thighs."

He breathed heavily, and my breaths matched his, my body igniting once more at his touch and reminding me he was right. Every time he spoke like that I just wanted to melt into a puddle of arousal and let him do whatever he wanted to do to me.

But he hadn't meant a word of it. Because he was a fucking liar.

I shoved him away. "Don't touch me."

His face was a mass of confusion, his brows furrowed, his head shaking, squinting like he couldn't work me out. Anger finally broke through all the rest. "Are you for real? You were damn near begging me to fuck you in the theater just a couple hours ago. And now you're getting drunk and don't even want me to touch you? What happened between then and now, because I have no idea what the hell I did? I know I'm not very smart, so take pity on me and spell it out. What happened in that bathroom, Kara?"

"Chaos," I spat out at him, unable to hold my tongue a second longer. "Complete and utter *chaos*." I put the emphasis on the last word, staring Hawk dead in the eye so he'd know exactly what I meant.

Understanding dawned in his eyes.

And then guilt.

Fuck him.

"You knew he was alive, didn't you?" I whispered, knowing the truth but needing to hear him say it.

He looked away and then finally dragged his gaze to meet mine. "Yes."

I nodded. It was probably the first truth he'd ever told me. But it did nothing to ease the hurt inside. I turned away, taking another swallow of the liquid. "Just leave me alone, Hawk."

He paused for a minute, and I prayed he would listen.

Because I didn't know how long I could stand there and defy him when every second felt so wrong.

He gave a single nod and backed away, his gaze holding mine until I let Riot and his friends surround me.

Anything to not have to see the aching hurt and regret in Hawk's green eyes.

41

HAWK

Three drinks in, I stopped bothering with a cup and just took the bottle from behind the bar. I put it to my lips and swallowed mouthful after mouthful, needing the burn of the alcohol just so I could breathe.

"This is messed up," War said quietly from the stool beside me. "We should take her back to my place."

I shook my head, choking on the urge to do exactly what War said. "You think I don't want that? You think I don't want to go pick her up right now and get her the hell out of here? Trust me. It's all I can fucking think about. But she's made it very clear that's not what she wants."

Fang let out a frustrated groan. "She's wasted."

I strangled the neck of my bourbon bottle. "Lucky her. I wish I could say the same."

Except the liquor I was downing like water had absolutely no effect in the face of Kara dancing on the motherfucking coffee table with Kiki and Amber, while half the Louisiana chapter cheered and threw money at them like they were strippers.

Amber and Kiki picked up the money, pocketing every bill, but Kara was lost to the music and the alcohol Riot had been plying her with, seemingly unaware of anything else. She swung her hips from side to side, her hands raised in the air, moving to the beat of the music.

She was so damn beautiful it hurt.

But all I could see was the hate and anger in her eyes every time I came near her. And the crippling knowledge that I deserved it.

"We should have told her about Hayden a long time ago," I admitted. "Or at least, I should have. I screwed up."

War sighed heavily. "Maybe, but it's my fault too. I told you not to tell her. You thought you were keeping her safe."

"Did I?" I laughed bitterly. "Or was I just really sure she would pick him over me and too selfish to let that happen?"

I knew the answer. I swore and raked my fingers through my hair. "I deserve this. I fucking deserve to sit here and watch every other man in this room think about getting her naked." I didn't even know she could move like that. So seductively. So perfect my balls ached with need. I was supposed to be in her cabin right now, holding her, touching her, feeling her soft tits in my hands and her warm pussy around my cock.

I was supposed to be caressing her. Kissing her. Making fucking love to her.

I wasn't supposed to be sitting here watching every other man in the room think the same.

I'd seen some shit in my time as a VP. I'd been in

fights. Broken bones. Had knife wounds that had needed more stitches than I could count. Been shot in the leg.

None of it had hurt as much as the look in her eyes when she'd told me that she knew.

I'd lost her before she was ever really even mine.

I shoved to my feet. "I can't fucking stand here watching Riot mentally undress her. I'm going to pull my gun and shoot the prick if I have to look at it any longer."

"Don't do that," Fang warned quietly. "There's a lot more of them than there are of us. I know it's killing you, but just play nice."

Riot reached out and ran his fingers up Kara's leg, and a red haze dropped down over my eyes. I reached for my gun.

"Jesus fuck," War muttered. "Bliss is having a baby any damn day now, and I do not have the time or patience for this bullshit. Riot!"

The Louisiana prez lifted his head.

War jerked a thumb toward the small conference room off to the side. "Church. Now. Bring your VP and one other member. Everyone else waits out here."

It wasn't a question. It was a direct order.

Riot might have had superiority over me, his rank of prez making his status higher than mine. But War was the prez of the original Slayers' club. So even amongst presidents, he was top dog, and the entire room knew it.

They didn't like it.

But they knew it.

Riot stood and said something to Kara that produced a pink blush on her cheeks.

I wanted to fucking scream.

At least in church, Riot couldn't gawk at her. Pervy old

prick. He was twice her age. He probably had kids older than her.

My fingers twitched over my gun again, desperate to use it.

Fang clamped a heavy hand down on my shoulder. "You have any idea how much trouble you'd cause War by doing whatever it is you're thinking of doing? He can't be here dealing with this shit when his woman is about to have a baby. You're VP. Not a pussy-whipped prospect. Get your shit together."

I glared at him. "Like you can talk. Rebel has you wrapped around her little finger. Always has."

His eyes darkened. "Just the way I like it. But I'm not the goddamn VP. And Kara has made it pretty clear she's not your woman, even if you want her to be. So do your job, walk your ass into church, and leave that girl alone. She ain't yours."

He was right. If I'd had any chance of calling her mine, I'd killed it dead when I'd lied to her.

It didn't mean I could just turn off everything I felt though. I couldn't just walk away. I glanced over at Ratchet and Aloha. "Watch her," I demanded, pointing at Kara.

They both nodded.

"Breathe," Fang said quietly in my ear as he marched me into church. "You've got a job to do in here, and it ain't to shoot fucking Riot in the head. Kara's having a good time with Amber and Kiki. Aloha is watching her. Your only job right now is to put your personal shit aside and have War's back. You owe him that much."

He was right. I'd barely been around lately. I'd been missing phone calls. I still hadn't done anything about meeting with the new police chief. I was just letting all of that fall on War whose head was miles away, at his home where his family awaited their newest arrival.

Fang was right.

It pissed me off because the man never made a comment unless it was to hit so close to home it scarred.

I stopped dragging my feet and pulled my shit together, standing up tall and shaking Fang off before we walked through the doorway. Fang kicked it closed behind him.

War sat at the head of the table, leaning back in his chair, arms folded across his chest. I took the seat to his right, Fang sitting on my other side. Riot sat opposite me, smirking, while his VP, Torque, and his sergeant-at-arms, Acid, sat to his left.

We'd all met before. Many a time. There was no need for introductions.

Just explanations.

War cleared his throat and raised an eyebrow in Riot's direction. "How you been, brother?"

"Same old shit, different day." Riot grinned and rocked on the back two legs of his chair. "Riding. Working. Partying. Fucking."

War nodded. "And you got sick of doing that in Louisiana so you thought you'd come on over here for a change of scenery, or..." He waited expectantly.

Riot shrugged nonchalantly, sitting his seat back down on all four legs and pulling out a packet of tobacco from his pocket. "Or."

War waited, but I could feel the irritation rolling off him in waves. He was trying to keep his calm and controlled exterior when I knew him well enough to know that he was mentally thinking about reaching for his gun as much as I was.

Fang's warning to step up and do my job rang in my ears. "What War is too fucking nice to say, is why the hell are you here without so much as a word of warning and with your entire crew? How long are you planning on staying?"

Riot glanced up at me from tapping out his tobacco. "War wants to know that? Or you want to know how long I'm going to be hanging around, pouring drinks for your girl?"

War shot me a sharp look that clearly said, *Don't you fucking dare react. He's a prez.*

Riot's guys wore identical expressions, the tension in the room so thick you could have cut it with a knife.

Preferably one I could later stick right through Riot's kidney.

Riot laughed suddenly, like the entire thing was hilarious. "Relax! Relax! I'm not here to take your girl, Hawk. If you say she's yours, then I'll back the fuck off."

"She's mine."

He held his hands up. "Done. Forget I ever saw her."

I leaned across the table, making a show of putting my gun down in the middle of it. "Don't expect me to thank you. Just tell us why you're here."

"Got some pickups to do."

War narrowed his eyes. "And you needed your entire club for that?"

Riot chuckled. "Fine. Got a lot of pickups to do. Needed the extra bikes to guard the vans on the way home. Got some clients desperately waiting on...stock."

"What kind of stock are you getting from our territory? Drugs? Guns? Anyone in Saint View or Providence and the surrounding areas is our turf. Not yours. You want something, you need to come through us," War practically growled.

It was the way the clubs had always run. You couldn't just walk into another club's territory and start making deals like you had every right. That was the biggest disrespect to War, and hackles rose on the back of my neck.

Fuck this guy. I'd never had a problem with him until now. But tonight we definitely had a problem. A big one.

Riot rolled his cigarette and then lit it, blowing a small ring of smoke into the air when he was done. "Cool your jets, hothead. We wouldn't dream of stepping on your toes. We came here for product you guys aren't interested in."

"Want to tell us what that might be?" Fang asked, his quiet presence as menacing as he was tall.

Riot took a long drag on his smoke and blew it out before he bothered answering. "Women."

The tenuous hold on my patience snapped. I threw myself across the table, fingers clenched into fists, the first one connecting solidly against his cheekbone.

Chaos erupted around me, War and Fang and Riot's two guys all pulling guns and pointing them at each other.

Pain exploded through my knuckles, an instant throbbing taking up residence in my fingers.

The momentum of my punch had forced Riot to turn his head, and he straightened it now to glare at me, his expression twisted with a scowl. "I'm going to give you that one for free because I did you dirty, hitting on your girl. Next one won't be. Jesus fuck. You love her or some bullshit?"

I shook my hand out and settled back in my seat, leaving the others to their guns. "Ain't none of your business. But don't walk into my club talking about taking our women."

Riot snorted. "Didn't you see how many we already had out there? We don't need your fucking club women. We got plenty of our own. And hey, I like the ones we have. I didn't want to go giving them away when we were approached about making a deal. You guys have made it real clear over the years that you don't do deals for women, so we came out here to talk to the contact ourselves."

"Let me fucking guess," Fang said darkly. "Luca Guerra?"

Riot raised an eyebrow. "Yes, actually. I thought you guys didn't want nothing to do with that game?"

"We don't," War practically growled. "Slayers don't traffic women."

"*Saint View* Slayers don't," Riot argued. "You might be sitting in the head honcho seat, War, but you ain't my prez."

War wasn't happy. Frost rolled off him, and his fingers gripped the table so hard his knuckles were white.

Riot didn't give an inch, facing off with him. "If we aren't welcome here, we'll leave. I didn't come here to ask your permission. It was just an easy drop-off point to collect the women. We're doing it whether you like it or not. The Jesus folk asked us to get them more women for their men, and they're willing to pay for them, so that's what we're here to do. We all got bills to pay, War. We aren't all you, shacked up in a multimillion-dollar mansion with your pansy-ass boyfriend."

War stood, never one to take any mention of his family lightly. He towered over Riot. "I'm going to give you exactly thirty seconds to get the fuck out of here before I make you wish you hadn't said that."

But something Riot had said didn't sit well with me. It took me a second to place it, but when I did, my blood ran cold.

Fang seemed to be thinking along the same lines. "Kara's people are from out Riot's way."

I shot him a look and then transferred it to Riot. "Who are they? Your Jesus people?"

Riot broke his stare-off with War, though he kept one hand resting lightly on his gun. "What? I don't know. Live on some homestead in Texas. Guy's name is Josiah or something, I dunno. Thunder did most of the back-and-forth with him."

Fear seized my heart.

I didn't believe in coincidences. It was stupid to downplay what was right there in your face.

These men knew Josiah.

And they were here for women.

I shoved to my feet and stormed for the door.

Behind me I was vaguely aware of Riot asking where I was going.

I yanked open the door only to be blasted in the face by music and talking and yelling and laughter. The room was twice as full as when I'd left, more people than I'd ever seen in the damn room, probably because it had started raining and there wasn't much in the way of shelter.

Kara was no longer on the coffee table with Kiki and Amber.

Amber was on her knees, sucking off one of Riot's guys. Kiki next to her, bouncing up and down on some asshole's cock while a third guy groped her tits.

All around me, just like our parties often did, the clubhouse had turned into a "nothing was off-limits" gang bang.

We'd all done it. We'd all had women in this room, everyone getting off on fucking in public.

But today the sight just left me cold.

"Kara!" I said sharply, scanning the room for her, heart pumping with the fear I was going to find her in a similar position as Kiki or Amber or one of the other women wandering around in various states of undress and fornication.

My gaze landed on Aloha, Queenie grinding over his lap in a display that shocked me since they weren't normally ones for public shows. "Aloha," I ground out, trying not to look.

His eyes opened, and I realized how drunk he was. His gaze was unfocused, and he laughed. "Hawk. Can't talk." He snorted. "Hey. That rhymes."

I glanced at Queenie, exasperated and awkward as fuck that I was trying to talk to her while she was impaled on her old man's dick.

I didn't want to see that. It was like watching my parents fuck. "Jesus, you two. Can you knock it off?"

She gasped, out of breath from her efforts, but then glared at me. "Hey. Don't come up in here, giving me your shitty attitude about me getting mine. We've had Hayley

Jade in our room for so long so you can get yours. We gotta take what we can."

I made a face when Aloha dragged her top up, exposing her tits. Both of them laughed hysterically at my expense.

Oh, this was too much. They were both drunk off their asses, and Queenie was going to die of embarrassment if she remembered this in the morning. I sincerely hoped I didn't.

But I needed her to focus. "Where did Kara go?"

Queenie shrugged and then pointed to the door. "Oh, wait. She said she didn't feel well and was going to her cabin."

I gawked at them. "And you just let her?"

She paused in her rocking over Aloha's lap, steeling me with a look of disapproval that I'd dared to sass her. "I let her go to her room, yes. Because you devastated that girl tonight, Hawk. She needed a goddamn minute. Just like I do now. So go out there and find her and make whatever the hell you did better and leave me to my orgasm."

I'd never run out of the clubhouse so fast.

Down the path. Up the stairs, shoving open the door that was never locked.

Why the fuck hadn't I gotten her a lock? "Kara!"

There was nobody in the living room. The kitchen. I slammed my way into the bathroom only to find it empty, and then into her bedroom.

Her clothes were all cleared out.

There wasn't anything left.

Not even a note.

She was gone.

42

HAYDEN

I paced back and forth, boots crunching over the gravel on the edge of the road, and checked my watch for at least the third time in twenty minutes. The bluff road didn't get a ton of traffic in the middle of the day, let alone at nearly one in the morning, but I felt like a goddamn sitting duck, waiting for Luca to show.

Impatience had my muscles all locked tight, and it was a minute-by-minute fight to just stand there and wait, when Kara was just a few miles away through the woods, packing her bags, readying to run with me.

At least I hoped she was.

"What the fuck are you doing?" I muttered to myself in the darkness. "What the actual fuck business do you have asking anything of that woman?"

I'd tried convincing myself that anything I'd felt for her hadn't been real.

But those few minutes we'd stolen in a theater bathroom tonight called me a liar. Those few minutes had told me that the last five years of thinking about her had been beyond my control. I couldn't have stopped it, even if I'd wanted to.

There was no forgetting what she'd suffered. No forgetting what I'd put her through or what we'd survived together.

No woman would ever understand. No woman would ever compare.

There was no walking away. I was in this up to my fucking eyeballs.

So I stood on the side of that goddamn road, praying Luca had some sort of plan for getting her out.

And she'd come with me.

I wouldn't force her. I wouldn't be that man.

She had to want me as much as I wanted her.

From the darkness, two vehicles approached, slowing down when their headlights lit me up. A black van with the name of one of Luca's Italian restaurants painted on the side. And behind it, Luca's silver Porsche.

I nodded at the guy behind the wheel of the van as he got out. I vaguely recognized him as one of the guys Luca had working at our restaurants. "Steve, right?" I held out my hand for him to shake.

The man nodded and offered me a smoke from the pack he pulled from his glove box.

I shook my head and went to Luca's car, since he seemed to be making no effort to get out of his vehicle. He wound down the window as I approached.

He leaned on his elbow. "When you get to the Slayers' gate, tell them you have a pizza delivery for Riot. No one will stop you. Once you're inside and you've made the delivery, what you do afterward is on you. There's a lot of people in there, if sources inside are to be believed. And the Slayers have a ton of land behind those fences. Maybe if you're lucky, they won't recognize you in the crowd."

There was fat fucking chance of that. The Slayers, at least the Saint View chapter, knew exactly who I was.

And I knew going back inside that compound was suicide if they discovered me.

It didn't matter though. I already knew I was going anyway.

Kara hadn't said yes. But she hadn't said no either.

I couldn't stand the thought of her in there, Hawk with his hands all over her. Not going in there wasn't an option.

I refused to let another man clip her wings. I'd done that to her once. I owed her the chance to fly.

I just wanted her to fly to me.

Steve whistled between his teeth, getting my attention, and then tossed the keys to me.

On instinct, I caught them before they could hit the ground.

Steve walked around to the passenger seat of Luca's car and got in.

A sinking feeling of dread washed over me.

I hit the button on the key fob that unlocked the back doors of the van and yanked one open.

At least ten sets of terrified eyes stared back at me.

Ten pairs of bound hands.

Ten gagged mouths.

I spun around, glaring at Luca. "No."

Luca raised an eyebrow at me. "That's not what you said earlier when you agreed to this job."

"You told me I was delivering pizza!"

Steve snorted. "Yeah, because bikers order pizza from five-star restaurants, and five-star restaurants deliver at one in the morning."

Luca's smile widened. "The man has a point, don't you think?"

I didn't fucking care if he did. I'd known pizza didn't mean pizza. I'd known there'd be drugs or guns in that van.

And I would have moved either without saying a word.

But women were different.

I was such an idiot. I'd known. I'd known from the very second Luca had walked back into my life that this is where I'd end up. Doing things so abhorrently awful I'd spent five years not sleeping while the goddamn guilt ate me alive.

I was weak.

That was what it came down to. I'd let him woo me with pretty words and opportunities I was too fucking poor and dumb to create for myself. I'd let my own damn desire for more overrule any common sense I should have had.

You couldn't be mad at a leopard for showing its spots when you were the one who got into bed with it.

I could live with guns and drugs. But I wasn't helping him traffic women. "Take your fucking keys. I'm not doing it. Go to hell."

Luca shrugged, taking them back. "If you don't want to do it, then Steve can."

Nothing was ever that easy with Luca.

I only had to wait a second for the slow, snakelike grin

to spread across his face. He leaned across the console and picked up his phone, pressing a button on it so the small screen lit up his face in the dim light. "Steve," he said with a chuckle. "You're good to go on in there and party it up with Chaos's girl, right? Want a sneak peek of what she's doing in there? I figured he might need some encouragement so I had Thunder send me a homemade movie."

I froze as sounds of a party poured through the tinny speakers on Luca's phone, a video rolling.

Steve let out a holler. "Big titty baby, come at me!" He glanced past Luca at me. "She dance like that for you, Chaos? All big tits in your face?"

Luca turned the phone around and let the video play for me.

Kara, still dressed in the clothes she'd been wearing at the movie, danced on a table with two other women, both in various states of naked. She swung her hips side to side, swaying seductively, her eyes closed.

Around her, a large crowd of bikers watched on. Some threw money at the women. Some catcalled and whistled. Hands reached for her, running dirty fingers up her calves and thighs, that she seemed wholly unaware of in her drunk or drugged state.

Something deep inside me erupted into anger as men around her started undoing their pants, stroking their cocks, getting off on watching her when she was too fucking out of it to consent.

"That's your girl, right, Chaos?" Luca asked innocently. "You just gonna leave her in there for that entire club to plow like a field?"

Hawk had turned her into one of his club sluts.

Over my fucking dead body was another man going to use her the way Caleb had. Or hold her against her will the way I had.

Luca tossed the keys back at me. "Make the delivery, Chaos. Go get your woman. We both know you aren't going to stand here doing nothing, knowing those men are going to take whatever they want from her pretty little pussy."

Luca held the keys out the window again, and when I didn't make a move to take them, he dropped them at my feet. His tires spun in the gravel, and I turned away instinctively, shielding my eyes.

By the time I turned back, he was gone.

Leaving me alone with a van full of women I didn't know.

And one I did, just a few miles away inside the Slayers' clubhouse, surrounded by men who didn't give a flying fuck about what kind of state she was in. Just that she was there, and theirs for the taking if they so felt like it.

But I couldn't drive in there and swap these women for the one I couldn't stop thinking about.

"Get out," I muttered to the woman closest to the door.

She stared up at me with huge eyes that leaked with tears as I untied her restraints. When her hands were free she pulled the gag from her mouth.

"What are you doing?" she whispered.

I shook my head, unable to even look at her. "Help the others."

She did, turning to the woman next to her and

yanking off her bindings. I did the same to a dark-haired woman to her left.

Her cheeks were wet from crying. "You're letting us go?"

I nodded, not caring about the consequences, only knowing that I had to get to Kara and this van was my way in. But I wasn't driving it past those gates with these women in the back.

"Where are we supposed to go?" one of the women asked.

I shook my head. "I don't know. I'm sorry."

Another gazed around wide-eyed. "We're in the woods! You can't just leave us here!"

It was near pitch-black, and we were in the middle of nowhere. But other cars would drive past eventually. Someone would come. "You can hitchhike. Go back into town. Into the police station. Someone will help you. But it can't be me. Just go. Please. Just fucking get out and run."

Headlights lit up the road once more, and I shouted to the first woman. "Hail that car down!"

There were still five more women in the van, all of them making desperate noises behind their gags.

I couldn't get to them fast enough. Kara's face was all I could see in each of their terrified eyes.

"They're stopping!" the woman called.

I didn't stop what I was doing to check. I just needed these women out of the van so I could get in it.

All I could see in my head was those men dragging Kara down off that table. Touching her. Taking things from her that they didn't deserve.

Car doors slammed.

Women spoke in frantic tones that echoed around my head, along with silent screams that belonged to Kara.

"Where. The fuck. Is Kara?" a deadly low voice came from behind me.

In the next instant, the barrel of a shotgun pressed to the back of my head.

Of all the people to stop, it had to be Hawk, didn't it?

I froze, fingers wrapped around the ropes tying down the last woman. Her huge eyes frantically flicked between me and the man standing behind me with a weapon held against my skull.

Hawk's voice held barely concealed rage. "Start talking, you piece of shit, because I swear to God, I'm barely keeping it together. Where the fuck is my woman?"

I spun around, not caring that it put me face-to-face with his gun. "Your woman? Are you joking me? You're feeling her up in movie theaters. You have her dancing on tables for your 'brothers.' She's not your fucking woman. You've turned her into your whore."

Hawk pressed the gun to my lips. "Call her a fucking whore one more time and I swear I'll pull the trigger. I'm going to ask you again, but you better believe this will be the last time. Where the hell is Kara?"

I stared at him, wide-eyed at his goddamn ignorance. "She's at your club! I just saw a video of her."

He shook his head. "She's not there. She's packed her bags and left. Where was she meeting you?"

Hope smacked me in the face, so stupid and out of place considering the situation I'd put myself in. But something deep inside me was damn giddy over Hawk's confession.

She was coming. She wanted to leave with me.

I was every bit the smug bastard, knowing she'd picked me. "Why would I tell you that?"

"Because we have acres and acres of land and about fifty bikers in there just waiting to take women back to her fucking cult leader of a husband."

I blinked. "Her what?"

Hawk lost any semblance of patience, his roar of frustration a scream of desperation. "Just tell me where she is, Hayden!"

For the first time, I saw past Hawk's bravado. Past the asshole biker front he put on.

And saw the pure terror in his eyes.

In an instant, I believed every word he'd said. Knew in my gut that Kara was in danger and I was just as responsible for putting her there as he was.

"She was meeting me at the back gate," I whispered.

"Try again, asshole. That was the first place we looked." His fingers trembled over the trigger.

"I swear. That was where we were supposed to meet."

"She's not fucking there, Chaos!"

I stared at him. "Then where the hell is she?"

He dropped the gun to his side and shook his head. "I don't know."

43

KARA

ONE HOUR EARLIER...

*M*y head spun. The room moved in dizzying circles, and my stomach churned.

Men touched me. Fingers sliding up my legs. Tucking notes into the elastic of my underwear.

I jerked away sharply, teetering on the edge of the table and then stepping down off it on wobbly legs.

Amber caught my wrist. "Hey. You okay?"

I wasn't. "He's a liar," I mumbled drunkenly. "And Hayden is alive."

Amber had been drinking too, but clearly holding it better than I was. "All men are liars," she told me. "Just don't expect more from them and then you won't be disappointed." She pointed at the men on the couch, watching us with their hands down their pants. "See? All I expect from men like this is a good time and enough money to pay my rent. Then nobody gets hurt."

She straddled one of the biker's laps, wrapping her

arms around his neck. "Hey, Thunder? You're going to put a hundred down my bra before I let you fuck me. Right?"

He took the money from his pocket and pressed it between her cleavage.

She glanced back at me. "Take your pick, honey. Hawk ain't worth getting upset over when there's a whole room full of men here just dying to fuck your practically virginal pussy."

I couldn't listen to it anymore. Couldn't take the jeers and the taunts from the men. There were suddenly too many of them. Too many unfamiliar faces, all of them seemingly focused on me.

I'd felt safe here for weeks.

Now suddenly that bubble had burst.

The door to the club's "church" was still closed, Hawk behind it somewhere.

Along with Fang and War.

They'd all lied.

Everyone but Hayden. He'd done bad things. But at least he wasn't a liar.

I didn't know what time it was, but he'd be waiting for me at the back gates by now, surely.

Queenie and Aloha were all over each other as I stumbled past, her hips grinding over his while he drank from his beer bottle.

"Hey, sugar!" she called. "You enjoying your first Slayers' party?"

"I don't feel well," I mumbled. "Going to my cabin."

It wasn't a lie. But I wasn't sure if I felt sick because of the amount of alcohol I'd poured down my throat in the last hour, or if it was because even through my drunken haze, I knew the decision I made tonight was one that couldn't be undone.

I was choosing between Hawk and Hayden. The man I'd spent weeks with, who I was falling for day by day, and the man who'd saved me all those years ago. Who I had a connection with like nothing I'd ever felt before. One so strong, I'd named my daughter for him.

If I chose wrong, there was no coming back.

Hawk wasn't the sort of man who would just forgive me if I left with Hayden.

He was the sort of man who would declare me dead to him and never look my way again.

Even though he'd lied, my heart didn't care. My heart only remembered the soft touches. The sweet words he saved only for me. The fire only he could ignite in my body.

The way he'd started to put me back together after Josiah's years of abuse and Alice's death had ripped me to shreds.

I didn't know how to walk away.

The party followed me down the path. The music. The voices. The footsteps. It should have got quieter the farther I got into the woods, but it was all just a mess of noise and confusion. My steps became faster, until I was running, desperate to leave it all behind, to find some quiet, so I could just think.

Tears fell as I reached the cabin and shouldered my way inside.

I needed to pack a bag.

I needed to leave.

I wasn't safe here.

Through sobs that spoke of the way Hawk had betrayed me, I pulled clothes from the closet and underwear from the chest of drawers. I threw them into the bag Hawk had brought me groceries in and then sat heavily on the edge of the bed.

He'd bought me clothes. Food. Made a place for me in this club, even after I'd broken his nose.

He'd taken care of me.

Taken care of my daughter. How could I just leave?

But once upon a time, Hayden had done all those things for me too.

I curled up on the mattress, paralyzed with fear and indecision.

I'd spent most of my life following the rules made by men. Every time I'd tried to make one of my own, it had ended in tragedy.

I didn't want to make another bad choice.

I didn't want to take Hayley Jade away from the home we'd started building here.

I didn't want to be out there in the world, all alone with no money, no job, no support.

I didn't want to leave Hawk.

I didn't want to leave Hayden.

I closed my eyes, clutching my knees to my chest.

I'd decide when the room stopped spinning.

The veil covered my face.

For weeks, I'd gone without it, breathing easily without the heavy fabric covering that kept me from being seen by Josiah's followers.

I hated the veil. I didn't want it back.

I tried to lift my arm to pull it away so I could breathe better but I couldn't find the edge. I shifted and squirmed, but something clamped around my arms.

"She's waking up," a muffled voice said.

"Put the fucking cloth back over her face then!"

The veil clamped down over my nose and mouth, an oddly sweet smell permeating through.

I slipped back into sleep before I could tell them I didn't wear the veil anymore. That I was no longer wife number one. That I'd left.

That I was free.

The darkness said otherwise. The darkness whispered taunts. Teased out fears I'd tried so hard to bury. Chuckled darkly as black consumed me.

Pain through my back woke me. Dull, thudding pain that radiated from my neck, along my spine and ribs, and into my hips. It wasn't sharp, or intermittent, more like a fresh bruise that covered most of my body.

I groaned, opening my eyes, but still only seeing black.

I reached for the veil, but it was gone.

My head spun in confusion. Why had I been wearing the veil?

There was a vague, sweet smell that lingered, but it wasn't as strong now. Something else overpowered it.

A scent I knew well from planting seeds in the commune plots and pulling vegetables.

Dirt.

I racked my brain, trying to make sense of the fuzziness inside it. I'd been in the clubhouse. Then at my cabin. I'd packed my bags. Had I been choosing

Hayden? Had I left the cabin and fallen somewhere in the woods?

The pain in my back made that a plausible explanation but didn't explain why I couldn't see.

Josiah's voice cut through the confusion.

"Women look to us for guidance. They are lost sheep, while you are their shepherd. It is your job, men of the Lord, to guide them to their rightful place. To teach them how to behave and how to honor the Lord by honoring the men the Almighty made in his image."

I twisted. Turning. Hitting something hard in the darkness.

"Women lose their way. They are weak creatures, easily tempted by evil. And when they are tempted by the Devil, it is your job to bring them back into the light of the Lord."

Panic crept up my throat. He was here. He'd found me.

I reached out blindly, groping the dark, fingernails rasping over rough wood.

"Women need to be reborn when they have sinned. They need to prove their worth. Prove that the evil can be leached from their souls."

I rolled over, ignoring the agonizing pain in my back, only to come face-to-face with another barrier.

More wood.

The panic spread. Josiah's voice in my ears.

I lifted an arm, reaching above me for what should have been sky, even though I couldn't see the stars.

More wood.

I managed to move my leg, and my ankle knocked against something, Josiah's voice suddenly becoming clearer as the speaker rolled along beside my body, taking up a new resting position by my ribs.

"Are you sure about this?" a muffled voice asked from somewhere above me. "This is...shit, man, this is a lot."

"Just fucking do it!" a second voice snapped. "You heard his words. Women need to be reborn to cleanse their souls of their sins! Put your foot on the motherfucking shovel and do what you were told to do. Stop questioning me!"

Josiah wasn't here.

But that no longer mattered.

Because his teachings were. The podcast he'd recorded, playing over and over through the speaker, not only for me to hear, but for the two men I couldn't see.

Heart-stopping terror cut through the last of the sweet-smelling, chemical odor on the cloth beside my head. Everything suddenly became so crystal clear I wished I could turn back the hands of time, and again inhale whatever it was they'd drugged me with.

A thump came from above. Something hitting the wood.

Not just wood.

A wooden box, surrounding me on all sides.

Thump. Thump. Thump.

Tiny particles filtered through the cracks of the coffin, grains of something cold and damp falling around my face.

Until all I could smell, and taste, was dirt as they buried me alive.

The end...for now.
The story continues in Torn in Two, book 2 in the Saint View Slayers vs. Sinners trilogy.

Check out www.ellethorpe.com for Saint View special editions, merch, and free bonus scenes.

ALSO BY ELLE THORPE

Saint View High series (Reverse Harem, Bully Romance. Complete)

*Devious Little Liars (Saint View High, #1)

*Dangerous Little Secrets (Saint View High, #2)

*Twisted Little Truths (Saint View High, #3)

Saint View Prison series (Reverse harem, romantic suspense. Complete.)

*Locked Up Liars (Saint View Prison, #1)

*Solitary Sinners (Saint View Prison, #2)

*Fatal Felons (Saint View Prison, #3)

Saint View Psychos series (Reverse harem, romantic suspense. Complete.)

*Start a War (Saint View Psychos, #1)

*Half the Battle (Saint View Psychos, #2)

*It Ends With Violence (Saint View Psychos, #3)

Saint View Rebels (Reverse harem, romantic suspense)

*Rebel Revenge (Saint View Rebels, #1)

*Rebel Obsession (Saint View Rebels, #2)

*Rebel Heart (Saint View Rebels, #3)

Saint View Strip (Male/Female, romantic suspense standalones. Ongoing.)

*Evil Enemy (Saint View Strip, #1)

*Unholy Sins (Saint View Strip, #2)

*Killer Kiss (Saint View Strip, #3)

*Untitled (Saint View Strip, #4)

Saint View Slayers Vs. Sinners (Reverse harem, romantic suspense)

*Wife Number One (Saint View Slayers Vs. Sinners, #1)

*Torn in Two (Saint View Slayers Vs. Sinners, #2)

*Three to Fall (Saint View Slayers Vs. Sinners, #3)

Dirty Cowboy series (complete)

*Talk Dirty, Cowboy (Dirty Cowboy, #1)

*Ride Dirty, Cowboy (Dirty Cowboy, #2)

*Sexy Dirty Cowboy (Dirty Cowboy, #3)

*Dirty Cowboy boxset (books 1-3)

*25 Reasons to Hate Christmas and Cowboys (a Dirty Cowboy bonus novella, set before Talk Dirty, Cowboy but can be read as a standalone, holiday romance)

Buck Cowboys series (Spin off from the Dirty Cowboy series. Complete.)

*Buck Cowboys (Buck Cowboys, #1)

*Buck You! (Buck Cowboys, #2)

*Can't Bucking Wait (Buck Cowboys, #3)

*Mother Bucker (Buck Cowboys, $#4)

The Only You series (Contemporary romance. Complete)

*Only the Positive (Only You, #1) - Reese and Low.

*Only the Perfect (Only You, #2) - Jamison.

*Only the Truth - (Only You, bonus novella) - Bree.

*Only the Negatives (Only You, #3) - Gemma.

*Only the Beginning (Only You, #4) - Bianca and Riley.

*Only You boxset

Add your email address here to be the first to know when new books are available!

www.ellethorpe.com/newsletter

Join Elle Thorpe's readers group on Facebook!

www.facebook.com/groups/ellethorpesdramallamas

ACKNOWLEDGMENTS

I'm rapidly losing track of how many Saint View series there are. I actually had to stop and count, and Slayers Vs. Sinners makes six! And that's if you don't include the Saint View Short and Smutty line exclusive to my digital book store.

What an absolute honor to get to write in this world for a fifth year. That's only possible because of the love you, the reader, have shown this series.

I can't even imagine what I would write if I wasn't writing Saint View anymore, so thank you for loving these characters like I do. As I always say, I'll keep writing them as long as you keep reading them!

There's an ever growing group of people who make these books possible and they all deserve the hugest thank you.

Thank you to the Drama Llamas. You guys make my days fun. If you aren't already a member, it's a free reader group on Facebook where I share all sorts of stuff. Come join us, everyone is welcome. www.facebook.com/groups/ellethorpesdramallamas

Thank you to Montana Ash/Darcy Halifax for writing with me every day and being the best office buddy/work wife ever.

Thank you to Sara Massery, Jolie Vines, and Zoe Ashwood for the constant support, friendship, and book advice.

Thank you to the cover team:
Emily Wittig for the discreet covers and Michelle Lancaster for the photography.

Thank you to my editing team:
Emmy at Studio ENP and Karen at Barren Acres Editing.
Dana, Louise, Sam, and Shellie for beta reading. Plus my ARC team for the early reviews.

Thank you to the audio team:
Troy at Dark Star Romance for producing this series. Thank you to Michelle, Sean, Lee, and E.M. for being the voices of Kara, Hawk, Chaos, and Grayson.

And of course, thank you to the team who organize me and the home front:
To Donna for taking on all the jobs I don't have time for. Best admin manager ever.
To my mum, for working for us one day a week, and always being willing to have our kids when we go to signings.
To Jira, for running the online store, doing all the

accounting, and dealing with all the 'people-ing.' Not to mention, being the best stay at home dad ever.

To Flick and Heidi, for helping pack swag, and to Thomas, who refuses to work for us, but will proudly tell everyone he knows that his mum is an author.

From the bottom of my heart, thank you.

Elle x

ABOUT THE AUTHOR

Elle Thorpe lives in a small regional town of NSW, Australia. When she's not writing stories full of kissing, she's wife to Mr Thorpe who unexpectedly turned out to be a great plotting partner, and mummy to three tiny humans. She's also official ball thrower to one slobbery dog named Rollo.

When she's not at the office writing, she's probably out on the family alpaca farm, trying not to get spit on.

You can find her on Facebook or Instagram(@ellethorpebooks or hit the links below!) or at her website www.ellethorpe.com. If you love Elle's work, please consider joining her Facebook fan group, Elle Thorpe's Drama Llamas or joining her newsletter here. www.ellethorpe.com/newsletter

        facebook.com/ellethorpebooks
        instagram.com/ellethorpebooks
        goodreads.com/ellethorpe
        pinterest.com/ellethorpebooks

Made in United States
Cleveland, OH
23 August 2025